BROK

Robert broke through into a clearing, the flames raging around him but not touching this section of the forest. In fact the only thing on fire was the figure directly ahead of him. Robert sucked in air, coughing, then refocused. He soon realised his mistake. This wasn't Mark at all; nothing like him. There, not ten feet away from him, was his old enemy: De Falaise.

Yes, he was on fire – the yellow and red rippling over him but apparently not eating him up. Robert was shocked. The last time he'd seen this man he'd killed him, and a blaze had played around them that day too. There was evidence of Robert's attack, because De Falaise no longer had eyes – and even though he was opening and closing his mouth, the Frenchman couldn't speak (a consequence of Robert having shoved an arrow as far down his throat as he could ram it). The arrow that had penetrated his heart – like a stake finishing off a vampire – was missing, but the hole was plainly there. De Falaise was saying something, but it was so faint Robert couldn't make it out.

It sounded like one word over and over.

Vengeance.

An Abaddon Books™ Publication
www.abaddonbooks.com
abaddon@rebellion.co.uk

First published in 2009 by Abaddon Books™, Rebellion Intellectual Property
Limited, Riverside House, Osney Mead, Oxford, OX2 0ES, UK.

10 9 8 7 6 5 4 3 2 1

Editor: Jonathan Oliver
Cover: Mark Harrison
Design: Simon Parr & Luke Preece
Marketing and PR: Keith Richardson
Creative Director and CEO: Jason Kingsley
Chief Technical Officer: Chris Kingsley
The Afterblight Chronicles™ created by Andy Boot and Simon Spurrier

ISBN: 978-1-906735-27-2

Printed in Denmark by Norhaven A/S

THE AFTERBLIGHT CHRONICLES

BROKEN ARROW

PAUL KANE

Abaddon
Books

WWW.ABADDONBOOKS.COM

For Simon Clark. Mentor, master of post apocalyptic
fiction, and friend.

**"Nothing's forgotten.
Nothing's ever forgotten."**

Robin of Sherwood, by Richard Carpenter.

CHAPTER ONE

It was a blood moon. A hunter's moon.

And she was most definitely being hunted. As she ran down the road, almost slipping on the icy surface, she looked over her shoulder. She couldn't see her pursuer, but she knew he was there – and he was close.

The light from above gave the snow-covered streets a crimson tinge. She pushed on, dodging the rusted carcasses of vehicles that hadn't been used in an age. Not since before the world went to Hell – and you could actually believe you were there tonight. Once this road would have been jam-packed with motorists making their way through the city. Now it was simply full of memories and ghosts.

It was a different place, and it wasn't safe anymore to be out at this time of night. She knew that, yet she'd ventured out anyway. Clutching the bag containing a half dozen cans she'd managed to scavenge from various shop storerooms, she was beginning to wonder if it had been worthwhile. After this amount of time most of it had already been picked over by the starving survivors of the virus. There weren't that many, granted, but they'd been living on their wits and whatever they could find for a long while.

Folk had raided houses first, homes on the outskirts – rather than head into the towns and cities; because gangs of thugs had banded together there, hoarding the lion's share of food and other items. Only those stealthy enough to creep in and out could get away with it.

Or at least that had been the case before...

Word had reached people far and wide that the gangs were no longer in control. That they were being driven out. Whether it was true or not, nobody could confirm, but when people are hungry enough they'll believe anything. She'd believed it. And she'd risked her life because of it.

Now she was paying the price.

She ran as fast as she could, skidding as she turned a corner, legs everywhere. Looking up, she saw it: a dark shape on top of a hill, the edges defined by that glowing red sphere above. A castle; the very heart of the city. For a moment she considered making for it, but she knew she'd find no refuge there. Whoever was following just out of sight would surely follow her there, too. Then she'd be trapped.

Might be help up there? Might be someone who could–

She shook her head. There was no-one living there, no lights, not a sign of life at all. No, her best bet was to try and lose her persuer in the narrow streets.

She heard the footfalls behind – boots crunching the snow. She had to keep moving, didn't have long before they caught up with her. Pulling the bag in close to her chest, like a mother cradling her baby, she ran into the labyrinth: a warren made up of houses that seemed to be leaning in to watch her progress. It shouldn't be too hard to get lost in here, to hide until the hunters had passed by.

Another quick glance over her shoulder told her it would be harder than she thought. Now she saw him, and the fact that he was revealing himself meant the hunt was almost at an end.

The man was wearing a hooded robe, which prevented her from getting a good look at his face. She caught something glinting, something the man was raising up.

A knife, twenty inches or more long. She'd seen their like before in old horror movies back when she was in her teens, usually wielded by masked killers. One slice could cleave someone in half.

If he had been alone, she might have reasoned that this was just some nut, using the apocalypse as an excuse to live out his fantasies. But there were more where he came from. Many more.

They emerged from the shadows, all hooded, all wielding those deadly weapons. She froze, realising that her situation was so much worse than she'd imagined. The lead figure came closer, reaching a hand up to pull down his hood.

She let out a gasp when she saw his face – or what there was of it.

Perhaps this place wasn't only populated by ghosts, but by the living dead as well? The skull was white – or at least would have been were it not for the moon's influence. The eyes were sunken and black, merely sockets from which this thing stared out. In the middle of the forehead was a symbol she couldn't quite discern, etched into the bone.

I'm going mad. I must be.

When she finally found she could move again, what she'd witnessed gave her feet wings. Head down, she sprinted faster than ever: up one street, down another. The ground beneath her was still treacherous, but somehow that didn't matter anymore. She lost her footing a couple of times, but ignored it, desperately trying to get away from the nightmare she knew was behind her.

Rounding a final corner she let out gasp. It was a dead end. The houses seemed to lean in closer, as if to ask: 'Well, what are you going to do now, then?'

She had no answer. Looking quickly to the left and the right she thought about trying a few doors, bobbing inside the buildings that were mocking her. But she'd be just as trapped inside as she would have been back at the castle.

Instead, she headed back up the street in the hopes she might find a way out before the dead men arrived. She'd taken only a few steps before her exit was cut off.

A figure appeared at the mouth of the street, seemingly materialising out of nowhere. Then, seconds later, others joined him. She counted ten at least. The leader, slightly taller than the rest began to walk towards her. She backed off, knowing that she didn't have much street left before she hit a wall, but in no rush to meet her fate.

"P-Please... Please just leave me alone..."

He took no notice – *they* took no notice – approaching now as one, swinging their machetes.

"*What do you want from me?*"

The dead man at the front paused, contemplating this question. Then he answered in a hollow voice: "Sacrifice."

They didn't want her physically, as so many had before. Didn't want to paw and molest her – why would dead men want that? They wanted her to join them; to become one of them. To give up her life so that she could exist forever walking these streets, preying on the warm blooded. Maybe living forever wouldn't be so bad?

But what if, when they killed her, she stayed dead? Or, even worse, went to a place that made this look like Heaven – as impossible as that might seem? She looked again, searching for a way out, a way *up* perhaps?

Then she saw another hooded figure on the rooftops. The bastards were up there as well! She was well and truly finished. The hunt was over. Bowing her head, she sobbed, accepting the inevitable.

One of the walking dead fell. At first she thought he might have slipped on the wintry ground. Blinking tears from her eyes, though, she spotted something sticking out of his shoulder. Something long and thin and feathered.

She traced the shot back to the figure above her. Even as she looked up, he was falling, legs bent to take the strain of the landing. The shape rose, standing between her and the dead men... except she knew now they weren't dead at all, not if an arrow from this man's bow could fell them. This man who wore a hood just like her enemies.

With his free hand he waved her back. Then he plucked another arrow from the quiver on his back. He'd loaded it and fired quicker than she had time to register, already reaching for another.

Two more of the 'dead' men dropped. But that didn't stop others taking their place, charging at her rescuer. He had time for just one more shot, but it went wide – his aim spoilt because he had to avoid a blow from one of the swinging machetes. Too close to rely on his bow, the hooded figure let go of it and pulled a sword out of his belt. He used this to block first one machete swipe on his left, then another to his right. Metal clanked against metal, but the man seemed as quick with this weapon as he had been with his arrows.

As she watched, he pushed one of the robed men back, headbutting a second – dropping the man like a stone. A roundhouse kick sent a third into the wall, and she heard a definite crunch of bone. But he couldn't be everywhere at once, in spite of how it seemed. A couple broke through, machetes high, ready to be planted in her.

The hooded man punched one attacker in front and elbowed another, before swinging around and chasing after the ones making for her. He leapt and landed on them, taking them both down just inches away. She fell backwards, landing on the snow, bag falling from her grasp.

The three men struggled to their feet, each one determined to get up first and have the advantage. The hooded figure narrowly avoided a machete swipe to the stomach, arcing his body then bringing his sword down to meet the challenge. No sooner had he thrown off that man than he had to meet the other's blow. This he did but the force knocked him back, hard, into the wall. A flash of gritted teeth, and he slid the hilt up to the man's hand as they struggled to force the weapons out of each other's grip. The stalemate was ended when the first assailant, now recovered, swung again; but the hooded man dragged the figure he was locked onto around, creating a human shield, and the sword buried itself in him instead. The injured man fell to the ground, but her hero wasn't quick enough to avoid a punch that caught him a glancing blow on the chin. Shaking his head, he brought his sword up and into that first attacker, the point emerging from his back.

Breathing heavily, each puff turning to steam in the night air, he looked across at the woman and she caught just a glimpse of the intense eyes under the cowl; searching her face. Then she saw one last glint of metal just behind him, a machete whipping through the air. She didn't have time to scream or point, but he heard the sound anyway... just not in time to do anything about it.

The machete halted in mid-air and the blade quivered. As she lifted her head she saw what had stopped it. A large wooden staff, being held by an equally large man. He was wearing a cap and sported a goatee beard.

"Whoa there, fella," said the big man, with a trace of an American accent. "That's enough of that." Taking one hand off the staff, he punched the robed man in the face, knocking him clean out. The machete clanged to the floor.

Beyond the giant she saw others: *his* men. The Hooded Man's. They were armed as he was, with bows and arrows, with swords. They were grabbing hold of her attackers, pinning them against the wall. Two or three of her assailants who'd been taken down by Hood seized their chance to get up and barged past these newcomers, shouldering them out of the way.

"Don't just stand there," the large man barked, "get after 'em!" Then he held out his hand, helping her saviour to his feet. "Don't worry, they won't get far."

"They'd better not," said the man in the hood – a hood she realised was not attached to some robed outfit, but part of a winter huntsman's jacket (sliced across the front where the machete blade had almost cut him).

"If you'd waited for the rest of us, we'd probably have got them all," replied the man in the cap.

"This woman was in serious trouble."

"Yeah, and so were you Robbie."

"What's that supposed to mean, Jack?"

"You've... Well, you've been out of the game for a little while, boss. You're rusty. That psycho almost had you."

Robbie grunted, ignoring his friend. Then he turned to her, pulling down his hood as he did so. She saw him for the first time, in the glow of the moon – a glow that gave his features a strange kind of warmth. He was clean-shaven and handsome, just like folk said. Oh, she'd heard the stories all right. Who hadn't? It was why she figured it might be safe to come into York tonight. The Hooded Man and his forces were cleaning up the area, or so went the rumour.

Finally, she found her voice. "Y-You... You're him, aren't you? The Hooded Man?"

"What gave it away?" Jack answered before the man could say a thing.

Though it was hard to tell in this light, she could swear Hood's cheeks were flushing. He nodded shyly, like he was embarrassed to admit the fact.

"Are you going to help the lady up then, Robbie, or should I offer my services? Which, I might add, I'd be happy to do..."

The Hooded Man held out his hand and she took it, feeling its strength. Her heart was pounding, not because of the skirmish, not because she'd been seconds away from dying, but because she was this close to *him*. Could he feel it too? Their connection?

As she rose, she stumbled slightly, unsteady on her feet. She fell into him and he held her there for a second... before the embarrassment crept back and he righted her, letting go. She felt somehow bereft, but still managed: "Thank you... Robbie."

"It's Robert," he corrected, stooping to pick up her bag and handing it to her, "or Rob."

"Or sometimes even Robin," added Jack, grinning.

Robert sighed. "Only this big lug calls me Robbie, I suspect because he knows how much I hate it."

The big man feigned a look of mock offence, then grinned again, resting his staff on his shoulder. "And I'm Jack. Always a pleasure to help out a damsel in distress... 'specially one as pretty as you are, ma'am." Once he'd got a smile from her, Jack turned to address his superior. "Looks like all those hours of stake-out actually paid off. We got most of 'em."

"I wanted *all* of them," said Robert.

"Who are they?" she asked as they walked towards the men having their hands bound behind their backs.

"We're not entirely sure; some kind of cult," Robert informed her. "We've had reports of them cropping up in various locations. It never ends well for their victims."

She remembered what one of the 'dead' men had said to her during the chase: *Sacrifice...*

She could see now, though, that they were merely wearing make-up. Their faces and shaved heads had been painted white, with the area around their eyes black in contrast. They'd done this on purpose, of course; imitating the deceased to intimidate the living. She peered closer at one of them, trying to make out the tattoo on his forehead. The robed figure bared his teeth, snapping like an animal before the young man holding him could pull him away.

"You might want to get back a bit, miss," he told her.

Jack clapped him on the shoulder. "You did good work tonight, Dale. I'm proud of you."

The youth beamed, clearly delighted by the praise. "Are we taking these back to Nottingham?"

"I believe that's the plan."

"You're going back to the castle? To Nottingham Castle?" The woman asked Robert.

He nodded.

"Then please... take me with you." Robert was silent and she looked at him pleadingly. "I'm begging you. I have nowhere else to go. I've got no-one... not since my mum... my family..." She didn't need to finish that sentence; they'd all been there, it was reflected in their eyes. *His* especially. The hurt, the pain he'd tried to bury but which still lurked there, slumbering in his mind – and only took a prod like this to wake.

"Come on, Robbie," said Jack. "The lady's been through a lot tonight; what harm can it do?"

"All right, all right," said Robert. "You can come along."

She flung herself at him, giving him a big hug. "Oh thank you, thank you." Jack coughed and she felt Robert tensing up. This was obviously too public a display of affection. Pulling back, she then gave Jack a hug as well. "Thank you. Thank you both."

"Er... Jack, when the others get back ready the horses."

"Sure thing," said a happy Jack, walking away, out of the alley, and taking the men and prisoners with him.

"So," Robert continued, turning to her; he'd looked more comfortable facing death than he did right now. "What's your name?"

"Me?" She hesitated for a second or two. "Do you know it's been so long since anyone asked me that? It's Adele."

Robert stuck out his hand. "Well then, Adele. Pleased to meet you."

She smiled. "And I'm so very pleased to meet you, Robert... The Hooded Man."

CHAPTER TWO

So much had changed, and yet so much remained the same.

Take this place they now called home, for example. The castle itself still looked the same, on the outside at any rate. But inside things were definitely different. Instead of a barracks for an army, this was now a headquarters for the fledgling constabulary they'd built up over the past year and a half. Ever since they'd kicked that Frenchmen's arse; just a handful of them against his entire militia. Robert had killed the self-styled Sheriff of Nottingham himself, while the rest of the men had mounted a covert attack on the castle.

The castle doubled as a home for Robert and those closest to him. Like Mary, the woman who'd coaxed him out of the forest, who'd taught him to love again after his own wife and son had died from the virus. Like his second-in-command, Jack, a former wrestler from the US who had come to Sherwood to join Robert's fight against injustice.

And it served as a home to him, Mark, the boy who'd had to

grow up way too quickly: a former scavenger on the streets who finally found a new family. He'd first met Robert at one of the make-shift markets on the outskirts of Sherwood, and soon after the man had saved his life – just like he had so many others. He and Mary had taken on the mantle of adoptive parents, loving and protective. But like all good parents, they also set the rules – some of which Mark completely disagreed with.

Like the one about his training. He was ready, but Robert kept putting him off.

"You need to face your fears properly first."

As Mark walked down the East Terrace, towards the Middle Bailey, memories flooded back to him of the first time he came to this place. Bundled into a truck, hands tied, then deposited down in the caves beneath the castle – which now held all of De Falaise's modern weapons (as Robert often said, "His way is not *our* way."). There he'd been tortured, used to lure Robert from Sherwood. Mark looked down at the stump of a finger, all that was left of the digit that evil psychopath Tanek had cut off and sent to Robert. The stump ached sometimes, especially in winter, and he even felt it there wiggling occasionally. Phantom pains they called it. The mind not letting go of the past.

Mark shook his head and walked towards the Bailey where Robert's men – his 'Sherwood Rangers' – were being put through their paces. Swordplay (techniques mainly gleaned from books: "You can find out everything about anything from books," Mary had said); archery; hand-to-hand combat. It was all going on down there. In lighter moments Mark couldn't help comparing their training ground to something out of an old James Bond movie.

Jack would just love that, he thought to himself, knowing the big man's fondness for old films.

Mark watched as arrows thudded into round, painted targets; as men tackled each other with wrestling moves Jack had imparted, and martial arts skills either taught by Robert or passed down from Reverend Tate's time. The holy man had returned to the village formerly known as Hope, along with Gwen, who he'd known from before his time in Sherwood. They'd left right after

Gwen had given birth, in spite of Mary's concerns about letting them go. Gwen had wanted to put the failed community of Hope back together, in memory of her beloved Clive – who the Sheriff's men had so brutally killed. Tate had gone with her, arguing that the people out there needed spiritual guidance much more than they all did. Mark wondered though how much it had to do with Robert's personal thoughts about faith.

Not that Tate had been the only member of their family they'd said goodbye to. Bill had also gone off to start again after constantly butting heads with Robert. The outspoken local hadn't agreed about the gun situation at all, especially when it came time for him to relinquish his canon of a shotgun. "He's daft as a brush," Bill had told Mary. "Judas Priest! With them weapons rusting away down in the caves we can really make a difference, an' what's Robert want to use? Bloody swords and sticks!" Last Mark heard Bill was back running markets, up the coast this time. He was doing all right, too, by the sounds of things. Oh, Robert kept tabs on him all right – just in case he needed help. He was still very fond of the man who'd once been his second, even though he was too proud to admit it.

Arriving at the top of the steps, Mark suddenly had a flashback to when the Bailey had been used as a staging ground for De Falaise's executions. The men below were clanking swords together – swords which, along with other ancient weapons, had either been gathered from various museums or made on the grounds by their budding blacksmith, Faraday (who also shoed horses and gave the men riding lessons). Robert and his Rangers shunned the jeeps, tanks and motorbikes left behind, not only because fuel was becoming a rare commodity, but, again, because they represented a different time. They'd rely on other defences to protect the castle, like the projects some of the men skilled in woodwork had been drafted into. Robert promised they'd be as effective as anything modern weaponry could offer.

Now in Mark's mind the training session was replaced by the wooden structure that mad Frenchman had made, a gallows.

Of all the times Mark had come close to death, that had been the worst. The feel of the rope cutting into his neck, the agonising wait for De Falaise to give the signal for them to be dropped; how helpless he'd felt...

The Hooded Man had intervened, of course. Or more accurately Mary *dressed* as The Hooded Man, walking in through the gates down there. That had taken some guts, switching places with Robert because she knew he'd be killed. It had proved distraction enough for the rest of Robert's forces to attack, but it could all have ended so differently.

Phantom pains... Just phantom pains...

Robert told him once what De Falaise had said right before he'd killed the man, ramming arrows into his throat and eyes, breaking them off. *"It is only just beginning, mon ami."* What he'd meant was anyone's guess, but in a sense he'd been right. As they'd begun their policing of the region, Robert had discovered just how hard it was to keep the peace. Even though people came every day to join his ranks, volunteers like the new recruits below, he still only had a limited supply of men to draw on – and now they were widening their protection to surrounding cities like Sheffield, Doncaster, Leeds, Manchester... things were even tighter.

Which was one of the reasons Mark couldn't understand Robert's decision.

"You're just not ready yet," he'd told him when he asked again.

"I'm almost fifteen, not that much younger than Lee and his friends." Mark was referring to the group from St Mark's School down south, who'd showed up a while back asking Robert for help in defeating some bad guys they called The Snatchers. He'd eventually loaned them some Rangers, in spite of being stretched so thinly. "I'm not a kid anymore... I haven't been for a long time."

"That's not what I'm talking about. You're simply not prepared, Mark."

"After everything I've been through? You're joking."

"It's *because* of everything you've been through. You need time, son."

"You mean like you're taking?"

Robert had flinched and Mark regretted it as soon as the words had tumbled out of his mouth. It had never been Robert's intention to run this operation; he'd never imagined he'd have to organise patrols or help squads on this scale when he gathered together his band of men in Sherwood. Hell, he'd taken enough convincing to get involved, even after saving Mark's and Bill's hides. By doing so, Mark knew he'd exorcised some of the demons from his past. But once that had been done he'd spent more time in his office than he had on the streets. When it came right down to it, the responsibility rested on Robert's shoulders alone. And it wasn't fair to criticise him for that.

Nevertheless, the man had seen little action since undertaking his work at the castle. The legend of The Hooded Man might have spread, but the reality of the situation was very different. Which was probably why he'd started to brush up on his basics again, why he'd begun going out on missions in spite of the fact Mary didn't want him to. She said there was no reason to risk his life anymore, but every reason to stay safe. Mark felt guilty about that; like maybe he was the one who'd started Robert thinking about it again. But he was only saying what all the men thought. If they felt like he was hiding away behind a wall, while they tackled who knows what, then their respect for him wouldn't last.

As Mark made his way down the steps, he spotted something that cheered him up. Coming down the main path was Mary, and she wasn't alone. Walking with her, on this crisp February morning, was a girl he'd recognise anywhere. He remembered the first time he'd seen her, in a small village, standing across the way in that yellow summer dress, freckles dotting her cheeks.

Sophie. Lovely Sophie. A couple of years older than him, she'd fixed Mark a drink and then quizzed him about his time with The Hooded Man, flashing that gorgeous smile of hers.

But even that memory was tinged with sadness. The Sheriff's men bursting in, attempting to take her with them... until Mark intervened; until he'd taken her place as a hostage. Then outside, the guys he'd travelled there with to return stolen food: all dead. Massacred in cold blood.

When things had died down, when he'd recovered from his ordeal at the castle, he'd been surprised to get a visit from her. Mary had knocked on his door and told him there was someone to see him. "She came looking for you."

"Who is it?"

It had been so unexpected, but he was delighted to see her. So delighted he'd almost tripped over on the way to give her a hug.

"Sophie! What are *you* doing here?"

"That's nice."

"No, no... That's not what I meant... I just..."

"Relax," she said, grinning an impish grin and hitting him on the arm playfully. "I'm just messing with you. I came to bring you this." Sophie reached into a bag and brought out a battered photo album. "Here you go. I found it after the soldiers left."

Mark's mouth dropped open. He thought he'd never see that again. It had been taken off him as he was bundled into the back of one of the Sheriff's armoured trucks. He turned the pages, and they transported him back to a time not just before the castle, but before the world went crazy.

"Oh, and here," said Sophie, handing him a single photograph. It was the one of Mark with his real parents that the scarred soldier, Jace, tore up. Sophie had picked up the trampled pieces and taped them together again.

Mark didn't know what to say, so he hugged her again.

"Easy tiger," she'd said, laughing.

"I'm... I'm sorry," Mark said when he let go. "It's just this is the nicest thing anyone's ever done for me. You came all this way."

Sophie looked him in the eye. "You're forgetting, I owe you mister. If it hadn't been for you I'd have been driven off in that truck, and God knows what would have happened to me. I certainly know what those men *wanted* to do."

"It was my pleasure."

"Hardly," said Sophie, taking his hand. "Mary told me about what happened. Thank you." Then she kissed him gently on the cheek. As Mary had taken her away to get some food, Mark rubbed the spot on his face where her lips had just been, and couldn't help imagining what they would feel like brushing against his own.

He'd asked Robert immediately if Sophie could stay and he'd said of course. He remembered her, too, from the village – after they'd gone there looking for Mark. He also recognised a certain look in Mark's eye. One that told him exactly how Mark felt about the girl.

Even now, after months of her being here, his heart felt like it would break out of his chest whenever he saw Sophie. Hormones, his head told him. That's all. But he couldn't help the way he felt. What he didn't know was whether Sophie felt the same. They'd spent a lot of time together, but he still had no idea whether she just wanted to be friends or something more. And now things were even more complicated.

Mark made his way past the trainees and down the path. Sophie was dressed in a thick parka, trousers and boots. It was a million miles away from what she'd worn the day they met, but she still looked beautiful.

He was about to shout across to them when he heard a bellow come from one of the gatehouse crew. "Green Leader is back!"

Both Mary and Sophie turned at the same time, to see the gates open wide. A number of men on horseback rode through, Robert – hood drawn – leading the way, with Jack not far behind. It was good to see them again, and in one piece, because Mark knew they'd been after some very dangerous men in York. There were no prisoners with them, however, which meant that they'd either been unsuccessful or they'd already dropped them off at one of the nearby hotels they used as jails – a step up from the caves De Falaise had favoured, and more than some of the prisoners warranted.

Mark watched the rest of the men ride in, spotting another figure he knew all too well.

Dale.

The twenty-three year old had joined them the previous summer, breezing in like something out of a US soap opera. His cropped hair and model looks belied the skill with which he fought. Many of the women under their protection had gone nuts over this guy – in fact he would be the pin-up hunk of the castle if such a thing existed any more. It didn't help that he'd once sung lead vocal for a band called One Simple Truth, and insisted, even now, on writing songs and strumming them out on that guitar of his to pass the time.

Mark knew it was only jealousy; not only was Dale older than him, he was also much cooler. In fact he was everything Mark should be, including the first choice for missions like this one. And here *he* was, not even on the long list for training sessions yet. It just wasn't fair.

Watch those hormones, Mark...

But his jaw set firm when he saw Sophie run over to the men on horseback. Over to Dale's horse. Mark carried on down the path, noticing how Mary hurried over to Robert, who was climbing down off his horse, wincing as he did so.

"Robert! Oh my God, are you all right?" Mark heard her ask.

Robert gave one of his trademark silent nods.

"He's just a little sore, aren't you, Robbie?" Jack swung down from his own mount, handing over the reins to a lad who'd come down from the castle's stables. "We saw a bit of action, y'see."

"Action?" Mary looked from Jack to Robert, her forehead crinkling; then, carefully, she pulled down his hood. "Oh no, look at you." There was indeed a nasty purple bruise on his chin. "Are you hurt anywhere else?" She was examining him now for any other wounds, and stopped dead when she saw the cut across the front of his jacket.

Robert pulled away. "Mary, don't fuss... please. I'm fine."

"But you might not have been. I asked you not to go, but you went anyway and –"

"If he hadn't *I* might not still be alive." Mark looked up to see a woman riding behind one of the Rangers. She had short, black hair, and a striking face; high cheekbones and perfectly plump lips. The Ranger helped her down from the horse and she walked over to Robert and Mary, then stood between them. "He saved my life."

Mary looked the woman up and down. "And who are you?"

"Her... her name's Adele. I said she could return with us to the castle."

Adele smiled and held out her hand to Mary, who took it after some hesitation, and only held onto it for one shake. "I see," said Mary.

Looks like I'm not the only one feeling jealous, thought Mark, eyes darting across to Dale and Sophie again. She was giggling at something he'd just whispered.

"She has nowhere else to go, Mary," explained Robert, drawing Mark's gaze back. "So I said she could stay here for a while."

"I see," repeated Mary and gave him a look that really said: *We'll talk about this when we don't have an audience.*

"I'm really grateful for everything he did."

Mark raised an eyebrow. *I'll bet you are.*

"You should have seen him in action."

Mary gave a tight smile, then replied: "I've seen him in action, thanks."

"He took on all those men on his own." Adele was gazing up at Robert with what could only be described as adulation. "I don't know how I can ever repay him." She placed a hand on Robert's arm, completely ignoring the look of disdain from Mary. Robert saw it, though, and shifted awkwardly around, closer to the woman who'd been at home worrying about him, wondering if he was alive or dead.

"Jack," he said, "would you mind taking Adele up to the castle, showing her what's what, getting her some food. She must be starving."

"My absolute pleasure." Jack offered the woman his arm. "Come on, little lady."

Before she took it, Adele leaned in and gave Robert a peck on the cheek. "Thank you again for everything."

When the pair were gone, Robert turned to Mary, who had now folded her arms. "What could I do? She has no one. Just like you when we first met."

It was absolutely the wrong thing to say. "Lining up a replacement, are we?"

"Don't be silly, Mary. It's just –"

"Silly? *Silly!*" Mary breathed in an out slowly a few times.

She looked like she was about to say something else when Mark decided he'd better cut in.

"The men you fought, they were the ones you'd been tracking? The cultists?"

Robert appeared grateful for the reprieve. "Yes. We took several of them into custody. They're at *The Britannia* right now." This was their main penitentiary, a hotel not far from the castle, guarded by Robert's men. "We're in way over our heads with them, though. They're fanatics, religious nutters. I think I'm going to need Tate's help to figure out their overall game plan."

Mark nodded, glancing over briefly to see Dale and Sophie still laughing and joking. He looked back at Robert, a serious expression on his face. "So they're potentially a serious threat?"

"Potentially," Robert conceded.

"Then you're going to need all the men you can spare to tackle them."

"I suppose I..." Robert suddenly realised where this was heading. "Look, Mark, we've talked about this before."

"I know, and it never gets any further. I'm ready; you know it and I know it."

Robert sighed, looking from Mark to Mary, then back again. "What is this, some kind of ambush? I've only just got back, I'm tired and hungry, and you two are on me as soon as I get through the gate. We'll discuss this some other time."

Mark wasn't sure whether he meant his problem, or Mary's, but persisted. "I want to talk about it now." Robert began to walk away from both of them. "*Please!*"

The man stopped, hung his head, then said simply. "I'll have a word with Jack about beginning your training." With that, he carried on up the path towards the castle.

Mark smiled, then saw Mary was still frowning. He put an arm around her shoulder. "Hey, you don't have to worry about him. He really loves you, you know."

She shook her head. "I just wish sometimes he'd show it more."

"Yeah, I know what you mean."

Mary followed his gaze across to Sophie. "They're friends.

That's all."

Mark shrugged. "I can understand it. He's older than me, gets to go out, play the hero..."

"Is that what all this is about? The thing with the training?" Mary asked him. "Because if it is –"

"No," he replied, but didn't sound very convincing. "Not really... Mary, do you ever think about the past, about what we all went through? About what happened here?"

"You mean, do I miss it? Being in the thick of things, even though we were all nearly killed?"

That wasn't quite what he meant, but he nodded anyway.

"Sometimes. But not as much as he does." She gestured towards the figure heading towards the castle. "I just don't know what I'd do now if I lost him."

Mark pulled her in closer and she put her arm around his shoulder. He thought about saying, "You won't" but they both knew he couldn't make that kind of promise.

"Come on," Mark said to her, more to get away from Sophie and Dale than to follow Robert.

So much had changed, thought Mark again. Yet it was true: so much was still the same. But there were so many questions left unanswered. Questions he was trying not to think about as they walked towards the castle.

Questions like what exactly had happened to Tanek's body during that final battle? Mark had seen him go down, seen him die. So why did the man who'd tortured him haunt his thoughts? Another phantom pain that refused to go away? Or something more?

It was then those words of De Falaise's came back to him and he gave a shiver that had nothing whatsoever to do with the cold.

"It is only just beginning, mon ami. It is only just beginning..."

CHAPTER THREE

It was cold, the snow was falling.

But then, wasn't it most of the time here? And he liked that; it reflected how he felt inside. He'd grown up in this environment, learned to block out the freezing temperatures. No, not block them out – welcome and embrace them. Let them influence who he was, who he would become. Let the cold touch his very heart.

To be fair, the temperature wasn't the only thing that had frozen that particular muscle. The death of his parents in one of the 'post war' Gulags – they were among the last to still be held after Khrushchev began his de-Stalinisation of the homeland – saw to that. Though officially their camp should not have even existed in the '60s, somehow it had slipped through the net – probably because it was in such a remote region, but also it paid to keep just a few of them operating. It contained some very dangerous prisoners, though in his mother and father's case it had just been an excuse to keep those with certain political or religious views out of circulation. He was too young to remember much of his infancy, just his mother's eyes, so full of love for him...

He found out later that the men who ran the camp treated prisoners like dogs. His father had been tortured regularly, his mother raped and beaten (the thought sometimes occurred to him that the man he thought of as his father might not actually have been that at all, but in the end did it really matter?).

When the camp's activities had finally come to light – or rather whoever had been sheltering and subsidising it finally decided to tie up a few loose ends – it was too late for his parents. He'd been shipped off to an orphanage in southern Siberia, to allow the weather to finish the job the Gulag had started.

In charge of that place was one Leonty Kabulov, a sour-faced man who believed in discipline to the nth degree. The slightest step out of line was met with severe punishment. Kabulov's role models were the Emperors of old, and he ran the place as one – delegating power to his underlings, including a brutish physical education teacher called Nikolin, who would run the children ragged on treks through the snow. But even Kabulov realised the necessity of letting his 'subjects' blow off steam every now and again. Which was why he often turned a blind eye if a fight broke out in the orphanage's playground. Many children had been badly injured that way, though the crowds that gathered round were thoroughly entertained.

He himself had been picked on by one lad called Yuri and this had ended in a fight. Yuri had pummelled him with his fists, breaking a couple of ribs and putting him in the infirmary, tended by a nurse who looked like something Dr Frankenstein had created in his spare time. He never complained; as bad as it was there, it was nothing compared to what his parents had endured.

When he was old enough, he was conscripted into the army. If he'd thought tolerating the orphanage was hard then training in the military taught him how easy he'd actually had it. They taught him how to kill, and it wasn't long before he'd had to use that particular skill fighting in the Soviet War against Afghanistan. It wasn't his natural environment – dealing with the heat to begin with had been difficult; it made the mercifully short summers back home seem chilly in comparison – but he'd soon proved himself one of the best fighters in his squad, eventually gaining the rank of Commander. During the '80s, and fuelled by the aid the USA was giving the enemy, his hatred for the West – and especially America – grew. Nuking would have been too good for them in his opinion. It was just a pity that plans to invade Western Europe, which were only uncovered much later, never came to fruition. By the time the Cold War ended, he was back in the motherland and, though he was grateful for the cooler air, he was not so enamoured with the way things were suddenly changing; spitting every time he saw a McDonalds. He fell victim to the army cutbacks Gorbachev initiated, and witnessed, with disdain, the eventual collapse of the Soviet Army.

But there were still jobs to be had for a man of his talents. He began working for the mafia, operating out of central Moscow, during the '90s, with a hand in everything from extortion and porn to caviar smuggling. The opening up of trade routes with other countries helped build up organised crime, with the mafia itself taking on more of a Westernised, business-orientated approach. On the other side of the law now, it left him just as much scope to get his hands dirty; a bullet in the head here, a snapped neck there. Little wonder he rose in the ranks, from general muscle and bodyguard, to actually getting involved behind the scenes. Before long he was in charge of one of the largest criminal networks in the country, soon gaining the name he still went by today: hiring others to do the dangerous stuff for him. While his former comrades struggled to earn a pittance, he was actually better off than he had ever been. And he liked the feeling of being in control. One day soon, he knew, he would be running more than just this operation. In fact he already had plans to expand ever further abroad.

Then it happened; the whole world froze.

He could remember seeing reports on television about the epidemic, and in his mind there was no doubt whatsoever that it was of Western origin. Probably from the US – an attack on his country! He took every precaution against catching it, including wearing a gas mask. But when people in his organisation started dropping like flies – one of his closest aids, Gerasim, virtually exploded right in front of him, blood jetting from every orifice – he figured it was already too late. It was in his system already, so he might as well face his inevitable demise.

Except it didn't come. The more he waited, the more he found out about this thing they were calling the A-B Virus. It wasn't just affecting his nation, it was killing people all around the globe. Whether it had started out as a weapon in the West was still unclear, but if it had then the plan completely backfired. The only ones safe were those with a certain blood type: *his* type of blood. At least here they were spared the secondary infections from the dead littering the streets. Such was the climate during those long winter months that the corpses were preserved and, yes, they were still out there – rotting much more slowly than in other parts of the world: a reminder of what had happened. Icy, once-living statues.

At first he had been frustrated. Just when he was getting somewhere, he suddenly found himself right back at the bottom.

But, in time, survivors began to emerge. He saw them flitting between the buildings in Moscow, chased some of the first few down, armed with his custom-made machine gun and Gursa self-charge pistol. Most had already heard of him and surrendered gladly, welcoming someone to show them the way. Others had been less easy to persuade, so he'd put a bullet in them.

It wasn't long before he'd gathered a decent force, just like the one he'd commanded in Afghanistan – and he soon had a protective ring around himself once more. What worked in their favour was that the amount of survivors here reflected the fact that this was the largest country on the planet. Of course, that also meant that there were pockets of resistance dotted all across the land, in towns, villages and, especially, in the cities. There were some even now who were not a part of his new Empire, but given enough time...

For that's what he was building, he'd decided. An Empire. If Kabulov and the Cold War had taught him anything it was that the old ways were the best. He would rule with an iron fist, ensure that, once again, they would be *the* force to be reckoned with; even in this post-apocalyptic world. In fact, hadn't the virus done them a favour – weeding out the influence of the West so they could start again as something purer?

How much more fitting his mafia name was now. The Tsar. A monarch whose influence had steadily spread as far East as Magadan, using Moscow as his base. Loyalty was rewarded with protection, treachery with death. Once he had enough troops to spare, he would think about branching out further, reaching into other territories. That day was coming soon and he knew it. A day when he'd have enough power to tackle America itself. Stories had reached him of what was going on there, of factions taking charge and organising themselves, just as he was doing. It was simply a question of who would assemble a big enough army and how quickly. He already had access to all the military equipment and weapons he'd ever need.

The Tsar was pleased when he realised his reputation was already stretching beyond borders. Indeed, his most trusted allies were from China and the Ukraine. The female Liu twins – Xue and Ying – never far from his side, had come to him and offered their services, mistakenly playing the Communist card. As if he gave a shit about that. He was more interested in their ability to carve up half a dozen of his guards without breaking a sweat, using those deadly Hook Swords of theirs, before surrendering and kneeling before him. Their oriental beauty was captivating, and so he kept them around not only as his personal bodyguards, but also his lovers.

Bohuslav was a different matter altogether. In him, The Tsar had recognised a kindred spirit: a soul as cold as his. It was there in those steely eyes. His methods were different to all the others in The Tsar's service, coming as he did from a background of serial killing. He had murdered more than fifty people even before the virus swept Russia, using his favoured weapons – small hand-held sickles – but had never come close to getting caught. No-one should ever trust Bohuslav, yet oddly The Tsar did. He trusted him with his life, which he knew Bohuslav could take at any moment if he chose to. He also trusted him with authority over the day-to-day running of his realm.

All three were with him today, riding in his bulletproof limousine. Bohuslav was driving, with the twins in the back, flanking The Tsar. As they travelled the distance between the Mariott Grand Hotel to one of the warehouses that had once stored goods for his business, The Tsar looked out at the falling snow. Where others might have seen nature's magnificence at work, he was comforted by the fact it showed temperatures would be well into the minuses. The white spots fell on those human statues outside, like Pompeii's ash. His face showed no reaction, no emotion. It wasn't just that he'd seen them many, many times: it was the fact that there wasn't any emotion to show. On the road ahead of them were two guards on motorbikes, and he knew the same number were behind. They pulled in at the rear entrance of the warehouse, and Bohuslav followed, bringing the limo to a halt by the pavement.

His second, dressed in his usual sharp suit, got out first and opened the car's back door; there was the merest glint from the sickle hanging at his belt. Xue hopped out next to check that it was safe for their important passenger. He watched the tight black leather of her outfit mould itself to her body as she did so, sword up and ready almost before she cleared the car. Her head appeared then, nodding that it was safe for him to get out. The Tsar's own red leather outfit – more military-based than hers – creaked as he stood up, and he pulled his greatcoat around him. Then he placed the peaked cap on his head, tugging it firmly down. Ying wasn't far behind, as elegant as her sister, and just as dangerous. With the specially trained guards now in tow, the group entered the building, striding through a series of corridors and climbing steps to reach a converted office with an open front; a good fifteen feet or more above ground level. It had once been used to oversee production at this facility, but now it was his official box. The noise drifted up to meet them even before stepping out onto this: raised voices, whistling and whooping.

Once they were sure it was safe to do so, Bohuslav and Xue parted, allowing The Tsar to stand at the front, viewing his subjects below.

Crammed into the warehouse were dozens on dozens of people, and in the centre itself was a raised, cordoned-off ring. Inside this were two men, each armed with axes and shields. One was taller and bulkier than the other, the vest he wore showing off his well-developed biceps. His dyed-blond hair was spiky, and his fair eyebrows made it look like he had none at all – giving him a slightly alien appearance. In spite of his size, he moved like a cat, dodging a blow from the other man, whose clothes were virtually rags. His tattered shirt and trousers, coupled with his untidy beard, made him look like a tramp. He was certainly no athlete like his opponent, and that was also clear from the way they both moved. One of them had done this before... and it wasn't him.

The man in the vest avoided yet another clumsy blow, much to the crowd's delight. They cheered again for their favourite, for The Tsar's favourite: Glazkov.

He was pleased they hadn't missed the first kill of the evening. Sitting down on what could only be called a throne, The Tsar watched the match. It was yet another idea he'd taken from Kabulov and the orphanage; a way for his subjects to let off steam. It was just like the fights in the playground, except this was organised. It gave his people something to look forward to and indulged their bloodlust, turning it away from any thoughts of rebellion which might arise. This way he could control them more easily, and it made his iron rule much more palatable. It was also a good way to get rid of the dregs of humanity who didn't fit into his vision of a future Russia.

Sometimes the men would fight with their fists alone, sometimes – like tonight – they would be given weapons like the gladiators of old. At any rate, it provided much needed entertainment, not only for the crowds, but for The Tsar. Nobody had even noticed he was here yet, and he would have been well within his rights to draw their attention to the fact he was observing. The fact that they should all be saluting. But he was loathe to stop the proceedings at this critical juncture. After all, he'd granted permission for them to start without him while he oversaw some pressing issues of state.

Glazkov was obviously having fun with this one, dancing round, tiring him out before having his turn.

Which came now, as the tramp swung his axe again, and missed. Glazkov pivoted, hitting the man on the back with the flat of the blade – sending him sprawling across the ring onto his hands and knees. Glazkov smirked at the audience's bellows and claps. His opponent picked himself up, and came running back for more. He growled as he swung his axe again and Glazkov easily blocked it with his shield. This time, though, Glazkov struck with the sharpened edge of his axe, plunging it into the tramp's thigh. It buried itself deep; so deep that when Glazkov yanked it out, a warm redness came jetting out with it. The man let out a cry, immediately dropping his own shield to clutch at his wound. He hobbled back out of Glazkov's reach.

At the sight of the blood the crowd went wild, chanting Glazkov's name over and over. He held up his bloodied axe triumphantly, and they cheered even more.

The Tsar leaned forward in his throne, hand on his chin.

Tossing his shield aside, Glazkov was on the offensive. He ran at the wounded man, twirling his axe like Fred Astaire with a cane. The tramp's survival instinct kicked in, urging him to meet the next blow with his own axe. They clashed together, but it only succeeded in pushing the weaker man back once more. He barely avoided the blow that followed, aimed at his chest, the wind whistling as the blade swiped through the air.

Glazkov was all for a good show, but it was time to finish this and get on with the next fight. Perhaps it would offer him more of a challenge. Springing forward, he swung the axe twice again, this time almost severing his opponent's arm below the elbow, causing him to drop his weapon. The tramp shrieked in pain, looking from the damaged appendage – hanging by threads of tendons – to Glazkov's face in disbelief.

Before there was any more time to react, Glazkov spun around, planting the blade of the axe in the tramp's stomach, causing him to double over. Glazkov supported his weight for a moment or two, then dragged the axe backwards and forwards in a sawing motion. When he let the injured man go and pulled out his axe, the tramp's guts came with it.

Rolling around on the floor, the man was still alive and – given enough time in a working operating theatre, and with the right doctors (an extremely slim hope in these times) – might yet pull through. But that wasn't an option. Glazkov held the axe high above his head, ready to bring it down on his felled adversary. The throng around the ring were whipped into a frenzy.

"*GLAZKOV!*" came a voice, cutting through the atmosphere like the axe had through the tramp. The crowd, who had been baying for blood only seconds before, were instantly quiet. Glazkov stayed his hand, breathing deeply, the sweat pouring over his face and arms. Even the tramp on the floor dampened down his cries. For they all knew who the voice belonged to. And with whose authority he spoke.

Bohuslav was at the railing of the office. He didn't have to say any more, because everyone below him could now see that The Tsar was in residence. Their Lord and Master had arrived. And when *he* was present, it was his say who lived and who died. Glazkov waited patiently for the outcome. Did The Tsar want him to finish this specimen off, put him out of his misery, or leave him alive for some reason – possibly so he could die more slowly? Glazkov wouldn't be surprised by that one, although it would leave a sour taste in his mouth after working up an appetite for killing.

The Tsar stood, approaching the rail. All eyes were now on him, everybody wanting to know what he would decide. He was not so pretentious that he would use the old symbol of a thumb up or down. No, The Tsar would simply shake his head or nod: life or death, as if there was really a choice. Today he felt lenient. He ordered the swift execution of the injured man. The crowd roared with delight.

Glazkov smiled and finally brought down the axe, cleaving the tramp's head from his body. It rolled across the ring, coming to a standstill near a little boy in the crowd, its eyes staring wildly into his. (And did it blink a couple of times or was that the child's imagination?).

The Tsar took his seat again as Glazkov was relieved of his weapon and given a towel to dry himself. The victor risked a glance up as he rubbed his face, but not at his master – rather at the twins that flanked him, appraising first one, then the other. The Tsar noted this, and the looks of admiration Xue and Ying returned: whether they just admired his fighting ability or his physique, he couldn't be certain, but he would watch what developed with interest from now on. The twins were his and his alone.

There was a brief pause in the proceedings, during which Glazkov took a seat on the stool in his corner of the ring – sipping from a water bottle – and the body of the tramp was gathered up. This respite didn't last long, however, because by his yawns it was clear The Tsar was eager for more action. He saw very little himself these days, instead getting his fill of killing vicariously. But he missed it, oh God how he missed it. Maybe if Glazkov kept looking at his bodyguards that way he would find himself facing The Tsar in the ring? The thought both excited and troubled him.

But that wouldn't be tonight. Because the next participant was already being forced to the ring, the crowds parting so that he could be brought through. The man wore what looked to be sacking or a large blanket and appeared to be in even worse condition than the previous fighter. Obviously picked up off the streets, like the majority of them, his long, greasy hair was straggly and he was having trouble standing, limping into the centre of the ring.

In fact, it looked like this newcomer was about to collapse.

Glazkov rose from his stool, spitting out a mouthful of water. He wandered over to the man, looking down on him in disdain. Rubbing his hands together, Glazkov got started, much to the audience's satisfaction. He threw a punch that landed squarely in the man's kidneys. Then Glazkov clasped his hands together, leaping up and bringing them down hard on the man's back. The figure toppled onto the floor.

The Tsar yawned again. This fight was barely going to be worth watching; it would be over in seconds at this rate.

The people's champion kicked this beggar creature in the side, rolling him over once, twice, so that again he faced the floor. Then Glazkov raised his booted foot to bring it stomping down on the man's head.

Only it stopped in mid-trample. Glazkov looked down the length of his leg, realising that this man, this frail example of street scum, had actually caught his foot and was holding it fast.

Pushing, the man toppled Glazkov over. He landed on his back, an explosion of air being forced out of him. The spiky-haired gladiator scrambled about, clambering to get up quickly; he wasn't used to being the one on the floor. And it wasn't good for the crowd to see him that way.

As he was rising, so too was his new foe. Only this one *kept* rising, and rising... and rising. Letting go of the sacks and blankets he'd wrapped around him, Glazkov's opposite number revealed his true size for the first time.

He stood a good few feet above the champion, and his muscles, visible beneath the khaki T-shirt he wore, were easily bigger than Glazkov's – as impressive as those were. The crowd, who'd been cheering, though not quite as loudly as they had in the previous match, suddenly took notice of what had happened. There was deathly silence.

The Tsar frowned and inched forward in his seat. Bohuslav placed both hands on the rail and peered down while the twins looked on. It was like they were all watching the miracle of birth, and in a sense they were. A transformation akin to a butterfly emerging from a cocoon. Only this insect was olive-skinned and, as he swept back his greasy black hair, he sneered first at the people in the 'royal box', then at Glazkov.

The champion swallowed. The roles had suddenly been reversed, and Glazkov now found himself being towered over.

It was small comfort, but he was tossed a mace as spiky as his hair, while his opponent had to make do with receiving a length of chain. As Glazkov hunched down, circling the larger man and trying to weigh up his options, the olive-skinned colossus moved to follow him, obviously still having trouble with one leg... or was it his foot? Yes, The Tsar noted that he wasn't putting as much weight on one side, as if an old injury was bothering him.

Glazkov struck and the blow glanced off the bigger man's forearm, cutting him, but not badly. At the same time, the bigger man unfurled his chain, throwing it out like a whip and snaking it around Glazkov's neck. Tugging, he yanked the champion towards him, then punched him hard in the face.

Glazkov unfurled along the chain, spinning away. His legs gave out. He ended up on the floor again with a thud, shaking his head.

The giant, seemingly in no rush at all, gave Glazkov time to recover and get to his feet as he wrapped the chain around his fist. This time when Glazkov took a swing with the mace, the newcomer batted it out of his hand, then punched the champion again, using the chain as a knuckle duster. Teeth and blood flew from Glazkov's mouth, as his head rocked to one side. Regardless of the fact it was their hero who was getting thrashed out there, the crowd responded well, cheering louder than ever.

"Who *is* this?" Bohuslav muttered to himself, but loudly enough for The Tsar to hear.

Glazkov was crawling around, spitting out more blood and teeth. When he looked up, his jaw was a mess. But he wasn't defeated just yet. Someone, probably one of The Tsar's guards, threw him a metal fighting pike.

He used this to help himself up, then turned it on his enemy, running at him – trying to skewer him on the end. In spite of his bad foot, the large man evaded the ungainly attack, whipping out the chain and lashing Glazkov across the back of the neck.

"*Mudak!*" growled the spiky-haired Russian. Livid, he tried again, but the giant used his chain to snag the pike, spoiling Glazkov's aim. Try as he might, the champion just wasn't strong enough to bring the weapon back towards his target. Then suddenly it was snatched from his grasp.

Before Glazkov could do anything, the pike had been turned on him and thrust through the Russian's shoulder until it came out the other side. Then, holding onto the pike, the man brought up a boot and kicked Glazkov off. He staggered, not quite grasping what had just happened. Then the pain registered and he howled.

The giant didn't give him long for self pity. Hefting the pike like a staff, the man struck Glazkov first in the stomach, then under his chin; with such force that Glazkov was lifted into the air, before landing heavily on the floor.

Glazkov didn't have a clue what was coming next – and that was probably for the best. The stranger bent and aimed the pike at Glazkov's head, forcing it in just behind the right temple. With his considerable bulk behind the strike, the man was able to push the sharpened end right through Glazkov's skull. Like the last time, the giant kicked Glazkov off the spear and the former champion's now lifeless body hit the ground.

The audience was speechless. They'd seen Glazkov in some challenging fights but never known him get more than a few cuts or bruises. What were they supposed to do now? They couldn't chant this *new* champion's name, because they didn't know it. Besides, he didn't look like the kind of man you applauded. More like trembled before.

The Tsar was equally shocked, not least when the bear of a man holding the pike and chain looked up and pointed at him. Bohuslav immediately nodded to the guards at the ring, who entered, raising their AK-47's and demanding that he put down his weapons.

"Call them off!" shouted the stranger in perfect Russian. His voice was deep, his words to the point. When the men remained where they were, and then actually moved closer, the man cocked his head as if to say, *That was a big mistake.*

Seconds later, the chain was unfurled and the pike was flicked to the side. The Kalashnikovs all fired at the same time, but were quickly knocked out of the guards' hands, completely missing the man in the middle. Having disarmed them, the giant set to work on the men themselves, taking out the closest by simply charging into them like a juggernaut – or flinging the chain at their faces. The others he dispatched with a series of kicks and blows with the pike.

Then, limping towards the edge of the ring, he used that

weapon like a pole-vaulter to clear the cordon. At the same time Bohuslav was ordering the guards with him to open fire into the ring. By the time they'd got their act together, the giant was already part of the crowd, crouching, moving from side to side so they couldn't easily track him.

"There!" shouted Bohuslav when he saw the tip of the pike above the mass of heads. The guards looked at each other, then at The Tsar, obviously troubled about firing into the throng. The Tsar nodded firmly and they did just that, picking off the people around the troublemaker, but not touching him. It only made the confusion worse. Those who remained panicked, slamming into each other, pushing each other out of the way. At one stage, when the giant saw he was close to being shot, he grabbed a woman and pulled her in front of him.

"Enough!" shouted The Tsar. This was only losing him subjects; it was obvious this had to be handled at closer range. "Xue, Ying." His bodyguards nodded, and ran to the viewing rail, leaping over it, into the crowd. Pockets of clear floor were opening up and in one to their left rose the olive-skinned man.

The twins drew their Hook Swords, circling him. He grimaced.

They attacked in a flurry of gleaming metal – and he blocked each and every swipe with the pike. The Tsar had never seen anything like it, never seen fighters move so fast; the giant's parries causing the girls to step up their game considerably. The space cleared much quicker and, were it not for the twins, The Tsar might have ordered his guards to start shooting again.

Swish, clack! Swish, clack! The three of them fought all the way to the base of the viewing platform. The Tsar got up and walked towards the rail, ignoring Bohuslav's gestures to remain out of harm's way.

He saw Xue duck as a pike blow whipped over her head; Ying almost ended up with the sharp end in her thigh. As confident as he was in them, he could also see that this interloper was highly trained. And people this skilled always wanted something... But what? Did he want The Tsar dead?

The giant took his eyes off the twins long enough to find his mark standing at the rail. "Call... them... off," he said, still blocking attacks, then added, "I would speak with you."

The Tsar rubbed his chin, still unsure.

Snarling, the giant elbowed one of the twins out of the way, kicked back the other – and lifted his pike like a javelin, aiming at The Tsar. Bohuslav's sickle was already out and he was about to throw it when The Tsar held up his hand.

"Wait... Wait!" Both men halted, staring into each other's eyes. The twins were about to attack again, but The Tsar ordered them to stand down. "Bohuslav, put that away. You men, lower your guns."

When the attacker saw this, he lowered the pike, placing it by his side – though his body was still tense, ready for any surprises. "I came here seeking an audience," he said in those clipped tones.

"You... you came here? You were *brought* here."

"I *let* them bring me."

Bohuslav's eyes narrowed.

The Tsar nodded; it did seem unlikely that he would have been captured on the streets if he hadn't wanted to be. "Who are you?"

"I am Tanek."

That name was familiar, but the Tsar couldn't remember why. It would no doubt come to him, but in the meantime he asked: "What do you want?"

"As I said, I would speak with you."

The Tsar frowned. "What about? What is so important that you would risk your life like this?"

The olive-skinned man brushed the long, greasy hair out of his eyes and said: "I have a proposition for you."

CHAPTER FOUR

Robert missed the dreams.

He'd never mentioned it to anyone, because he doubted whether they'd understand – not even Mary. But God did he miss them. Those vivid – sometimes nightmarish – visions he'd experienced during his time in Sherwood had saved his life. He'd seen his friends in those dreams, before he'd even met them, and he'd seen what The Sheriff, De Falaise, had planned during their final confrontation – allowing him to twist as he plunged the knife into Robert, avoiding a fatal belly wound and taking the blade in his side instead. It had taken him a while to recover, but he would surely have been dead if it hadn't been for the tip-off.

Since moving into the castle, though, he hadn't been able to remember a single dream. Of course, you needed to *sleep* to dream – and that was something Robert had been doing very little of lately. The mattress he lay on seemed far too... luxurious. He'd slept much more soundly on a blanket of grass and moss, in his handmade lean-to or outside, looking up at the stars. All he saw these days when he looked up was the ceiling.

But it was more than simply missing the dreams. They were part and parcel of missing a way of life. Missing a place where he'd felt completely at ease.

Yeah, except when intruders were coming in after you with guns, or firing grenades off into the trees.

No, before. The time when he'd been alone in the forest, just him and nature – with only the birds, animals and foliage for company. He'd been happy–

Happy? You went there to escape, have you forgotten that? You went there because you didn't have anyone else in the world, not after... Now you have. People who love you, people who care about what happens to you.

People who counted on him, every minute of every day. Responsibilities the likes of which he never could have imagined; not even when he was after those promotions on the force. Everything seemed to have snowballed since they came here. He'd turned around and suddenly he was this mythical figure in charge of his very own policing network. How exactly had that happened?

Because you made *it happen. You wanted people to be safe, for there to be some kind of law, some justice after The Sheriff's rule. You did a good thing, Robert.*

But at what cost? Leaning up against the headboard, he sighed. If he'd had a dream about this when he'd been back in Sherwood, he might not have got involved. Who was he kidding? He wouldn't have done a thing differently. He'd still have saved Mark and Bill; been persuaded by Tate to fight, to build an army that could take on De Falaise; taken in Granger – rest his soul – and Jack.

And Mary...

He looked down at the sleeping figure, her dark hair splayed on the pillow. If anyone had told him, even a year ago, that he could fall in love again – even if he'd dreamt about it – he would have thought it madness. But then, wasn't love a kind of insanity, or so the old pop and rock songs said. Songs like Dale used to sing... still sang on some occasions when the residents of the castle needed their spirits lifting.

Robert remembered how awkward it had been at first with Mary. He'd pushed her away, the thought of being with anyone again after Joanne was just... But somehow she had broken down his defences, or rather slipped past them just as his troops had done when they took the castle. When he remembered what had almost happened to her at the hands of De Falaise, it tore him up inside.

So why was she giving him such a hard time? Why had she barely spoken to him all evening, turning her back on him when they got into bed? She had to know that there was nothing going on with him and Adele – he'd only known her five minutes! How could Mary possibly believe he was trying to replace her?

But wasn't it partly down to Mary that he was stuck in this castle when he should be out there doing more of what he'd done in York? Was it really the fact that he'd saved Adele that bothered her, that the woman was so grateful, or was it because he'd gone there regardless of Mary's wishes?

"You've been out of the game for a little while, boss. You're rusty. That psycho almost had you."

He'd dismissed Jack's words, but the man had been right. If he hadn't been there, Robert wouldn't be alive right now. Out of the game. Too much time stuck behind a desk. Now where had he heard that before?

Sitting in the dark, a face from the past floated into his mind. Now he flashed back to his very first days as a rookie, to his old station house in Nottingham, just south of this very castle in fact – before Joanne had made him move away from the city. To seasoned Constable Eric Meadows, who'd 'puppy walked' him through his first weeks, pounding the beat alongside him.

Robert watched as a mini-movie played in his head, of them chasing a thief who'd just snatched a woman's purse in broad daylight before disappearing up a side street.

"You go after him," Meadows had instructed. "I'll go this way, try and head him off." Holding onto his cap, Robert raced after the man.

The felon, checking back over his shoulder, saw that there

was only one young copper chasing him – and he'd slowed down, fancying his chances. Robert skidded to a stop only metres behind. "N-Now don't try anything funny," he said, with absolutely no confidence. "Come along quietly and it'll be better for everyone."

"I'm not going back to jail," the scruffy-looking man had warned him, then approached, balling his hands into fists.

Robert knew how he *should* tackle a situation like this, he'd been trained after all. But reality was completely different. Here was a real criminal, a *desperate* criminal, and only one thing stood between him and his freedom: Robert.

The thief ran at him, readying to punch. But before that blow could land the man was falling over sideways. A puzzled Robert lowered his gaze and saw Meadows there, rugby tackling the fellow to the ground. His plan had worked, going round the houses to take the villain by surprise while Robert distracted him. It was a good strategy; one Robert would later use on a much larger scale.

The thief tried to fight, knocking off Meadows' cap to reveal his salt and pepper hair. "Well, don't just stand there gaping," Meadows shouted, struggling to hold the scruffy man down. "Get your arse over here and help me cuff him!"

Snapping awake, Robert had gone over and assisted, listening while the veteran officer read the thief his rights. Then they'd escorted him back to the station, putting him in a cell.

"Nothing quite like it, is there?" Meadows said to Robert as they'd come away again, the job done.

"What's that, sir?"

"That adrenalin rush when it's you or them." Meadows' eyes were twinkling. "Facing your fear, lad. Did you feel it?"

Robert nodded, but all he'd really felt was scared. He suspected he wouldn't actually know what Meadows was talking about until he arrested someone himself, until it was just him and the other guy... or guys. In the years since that day, he'd felt that rush many, many times.

"Never let them put you behind one of those," Meadows told him, gesturing to the officer behind the duty desk. "You stay out there, young Stokes. Stay where you can make a difference and leave all that to the paper pushers."

Sadly, they'd all become paper pushers by the time the virus struck, with more and more government bullshit tying them up. But in the period before that, Robert had learned a lot from his old mentor: not least of which was that guns were not the real answer to tackling gun *crime*. "It all escalates, you see," Meadows had warned him. "And then where's it all going to end?"

Another memory crept in now; that of Meadows the last time he'd seen him, before Robert moved to the outskirts of Mansfield. A combination of injury – sustained on football match duty when one crazed supporter had broken Eric's leg – and old age meant that he'd found himself in the last place he wanted to be. Oh, there'd been a promotion that came with the office, to Sergeant no less, but the fact remained that Meadows was trapped, drowning in responsibilities. When Robert shook his hand and thanked him for everything, he could see the spark had almost completely gone from those eyes.

"You're awake." The voice made him jump. Robert hadn't even noticed Mary had stirred; he'd been so wrapped up in his recollections. "What are you thinking about?"

In the half-light, Robert stared down at her face and shrugged. "Nothing."

"Liar." It wasn't said in a nasty way, but it stung nonetheless.

"Am I not allowed to just sit here peacefully now?"

"That's not what I said. I asked you what you were thinking about?"

"The past."

Mary sat up, resting against the headboard beside him. "You were thinking about Joanne and Stevie again, then."

Robert sighed. "No... why does it always have to come back to that? Why can't you let it go?"

"Why can't *you*?"

"This isn't even about... If you must know I was remembering an old friend of mine from the force. And before you ask, no, he wasn't a woman." Mary's turn to be stung. "I've been thinking about what's been happening, what I'm doing here."

"With me?"

Robert sighed again. "No, you're twisting it all... What I'm doing *here* at the castle, Mary. How I've become rooted to this place, been hiding behind its walls for too long. It's not where I belong."

"And *where* should you be? Sherwood? Alone?"

"No..." Robert shook his head, but there was no conviction in it, only confusion. "I don't know... Anywhere but stuck here organising the men, sending them out on missions."

"I help you as much as I can, you don't have to shoulder it all on your own."

"No, that's not what I'm talking about. I'm not the man you met anymore, Mary. Staying here's done that. I'm... rusty."

"So this is about what happened in York? I said it was a bad idea to –"

"Mary, you're not listening. That's not the issue. The men we saw out there, the cult. They're dangerous."

"More dangerous than the Frenchman?"

"They have the capacity to be. And they're not interested in wealth or power like he was. They'll fight until every last one of them is dead."

Mary was silent for a few moments. "We have men, loyal men," she said eventually.

"And what if they fall? What if the fight is brought here again? How am I supposed to defend the people I care about, how am I supposed to lead men into battle, when I've lost my edge? When I've become..."

"What? A family man? A leader?"

"You just don't see it, do you? I'm no better than De Falaise."

Mary pulled a face. "How can you say that?"

"Because it's true. He stayed here in his ivory tower with Gwen while he sent his men off to their deaths, to do his dirty work for him."

"To do his *killing*. And he wasn't exactly the dutiful partner when it came to Gwen, was he? She was his plaything, Robert. His toy. You care about your men. You care about me... don't you?"

"You really need to ask that?"

Mary gave a little shrug which he could barely see in the dark. "When girls like Adele –"

"Adele again?" Robert snorted. "What the bloody hell's she got to do with this?"

"It's another consequence of going out there. You're a living legend, Robert; women fall at your feet."

"That's your paranoia again."

"Is it? I saw the way she looked at you. You can't have missed it; and you invited her back here of all the things to –"

He pulled the covers aside, climbing out of bed.

"Where are you going?"

"For a drink of water." Robert pulled on his robe, making for the door.

"Robert, I –"

"They don't mean anything to me, Mary. None of them. You'd know that if you really knew *me*." He took one last look at her, then he opened the door and slid out, whispering under his breath, "I love *you*." Robert wasn't sure whether she'd heard him or not, but he'd said it and as far as he was concerned that was enough. As he shut the door he thought he heard a faint sob, and almost went back in. But he was in no mood to keep talking that particular subject to death.

Robert crept down the darkened corridor, careful not to wake the others sleeping in this part of the castle. He padded down the stairs, heading for what had once been the castle café. Striking a match on the counter, he lit a couple of candles. Then, taking a glass, he opened a cupboard and took a bottle of water from a pack, one of a batch his men had found out on their travels. He looked at it. There weren't many still around, but even this was somehow mocking him – reminding him he'd returned to a life he'd once turned his back on. When he'd been in Sherwood, he'd caught his own water and filtered it. Now, it was like that had never happened. Hanging his head, he unscrewed the lid and poured.

He felt a hand on his shoulder and dropped the glass, spinning round, simultaneously grabbing whoever was behind him by the throat and shoving them against the wall.

Robert was breathing hard. He blinked, and realised the figure he was holding was a woman with short hair.

"I... I'm sorry..." croaked Adele. "I..."

Horrified, Robert let her go. "No, I'm... You shouldn't creep up on me like that."

She rubbed her throat and said hoarsely: "I... I wasn't creeping, Robert. Honestly. I had to go to the loo and got lost finding my way back. This place is so huge, and I'm still figuring it all out."

Robert's breathing slowed. God, he really was losing his touch; there was a time he would have heard... *felt* someone come up behind him. If it had been an assassin, they'd have plunged a knife into him before he could even turn.

"I saw the light and, well, if I'd realised you wanted to be alone..." Adele said sadly.

"It's not that. I just..." Robert shook his head. "Did I hurt you?"

Adele coughed and smiled. "Nothing a glass of water won't fix."

Robert walked back to the counter, then stooped to pick up the bits of broken glass. He looked across when Adele followed him, noticing what she was wearing for the first time. A man's shirt – probably Jack's because it was so big – with the sleeves rolled up... and nothing else. Her long legs looked pale in the light from the candle, and he chastised himself for letting his eyes linger on them before getting back to his task.

"You're very fast, you know."

"Hmm? Not nearly as fast as I used to be."

Adele leaned on the counter, watching him pick up the final pieces of glass. "You're joking? You really had me back there. And the way you tackled those hooligans back in York!"

Robert put the glass in a bin. "It was nothing." That sounded better in his head than it did out loud. *Why didn't you go the whole way and add, aw shucks?* "It's what I do. Well, what I did."

"Did?"

Robert joined her at the counter, then rounded the other side – partly to fetch another couple of glasses, partly to put a physical barrier between them. He poured her some water and she sipped it gladly. But she wasn't going to be distracted. "You said *did*; past tense?"

Robert took a swig of his own water. "It's just that lately I've felt like I'm not doing any good anymore."

"I don't understand."

"I'm stuck here all the time. Organising."

"Then if it makes you feel like this, perhaps you shouldn't be." Adele put the glass down and absently ran her finger around the rim. "I've always been a big believer in following your heart." She looked up at him. "What's it telling you?"

"That's the thing: it's not telling me anything. Or at least nothing I can trust." Robert let out a breath. "I don't know why I'm dumping all this on you. I barely even know you."

Adele smiled again. "Sometimes it's easier to talk to a stranger than someone... Well, you know."

Robert nodded. "Sometimes I guess it is."

"This Mary you're with," said Adele after a pause. "She seems really nice."

"She is," Robert said without hesitation, then took another drink.

"It's really late. I should be at least trying to get some rest I suppose. Not that it's easy in a new place."

"If it helps, you're safe now."

"That why you're so on edge, jumping at shadows?"

Robert laughed softly. "You have a point."

"And you should try and get some sleep as w–" She let out a yelp, sucking in air through her teeth as she hobbled backwards.

"What? What is it?" Robert had rounded the counter in seconds.

Adele was hopping towards a chair, clutching her foot. "I don't think you got *all* the glass."

"Oh no, hold on..." He brought one of the candles from the counter, placing it on the floor as he crouched down and took hold of her heel. "Let me have a look. I can't see anyth... wait, there it is." Holding Adele's foot steady, Robert squeezed the area and drew out the splinter. "It needs washing, we don't want it to get infected."

Adele looked down at him. "You really are sweet you know, Hooded Man or not. I hope Mary knows how lucky she is."

Once Mary had begun to cry, she couldn't stop.

All the tension, the stress, the worry flooded out of her – not just from tonight's argument, but from the days preceding it. Waiting to see whether the man she loved more than life itself would come back to her.

And when he did, what had she done? She hadn't even given him a kiss, she was too busy firing off questions, checking for injuries (she hadn't seen the worst of them till he'd undressed, his back a mass of bruises), giving him a hard time about bringing the woman he'd saved back to *their* home. What was she, some kind of jealous teenager?

But then, she'd never done the whole teen in love thing. Hers had been a small locality and, apart from break times at school, she hadn't really mixed with boys. She certainly hadn't been able to go out in the evenings; her brother, who'd looked after her when their father had died of a stroke, would have gone mad.

Damn right I would, Moo-Moo, said the voice of that dead sibling in her head; the one she still heard occasionally, even though David had died from the virus long ago. And who still called her by that ridiculous childhood name, a contraction of Mary Louise. *So would Dad if he'd still been alive.*

In some ways it had been a drawback having two strong male role models, living all that way out on the farm. But it had made her the woman she was today; taught her to fight and stand up for herself.

But in fighting for Robert, maybe she was also pushing him away. If you love something so much, sometimes you have to let it go – isn't that what people always said? When you let them go, however, you run the risk of them never coming back.

To her mind, the jealousy was justified anyway. It hadn't

been easy for her, competing initially with the ghost of Robert's late wife – the one he'd loved so much he cut himself off from civilisation and swore he'd never care about anyone again – and then with this character people thought he was; this symbol of hope. It was tough being in love with an icon.

Though probably not as tough as actually being *one, Moo-Moo. You should cut him a little slack every now and again.*

"What are you talking about?" Mary caught herself saying out loud.

Remember when I asked you if you were sure about him?

Mary nodded.

Well, you were right. He risked everything to save you when you pulled that stunt impersonating him.

"He'd have done the same for anyone. He just *did* for that woman he brought back."

It's not the same thing, and you know it. He came after you because of how he feels. Not out of any sense of duty. But you're in danger of losing him, unless you're careful.

"I don't need relationship advice from someone who never had a date in his life."

Suit yourself, Moo-Moo. Just trying to help.

She knew he was right, of course. Robert had come after her that day because he loved her. She'd seen the way he fought when De Falaise took her captive.

And even though the months after that had been hard, Robert moving from Sherwood to the castle, them trying to build something up out of the aftermath of the Sheriff's rule – both in terms of the Rangers, and with regards to their personal feelings – there had still been moments to cherish.

Like the first night they spent together, after last year's Summer fête. Jack had the notion that it would be good to give the men and their new family a party, and though Robert had been resistant at first he'd finally been persuaded by Mary.

"We could all use a bit of... what was it Jack said? 'Down Time'," she'd told him.

The grounds of the castle had been open to all that day, with food and drink and music; some of which had been provided by a battery-powered stereo, some by Dale and his guitar. People from New Hope and other villages under Robert's protection had visited Nottingham, and said afterwards it had been well worth the trip. It reminded them that not everything in this post-virus world had gone sour. They were still alive after all, and still human. Even Robert, who'd been on tenterhooks waiting for some emergency or other to happen had loosened up after a couple of drinks.

"Come on," Mary had said, after some Dutch courage herself. "Dance with me."

Robert shook his head, so she'd leaned in then, whispering in his ear. "Please."

He'd allowed himself to be pulled up, and when he held her she could tell he was relaxing. Several dances, and several beers later, they'd found themselves walking through the grounds of the castle, alone in the moonlight. She'd pointed up at the stars and when he looked down again she'd kissed him. Not the kisses they'd shared since first meeting, the awkward, tentative brushing of lips they were used to – but a long, lingering kiss. Mary had felt her body turn to jelly as Robert responded: his hands on her back just as hers were clutching his shoulder-blades.

When both their hands started to explore further, they'd pulled apart – and it had been Robert, surprisingly, who'd suggested they find somewhere a little more private. "Maybe there's a room where people have left their coats," he suggested, and she'd laughed, feeling truly happy for the first time in a long while. Though she should have been scared because this was her first time, Mary was far from it. Even if things had felt uncomfortable before, nothing on that special night did. It felt right, *so right.*

Sure, she could put it down to the alcohol, the atmosphere of the party. But to her it just felt like they were finally on the same page. That now he wanted her as much as she'd always wanted him. And it had been amazing, truly amazing. She'd placed herself in Robert's hands and he hadn't failed to live up to her imagination.

Then, waking up that morning with Robert lying next to her, she'd experienced a horrible sinking feeling. What if he regrets what we did? What if he rejects me? She'd kept quiet, frozen, just watching – waiting for him to rouse, but at the same time hoping he'd sleep forever so she wouldn't have to face the disappointment.

What a relief, then, when he'd woken up and smiled.

"Hello sweetheart," she said.

His smile had widened.

Yay me, she'd said to herself.

It was a million miles away from sitting here in that same bed and crying her heart out. When she thought back to those first couple of months of being together, properly together, it just made her feel worse. They'd spent as much time as they possibly could in each other's company, working around schedules, finding private moments. Most of the castle – and most of Robert's men – knew. Had to by the daft grins on both their faces.

Lately, though, they'd spent less and less time together... especially in *that* way. Admittedly, Robert had been worrying about this cult – and who could blame him? She had been busy too, dealing with the day-to-day running of the castle, tending to any injured men that came back from patrols with nursing skills she'd built on since Robert had found her at her farm; studying from text books she and the men brought back, not to mention teaching those same skills to others. They were both tired and, more often than not, would just go to sleep at night.

She'd read about this in women's magazines and the glossies that were delivered with the weekend papers, back before the world changed. The problem pages were full of stuff about 'Honeymoon Periods' and what happens afterwards when real life intrudes. And although Mary knew this was meant to signal them being more comfortable with each other – solid couples didn't have to show affection like that *all* the time – she couldn't help feeling more than a little unwanted.

At the same time he was growing increasingly distant. It came to a head when he'd begun training again, working out to try and get fit; exercising muscles that had grown flabby from lack of use.

Then one day he announced he was going out with the patrol

again, going out to assess the threat of the cult personally. They hadn't even discussed this and it had thrown her completely.

"Why, Robert? Why does it have to be you? And why now? Jack can-"

"I'm *going*, Mary. And that's that."

They'd rowed, he'd stormed off, and he'd left without even saying goodbye. Maybe she should have been more laid back – after all, he'd been leading a band of men when she first met him, fighting De Falaise's troops. But he'd also got himself blown up that day, would probably have died if she hadn't been there to tend to his wounds. She couldn't shake that image from her mind – of him unconscious in the back of the truck, on his way to Sherwood...

He'd recovered, of course, faster really than he should have. But what if he didn't next time? What if she had to cradle his head as he died? What if she didn't even get the chance to say goodbye?

It was why she'd pulled that 'stunt', as her brother called it: drugging Robert and taking his place for the final battle with the Sheriff. She'd wanted to keep him safe, that's all. Wanted to protect the man she loved.

He can look after himself, David had told her, and she knew deep down he was right.

That didn't stop her worrying. And none of this would help them get back to how they'd been during those summer and autumn months.

Mary dried her eyes with the bed sheets, then got out and wrapped her robe around her. She'd go down and drag him back to bed if she had to, talk to him, maybe do more than that. Show him how much she'd missed him, how much she still *loved* him.

He'd said he was going for a drink of water, which he often did when he couldn't sleep. She knew she'd find him in the café probably looking out through those big windows.

Mary stopped dead in her tracks when she heard voices from inside. Two voices: one Robert's, the other a woman's. As she drew closer, keeping quiet, she saw them inside. Lit by candles, they were sitting at one of the tables. Mary realised she could have marched past with a brass band and they wouldn't have noticed, they were so wrapped up in conversation. Though try as she might, she couldn't hear what was being said.

The woman with Robert – *her* Robert – had her back to Mary. But she knew who it was, even without the short hair as a clue.

Right, that does it... I'm going to...

Do what, Moo-Moo, storm in there and make a fool of yourself? They're only talking.

I know, but–

But nothing. Leave it, sis.

David was right. Again. There was no way she could make her presence known that didn't look like she was spying on them. Checking up on Robert. Dammit, right now that's exactly what she *was* doing.

Mary watched them for a little while longer, but had to turn away when she heard Adele laughing at something Robert had just said. So happy. Just like Mary had been the night of the fête.

Feeling the tears coming again, she retreated to their bedroom where she waited. Not for Robert to come back from patrol this time, but for him to return to her. If he ever would.

Mary tried to stay awake, but eventually sheer exhaustion and all that crying took their toll. Sleep claimed her, and she never heard Robert come in, or felt him climb into bed with her.

If she had she might also have heard him tell her again softly, as he kissed her shoulder, how very much he loved her.

CHAPTER FIVE

The village had been named Hope.

But that Hope had died along with its founder. Clive Maitland had been killed defending this place against De Falaise's men, murdered by the fat Mexican, Major Javier. The Reverend Tate knew that Gwen had taken her revenge on Javier for that, shooting him just like he'd put a bullet in Clive. Although Tate could forgive her for that – many terrible things had happened in the heat of that final battle – he wasn't altogether sure The Lord would be able to without repentance. It hadn't been her place to take that life, and more than likely there would be a punishment, one way or another.

Gwen probably thought she'd served her time in purgatory, held prisoner at the castle and made to do unspeakable things at the behest of that mad Frenchman. Tate had to admire her for not going completely stark, staring mad over those months. But she would have killed De Falaise as well, given the opportunity, and was on her way to do so when Tate had been hit in the shoulder by a stray bullet.

"God will provide his own revenge."

Tate had shouted this after her, but she'd taken no notice, headstrong as she was. She hadn't succeeded anyway, apart from stabbing De Falaise in the leg and managing to get shot herself by one of Tanek's crossbow bolts. It had been left to Robert Stokes, their leader, to end the Frenchman's reign. Tate had often wondered if The Hooded Man had actually been an unwitting part of The Almighty's plan for revenge, but almost always dismissed these thoughts. Robert was a law unto himself and still continued to be so. That man no more believed in God's overarching design than Tate believed he was the reincarnation of St Francis of Assisi.

Not that you had to *believe* in God to be a part of his plans. But you did have to have faith, something Robert was sorely lacking. It was one of the reasons why had Tate left the castle in the first place; the two of them were never going to see eye-to-eye on that. The holy man knew he could do more good out in the fledgling communities, as Clive had told Tate when he'd found him. The man had a vision of what Hope and other villages could be like, how the survivors of the human race might all rise again, Phoenix-like, from the ashes of The Cull. He'd had the necessary leadership qualities to draw together his own community, and if it hadn't been for Javier wrecking it that fateful day – riding in and casually shooting up the place – Clive might just have succeeded.

Of course, he might yet: through Gwen. She'd inherited a lot of Clive's determination, seemingly channelling his ability to make people listen. (It was a quality, coincidentally, Clive had also shared with Robert.) She was dead set on pursuing his dream, putting Hope back together, making a place to fit to raise their child, Clive Jr.

"I want him to grow up in a loving atmosphere, away from the city and out of the shadow of that castle," she informed Tate, not long after the birth. The first part was fair enough, what parent doesn't want such an environment for their child? Yet Tate had to question whether the second part had more to do with the question mark hanging over the baby's origins. Did she really want to get away from the castle because some part of her recognised it was where Clive Jr had been conceived?

Robert, Mary, Jack, even Tate himself. They all suspected the truth of the matter, even if Gwen steadfastly refused to. She didn't want to hear it through the pregnancy and certainly didn't want to talk about it after her son was born. Regardless of the fact there was only a slim chance Clive was the father, Gwen was adamant he be listed as such in the new records system being initiated in Nottingham ("If we start with our own people," Mary had suggested, "then we can add others we find out about as and when."). Tate couldn't blame Gwen for wanting to pretend the boy was Clive's. Who would want to think that their offspring was the product of rape? Especially by a man whose genes, Tate suspected, had been given to him by Satan himself. He'd certainly been put on this Earth to do the Fallen Angel's bidding.

Tate always felt more than a little responsible for what had happened to Gwen. Perhaps there had been something more the holy man could have done to prevent Javier from taking her back to Nottingham. Or maybe if he hadn't tackled Javier in the first place, struggling with the man as he held the pistol... Was it as much his fault the gun had gone off and shot Clive? No, Javier was about to shoot him anyway, Tate was sure of it, that's why he'd felt compelled to intervene.

Then later, when he'd joined Robert's band, Tate should have tried harder to convince the man to mount a rescue. There again, they both knew it would have been suicide. Plus there was no way of knowing for sure Gwen was even alive.

Robert had done it for Mark, though, hadn't he? Tate would say to himself, then feel guilty for such thoughts. Mark was just a child, being held and tortured, then sentenced to execution. There had been other villagers that were going to die as well. It had been that which had forced Robert to move against De Falaise. In any event, Gwen had remained at the castle, subject to the Frenchman's sadistic whims.

For all these reasons, Tate decided to go with her when she left. It had been a tearful goodbye, but he knew he'd see everyone again. Nottingham wasn't *that* far from where they were heading, and he'd made the trip a few times, like when the castle had hosted a fête last summer.

He recalled now the day they left, though, and what each of his friends had said.

"Thank you for everything," had been Mary's words, giving the Reverend a kiss on the cheek.

"Gonna miss your words of wisdom. Take it easy," Jack had told him, clasping his hand and shaking it firmly.

"Are you sure you have to go?" Mark had asked. And when Tate nodded, he saw the boy's eyes moistening. Tate had rubbed his tousled blond hair and Mark had laughed.

"See you around, I s'pose," Bill had said next – and it wasn't long after that he had made tracks himself, after some disagreement or other with Robert.

Then came the man himself. The Hooded Man, who Tate had talked into leading these people. They might have had their differences, and Tate might not have agreed on some of his methods, but he knew fundamentally that Robert was a good man. And he knew he was going to miss him.

"If you ever need anything, even if it's just to talk, my son –"

"I know where you are," Robert said, fixing him with those intense eyes of his. "You look after yourself, Reverend."

"You too." He'd leaned in close so the others couldn't hear and added: "Look after them all." It was Robert's turn to nod. "You did a good job, you know," Tate said finally. And he thought then that he'd detected the slightest of smiles playing on Robert's lips.

They'd driven off in one of the jeeps De Falaise had left behind, packed with enough food and water to last them the journey, in addition to whatever items Robert's men had been able to find for the baby: nappies, bottles, jars of baby food (there were actually plenty of these kinds of stocks still left in shops and warehouses; Tate didn't like to think about why). Neither of them had known what to expect when they finally arrived, having heard nothing of the village since they'd left. When Tate had gone in search of The Hooded Man, there had only been a handful of the original members of Hope still living there. Young Darryl Wade, for example, who'd been helping Clive fix up the village hall the day Javier arrived – turning it into a school for future generations. Graham Leicester, as well, who'd been attempting to grow food in gardens and fields. But most had fled the village, fled the region, once the new Sheriff's stranglehold on the area had taken effect. Tate knew for a fact that former midwife June Taylor had done so with Gwen and Clive's adopted kids, Sally and Luke.

"They've seen enough of fighting and death," June said to Tate as she was packing up their things. She was referring, of course, to the kids having witnessed Clive's brutal demise – something they'd probably never get over as long as they lived. "After everything they've been through, even before Hope, they need some kind of stability." He'd tried to talk her out of it, saying that one day Gwen would return, he felt it in his bones, but it was a half-hearted protest at best. Deep down Tate realised June was right: Sally and Luke *should* be away from this place. He hoped they were living a peaceful life somewhere.

Strangely, Gwen had not asked about them when they'd both recovered after the battle. And when he'd told her anyway, she'd nodded as if taking the information in, but had been more concerned about the baby she was carrying inside her. Tate liked to think she felt the same way as him, that she wished them happiness wherever they were. It was what Clive would have wanted. But there was always that niggling feeling – and again, he hated himself for it – that she was okay with them being somewhere else, because now she had a *real* child that belonged to Clive. Sally and Luke must have seemed like something from another lifetime, after her trials at the castle.

They'd driven into the village and it seemed like a ghost town. Nothing much had changed in the time since Tate had been there last. The cottages still had pock-marks on the walls where the bullets had struck, and there were charred sections of road where grenades had gone off.

Gwen had parked the jeep and climbed out. Unlike Tate, this had been the first time she'd returned since Clive's death. Leaving the Reverend behind for a moment, to look after Clive Jr, she'd wandered down the street as if in a daze. When she reached the bit of the road where Clive had fallen, she'd knelt.

Maybe this wasn't such a good idea after all, thought Tate. Like the castle, there were too many memories here. They should have sought out another village to start again, dedicated it to Clive – somewhere his ghost wasn't on every street corner.

There was a clacking sound, and Tate leaned forward in the jeep's front seat. Gwen had heard it too and was rising, pulling something out from under her jumper; something she'd tucked in her jeans without telling Tate. It was an automatic pistol, another parting gift from the previous tenant of Nottingham Castle. Gwen held the weapon like a professional, just like she had the machine gun she'd used during that last battle in the city.

"Come out, whoever you are," shouted the thin, auburn-haired woman. "I'm not messing around." The more Tate saw of Gwen like this, the more he realised how she'd changed – or rather how circumstances had changed her – and how much he didn't care for it.

Behind him, Clive Jr began to cry.

Then, at the side of one cottage, Tate spotted a figure. It was Andy Hobbs, another resident of the old Hope, standing with a hunting rifle – aiming it at Gwen's head. She'd spun on him in a heartbeat, bringing her pistol to bear.

"Gwen, no!" called Tate. But she'd already spotted who it was... and so had Andy.

"It can't be," said the man, lowering his gun. "Gwen? Is that really you?"

She began lowering her pistol, though not letting her guard down quite as quickly as Andy. Gwen approached him, eyes darting left and right. "How have you been, Andy?" Tate heard her ask.

"Never mind about that, come here." Andy went to give her a big hug, but Gwen pulled back before he could get anywhere near her. This was Andy, who'd once tended the fields, who'd sat and laughed and joked outside the local pub with Clive and Gwen on balmy summer evenings. She recognised him; she'd even said his name. But the trust was gone – maybe Gwen's trust in *all* men except Tate. It would take time, but she'd need people like Andy if she was really going to fulfil Clive's dream.

"Andy!" Tate called, in an effort to take the embarrassment out of the situation.

"Reverend? I can't believe it. I never thought... Well, I didn't think I'd see either of you again to be honest."

Clive Jr. was crying louder and Gwen returned to the jeep. Andy called the all clear, and other familiar faces appeared: Graham and Darryl, along with a few others Tate had never seen before. They gathered round, old friends swapping hellos, introductions being made.

"I still can't believe you're really here," Andy said again to Tate. "It's so good to see you."

"You too, my son," Tate replied, leaning on his stick.

"We heard snatches about what happened in Nottingham, but nothing concrete."

"Something about a big fight?" Darryl added.

"We figured something big must have happened because no more men came to take our food."

"We were ready for them anyway, even if they did," Andy said, holding up the rifle.

Tate grimaced. "I wouldn't have thought that was your style."

"Neither is being hit in the back of the head with a rifle butt."

"Granted," said Tate.

"So, you went off to join Hood's men?"

"Not intentionally," Tate pointed out. "But I suppose I did end up getting dragged along for the ride. That's a story for another time, though."

Gwen was standing by the jeep, cradling Clive Jr, feeding him a bottle of milk. Darryl came over and smiled at the little one. "So who's this then? He's really cute."

"This is Clive's son."

"Clive's..." Darryl frowned. "But I thought–"

"Darryl, Darryl." Tate interrupted, limping round the side of the jeep. "Enough of your questions. We've been on the road a while and there's still food and drink in the back of the jeep. Enough for a celebratory dinner, I'd suspect."

So that's how they'd spent their first night back; inside *The Red Lion*, filling their bellies and swapping stories about what had happened in the time since they'd all last seen each other. The remaining members of what had once been Hope had carried on with their lives, but lived in fear that the soldiers might return. That was one of the reasons why they hadn't cleaned up the place much.

"It was a reminder of what could happen again," Graham told them. "A reminder not to get taken unawares again."

"That's why when we heard your jeep... well, you know," said Andy, now feeling slightly foolish.

"De Falaise is no more," Tate assured them, nursing a brandy. "His men have been defeated, his legacy replaced by a new law in the land."

Gwen pulled a face at this and Tate caught it out of the corner of his eye. As far as she was concerned, she'd got herself out of the mess at the castle. Robert Stokes had been far too late to save her, in every sense of the word.

"Do you really think he can protect us?" asked Darryl, also seeing Gwen's expression.

Tate nodded. "I think he'll try his best."

"So what now?" asked Graham, putting his feet up on one of the tables.

It was Gwen who answered, rocking the baby in her arms. "We start again. We turn this back into the place Clive always wanted it to be. With one or two exceptions."

Graham frowned. "What do you mean?"

"It's like you said." Gwen held Clive Jr in the nook of one arm and picked up the pistol that was resting on the table in front of her. Tate raised an eyebrow, which she completely ignored. "We're never going to be taken unawares again. This time, we make sure we can defend ourselves. There are more in the jeep; rifles and pistols, plus ammo."

"What? Gwen, you stole–"

"I *borrowed* them from the caves," she said, cutting Tate off. "Besides, from the sound of things they won't be using them any time soon."

Many of Clive's ideas had been sound, she went on to explain, but in attempting to start again with a bunch of people skilled in various areas – Graham's knowledge of agriculture, for example; Darryl's handyman ability – he'd left out the very people who could fight off an attack like the one they'd encountered. Now, every single person in *New* Hope, as Gwen suggested renaming the village, would know how to fight as well. With guns, with their hands. This met with nods of approval from the folk in *The Red Lion*.

All except Tate.

He'd talked to her about it later, asking her if a community based on violence was what Clive would really have wanted. It certainly wasn't the 'loving atmosphere' she'd said she was looking for when they'd left the castle.

"We also need to be safe, Reverend. I don't want to be reliant on Stokes and his people."

"You'd rather create a mini army of your own, is that it?"

She shook her head. "We'll leave the outside world alone, if they'll do the same with us."

While Tate conceded that she had a point about defending themselves, he still wasn't mad on the idea of these ordinary men and women being on a state of constant alert, trained in using firearms and hand-to-hand combat. "How is it any different to what you did for Robert?" Gwen had said after she'd asked Tate to teach his self defence tactics.

"That was a war," Tate replied. "Desperate times..."

"These are *still* desperate times, in case you hadn't noticed. What happens if another threat comes, if another De Falaise decides to try and take over?"

He didn't have an answer. But nor would he willingly teach these people how to fight in what he saw as a time of peace. While it was true he'd taught classes before The Cull, Tate was only trying to keep people safe. So what was the difference here? He couldn't explain it; he just knew that it was wrong and it wasn't what he'd come here to do. These people needed spiritual guidance, not advice on how to disable a person using the flat of your hand. Gwen might not have any faith in Robert to police the area, but Tate at least had that.

"Suit yourself," Gwen said in the end, realising she wasn't going to talk him round.

Thankfully, the task of revitalising Hope had kept a lot of them busy, including Gwen. The first order of business had been to clean up the streets, the cottages – to make it look as good as, if not better than it had been before. Darryl was put in charge of that operation, while Graham and Andy headed up the task of planting crops in time for the coming harvest (and it had been a good one, Tate had to admit). Meanwhile some of the newer people had been sent out to look for more skilled workers who might want to boost their numbers. Gwen had gone on a number of these missions, just as Clive had done before her. Tate found out later that she'd even poached people from other villages: like their doctor Ken Jeffreys, who they'd discovered in a community near Worksop. Somehow Gwen had managed to persuade Ken to join them, leaving behind the people he'd tended to up there. "I told him we needed him more," was all Gwen would tell Tate. "It was *his* choice." But something told Tate that the woman hadn't taken no for an answer.

When she went away on these 'head-hunting' trips (which invariably were getting shorter and shorter), Gwen would leave Clive Jr with Tate. It showed how much she trusted the holy man, as she wouldn't let anyone else within a mile of the little one, but for Tate it always proved a difficult undertaking. Many a time he'd look down on the boy and those dark eyes would stare back. He'd shiver then, but couldn't explain why. This was only a child, after all.

But hadn't their very own Jesus Christ once been a baby just like this one, and look how he'd changed the world.

Tate shook his head; these were ridiculous thoughts. The whole next generation of infants had the capacity to change the world: for better or for worse. What made Clive Jr so special?

Yet he couldn't help thinking...

When she returned, Gwen would always go to the child and make a fuss of him. As she'd rest him on her shoulder, whispering to him, the baby would look over and find Tate again. The

Reverend would smile when he saw Gwen looking, but it was pasted on. Was that one of the reasons why he'd stayed so close to New Hope? So he could keep an eye not only on the welfare of this community but also so he could watch Clive Jr?

Before they knew it, Spring and Summer were a distant memory, Autumn had come and gone, and Winter had set in. They'd celebrated Christmas, this burgeoning group of people, and Tate had led them all in carols in the renovated chapel. All except Gwen and her son.

"I won't be coming," she'd told Tate long before the celebration. "I don't feel it would be right. I don't... I'm just not that religious, especially after..." Gwen's sentence tailed off and he didn't push it.

But her actions, her attitude, troubled Tate more and more as the months crawled by.

That morning, Tate had called round to see Gwen, only to be told she was visiting Clive's grave again; a burial Tate himself had presided over, in the small graveyard behind the chapel, after Gwen had been taken to the castle. Now he returned to see Gwen and her baby, wrapped up warm against the icy chill which also bit into his leg. Clive Jr was in a pushchair, a bobble hat covering his head and thick woollen blankets tucking him in.

Gwen didn't notice Tate's approach until he was almost at the grave – not a stone one, like most of those here, or even marble, but a simple cross made by Darryl. It was all anyone had been able to manage in these times, and it was more than some poor people had been granted. He heard Gwen talking to her baby, then to the grave, before waiting – as if expecting an answer from the man buried there. It was only when she heard the crunch of snow under Tate's feet that she stopped.

"You shouldn't be out here, Reverend," she told him when she did finally look round. He wasn't quite sure what to make of that statement. Was she telling him he wasn't welcome? "It's treacherous underfoot." Gwen nodded at his stick.

"I'm not an invalid," he pointed out. Far from it; even with his disability Tate could put an able-bodied person through their paces. "I'll be all right. I'm more concerned about your welfare."

"Me?" She looked mystified. "I don't know what you're talking about."

Tate let out a sigh. "This isn't healthy, Gwen. It never has been."

"What, visiting the man I loved? Clive Jr's father?"

"That's not what I saying and you know it. You're not facing... certain facts."

Again, she gave him a confused look.

"Facts like–" Tate was interrupted by someone shouting from the gate. It was Andy. He was holding a different rifle to the one he'd brandished when they first arrived, one of the automatics Gwen had taken from the castle.

"Someone's coming," he yelled.

Tate and Gwen exchanged glances, then set off down the path. The holy man *had* nearly stumbled, but only in his haste to reach the street. He saw Gwen take out her pistol, ready to protect her child, and it didn't even seem strange this time – that's how much she'd altered. Gwen with a gun seemed like a natural thing.

They joined Andy out on New Hope's main road and he pointed. "There."

Tate squinted. There was a lone figure heading up the street on horseback. The Hood pulled down over the figure's face betrayed his identity. As if that wasn't enough, the bow and quiver on his back provided more evidence. And though you couldn't tell for sure just by that – look how Mary had fooled *everybody* on the day of the attack – something told Tate that this was indeed the man he'd first encountered in Sherwood Forest some time ago.

"You can put those weapons away," he told Andy and Gwen, then he hobbled up the street towards the horse.

The rider brought his steed to a halt, then climbed down. As Tate drew near, the man pulled down his hood and the Reverend saw he'd been right. It was Robert Stokes, but he looked older, more tired than he had the last time he'd seen him.

"Hello, my son. What brings you to New Hope?"

"Trouble."

"Yes, I can see that by the bruise on your face."

"Could someone fetch my horse water and hay?"

"Andy," Tate said, waving his hand for the man to approach.

Robert handed over the reins. "Much appreciated."

"I'm surprised to see you travelling alone," Gwen said by way of greeting. As she pushed the buggy towards Robert, she tucked the gun back in her jeans. "Someone of your importance, I'd have thought you'd have two or three men with you."

"I don't need any protection. I never have." There was something in his tone which said she'd hit a nerve.

"You say there's trouble, Robert," Tate said. "What kind?"

"Can we talk inside, Reverend? Somewhere a bit more private?"

"This isn't the castle," Gwen informed him. Tate balked at her rudeness. "It's *my* village. You can talk in my house if you're talking anywhere."

Robert nodded. "Understood. So lead the way, we've got a lot to discuss."

Robert sat down at the kitchen table while Tate put a kettle on the range.

Their visitor had taken off his bow and quiver but kept them close – and he kept the sword he always wore now at his hip, even though it stuck out behind his chair. Looking at the scene, Tate mused what a curious blend of ancient and modern it was, perhaps that was the way of the future after all?

Gwen, having placed Clive Jr in his playpen, leaned against the edge of the work surface, her arms folded. The silence was deafening, and in the end it was Gwen that broke it. "So, how are things back up at the castle?"

"Ticking over," Robert replied.

"You managing to keep on top of everything, keeping the area safe?"

"I'm working on it."

"Quite a task you've set yourself, though. And quite an ego to think you can right the wrongs of the whole world."

"Gwen, that's not fair," Tate said.

"Let her speak, Reverend. She's obviously got something on her mind."

Gwen's smile was tight. "I'm just making idle conversation."

"Those heavy duty guns you and your friend were waving around, they looked awfully familiar."

"How's Mary?" Gwen said quickly, changing the subject. "I liked Mary. She was good to me when I had Clive Jr."

"Ah yes," said Robert, glancing over at the baby. "Clive Jr."

The whistling of the kettle broke in, and moments later Tate was announcing that tea was ready.

"No cucumber sandwiches for our guest?" Gwen tutted. "I'm surprised at you."

"Look, what exactly *is* your problem?" Robert said.

"What's my problem? I'll tell you what my problem is-" Gwen was about to say more when Tate called for her to fetch the tea, his voice firm. When she placed the tray down on the table, the china rattled.

"You two knock yourself out," said Gwen, then she picked up Clive Jr and left the room.

Tate eased himself down on the chair opposite Robert, rubbing his temple where he felt the beginnings of a headache. "I'm sorry about that. She's been through a lot."

"We all have. It's no excuse."

"I know. I know. But, well, seeing the man you love get shot right in front of you and then... Well, I don't need to refresh your memory about what that creature did to her."

Robert shook his head. "She blames me for not coming sooner, doesn't she?"

"I think that's part of it, yes."

Tate suddenly recalled the moment Mary told them Gwen might still be alive.

"Are we finally going to do something about this Sheriff now, once and for all? Are we finally going to go in there and get those people out?"

"Like your Gwen, you mean?"

Yes, like Gwen, who he'd failed so spectacularly. Who Robert had failed, too.

"So," said Tate, drinking his tea and feeling the headache waning slightly, "are you going to tell me what this is about?"

Robert explained that they'd been tracking members of a cult, how they painted their faces like skulls and were growing in numbers. How he and his men had caught a few of them. "They're incredibly dangerous, intent on killing whoever they come across. I really need you to come back with me and–"

"Robert, I'm afraid my fighting days are over. I never really wanted them to begin in the first place. If circumstances hadn't forced me to..." Tate didn't feel like he could continue with that line of argument.

But Robert was shaking his head. "You misunderstand me, Reverend. I need your help figuring out the religious side of all this, maybe to sit in while I question the prisoners. I'm afraid I'm in over my head where all that stuff is concerned."

Tate could feel the headache building again, this time with a vengeance.

"Take this..." Robert reached into his jacket and pulled out a folded piece of paper. "I got Mary to draw it, based on our descriptions of the tattoos the men have on their foreheads. I didn't want her getting too close to any of those lunatics."

Tate put down his cup and took the paper, casting his eyes over the symbol. It was an inverted pentangle within a circle. There were markings around the outside of the ring, and at the tips of the cross: some kind of lettering. Inside the pentangle was an inverted cross. "These people are Satanists, Robert."

"Yeah, I kind of got that."

Tate tapped the paper. "This is a variation on The Sigil of Baphomet, which used to be used by the Official Church of Satan back before The Cull. The symbol of Baphomet was also used by the Knights Templar to represent Satan. It was known as The Black Goat, The Goat of Mendes, The Judas Goat, The Goat of a Thousand Young and The Scapegoat. That particular sign had a picture of a horned goat in the middle of the pentangle, whereas this has an inverted cross – which is actually the Cross of St Peter, a common mistake made by those practising this kind of thing. St Peter was crucified upside down, you see..."

"I see I've come to the right person."

"They've done something else to the symbol, though," Tate continued. "Usually there are two circles around the pentangle, and between those, at the edge of each point, there's a letter in Hebrew which, when brought together, spell LVTHN anticlockwise."

"I don't follow," said Robert, his brow furrowing.

"Leviathan, my son. The Horned One. The Devil. Here, though, the letters are reversed Latin."

"What do *they* spell?"

"Well, the outer five spell MRNIG."

"What the Hell is that supposed to mean?"

"Probably exactly that. Because if you look at it in conjunction with the letters around the cross as well..."

"Go on."

"Those spell STAR."

Robert shrugged. "Still not getting it."

"Morningstar? Lucifer. The Fallen Angel."

"Oh God..."

"Quite the opposite." Tate let out a long, slow breath. The headache was worsening by the second. He was about to pick up his tea again, but his hand wavered as if something had suddenly struck him. "Did you say these men were killing people?"

Robert nodded, then rubbed his bruised jaw. "It's how I got this. They were after a young woman in York, and if we hadn't been there..."

"Then it's even more serious than I thought."

"Isn't it serious enough?"

Tate gripped the side of the table with one hand, and pointed at Robert with the other. "If they're killing, *sacrificing*, then there can only be one reason."

"They enjoy it?"

"They're attempting to raise Him."

Robert looked at Tate sideways. "Come on! Satan? You're telling me they're trying to conjure him up or something? That's ridiculous."

"No more ridiculous than our Lord Jesus Christ coming back

from the dead. They want him to appear in the flesh, Robert. After all, hasn't this world been called by many a Hell on Earth? Wouldn't He be right at home here?"

"You don't seriously believe that."

Tate held up his hand. "What I believe is irrelevant, *they* believe it. And they will carry on executing people until He appears."

"Then what will they do?"

"Anything He tells them to. He's their master."

There was silence for a few minutes, during which Robert looked down at the table. "They have to be stopped. Regardless of what they think is going to happen, I can't just let them carry on."

"I know," replied Tate.

He studied the Reverend. "Will you come back with me to the castle? I could really use your insight."

Tate breathed out wearily before answering. "When God calls me, I must answer."

Robert thanked him and got up, leaving the cottage to fetch his horse. They would set off immediately for Nottingham. Gwen came back into the room when she heard the door slam. She was still cradling Clive Jr in her arms.

"Don't bother to explain. I heard everything."

"You were listening?" Tate was more than a little surprised.

"Of course. I can't stand to be around that man, but I wanted to know what was going on. Seems I was right all along about another threat coming." Gwen fixed Tate with a stare. "Still think Robert and his men can protect us?"

"As I said before, my child, I know he will try."

"And you will help him?"

"I will."

"Then I wish you all the luck in the world," Gwen said, before walking out again.

"And I," whispered Tate, his eyes trailing her as she disappeared, "pray that God might deliver you from this darkness." Whether he meant the darkness of the conflicts to come, the Morningstar cult and whatever waited for him at the Castle, or the darkness inside Gwen's own soul, not even Tate knew for sure.

CHAPTER SIX

The blade swished as it whipped past his ear, narrowly missing his head.

He rolled out of the way then leapt up to avoid another stroke, beneath him this time. Landing badly, he toppled to one side – recovering just quick enough to fall backwards when he saw the blade about to run him through. He hit the ground hard, emptying his lungs. Laying there, sucking in a deep breath, he saw a shadow fall over him.

Then the blade was at his throat.

If it had been a real sword, he'd be dead by now. As it was all he'd suffered were a couple of splinters in his neck.

A hand reached down and he took it, felt himself being hauled to his feet. The man standing opposite Mark said nothing, merely gestured that he was ready to go again if the boy was. Mark nodded to the dark-skinned soldier, his sparring partner today. Mark didn't know Azhar all that well, but the man wielded a sword like he'd been born with it in his hand. Jack had left Mark to 'do battle' with him over an hour ago, and as he now watched the man spin the sword Mark wished his tutor had at least given him a weapon to fight back with.

Azhar swung again, the wood clipping Mark's left shoulder. He let out a yelp, hopping back out of its way. He didn't stay there for long though, because his opponent was already moving forward, jabbing for his ribs. "Hey, *watchit!*" Mark cried when the tip poked him hard in the side. He had to react fast, as the wood flashed past his face. Now that one really would have hurt!

Azhar's feet were a blur as he positioned himself in front of Mark, preparing to swing the sword again. Mark dived beneath the next sweep, running at Azhar to try and shove him off balance. The man easily side-stepped the boy's attack, causing Mark to dive head-first at the ground. He came skidding to a stop on the slushy snow of the Middle Bailey field, where a pair of size 15 boots were waiting.

"Very impressive, kid. The old sliding on the snow manoeuvre." Mark cast his eyes upwards to see Jack standing there, leaning on his staff and chuckling. He helped him to his feet, then brushed the snow roughly from the front of his jacket.

"It's not funny," said Mark. "And it's not fair, either. How come he gets a sword and I don't?"

"You think you're always going to have a weapon to hand?" Jack shook his head. "Uh-uh. Nope. But your opponent might."

"What if my opponent has a semi-automatic?"

"Then you learn how to dodge bullets as well as swords."

"This is pointless."

"If it helps, think about it like Jedi training."

Mark moaned. "It doesn't. I was never a big movie fan, Jack, remember? I was more into sports – which is how I ended up following *your* career."

Jack smiled at the reference to his time on the wrestling circuit. "Still my number one fan, eh?"

"Depends."

"On what?"

"On how long I have to keep doing this shit for."

Jack clipped him around the ear. "That's cos Robert's not here, or he'd have done the same. It's not grown up to cuss like that."

Mark let his shoulders sag.

"Look, tell you what: Azhar, toss Mark your sword a second."

The soldier threw his wooden sword over to the boy, who almost dropped it.

"Okay, now you're armed. He's not. Think you can take him?"

Mark grinned, swinging the sword to test its weight. It was payback time. He stepped into the area of combat, while Jack watched from the sidelines. Azhar hunched down low and matched Mark's circling movements, eyes flitting from his enemy's face to his hands. Mark swung the sword experimentally. He'd practised before with one of these, sneaked away when no one was looking to get the feel of what it was like. He'd taken on trees and fences, fancied himself as pretty good too – not in Azhar's league, of course, but given enough time... Except Azhar didn't have the sword anymore, did he? Now the advantage was all Mark's.

He came at Azhar, swinging left and right. The darker-skinned man moved like a cat, making sure the sword never came within three feet of his body. Mark gripped the weapon with both hands, bringing it up in an arc which would ordinarily have caught his opponent beneath the chin – but Azhar had already leaned back. The difference between his move and the one Mark attempted earlier was that Azhar was soon upright again.

Mark showed his teeth, in an effort to put Azhar off, but there was absolutely no reaction. This made him even angrier. He swung the blade this way and that, as he figured he was bound to strike something sooner or later – an arm, a leg... a whack in the head might be nice in return for all the pokes and prods.

He hit nothing.

Mark was on his final swipe – Azhar right in front of him – when suddenly the man wasn't there anymore. He was at Mark's side, having dropped and slid around, and was relieving Mark of the sword, grabbing his wrists and wrenching the weapon free. In seconds Mark was again on the wrong end of the tip, which was hovering between his eyes.

There was laughter coming from somewhere. At first Mark

thought it was Jack again, but it wasn't deep enough. When Azhar stepped back Mark turned and saw Dale sitting on the steps to the East Terrace. He had his guitar with him, and was shaking his head, clapping his thigh at the sight of Mark's defeat.

"Nice one, Marky. You had him right where he wanted you," Dale brought his guitar around and started to play a melody, making up words on the spot.

> "You try your best, put to the test,
> But let's face it now you need a rest.
> Can't be easy, ohhh, it can't be easy...
>
> "Give it your all, but when you're small,
> You find out life just ain't no ball,
> Can't be easy, ohh, it just can't be that easy..."

"Shut up!" shouted Mark, but Dale continued playing. Mark turned and saw that some of the other men training had stopped to listen.

> "He's just a child playing at bein' a man,
> It's hard and he don't know if he can.
> Oh, it ain't easy... It simply ain't that easy..."

Mark's eyes narrowed and he marched towards Dale. "I said *shut up!*" Azhar came up behind to try and stop him, but Jack put a hand on his arm. This had been a while coming and the last thing Mark needed was anyone interfering.

"What's the problem, Marky-boy?" answered Dale, resting his guitar against the wall and standing to meet him. "It was just a joke. What's the matter, can't you take a–"

Mark grabbed him by the collar, swinging him around and onto the pavement between the steps and the field. He pulled back his fist, then struck Dale squarely in the face, making his nose bleed. Dale brought a couple of fingers up, touched the nostrils, and when they came away red he glared at Mark. "You little sod, look what you did."

"Want some more?"

Dale ran forwards, dragging Mark back onto the field. They slipped, then rolled over several times on the snow.

"Let them work it out," Mark heard Jack saying as they rolled past him and Azhar. "Bit of old fashioned wrestling never hurt anyone."

On the final roll, Dale landed on top of Mark, pinning him down. He brought his fist back, ready to retaliate, when there was a cry to their left.

"Dale... Mark..." It was a female voice, too young to be Mary's. Mark recognised it instantly. So did Dale.

"What's going on?" asked Sophie as she made her way down the steps.

"Some other time," Dale said to Mark, tapping him on the cheek.

Mark wrenched his head away and spat back: "*Any* time."

"Jack, what's happening here? Why didn't you break the training up when it was getting too rough?" Sophie said.

The big man held up a hand in mock surrender. "Hey there, little lady, it was nothing to do with me."

"Wait till Mary hears about this," she told him.

Dale was up and walking over towards her, wiping his bloody nose. Already, Sophie was pulling a tissue out of her winter coat to dab at it. "Look at you... You should know better. He's only just starting out."

"Yeah," Dale replied, looking back at Mark. "I'm sorry, mate." He grinned as he let Sophie clean up his face.

"You should go easy on him. Come on inside, let's get you cleaned up properly."

Mark stared in disbelief as Dale grabbed his guitar and trotted off back up the steps with Sophie. *Go easy on me! Go easy? I nearly bloody well broke his nose!* He got up just in time to watch the pair disappear from view.

Jack placed a hand on his shoulder. "All's fair in love and war." He said the words as if distracted.

Mark followed his gaze and saw he was looking towards the far end of the Bailey, where a woman with short, dark hair was walking past. It was the woman who'd arrived with Jack and Robert the other day. Adele. She'd gone off with Jack then to have a tour of the castle and its grounds, but it was Robert she'd had eyes for – much to Mary's chagrin.

"I'll remind you of that sometime," Mark said bitterly.

"Hmm... What?"

"Nothing," sighed Mark. Adele disappeared from view and Jack brought his attention back to his pupil.

"You up to carrying on with your training, or do you need to take a time out?" Even before Mark could open his mouth, Jack said: "Good, that's good, kid. Azhar, he's all yours again."

With that, Jack was off up the walkway, heading in the direction he'd seen Adele going. "I'm... I'm not a kid," Mark whispered.

But no-one was listening, least of all Azhar, who was urging him to get back on the spot they'd occupied before. The dark-skinned man picked up the sword and started spinning it around again.

Mark hunkered down, trying to recall what Azhar had just done in his position.

"Hey... Hey there, hold up."

Jack called out to Adele. The woman had certainly made tracks since he'd spied her, and was now past what had once been the main entrance to the museum. She appeared to be looking for something, when she heard his cries.

"Hey there, Adele. Wait up!"

She waved to Jack then waited for him to reach her. When he got closer he saw that, like Sophie, she was wearing a winter coat – only Adele's clung to her, pulled tight in all the right places. He recognised it as one of the long coats Mary sometimes wore. The kind-hearted woman must have lent it to Adele to keep her warm.

"Jack," she said, smiling warmly. "How are you today?"

"Well, I'm just fine. All the better for spotting you up here. Haven't seen you much since you arrived."

Adele's smiled broadened. "I've been... busy."

"Have you now? Doing what?"

"Trying to get my bearings mostly. One whiz around the block wasn't quite enough to familiarise myself with this place."

Jack looked up at the castle. "Yeah, I know what you mean. I used to come here sometimes, y'know? Visit in the week. It was always free to get in."

"I wouldn't have thought you were the type to wander round stately homes and castles."

"I'm a man of hidden depths," Jack announced proudly. "Do you mind if I walk with you for a spell?"

Adele hesitated for a second, then gave him another smile. "No, of course not."

"Forgive me for asking this, ma'am, but I figure I don't really know much about you and, well, I'd like to. It's kind of what we do around here when we bring someone into the fold."

"What would you like to know?"

Jack laughed. "Wanna hear somethin' funny? Put on the spot like that... I haven't a blessed clue."

Adele laughed too. "There's not that much to tell really. I was an only child, my mother brought me up alone because my dad died when I was very little. Average kind of education, did okay at school. Left school, did some travelling, you know how it is?"

"Indeed I do," said Jack, remembering the wanderlust that had taken him from his native upstate New York, into the lights of the big city, then finally to England where he'd made his home.

"Drifted from one job to the next, never really settling on anything. Never really had something I wanted to do, a life purpose like some people have." She paused to take in the stunning view of Nottingham. "Not like you; I heard you were a pretty good sportsman. A wrestler wasn't it?"

Jack nodded.

"I'm envious. Not of the wrestling, obviously." She laughed again and touched him on the arm. "But that fact you always knew who you were."

"Oh, I'm not so sure I *always* knew. But yeah, I guess you could say I was lucky. In more ways than one when the virus hit."

Adele pulled up sharply and her smile suddenly faded. "Hey, I'm sorry... I... That was real thoughtless of me. What you said back there in York, about having no-one. You lost your family, didn't you?"

"Can we change the subject, please?" Adele said, bristling.

"Sure. Hey, no problem."

She began walking again, without waiting for him to catch up. Luckily all it took for Jack was a couple of strides. "Do you know where Robert took off to in such a hurry?" she asked then.

"Robbie? Why do you ask?" Jack fought to keep the jealousy out of his voice.

"Oh, no reason. It's just that he left without saying goodbye or anything."

"You get used to that," Jack told her, resting his staff on his shoulder as they walked. "You should have seen him in Sherwood. One minute he was there, the next..."

Adele looked wistfully out at the view. "I really wish I could have seen that. It all sounds so... I don't know, romantic. Living in the forest, with the Hooded Man."

Jack shrugged. "I don't know if romantic's the right word. It was dangerous, I know that. Especially when we came up against the Frenchman's men."

She stopped again. "De Falaise?"

"You've heard of him."

Adele nodded. "You hear things. Rumours of what happened."

"It was a tough time."

"I can imagine."

Jack looked at her, searching her eyes. "Adele, you–"

"You never answered my question about where Robert went."

"To... To get help. We need to know more about the cult, the people who were chasing you."

"Right," said Adele, nodding. "When's he due back, do you know?"

"Anytime I guess. But–"

"Jack," said Adele, pulling him towards a set of steps with a locked gate across it. "You never did tell me what was down there."

"Oh, that's just the caves. You wouldn't like it down there."

"Is it where prisoners are kept?" she asked, biting her lip.

"Not anymore. Not since we took over. It's just where we keep the stuff De Falaise left behind. Y'know, weapons and such."

Adele looked puzzled. "Robert doesn't use them?"

"You've seen what Robert uses," replied Jack, a little more impatiently than he'd meant to. Here he was, trying to get to know this beautiful woman, and all she wanted to talk about was Robert.

"I'm sorry," Adele told him, sensing the mood. "I don't mean to ask so many questions. I'm just curious about what happens here." She took his hand. "Forgive me?"

"Er... Yeah, of course." Jack could feel the colour rushing to his cheeks.

"Listen, how about you give me a bit of time to freshen up – then maybe we could grab a bite to eat? God, that sounds so normal doesn't it? Sounds like what people used to do."

"It does."

"Okay then. Meet you in the dining area in about an hour?"

Jack nodded.

"And listen, thank you Jack. You've been really sweet to me." She leaned in and kissed him, before running off to the nearest entrance.

Jack beamed from ear to ear. "You're very welcome, little lady. Very welcome indeed."

It was a good few minutes before his thoughts returned to what she'd asked about: Robert. And Jack wondered how he'd got on himself, and whether his trip had been worthwhile.

CHAPTER SEVEN

The guards weren't that surprised to see the horse come trotting up St James Street. Robert had already checked in with Rangers positioned at the city's edge, telling them not to inform the castle yet, just his people at *The Britannia*.

"They'll only want to join us, and I'd rather this was just you and me, Reverend," he'd told Tate by way of an explanation. "I don't want Mary being placed needlessly in danger here." He'd registered the holy man's look of fear when he said that, possibly the only real time he'd ever seen Tate scared.

Robert tried to tell himself that these were just men whose minds had broken, probably during or after The Cull. It would have been an easy thing to slip into madness back then; he'd come close himself. But Tate's words about The Devil, about worship and sacrifice, had spooked him. Any kind of organised religion bothered Robert, but one which called for the death of innocents... He'd hidden it, but when Tate had been talking about Hell, Robert suddenly had a mental image of flames, of fire licking up around him.

His house burning to the ground, torched by the people in power trying to contain the virus. Robert's family, dead inside.

The lake he'd dreamed of at Rufford, ablaze and then–

The market square where he'd confronted De Falaise finally, their crashed vehicles catching light; the fire spreading out across their battlefield.

In spite of what Tate might think, Robert did like him. More than that, he respected him. They might never agree about their chosen professions – Tate would say callings – but the man talked a lot of sense. Depending on how you looked at it, Robert either owed him for making him face up to his responsibilities, or was the catalyst for everything that had happened since: leaving Sherwood, being put in charge of the Rangers, becoming a figurehead for something much greater than he could ever be.

Robert pushed all this to the back of his mind as they approached the hotel entrance, its glass doors cracked but still in place – the steps stained a faded red with blood that had long since dried.

The guard there, Robert searched for his name, it was getting much harder these days, the more his team grew – Kershaw, that was it – stood to attention. Robert thought he was going to salute and he'd have to go through that whole business of reminding them they weren't in the army. He wasn't their general.

"You just don't see it, do you? I'm no better than De Falaise."

Robert swung down off his mount, then helped Tate from the saddle. The holy man was stiff, and it took him a moment to regain the feeling in his legs. Robert tethered his horse to a nearby handrail.

"I'm here to see the prisoners, Kershaw," he told the guard, pulling down his hood at the same time.

The guard swallowed hard. "We... we thought it best to tell you when you got here. There's been a problem."

"Problem?"

"The men watching them tried to stop it but... Well, I think it's probably best you see for yourself, sir." Kershaw waved a hand for Robert and Tate to enter. They were met inside by another of Robert's men – and this one he did recognise. It was Geoff Baker, the man he'd left in charge of this improvised jail, having been a warder in a real prison for years until the virus struck.

Geoff ran a hand through his thinning hair before offering his apologies. "It all happened so quickly, there was very little we could do."

"What did?"

"Go easy," Tate said. "Give the man a chance to explain."

"They did it all at once. We managed to get to one of them, but..."

"Geoff, talk to me."

Instead of saying anything else, Geoff took them to a storage room just to the right of the lobby, past a huge wall-length mirror, and unlocked the door. Inside were several bodies, stacked on top of each other, all wearing the robes of the Morningstar cult. Robert looked at Geoff, confused. "They committed suicide, Rob."

"What? How? You had them secured, right?"

"Two or three swallowed their own tongues, another one managed to get one hand free of the ropes and tear his own throat out."

"Dear Lord," whispered Tate.

"One tipped the chair over that he was tied to, angling it so he struck his temple on the side of a nearby table. Another actually lifted up the chair and ran at a wall, hard enough to smash his own skull in."

Robert was having difficulty understanding. He'd never had to deal with these kinds of prisoners before, people who would gladly end their own lives rather than divulge any information.

"But why weren't you lot keeping an eye on them?" There was more frustration than anger in his voice, but Geoff reacted as if chastised.

"We were doing our best. I don't exactly have a full staff here," Geoff reminded him, his tone hardening. "And when a crisis crops up out there, a portion of my men always seem to be called away even though they're vital for guarding this place."

Robert nodded. "Point taken. You say you managed to get to one of them, though?"

"Yeah. We've been keeping him dosed up to try and stop him from doing anything similar." Geoff gestured for them to follow him.

"Just one moment," Reverend Tate said. He made the sign of the cross at the door and closed his eyes.

"Why are you wasting your time with that?" said Robert. "They don't want your help, and they definitely don't want to go to your Heaven."

"We're all God's children, whether we've strayed from the path or not. They deserve the chance of forgiveness. Of mercy."

Robert could see he wouldn't be argued with.

They left the room behind and headed for the stairs. Tate had trouble with these, but refused both Geoff and Robert's help, intent on climbing the two flights himself. Finally, they made it to what had been the bar area, an expanse of carpeted floor that once contained comfy chairs for residents, but now only boasted tables which ran into the restaurant section. On either side was a long glass window – the left one cracked in places – and the bar at the back was smashed to pieces, graffiti sprayed across the walls, probably by someone during or after The Cull who'd come looking for booze.

At each corner of the room stood a Ranger with a bow and arrow primed, keeping an eye on what was taking place. It was lunchtime, Geoff explained, and as they didn't have the time and resources to feed each prisoner individually, they had to do it *en masse*, bringing out vats of stew from the reclaimed kitchens located beyond the restaurant. Robert had to admit, it didn't look very appetising, but it was all they could manage under the circumstances.

There was a shout as one of the inmates spotted Robert and Tate. Then a figure broke away from the rest of the prisoners, making a dash for Robert. Immediately, bows and arrows were raised and the man stopped before he could reach his target. They needn't have worried, as Robert had his bow primed too, an arrow snatched from his quiver the second he sensed trouble.

"This is bullshit. I keep telling 'em, I shouldn't be here!" shouted the prisoner.

"Really?" said Robert, approaching, his weapon trained on the man. "How so?" The man's face looked familiar, but he couldn't quite place it. It was certainly distinctive, the way that scar ran the length of his jaw-line.

"You let some of the others that worked for *him* go. Fucking 'ell, some of 'em are even working for *you*, while I'm stuck in this bastard place with them lot."

"Come on, Jason – back in line," said Geoff, moving forwards and signalling to a couple of the guards.

"Fuck off, screw. I'm talking to the organ grinder now."

That was it. Jason... Jace. When it had come time to sort out who might be retrained from the remnants of De Falaise's army, several of Robert's people had warned him about Jace. Mark, Sophie and Gwen especially, detailing how he'd first of all kidnapped Hood's ward, then allowed himself to be 'seduced' by Gwen so she could knock him out and steal his uniform. A nasty piece of work by all accounts.

"You're talking to the wrong person," Robert told Jace. "He's the one who deals in forgiveness for scum like you." He nodded at Tate, who pursed his lips. "How about it, Reverend? Think we should let him go? Is there a place for him in God's plan? How would Gwen or Sophie feel about that? He would have raped them both given half a chance."

"That Gwen was up for it," sneered Jace. "She *enjoyed* being with De Falaise – told me as much."

It was the holy man who moved forward this time, whacking the youth in the stomach with his stick. He would have done more had Robert not pulled him back. The guards had Jace then, and were dragging him across the room.

"Put him in solitary for a day," Geoff ordered. "That should cool him down a bit." Solitary, Robert knew, was a locked storage room with no windows. It might seem barbaric, but for Jace and his kind it was better than some of the justice that was being meted out in other parts of the country. At least here, Robert was more or less sticking to the legal system of old. It was the only way they could build the tentative beginnings of a new civilisation.

When Tate had calmed down, Robert looked at him, perhaps expecting some kind of apology or explanation. Tate gave him neither.

He might represent a higher power, but he's still a man – with a man's emotions, Robert reminded himself. *And in spite of everything he's said, Tate's still a fighter.*

They were taken up to the next floor – to conference rooms that had once hosted presentations and lectures, but were now being used as holding bays for the more dangerous prisoners. In one of the smaller ones, they found a table with a woman and another guard standing next to it. There was a mirror to their left as they walked in. Strapped down with what looked like belts, buckled across the chest, stomach and legs – and ropes tied around the wrists – was the member of the Morningstar cult Geoff had referred to. It took Robert a second or so, but he placed the Ranger as a man called Lewis, the woman with features that looked too small for her face as a 'nurse' Mary had trained called Lucy Hill. Lucy had her scrubs on, her hair tied back in a pony tail. She was flitting about around the prisoner, around the *patient*.

"How's it going?" asked Geoff.

"He's stable. Still pretty out of it, mind," Lucy replied. "I gave him some Chlorpromazine to calm him down."

"Is he up to us asking some questions?" Robert inquired.

"You can ask them but I can't vouch for any of the answers you'll get."

Robert approached the table. Tate hesitated, and only when Robert looked back over his shoulder did the Reverend join him. Robert could see the cultist much more clearly now. It was the one who'd snapped at Adele, attempting to bite her like the animal he surely was. The white paint he'd used to mask his identity had rubbed off in places, run in others, giving him – if anything – a more nightmarish appearance than before. The only thing that remained was the tattoo on his forehead. The man's eyes – a steely blue – stared up at Robert, and he had no idea whether his presence had registered. He looked completely stoned, like so many of the druggies Robert had come across in his former life, but he had the feeling this guy's eyes had looked like that even before Lucy had come near him with a needle.

"Can you hear me?" asked Robert.

"Mmmnnnfff," was the reply he got.

Robert looked up at Lucy. "At least he's not trying to top himself," she offered.

"Let me try," said Tate, tapping Robert on the shoulder for him to move aside.

Robert watched as the bald man studied the cult member's features. "I know you're in there," said Tate. The words seemed normal, but Robert had seen the Reverend do this before, draw things out of a person, force them to answer, force them to *think*. He'd done it with him once, persuaded Robert to communicate. "Speak, my son."

The cult member's eyes locked on Tate's. Robert found himself holding his breath as the man spoke again. "I... I hear you," mumbled the prisoner, the words barely audible.

"What is your name?"

He continued to stare, as if he didn't understand the question – either that or didn't know how to answer. Tate repeated it and the man simply whispered: "Servitor. I serve."

"No, not your purpose. Your name. Your *Christian* name." The man shook his head slowly. "Who were you before?"

"No before," the man breathed. "We have always been here."

"Since before the virus, you mean?"

There was the slightest hint of a nod.

"All right then, tell me why your fellow... Servitors all killed themselves."

"S-S-Sacrifice."

So it wasn't just other people they were out to kill, Robert mused; when they were taken captive they were happy enough to kill themselves.

"A sacrifice? To whom?"

"Our master. The one true Lord."

"I beg to differ. You worship a false deity, can't you see that?" From the man's blank expression it was pretty obvious he didn't.

"He will come. It is written."

"Through your sacrifices?" Tate asked, and the man nodded.

"Looks like you were right," Robert chipped in, but Tate took no notice.

"You believe you will find Him here, in this world?"

"He will... He will rise again..."

Geoff whistled. "See? What a loon."

Tate whirled around and shot the warder a look that would have given Medusa a run for her money. Geoff kept quiet.

"You will see Him," the Servitor promised. "Feel... feel His power..." Tate's face was almost as white at the make-up the cult member wore. The holy man was clearly terrified. "You know, don't you? You feel it."

This was going horribly wrong. Instead of Tate's words having an impact on the Servitor, the reverse was happening. And his voice was growing stronger by the second.

"He's coming... He who is... who is... blood red... from head to.... to toe..." The man's mouth was foaming, and he was straining against his bonds.

Robert went over to hold him down. "Lucy," he called out. She already had the needle prepared, and was attempting to stick it into a bottle to draw more Chlorpromazine. Her hands were shaking though, and she almost dropped the bottle twice.

Then everything happened so suddenly. Robert looked down to see that the Servitor had snatched the knife he always kept at his hip. With another wrench, the man broke free of the ropes holding that wrist, and was in the process of cutting through the leather strap across his chest. Robert made a grab for the forearm, but the man tugged it free. His strength was incredible, as if he was channelling something.

"Lucy, stick him – right now!" shouted Robert.

The nurse brought the syringe across, but when she bent to administer the drug, the Servitor brought the knife up and sideways, slashing her across the arm. She stepped back, mouth wide, dropping the needle and clutching at the gash.

"Tate, I could use some help," Robert growled over his shoulder, struggling with the man. The Reverend was standing there, gaping.

Geoff and Lewis were racing to assist, but somehow the Servitor had managed to worm one leg free and he brought that up and kicked the Ranger in the face, sending Lewis crashing backwards into the wall.

Robert took one hand off the prisoner to punch him, but the man took the blow without even flinching. Absently, he wondered what Eric Meadows would have done in this situation: would even he have been able to secure this charge? The next thing Robert knew, the strap across the Servitor's chest was in two halves and he was rising, yanking free to attack the other bonds with the knife. When Geoff tried to stop him, he broke off to plant the knife in him up to the hilt, then pull it out again. Geoff looked down to see a bloom of crimson stain his top, then his feet buckled and he fell.

Robert was on his own.

This shouldn't be so difficult. I took a handful of them down back in York. But something was different. Whether it was the confines of the room, or the fact the Servitor appeared to be drawing on reserves of energy that could power this entire city for a week, he couldn't decide. One thing was for sure, if the cultist got free of the table–

And then it was done. The Servitor was standing. He was still staring at Tate, however, still had him in that hypnotic trance. Lewis was spark out, Lucy had retreated to the corner of the room – what Robert wouldn't have given for it to be Mary here instead now, or even Gwen! – and he didn't even know if Geoff was still alive

Robert kept the table between them. It was too small a space to use the bow and arrow, and the same went for his sword – one swing and he might end up hurting one of his own. No, this fight was going to be a nasty one: scrappy, clumsy. He hated that.

"I can't let you leave," Robert told him. "You know that."

The Servitor cocked his head, turning finally to face Robert – but in the process caught sight of himself in the mirror just beyond. He paused, frozen just as Tate had been moments before. Then he took the knife and drew it over his own throat. The blood sprayed across the table, across the room, and Robert held up his arm to shield his eyes. Remarkably, when he took it down again, Robert saw the man was still standing, thick gouts of red spurting from the wound at his throat, those cold, dead eyes now fixed on him.

Then he dropped face forward onto the table, almost upending it. Robert gaped at the scene. His mind couldn't quite take in what had happened. Why had this man struggled so hard to get free, only to take his own life? But then he remembered the other bodies down in the room on the ground floor, remembered what the Servitor had said about sacrificing themselves to their master.

Robert looked over at Tate, who seemed to be snapping out of his daze. "Evil faced itself," the Reverend whispered.

There was a groan from the floor. Geoff! Robert skirted round the table to see him laying there, blood welling from the wound in his chest. He applied pressure to it, then shouted again for Lucy. This time she came, tentatively and still holding her own arm, one eye on the man sprawled across the table, as if expecting him to rise at any moment. "Lucy, for Christ's sake!" snapped Robert. Blinking at the wounded man on the floor, she too snapped out of her daze, immediately crouching to help stem the flow of blood.

Robert shouted at Lewis to go fetch help – other personnel who had medical training. "And Mary..." he said. "Send for Mary. Quickly!"

Mary couldn't quite believe what she was seeing.

That cow was wearing her coat! It was such a small thing, and there were admittedly few items of female clothing in the castle so it made sense that she should have borrowed it – but it was precisely because of this that Mary was angry. There were *precious* few things that were hers, only hers. Worst of all, Adele had taken it without even asking.

Though she hated herself for it, Mary wondered what else the woman was intent on taking from her.

What do you want her to do, Moo-Moo, freeze to death out there?

She was tempted to come back with: "Do you really want me to answer that?"

Now, that's really not nice... her brother told her. She'd completely forgotten that whatever she thought, he instantly knew as well. Because he *was* her, wasn't he? The voice of her conscience, her reason.

I'm bloody well not, you know. I'm me. I'm your brother.

"Oh shut up," Mary said, drawing Adele's attention.

The woman, standing at the bottom of the steps, about to ascend, waved at her. Mary let her head droop, then lifted it again. She didn't want to give her the satisfaction of knowing she was upset.

"Mary, hi!" the woman called out, coming over. Reluctantly, she met her halfway.

"Adele."

"I was hoping to run into you. I wanted to say thanks." The woman's eyes sparkled when she spoke. Mary looked puzzled, so she continued: "For this, the coat."

"Oh, yes... That's..." Mary didn't know how to complete that sentence because, until a few moments ago, she had no idea Adele was even wearing it.

"Rob said it would be okay to borrow some of your gear."

My *gear?* "Did he?"

"Er... yeah. Hope that was okay? You've got a really nice room, you know. Love what you've done with it. Considering. I guess anything's a step up from the forest." Adele smiled, but there was no warmth in it.

"You've been in my... in *our* room?" What she was really asking was, had Adele been in there alone? Not because she thought her and Robert had snuck off there – apart from the fact he hadn't had time before leaving, Mary did know the man well enough that he wouldn't be able to hide that one. (What about the other night, what about the cosy little drink in the café? He still hadn't mentioned that to her.) No, it was just the thought of a complete stranger going through her stuff, poking around, maybe sitting or laying down in the bed she shared with–

"I... I wasn't in there very long," Adele promised, as if that made it all right.

Mary said nothing, but found herself clenching and unclenching her fists.

"Look," Adele went on, "you've all been really nice to me, and I'm so grateful. But, well, there aren't very many women around here, are there? Bit heavy on the testosterone. I suppose I was hoping you and me could be... well, I had hoped we could be friends. You know?"

"You're thinking of staying a while, then," was all Mary could muster.

Adele smiled again. "Thinking about it, yeah, if you guys will have me. Sure beats being out there on the streets, being chased by murderers and rapists."

"Right."

"I hope it isn't going to be a problem or anything?"

"I hope not as well."

Adele frowned. "Forgive me for saying this, Mary, but you seem to have a... I don't know. Have I done something wrong? Something to you?"

Mary felt like saying, "Cut the crap, you know exactly what you've done. And it's what you're *going to do* when Robert gets back I'm interested in." But instead she said: "No, not exactly."

"Only I'm getting some really weird vibes from you."

Mary shook her head, this wasn't the time or the place. "No, everything's fine. Really."

"Ah, okay." Adele's smile widened, but seemed even less genuine. "Right, well I suppose I'd better go and get ready."

"Ready?"

"I'm having something to eat with Jack."

Now it was Mary's turn to frown. First this woman had been flirting openly with Robert, then she'd caught them having a little late night rendezvous (*It was hardly that, Moo-Moo. Might've been completely innocent.*) now she was making a play for Robert's best friend.

Don't do it, warned David. *Seriously, keep your mouth shut.*

She couldn't help herself. "What exactly is your game, Adele? What are you up to?"

The smile faded fast. "Excuse me?"

"I saw you with Robert the other night."

Adele looked horrified. "What?"

"Don't act all innocent," Mary said, pointing her finger. "I could see what was going on. What you were trying to do."

Adele stepped back. "There was nothing *going on*. Robert dropped a glass and I got some in my foot."

Mary pursued her, moving forward, still pointing. "You're after him. And now you're leading Jack up the garden path."

"You're insane."

"Am I?" Mary let the words settle and neither of them spoke for a second or two. Then Adele turned to leave, and Mary grabbed her wrist.

"Let go of me!" she spat.

"I've got my eye on you, Adele."

Adele grinned. "You'd be better off putting your energies into hanging onto your man. There's obviously something lacking in your relationship if you're this insecure. Maybe you don't know Robert as well as you *think* you do."

Mary was about to bring up her hand to slap the woman, when she heard someone shouting her name. It sounded urgent.

"Mary... Mary!" It was coming from behind, so she let Adele go and whirled around. One of Robert's men was racing down the corridor. "You have to come quickly – bring your medical stuff. Someone's been injured at *The Britannia*."

"Injured?" asked Mary.

"Stabbed. You have to come quick, Robert said–"

"Hold on, *Robert*?" Mary looked at him, then back at Adele, who was still smirking in spite of the news. "He's back? But–"

The man pleaded with her to come with him, saying that there wasn't time, so Mary did. But before she'd got out of earshot, she heard Adele reiterate: "No, maybe you don't really know him at all."

CHAPTER EIGHT

He felt like Jonah in the belly of the beast.

Tanek sat in one of the cargo bays, working away on his secret project. He'd been labouring on this since they set off across the Baltic. It was important that he got it right. The various parts were all laid out in front of him on the table, which at the moment was vibrating slightly. Tanek reached for one of the pieces of wood and his sandpaper, running the rough side across the face with a sweeping motion. Every curve, every inch would be lovingly crafted, just like the last one.

He recalled the man who'd taught him how to build this particular piece of weaponry – a man skilled in the ancient arts of combat and defence. His name had been Liao and he'd been good to Tanek, offered him a place to stay when he'd had none, a stranger in their land. Liao had been an expert in all kinds of weapons, though the modern ones didn't interest him as much as those from the past.

"You can learn much from studying history, my friend," he'd

told Tanek in one of their late night drinking sessions. They were words that another man would echo years later. Both were dead now. The Frenchman, De Falaise, who Tanek followed without question, had been killed by The Hooded Man. Tanek had not been present at his execution, but he'd felt the man's passing.

Liao, who had looked so similar to The Tsar's twins he could have been their father, had died at Tanek's hands long before that. Once he'd learnt everything he could from the man, and it had been time to move on, Tanek had simply snapped his neck, leaving Liao for his wife and children to find. He'd had no qualms about doing it, the man had been of no more use to him. And to Tanek, a quick death was a merciful one – better that than to be tortured at his hands.

Oddly enough, he'd never foreseen a time when he would have done something like that to De Falaise. He felt The Frenchman would *always* have something to teach him, only disclosing his nuggets of genius tantalisingly slowly. Before they met, in that Turkish tavern when De Falaise had saved his life – something that didn't always guarantee the same in return from Tanek – he thought he knew everything about warfare, about killing. Listening to De Falaise, he realised he knew nothing at all. Not really. He also knew nothing about ambition. De Falaise's plans saw him one day stretching his hand out to rule the entire world.

With Tanek by his side.

So much for that plan. But The Tsar, oh The Tsar... Now *he'd* done what De Falaise had only dreamed about. Become the ruler of his country with a force under his command that made their army look like the bunch of disorganised yobs they'd been. Apart from some of the more seasoned veterans, like him, they'd been kids with toy guns and tanks. When it came right down to it they were no match for Hood's sheer deviousness. While De Falaise and his men had been up front about their business in Nottingham, their enemies had chosen to sneak in and attack.

However, it had worked. And one thing Tanek knew about De Falaise was that if something worked, you adopted it yourself. It was the tactic he'd been advised to use to get to The Tsar:

hide in plain sight. If you want to reach the very heart of your opponent's camp, let them think they've captured you, let them escort you into the belly of the beast.

The tipping of the floor reminded Tanek that he was inside an altogether different belly now. Of a Zubr class military hovercraft to be precise: one of a fleet The Tsar had dispatched for this trek across the sea. Tanek finished sanding and placed the part down on the table, picking up a rectangular box. He began to sand this also.

Anyway, just like Hood, he'd been delivered unto his target. The only difference was that this time he'd come to talk, not kill. Luckily, his reputation preceded him.

"The giant Tanek, De Falaise's right hand man. I heard you were both dead," The Tsar said to him after they'd retreated to a more private place, his luxury suite at the Marriott Grand. And after Tanek had been offered use of the facilities, including a working shower – something he hadn't seen since well before the virus struck.

Tanek had sat in a plush chair, eyeing up the twins that flanked The Tsar, swords resting on their arms. But, more importantly, The Tsar's second: Bohuslav. He was potentially trouble. "De Falaise is. I was," he replied, his face stern.

The Tsar's words transported him to the final moments on those gallows, fighting the man with the staff; the infuriating child Mark (oh, how he savoured the memories of torturing the boy, wishing he had the opportunity again, wishing he could go further this time... payback for ramming that knife into Tanek's foot); and finally the man with the shotgun who'd blasted him and sent him toppling backwards. In the confusion that had followed, as De Falaise had escaped in the armoured truck – driving into the platform and unwittingly giving Tanek the opportunity to crawl away once he was on the ground – he'd made good his own escape.

Tanek had staggered to his feet, stumbling towards the buckled side gates as best he could. The chest wound from the shotgun was stinging, but not instantly fatal, and with a painful summoning of strength, he'd made it out into the street. One of Hood's men spotted him and tried to take him down, but Tanek – as weak as he was – still managed to knock him to the ground and stamp on his skull.

He'd lurched from the scene, making for one of the narrow streets adjoining, flinging himself forward; onwards ever onwards – away from the castle. How he'd made it to the outlying regions of Nottingham, he still wasn't sure, exhaustion and blood loss taking their toll. Tanek had passed out by the side of a country lane, in a ditch in the middle of nowhere. The world around him started to fade. Then all he knew was darkness. He was surely dead – had been from the moment the man shot him. He was just too stubborn to lie down and let nature take its course.

But somehow he wasn't in that ditch anymore. He was in a forest. All the colour had bleached out of the scene. Greens and browns replaced by greys and blacks. Tanek approached one of the trees – apparently able to move quite freely now, his wounds gone. He touched the bark, and where it came away the wood was bleeding, red and moist. In the clearing beyond he saw an indistinct figure – the more he concentrated the more it came into focus. It was his superior, the Sheriff, except he had no eyes and didn't appear to be able to speak, though his mouth was opening and closing. Tanek walked towards him, and as he did so the forest caught on fire. The blind De Falaise held out a hand as if pleading for help. Tanek's pace picked up, running through the flames towards him. The injured Frenchman was mouthing the words, "Help me." Tanek ran and ran, towards the figure, fighting back the fire until–

He woke up panting. For long seconds he blinked, looking up at the ceiling. *How?* he wondered. How could he be awake when he'd died back there in the ditch? It didn't make any sense. And how could he be here? Tanek was in bed, covers pulled over him. When he moved, the pain in his chest and foot returned, proving that this was no longer the dreamscape. That he actually was still alive. Lifting the covers, he was suddenly aware of his nakedness – save for the bandages around his chest. And, yes, when he wiggled his foot there was one around that too.

All became clear when an overweight, middle-aged woman

with a tight home perm – wearing a hideous floral dress – came into the room to check on him. "Ah, you're awake at last," she said, "that's a good sign. I thought you were going to sleep away the rest of the year."

Tanek sat up slowly, looking at the woman sideways.

"Don't try moving just yet, your body's still recovering," she told him, sitting down on the end of the bed. "It's just lucky that William found you when he did. If we hadn't got you back to the cottage, Heaven knows what might have happened."

William? A husband? A son, or maybe a brother? More than that, a threat!

"How...?" Tanek asked, then realised that talking hurt.

"Brought the car back for you. Only an old Morris, but... It was too far to drag you, and you're very, well, very *big*." The woman smiled coyly, looking down. "I'm sorry, where are my manners? It's just been so long since we've had company." She rose and went to the door. "I'll fix you something to eat, you must be starved."

She disappeared, leaving a puzzled Tanek to take in his surroundings: the hideous floral wallpaper; the wooden dresser and wardrobe. From the window sill leered down photos from the woman's life. Her with several children, then at the seaside with a tall man much older than her, who had grey hair.

The woman returned about fifteen minutes later with a tray of scrambled eggs. "From the chickens," she explained, kicking the bedroom door shut. "They've been a Godsend." Tanek devoured the meal in minutes. "My..." said the woman, touching her hand to her throat, "you were hungry, weren't you?"

Tanek gave a single, curt nod.

The woman sat down on the edge of the bed again. "I'm Cynthia. Cynthia Reynolds." She looked like she was waiting for his name, but he didn't oblige. "It... It doesn't matter to me, you know."

Tanek cocked his head

"Your wounds. I don't care where you got them. I just wanted you to know that." She was playing with her obviously fake pearl necklace. "You don't have to tell me anything. I know what it's like, *out there.*" It was painfully obvious she didn't have the first clue what it was like. She reached out to touch his arm. "And don't feel you have to repay me or anything."

He didn't. Tanek pulled away sharply.

"I'm... I'm sorry." Cynthia looked like she was about to cry. "It's just that, like I said, I haven't had much company these past few years. Only William. But, well, you know, a woman has certain needs that *he* can't fulfil."

Tanek looked again at the man with grey hair in the photo.

"Others have come, but they've never stayed. Then, when we came across you while we were out walking..."

"I need clothes," he snapped suddenly. "And your car."

"You're not going?" It was phrased like a question, but it was also a statement. "You're not well yet."

Tanek was well enough. Better than he had been when he'd staggered away from the castle... how long ago? Days? Surely not weeks? He got up, letting the covers drop and not caring about Cynthia seeing his body. It must have been her who'd undressed him, anyway. But she seemed coy again, as if she hadn't just been suggesting he stay for more than his health.

Ignoring Cynthia, he checked the wardrobe first – finding a mixture of men's and women's clothes. The trousers, shirt and jumper obviously belonged to the man in the picture; large enough to fit him, but tight where Tanek was broader across the chest, shoulders and legs.

"Please," said Cynthia as he was getting dressed, "stay with me. I've looked after you, haven't I?"

Tanek grunted, tugging on a pair of shoes he'd found in the bottom of the wardrobe. He made his way over to the door, once again disregarding Cynthia's pleas. Then she grabbed him by the arm. That was it, he'd had enough. The woman should have known when to leave well enough alone. Tanek took hold of Cynthia by the shoulders and pushed her up against the wall.

It was then that he heard the growling.

Tanek turned to see the door had been nosed open by a large Doberman pinscher.

"William," he said.

Cynthia nodded. "I had hoped you might be different, William really liked you. I hoped you'd join us here, stay and be our guest for much longer. But, well, as you insist on being so rude."

Tanek never saw the command if there was one, but the dog leaped straight for him, teeth bared. His reactions were dulled from being flat on his back for so long, but the sight of that mutt coming for him soon sharpened them. Tanek let go of Cynthia, whirled around, and punched the dog in the side of the head. It fell across the bed.

Little wonder no one had stayed for very long when this was Cynthia's protector. Leaving the woman, Tanek ran across to the bedroom door, slipping through and slamming it shut just as the hound had recovered sufficiently to leap again. He held onto the door handle for a few moments, grimacing at the snarling and clawing on the other side, and taking in what was around him: a small landing, a steep staircase that led to the front door.

Tanek let go of the handle and pelted down the stairs, almost tripping on the final few. He scrambled to open the front door, only to find it locked. Meanwhile, Cynthia had flung open the bedroom door and was ordering William to attack. Bracing himself, Tanek rammed the door, causing it to loosen at its hinges. There was a growling from behind, very close behind, and he slammed into the door again – this time knocking it flat.

Ahead of him, parked next to the cottage, was the Morris car Cynthia had mentioned. Tanek lumbered towards it, aware the dog was only seconds behind. The car was locked as well, so he elbowed in a window, pulled up the knob and climbed into the driver's seat, barely fitting.

William jumped at the side of the car, desperate to climb inside and bite Tanek. He leaned over just enough to stay out of the reach of those vicious teeth, as he broke open the ignition housing and hot-wired the engine. Shoving the gear stick into first, Tanek drove off, and William lost his grip. Through the rear-view mirror he saw the dog chasing after him, Cynthia at the front door watching the pursuit. Tanek sped up and pretty soon he'd left the woman, the animal, and the cottage behind.

With no real strategy in mind, except to get out of the region because he knew Hood's men might be searching for him, Tanek headed east. There was nothing for him on this island anymore and his best bet was to retrace his steps, head back over to Europe. Maybe even head back towards Turkey.

The Morris had an almost full tank of petrol – Tanek doubted whether Cynthia had driven more than a few miles since the time of The Cull – and it was enough to get him to the coast. In a small seaside village, Tanek appropriated a sailing boat and made his way back across the ocean. It wasn't as easy as their bike ride through the Channel Tunnel, but he'd finally made it to the Netherlands.

On nights when he'd let the boat drift and slept down below, Tanek had been surprised to find himself dreaming. He hadn't been able to remember his dreams before. Now they were so vivid, always set in the burning forest and always featuring De Falaise. Somehow he knew, without it having to be explained, that the link his leader shared with The Hooded Man now extended to him. In each dream Tanek had got closer and closer to the man, and in one a stag had trotted up beside De Falaise, seemingly oblivious to the flames licking around it. The Frenchman had pointed to the animal.

"I do not understand," Tanek had told him.

The flames turned to snow, falling on cold, bare branches. De Falaise looked at him with those black, empty eye sockets. "Help me," he mouthed again.

"How?"

The dreams always ended at that point, leaving him none the wiser. That is until a few months ago. He'd been sleeping rough on the streets of Warsaw when he'd had his most vivid dream yet. This time it all fell into place: what De Falaise was telling him to do, where he was telling him to go. The stag, the snow... He wanted Tanek to avenge him, kill The Hooded Man – something that had crossed the big man's mind on more than one occasion, but he'd had no idea how to go about it. Now he knew. The trail was taking him to a person they'd often talked about – someone De Falaise had both hated and admired, because he'd succeeded where the Frenchman had failed.

It was how he'd ended up fighting in The Tsar's arena, then sitting in his hotel room. His fighting skills, built up slowly again after suffering his injuries, had impressed. And his statement about having a proposition had intrigued Russia's new monarch.

"So, what is it that brings you to our country?" The Tsar asked eventually, pouring a measure of vodka for himself and another for his guest.

"You obviously know what happened in Nottingham," Tanek said to him, at the same time accepting the drink with a nod.

"I've always kept my ear to the ground."

"Then you know the threat Hood poses."

The Tsar started laughing, almost choking on his alcohol. "Threat? *Threat*? What possible threat could that woodsman and his followers pose to me?"

Tanek scowled. "That is exactly what De Falaise thought."

"But your dead master was a lot nearer, wasn't he? The world's a much bigger place these days, my friend."

"Hood is already expanding." Tanek knocked back the vodka. "He has appointed himself protector of the region. Next it will be his country. Then he will look to Europe." It was the most Tanek had said in years, probably ever. But he felt he wasn't just speaking on his own behalf anymore.

The Tsar had leaned back, the leather of his suit competing with the squeak of the chair. "Let him come. He will have to deal with others before he reaches me." He was referring to the warlords who had taken over places like France, Germany and Italy. Those who drove De Falaise to England in the first place.

Tanek held up the glass, ready for another drink. "But your goal is to rule the whole of Europe eventually, is it not?" The Tsar was silent, so he took the answer as a yes. "Then sooner or later you will meet in battle. Why not now, when his forces are small and yours are great?"

"I've heard enough," snapped Bohuslav. "He just wants revenge, sire."

"True," Tanek agreed, before The Tsar could say anything. "But as I understand it, we could be of some use to each other."

The talks had continued, well into the night, fuelled by liquor.

Tanek could feel Bohuslav's eyes boring into him as he appealed to The Tsar's ego, assuring him that it wouldn't take much to stamp out Hood, thereby also gaining a foothold in the UK from which to mount attacks on his enemies in Europe, coming at them from both sides.

"I have to admit," The Tsar slurred, well into his second bottle of Smirnoff, "that the thought of conquering America's biggest ally does appeal."

Tanek nodded. "Once you have control of England and Europe, what is to stop you going after them, too?" The picture he'd painted was one of global sovereignty, with The Tsar well and truly on the throne. The man had lapped it up, as Tanek knew he would.

Placing Bohuslav in charge, The Tsar had ordered preparations for this fleet of Zubrs to set sail, with a pit-stop at Denmark before the final leg across the North Sea. It was then that Tanek truly saw the scale of The Tsar's power, the size of his army compared with the one that had been commanded by De Falaise. He also saw that the old-fashioned weaponry he'd used to fight Glaskov was thankfully limited to the gladiatorial arena.

Each craft carried either three T-90 MTB battle tanks or a mixture of APCs, BTR 60 or 90 Armoured Fighting Vehicles, IMZ-Ural motorbikes and UAZ-3159 jeeps, plus around 50 troops (Tanek was told that pre-virus this number would have been at least double). The men were equipped with the standard AK-47s, but also Saiga-12 semi-automatics, 9A-91 shortened assault rifles, PP-19 Bizon submachine guns, compact SR-3 Vikhrs and, for real stopping power, NSV-12.7 large calibre machine guns, RGS-50M modernized special grenade launchers and AGS-17 automatic mounted grenade launchers. The list went on and on, virtually making Tanek salivate.

As he glanced up from his labours, Tanek saw the impressive array of military vehicles and equipment in this particular Zubr's bay. But in spite of being given full use of a selection of rifles and pistols, there was still something comforting about fashioning his own distinctive weapon. The sight of a crossbow bolt entering someone was so much more satisfying than a messy bullet hole.

He was alone at present, the troops having gone off to eat, so Tanek had taken full advantage of the silence. Just the thrum of the engines and creaking of the hull as the hovercraft made its way across the water, taking him back again to the place he'd departed just over a year ago, where he hoped to use his new repeater crossbow on the people who'd cost him the old one.

There was a noise off to his left, at the back of the bay – someone behind one of the T-90s. Tanek licked his lips and began to assemble his chu-ko-nu, hands flying over the wood, pieces slotting together around the stock, sliding the fully loaded magazine on top last, and pointing it in the direction of the intruder.

"Impressive," said a voice. Somehow the man had appeared at Tanek's back, and there was a cold sensation at his throat. Tanek risked a look downwards and saw the curving blade of a hand sickle.

Bohuslav.

"Now that we're alone, I thought we could have a little chat. I don't know exactly what you're up to, but you're hiding something. And you should know this: If you cross me, or if your actions in any way interfere with The Tsar's designs, I *will* kill you. And I will enjoy it."

Tanek snorted. As he'd thought: trouble.

"You may have been able to talk him around, but I am altogether a different animal."

"Look down," said Tanek.

He couldn't see the man cast his eyes downward, but he heard the sharp intake of breath when Bohuslav saw that the knife Tanek held in his other hand was hovering inches away from his side.

"Now let me go."

Bohuslav reluctantly eased the pressure on Tanek's throat. The larger man stood, turning to face the serial killer. They each held their respective weapons high: Bohuslav's two sickles; Tanek's knife and crossbow.

"This isn't finished," Bohuslav told him.

"I know."

Then Bohuslav lowered the blades, exiting stage right, moving soundlessly – which confirmed to Tanek that he'd made the noise up front purely as a distraction.

Tanek sat back down and let out a long sigh. He looked up again at the machines of war, at the hull around him. He was in the belly of a much greater beast than this one when it came right down to it. So much had happened to him since the castle, and there was still so much at stake. More than Bohuslav or even The Tsar realised. *Especially* them.

He cast his mind back to the last of his dreams before entering Moscow. The last thing De Falaise – or the dream version of him – had said. "Help me..." the blind ex-Sheriff had attempted to say again. Then:

"Help me and help my child."

CHAPTER NINE

He'd never wanted to be in charge.

Not even when he'd helped to set up the floating markets in Nottinghamshire. He'd been content to be the person who guided everyone along, without actually being the focal point. People assumed he was organising things even then, though; had always come to him for advice about trading, to settle arguments and disputes. Mainly because he liked things to run smoothly. Even when he'd worked on the proper markets back before the big bloody hiccup that was the A-B virus, folk had done the same. He'd only have to point out the best use of space, where the fruit and veg stalls would work better, or make a few observations on buying and selling, and everyone would think he was running the whole damned thing, instead of just being another trader.

The fact that he'd wandered around the post-Cull markets with a shotgun tucked under his arm hadn't exactly helped in this respect, he had to admit. Good behaviour was a lot more likely when someone was standing a few feet away with a twelve bore.

He hadn't really thought anything of it. He'd always gone out shooting with it, even when he was a lad. And when things went wrong with the world it was a no-brainer for him to keep it close by. It was one of the reasons he'd been so reluctant to relinquish it to Robert at the castle.

Stupid idiot had been glad of the thing when they'd gone into fights together, and he would put it up against that man's bow and arrow any day of the week. He didn't have the time or the inclination to start training with those, or take up the staff like Jack, or swing a sword around. It wasn't the Middle Ages. There were people still out there, dangerous people. People like that mad bastard De Falaise, who had no such qualms about carrying a gun. And he, Bill Locke, was damned if he was going to get caught with his pants down trying to string a bow when someone was shooting bullets at him. He much preferred to be shooting them back, thank you very much.

Which was why the gun had stayed with him, and was with him today – by his side as he flew over the countryside in his Sud Aviation SA 341 Gazelle helicopter – 'borrowed' from the same place as his last one: Newark Air Museum. The Sioux had been smashed to pieces by Robert when he chased down the sheriff and rescued Mary, but flying that had given Bill a taste for it again. So he'd requisitioned the more heavy-duty Gazelle for his trip North-East, away from Nottingham and all the memories it held, good and bad.

Bill had really thought things would turn out differently after the fight for the castle had been won. He and Jack began taking care of things while Robert recovered – again, Bill hadn't been the one in charge, merely gave that impression to old and new recruits alike. For a while everything was okay, until The Hooded Man was back on his feet, dishing out the orders. And for some reason – Bill couldn't for the life of him work out why – Robert had decided to just lock up all the weapons that they'd confiscated from De Falaise's troops. Now they sat in the caves, rusting away, when Robert's men could be using them to really make a difference: to keep the peace, just as Bill had done with his shotgun at those markets. It stood to reason, didn't it? At least it did to Bill. But could he get Robert to see it? Could he bollocks.

There was no way he was staying after their last bust up – too many things had been said in the heat of the moment, including Robert still laying the blame for Mark's capture at Bill's feet. How long was he supposed to go on punishing himself for that? Okay, he'd cocked up – but he'd thought the boy would be safe enough with a whole group of armed men looking after him. How was Bill supposed to know that the Frenchman would begin rounding up people to execute unless Robert turned himself in? Mark had forgiven him, hadn't seen anything *to* forgive, really. So why couldn't Robert?

"One of these days ye goin' to come a right old cropper," Bill had shouted at Robert. "An' I hope I'm there to see it." He'd stormed out of the castle and – bar saying his brief goodbyes – hadn't hung around much longer.

He'd determined to start afresh, maybe see if he could encourage more market networks to start up, if they hadn't already. It had been hard at first, relocating to another area, but he'd soon found out who was who, and what was what. So fast, in fact, it had amazed him. Yes, there were some markets operating, but they were nowhere near as organised or well run as the ones he'd known. Bill recalled visiting one, drawing strange looks from some of the stall-holders (in fact the stalls were little more than things scattered randomly on the floor). They thought he might be there to cause trouble, especially when they spotted his weapon, but he'd soon assured them he meant no harm. "There's quite a bit o' potential here, if everyone pulls together," he'd told them.

Word spread, and soon Bill had found himself in exactly the position he hadn't wanted to be: running things. He had a team of personal helpers – no, more than that, they were his friends. Ken Mayberry, for example – a former social worker who now handled timeslots for the markets; chipper Sally Lane, who along with her boyfriend Tim Pearson (he hadn't been her boyfriend *before* the plague, in fact Bill remembered her telling him she'd been married, but that was happening more and more, people pairing off), they were in charge of location scouting. It was still sensible to steer clear of big towns and cities, just as they'd done back in Nottingham, so venues now included village community centres, playing fields and even some car parks if they were in relatively isolated places.

Bill and his team had set up shop not far from Pickering and had a radio network of marketeers – as Sally called them, though that always made Bill think of pencil moustaches and swashbuckling – that took in a good chunk of the upper east coast. He was managing to keep the chopper fuelled and thus kept an eye on what was happening. They'd branched out recently into ferrying goods up and down the coast, using rowing boats or whatever else they could get their hands on. Bill had even seen one ingenious soul using a RNLI boat; well, it might as well be put to good use.

Bill had heard rumours of the things going on in Europe, men who made De Falaise look like a novice. There were actually a number *in* France, apparently. Just as long as none of them came over to these shores again...

But that was always a possible threat. And when Bill got a call like the one he was answering this morning, he had to wonder. A lookout at Whitby lighthouse had spotted something coming in across the ocean. Several large somethings to be precise which looked to be separating out. "Can ye give me any more to go on?" Bill had asked over the crackling static. What came back was unintelligible – had he heard the word ships? – and they'd lost the signal not long after. It was still not a great way of communicating, but at the moment it was all they had, short of smoke signals or semaphore.

Bill had been *en route* within the hour, though it would take him a lot longer to reach his destination from where he'd been on the other side of the North York Moors. It wasn't necessarily bad news. Perhaps someone was trying to make contact to trade with them? That would open things up even more, make life easier for a lot of people. If supplies in the UK were dwindling, apart from those people were growing or farming themselves, then there was sure to be more abroad, wasn't there?

He had to hold on to that hope, because the alternative was too terrible to think about.

Several large somethings...

Tankers, freighters, ferries?

Or warships?

Inside the cockpit, Bill shook his head. He'd been conditioned to think like that, was letting his past experiences influence him.

(But didn't he still wake up in a cold sweat some nights after looking down the cannon of a tank? Standing there pointing his shotgun at the metal monstrosity which, in his nightmares, had features – pointed teeth and glaring eyes?)

You couldn't go through something like that without it affecting you. Nor could you look on the aftermath of a battle, see the bodies on either side, and not have it haunt you.

(The pain bit into his pelvis now. It felt like that olive-skinned bastard's crossbow bolt was still lodged in there sometimes.)

Wait and see... wait and see.

He did, but as he flew closer to the coast, coming in low as he had done through the city on the day of the castle run, he saw the smoke rising from one particular location. It was a community he knew, had traded with, and the irony of its name wasn't lost on him either.

In terms of line of sight, Bill had the advantage over them at the moment – as the angle down to the bay meant those at the bottom couldn't really see him. Landing quite a way from the upper entrance, the buildings at the top giving him some cover, he powered down the chopper and grabbed his shotgun, tucking it under his long winter coat as he got out to investigate.

He worked his way down the sloping, winding King Street. The picturesque quaintness of the buildings should have been a thing of beauty, especially with the light dusting of snow they had on them at the moment. But Bill was just filled with dread. It was a steep trek downwards – though not nearly as hard as it would be to get back up again – and when he was close enough, Bill saw where the smoke was coming from. Down by the dock of the bay itself. The buildings there – including the white Bay

Hotel – had taken heavy weapons fire, scarred black where shells had hit them.

And then he saw the bodies.

Judas Priest, not again!

Who had done this to such a small, inoffensive place? More importantly, why? What had they ever done to anyone, either before or after The Cull?

Bill saw a handful of figures. People still alive. His heart sank when he spotted they were wearing uniforms, grey in colour with fur hats that covered their ears. And they were carrying machine guns. A patrol left behind to guard this spot after... after what? It was obvious from the track marks in the snow leading from the dock, up towards the wider New Road, that military vehicles had barged their way through this village. An army. Another fucking army! Before he could wonder how they'd offloaded the vehicles and men from the sea, then simply disappeared, there was a voice shouting from behind him.

Bill didn't need to turn to know it was another one of the soldiers. And he was drawing attention to the rest with his bellowing.

Both the tone of voice and language was distinctive. *Russkies*, Bill said to himself. *What in the name of fuck's sake are they doing here?*

"Turn around!" demanded the voice again, this time in broken English.

Slowly, Bill did as he was told, but at the same time he brought his gun up from under his coat, finger squeezing the trigger even before he was fully around. The loud bang coincided with his first glimpse of the soldier, barely out of his twenties, but hefting a deadly AK-47 that would have cut Bill in half given the chance. The shotgun blast hit the man in the chest, knocking him clean off his feet. Bullets from the machine gun pinged off a wall to Bill's left, the soldier's finger automatically pulling back, but his aim completely thrown.

As the first soldier fell, Bill risked a look over his shoulder at the others below, rushing up the incline to take him out. He fired another cartridge at them, causing the group to scatter.

Then he ran towards the felled soldier as fast as he could. Ignoring the blood being coughed up by the wounded trooper, he reached down and grabbed the Kalashnikov, swinging it around at the others.

"Welcome to England, Comrades!" he shouted before crouching and spraying them with bullets. They hadn't been expecting that, apparently, because they all went down fast, barely getting a shot off. "Like t'see a bow an' arrow do that," he muttered under his breath.

Bill reloaded his shotgun, then rose, holding both weapons out in front as he traversed the slippery road down to where the soldiers lay. He was well aware there could be more in hiding – it was what he and Robert would have done once upon a time – but felt the risk was worth it for information. He'd killed some of the men, he could see, on approach, he'd only injured others. When he reached one of the soldiers who had multiple leg wounds, he picked up his booted foot and brought it down on the man's thigh.

Then he pointed the twin barrels of his shotgun in his face.

"What are ye doing here, Red? What d'ye want?" he asked him through clenched teeth. The man shook his head, so Bill leaned more heavily on the thigh. There was a howl of pain. "I'm not a patient bloke. Tell me!"

"*Poshyol ty!*" Bill had no idea what it meant, but the way the man spat this out told him he was getting nothing.

"Fair enough," said Bill, taking his boot off the wound long enough to kick the man across the face.

He made his way a little further down the slope, to the dead locals. The fact there were women and children among them eased his conscience somewhat about the killing he'd done that day.

Then he heard the groaning. One of the 'dead' was trying to speak. Bill whirled around and immediately went over, getting down on the ground beside him. The man was in his thirties, with a kind face. His thick woollen jumper was stained crimson where the soldiers' bullets had eaten into him.

"Easy lad," said Bill, and though it would leave himself

vulnerable to attack he placed the man's head on his knee. "What happened 'ere?"

The man's eyes were glassy, but Bill knew he could still see him. He winced when he tried to talk, but forced the words out anyway. "H... Huh... Hit us hard... without warning... jeeps and.... bikes...and..." The man attempted to shake his head. "We made a stand... but we were no m-match for 'em..."

"Judas Priest," Bill said under his breath. "I don't understand this." The man groaned again, in terrible pain from the bullet wounds. And something else. As Bill's eyes were drawn down the man's body, he saw an object sticking out of his side. It had snapped off almost completely when he fell to the ground – after being raked with bullets – but there was no mistaking the crossbow bolt that was wedged in there. Bill would recognise one of those anywhere.

Quickly, he cast his eyes across the rest of the bodies. Sure enough, he saw it at least a half dozen times. More of the bolts sticking out of people, a way of slowing them down for the infantrymen to pick them off.

"Who did this?" Bill asked the man.

He looked annoyed and answered, "Soldiers," as if he resented the waste of his dying breaths.

Bill shook his head and pointed to the broken bolt. "No, who did *this* to you? T' the rest of those people. I seen it before, y'see."

The man appeared confused, then it dawned on him what Bill meant. "The... the giant..."

"What?"

"B-Big man... olive skin..."

"Shooting people wi' a crossbow," Bill finished for him. The man nodded, then hissed in agony.

It couldn't be. I killed him.

Bill had certainly shot him, square in the chest as far as he could tell – though it had been pretty hard to concentrate on anything when that bolt had punched into him. They'd never found a body, though, had they? In spite of searching when everything had calmed down. Nothing in the wreckage from the platform; neither Jack nor Mark had seen anything. But still... How could it be? And what was he doing with Russians?

Well, he'd been with the Frenchman, hadn't he? He'd been with the German, the Italian and Mexican. *Used* them. Race meant nothing to Tanek, only the need to destroy and take what he could for himself.

Bill was brought back to the here and now when the man began to convulse. "Easy," said Bill again. But the man couldn't hear him anymore. Bill held him tightly by the shoulders. The convulsions ended suddenly, then the man went completely limp. Bill closed the dead man's eyes.

He stood, feeling numb: none of his original questions answered and a whole lot more lumped on the pile. If Tanek really had returned, bringing with him another army, then there was only one place they could be heading. As he was righting himself, though, at least one of the mysteries was solved. Across the sea, and almost obscured from view by an outcropping, he could see some kind of ship. Bill took a pair of binoculars out of his pocket and looked through them. Maybe it was just the light, but it looked slightly silvery, and it had three big fan-like things on its back. It resembled a grey slab of concrete on the water, except it wasn't quite *on* the water – a black ring was keeping it afloat like a fat man sitting on a rubber ring.

"A bloody hovercraft!" said Bill.

But only one of them, and now he remembered what that lookout at Whitby had said: "Several somethings." Bill had no clue what one of those brutes could carry in terms of equipment, men and vehicles, but he was guessing it wasn't to be sniffed at. Imagine what had come across in a handful, splitting up and branching out to land at different points along the coast so they could take out observers before a flag could be raised. Bill was betting the army would rendezvous somewhere inland before heading on for their final destination. "Shit," he added for good measure.

Time he wasn't here. Grabbing the other rifles – jamming them under his arm – and stuffing anything else he could find of use into a backpack one of the soldiers had been wearing (like grenades, knives and spare ammo) Bill began the task of climbing back up towards his chopper. Hopefully before anyone over at the hovercraft realised something was amiss.

What he was going to do first, he didn't have a clue. Deep down he knew not only was the region in danger again, but probably his friends as well.

And he realised they'd only been in the middle of the calm before the next storm. A lull which had made them complacent.

All of this and more was buzzing round Bill's mind as fast as the rotor blades on his helicopter when he started her engine.

Everything being mulled over, especially Tanek, always Tanek, as he made his way upwards and eventually away from Robin Hood's Bay.

CHAPTER TEN

"Are you sure this is such a good idea?"

If he'd been asked that once today, he'd been asked it a million times. By Mary – of course – by Jack, and now the one person he'd thought would be guaranteed to be on his side: Mark. This was for his benefit, after all.

Wasn't it?

Mostly. Robert was finally beginning to concede that the boy was getting older, that maybe it *was* time he started his training in earnest – and that didn't just mean messing about on the Bailey with Jack and the other men. It meant taking him out to where he himself had learnt his skills.

Where Robert had become The Hooded Man.

"Sherwood? Are you serious?" That had been Mary. "You can't go off again now, with everything that's happening."

Jack had broached similar concerns. They were only just starting to figure out the cult, with Tate's help, and for their leader to keep vanishing like this...

"I'm not vanishing. You know where I'll be if you need me," he argued. The first trip to Hope had been essential. This one they really didn't understand, and his flimsy explanation about Mark hadn't cut it. Especially after he'd been the one who kept knocking the boy back, telling him he wasn't ready.

Robert couldn't blame them for being freaked out, not after the incident at *The Britannia*. Mary had only just been able to save Geoff Baker's life. She'd set to work straight away after getting there, seemingly taking the dead body slumped across the table in her stride. Then she'd had Geoff moved somewhere they could treat him properly. Mary hadn't even acknowledged Robert or Tate's presence. Though that was understandable because she had her hands full, Robert still had a niggling feeling she was punishing him.

Later, when Geoff was stable – though there was still a good chance he wouldn't see the next dawn – Mary had demanded to see Robert and Tate alone in one of the small conference rooms at the hotel. That was when she'd asked them what they thought they were playing at, interrogating a prisoner without her present, with only Lucy on hand to deal with the medical side of things. "What were you thinking?" she'd asked, pacing up and down in front of them.

"There wasn't time, Mary," Robert told her.

"No time to let me know you were back, either," commented Mary with a sour face. "But time to send for me when Geoff had been attacked?"

"Lucy had given the Servitor–"

"The what?"

"It's what they call themselves. Anyway, Lucy had given him something to calm him down. He was secured. We didn't think–"

"No, you didn't, did you?" Mary sighed. "Look, some people's reactions to *any* drugs can be totally unexpected. Here, the Chlorpromazine obviously had exactly the reverse effect to calming him down."

Tate, seated on one of the chairs, was tapping his stick with a finger. "Can I just ask, Mary – and by the way, it's nice to see you again." His smile was weak, but sincere. "Could that same side-effect have made him stronger?"

"It's possible, yes," Mary admitted. "And it's nice to see you again, too, Reverend. I wish it was under better circumstances."

When they'd finished going over what had taken place, possible causes and reasons, and coming to no definitive conclusions, Tate had left to go and get settled back at the castle, he'd be staying there until this mess with the cult was sorted out. Robert and Mary had hung back in the room, at first hardly able to even look at each other. It was Robert who broke the silence first.

"I'm sorry."

"For what? For leaving so suddenly, or not saying a thing when you got back?"

"For whatever it is I'm supposed to be apologising about this time." It hadn't been the wisest thing he'd ever said.

"How about for giving Adele the run of our bedroom?" Mary had said, hands on hips.

"What?"

"You heard me."

Robert wracked his brains. Had he done that? He didn't remember it... maybe something about borrowing anything if she needed it, but he just assumed she'd ask first. Robert shook his head. This wasn't really about privacy, no more than it had been the other day. This was about him and Mary. About how strong they were together or, right now, the opposite.

"You've got to stop this, Mary. Adele is–"

"I know exactly what she is – and what she's after," Mary stated emphatically. "What I don't know is, if she's being encouraged."

"It's been another long day, I've just been wrestling with a maniac and almost seen one of my friends die right in front of me. I haven't got time for this nonsense."

"I understand," she'd told him; he could feel the chill in her words.

Robert followed Tate's lead, leaving Mary alone in the room. He hadn't seen her again until that night, when he'd felt her climb into bed. Part of him just wanted to reach out and put an arm around her, snuggle up tight and forget everything else. But his stubborn pride got in the way: *wait and see if she does it first.* She didn't. In fact she edged as far away from him as possible.

It was as he was lying there awake again that he'd thought of a solution. Of what he must do. Of a way of figuring out a direction. Things were falling apart rapidly, not only in his personal life, but in every other department. He didn't know how to fight monsters like the one who'd broken free at *The Britannia* – it was so far removed from his experience. He knew his men were being spread too thinly, both on patrol and looking after the prisoners they'd captured. Robert not only needed to get away from the chaos and confusion for a while, to rediscover who exactly he was, he needed some kind of guidance.

He needed to be back in his one, true home.

So yes, Mark had been an excuse if he was honest – but Robert saw no harm in that. If the youth was one day to take all this over, which was Robert's hope, then he needed to begin where Robert had. Needed to experience what he'd experienced out in the wilderness, or at least start his journey there.

It hadn't gone down well. Mary believed it was just another excuse to get away (from her, though she only implied the last bit). "Go then. It's obviously where you'd prefer to be right now," she'd sniped.

Meanwhile Jack was worried because of the new threat they were facing. "I thought *you* were too, Robbie. The kid's training's going okay on the castle grounds."

"There are things I can show him at Sherwood that no-one can show him here. Things I never taught any of the troops when we were living there."

Jack had accepted it, but didn't like it.

Tate, on the other hand, never said a word. It was almost like he knew why Robert was making this pilgrimage, and why he wasn't going alone. He'd merely blessed him and said he would pray for his speedy return. "Bring wisdom back with you," Tate had said.

"I'll try, Reverend."

Mark had been all for it initially. But now, on their way to the forest on horseback, he asked Robert if he knew what he was doing. "I don't want to take you away from important things at the castle," he said, riding at a trot alongside.

"This is important, Mark. What we're doing here. But you're not the only reason we're heading back to Sherwood."

"I'm not?"

Robert leaned across and clapped him on the shoulder. "No. This trip's for me as well. I need to reconnect with something I've lost."

"Oh, okay... Talking of which," broached Mark. "You and Mary."

"Not you as well!" Robert gave him a stern look. It was the face he'd pulled when Mark had first followed him into the forest, first begun pestering him to help them against De Falaise. He'd eventually accepted his other role as well, his relationship with the boy growing, each of them replacing something – some*one* – they'd lost during the virus. But that didn't mean he could be as cheeky as he liked. "There's nothing to discuss, Mark. Drop it."

"But you need to reconnect with something back there as well, don't you see?"

"Since when did you become the fount of all knowledge?"

Mark laughed. "I always have been, didn't you notice? You two are good together."

"You think I don't know that?"

"I do, and that's the pity. You've lost your way a bit, that's all. What is it you say to me, face your fear?"

"And how about you and Sophie? How's it going there, bigshot?" Robert knew it wasn't really fair to turn this around on Mark, but the boy had asked for it. God, teenagers thought they knew it all, didn't they? But Robert had to stop and remind himself that this kid wasn't any ordinary teen, not like those he used to see on street corners with their mates during his time on the beat. Mark had already seen more than he should have of life's horrors, and perhaps that afforded him some leeway. Only not to discuss Robert's private life, and not this frankly.

Mark reacted as if slapped. "There *is* no me and Sophie. That's the trouble. If we had what you and Mary had... still have, then..."

Robert held up his hand. "I told you, let that drop." But then he couldn't help digging himself deeper. "Jack told me about the fight, you know. You're a brave guy taking on Dale. He's one of the best fighters I've got."

Mark grunted. "He's not so tough."

"Heard you gave him a bloody nose." Robert smiled. "That makes you pretty good too in my book." Mark joined him in the smile. "Mind if I ask what he did to deserve it? Jack told me about the song. He was just pulling your leg, the men do it all the time with each other."

"The *men*," said Mark, hinting at the problem.

"Ah, I see. You're fed up of being treated like a younger brother or something."

"Brother?" Mark let out a long, mournful breath. "Yeah, I guess that's how Sophie sees me."

"I meant Dale and the blokes. But now I see what's at the bottom of all this. She doesn't treat *him* like a brother, does she? Dale, I mean?"

Mark shook his head.

"Women, eh?" said Robert, then waited for the smile to broaden; and for it to become another laugh. "They operate on a whole other level, Mark. Out here it's simple. Even in a fight, it's simple. But relationships..."

The horses made their way up one final road. Robert saw the faded brown signs saying 'Sherwood Forest National Nature Reserve', and indicated they should turn in there. Normally, he would have entered the less obvious way, but he wanted to show Mark something before they got to all the survival stuff.

"Come on," he said to the boy, urging his horse to speed up a little and taking them through the first and biggest of the car parks. He looked around, admiring the way the forest had taken back what belonged to it, punching through the concrete in many places, overrunning the dividing posts and benches where families would have had their picnics in summer months. Where he'd once brought Stevie and Joanna to do the same.

Swinging down from their steeds, the pair walked them down an overgrown trail, marked out by fences, and left them with plenty of hay inside the abandoned and rundown 'Forest Table' – once a thriving eating place for visitors to Sherwood. They walked on into the middle of the Visitor's Centre, with its focal point: the peeling statue of two legendary figures battling it out with staffs. "Reminds me of the night we met Jack, remember?" said Mark.

Robert did. He'd assumed – wrongly as it turned out – that Jack had been sent into the woods to assassinate him. He was actually auditioning, as he called it (Jack and his movies!) for the role of the man in front of them. One of the old Hood's most faithful companions. It had worked out similarly this time around as well, Robert had to agree. He didn't know now what he'd do without the hulking American by his side.

Robert lit a couple of torches, then led Mark inside a big building off to their left, forcing open a stiff door. As they stepped inside, Mark could see through into a deserted shop on his right. It looked like a cave filled with ancient treasure. Cobwebs covered everything: from toy bows and swords, to hats with feathers in them; from mugs and plates to pens, badges and notebooks. Ahead of them, though, was an exhibition – which, via winding corridors, told the history of the original Hooded Man. Robert took them past another statue of that man, in a more familiar pose, about to fire an arrow. This, too, was covered in cobwebs. As they ventured further inside, there were more representations, including one of the Sheriff of Nottingham in full panto villain mode, rubbing his chin.

"What are we doing here?" asked Mark. "It's all a bit creepy."

Robert knew what he meant: the parallels were too close for comfort. But there *was* a purpose, as he showed him soon enough. Behind the wooden walls of these displays Robert had hidden an entire arsenal of weapons. Dotted throughout the exhibition were dozens of real bows and swords, bolas made from twine and rocks, and quivers bristling with arrows, even spare clothes. It was his own private stash.

"The stock room we passed on the way in was far too obvious, plus I didn't want them all in one place," he explained. "I came back a while ago. Thought I'd leave all this in case of an emergency."

"What kind of emergency?"

Robert shrugged. "It wouldn't be an emergency if I knew in advance."

The boy was studying his features in the light from the burning torches. "You've never really considered that castle your home, have you?" Once again, he had to hand it to him – the fount of all knowledge. "Is that why you left this lot, because you thought you'd be back one day?"

Robert didn't answer that. "I just wanted to show someone. Not even Mary knows."

Mark gave Robert a hand to conceal the weapons again, then they made their way up and through the final winding corridor. Before they came to the exit, both of them paused. There was a display on their right. Behind cracked and smeared glass was an arrow embedded in some earth. "'And where this arrow is taken up,'" read Mark, "'There shall my grave be.'"

Robert pushed him out by the shoulder. "Not yet you don't."

The pair headed deep into the forest, with Robert preferring to make a new camp rather than seeking out an old one.

He'd noticed a change in himself almost as soon as he'd entered this place. His body had relaxed, but was still coiled and ready to attack if provoked; just like it had been when he'd first moved here. His mind was also more balanced than it had been in a long time. Robert had seen Sherwood in all seasons, so the bare trees were not a shock to him – in fact they only added to the beauty of the place on this winter's day, especially with that sprinkling of snow on them.

When they'd found the right spot – somewhere that was hard to locate if an intruder might be looking for it, but gave them a clear 360° view of the area – they set up their camp. "Your base camp should be the safest location in your territory," Robert said.

"This is all so cool," Mark told him. "Do you know how often I wished you'd teach me all this stuff when we were here before?"

Robert gave a half smile. "Well now I am, so pay attention."

He went through how to make a lean-to, using branches for poles and whatever foliage they could find – not easy at this time of year – then how to make a bed out of moss.

"Okay, time to go hunting," announced Robert. Nothing big at first, in fact just a couple of hares which they staked out near a warren. "Rabbits and hares don't hibernate in the winter," Robert explained in hushed tones, "but fortunately for us they become slower and less active to conserve energy. So they're easier to catch when they're rattled. Now keep well out of sight. Always let them come out into the open – then deliver your surprise."

Mark had grumbled a little about preying on such easy targets but, as Robert informed him, when you lived out here sometimes meat was in short supply. You took what you could find. Besides which, hare was tasty.

When they returned to camp, Robert taught him how to make a fire, tucking away the lighter and forcing Mark to use the tried and tested method of rubbing sticks together. When the boy had built up a sweat, Robert chuckled and finally showed him the easier way of using a little bow to create friction, feeding the flames when they began to catch light.

That night they cooked the animals over a spit and talked more about their time together here before. Most of the stories were preceded by: "Do you remember when?" and Robert was surprised by how many ended with them both laughing. It had been a trying period, out here waiting to be discovered or killed by De Falaise's troops, but it was also, in some ways, a happy time. With each moment that passed during that evening, Robert was more convinced he'd done the right thing by bringing Mark here.

As the fire died down a little, Robert caught Mark resting against his backpack and looking at his missing finger, lost in thought. "You still think about what happened back then, don't you?"

"Don't *you*?" Mark said, tossing aside a piece of bone that had been picked clean and taking a swig of the water they'd made from boiling down the plentiful supply of snow.

Robert nodded. "It takes a while to come to terms with our demons, whatever shape they take."

"Is this about facing your fear again?"

"Sort of. Only sometimes we get to face it in the flesh." Robert poked the fire, then jabbed a finger at it. "That was one of mine."

"Yeah, I remember what happened when the Mexican used those incendiary grenades. It sent you almost to pieces."

Robert stared directly at him. "It made me weak, that fear."

"Some folk might say it made you human," Mark countered.

"Then being human can get you killed."

"Or save you. Are you ever going to tell me why it frightens you so much?"

Buried memories intruded now: his house on fire, the knowledge that the men in yellow suits were cooking his wife and son, dead upstairs in the bedroom. His dog, Max, limping out, fur alight...

Robert ignored the question, and rolled onto his back, looking up into the night sky. "The stars seem so much clearer out here. Everything's clear, in fact. No distractions."

"You're going to have to open up someday," he heard Mark comment. "To me, Mary. Maybe even Reverend Tate."

"What I'm doing now," Robert broke in, totally off topic, "with you, I mean. Someone else did the same with me. His name was Eric Meadows. He showed me the ropes."

"I don't underst–"

"And do you know the most important thing, the first thing I learned from him?" Robert couldn't see Mark shaking his head, but he knew the boy was doing it. "To keep my mouth shut and listen." He rolled back onto his side, resting his head against his hand and looking past the fire at Mark. "He was older than me, more experienced. So I listened."

Mark looked down into the fire. "And was there ever a time when you were able to help *him*?"

Like most of Mark's questions, this caught him off guard, but his mind automatically supplied an answer. Another memory, not buried, just forgotten until now. Of Robert and Eric being called to a fight in a bar, where two twenty-somethings had decided to kick off over a girl who looked like she wanted nothing to do with either of them. By the time they'd arrived, the men were smashing bottles and throwing punches, so Eric had been the first to wade in. What he hadn't spotted was that one of the guys had mates in the corner, who came at Eric and were about to glass him when Robert stepped in. Several years down the line from the first collar he'd made, and he was a different officer. Confident, though not a risk-taker (because he had a wife to return to and they were planning on starting a family soon), but able to assess a situation like this and turn it to his advantage.

Robert had kicked the glass out of the attacker's hand, then followed up with a punch that sent him to the floor. Technically not the done thing, but Robert wasn't about to play nice in this powder keg of a situation. He'd been ready to tackle the others as well, but when the fighters heard sirens outside – Eric and Robert's backup – they'd fled the pub. Eric had cuffed the two original trouble-causers, leaving Robert to handle his. So he had no idea whether his mentor knew he'd probably saved his skin that night. Neither of them said anything to each other, as it was all in a day's work for Her Majesty's Constabulary, though Robert often wondered if he realised the favour had been returned.

But that wasn't what Mark had asked, was it? Had Robert been able to help him? Truly help him? Where was he when Eric had been injured at that football match? Robert couldn't even remember now. On holiday? Sequestered to one of the CID units? He hadn't been able to help Eric when it came to the real crunch, had he? Only postponed the inevitable.

"Never let them put you behind one of those. You stay out there, young Stokes. Stay where you can make a difference and leave all that to the paper pushers."

Was that what this was all about? Did he need to get back out there for Eric, do something for the man even though he was probably dead by now (Robert had absolutely no idea what his blood group was, but he had to be pushing seventy even if he had survived).

Robert realised that long minutes had passed and he hadn't

said a word in reply to Mark. "I'm... I'm sorry. Just remembering something."

"About when you were able to help this Eric guy?" asked Mark, looking up at him.

"I think in my own way I'm helping him right now," Robert replied, not even attempting to explain. He wasn't sure he understood himself.

The fire was really dropping now, so they said their goodnights and retreated to their lean-tos. Robert faster than Mark, if anything. Not to get out of the cold, but to do what he'd come here to do all along: sleep.

And hope that the forest would find it in its heart to speak to him.

CHAPTER ELEVEN

At first he thought one of the sparks from the fire must have caused it.

Set this whole portion of the forest alight. Robert felt dreadful; how could he have done this to his beloved home? The bark was on fire, the branches and twigs. It was a good thing there were no leaves because they would only have added to the conflagration. He looked around, frantically trying to find something to douse the flames with. If they'd been closer to the lake at Rufford then–

But they weren't. Robert had chosen this spot intentionally to be away from the locations he'd lived in alone, when he'd first come here. The locations he'd been drawn to so he could while away the rest of his time and die; be with his late wife and child. To run away from...

From the blaze.

But he was wasting time now, thinking about all that. He should be waking Mark, getting him to help put out this fire.

Robert couldn't see the boy's lean-to anywhere – couldn't see his own for that matter. Perhaps they'd both been burnt away? If that was the case was Mark all right?

A sudden wave of heat forced Robert to shield his face. He tottered backwards. Then, through the shimmering air, he saw a figure caught in the midst of the licking flames. Blinking, he tried to make out the features, but they were unclear. Once, he would have held back no matter what – not even attempted to go into the heart of this inferno. Now Robert braced himself and, head down, rushed in to get closer to the figure. It was about Mark's height, could easily *be* him. Robert hoped not, because even now the person was catching light, going up like the forest around them.

"Hold on," Robert shouted. "I'm coming." He was aware that he must be cooking as well, but had to push through, had to save this person. He'd lost too much to the fire already, he wasn't about to lose the closest thing he had to a son as well.

Robert broke through into a clearing, the flames raging around him but not touching this section of the forest. In fact the only thing on fire was the figure directly ahead of him. Robert sucked in air, coughing, then refocused. He soon realised his mistake. This wasn't Mark at all; nothing like him. There, not ten feet away from him, was his old enemy: De Falaise.

Yes, he was on fire – the yellow and red rippling over him but apparently not eating him up. Robert was shocked. The last time he'd seen this man he'd killed him, and a blaze had played around them that day too. There was evidence of Robert's attack, because De Falaise no longer had eyes – and even though he was opening and closing his mouth, the Frenchman couldn't speak (a consequence of Robert having shoved an arrow as far down his throat as he could ram it). The arrow that had penetrated his heart – like a stake finishing off a vampire – was missing, but the hole was plainly there. De Falaise was saying something, but it was so faint Robert couldn't make it out.

It sounded like one word over and over.

Vengeance.

De Falaise smiled, those broken teeth even more yellow in the flames. The Frenchman opened his arms wide and let the full force of the fire take him, and this time it did crisp his skin, blackening his face and exposed hands. His dress suit – the one he'd worn for the executions at the castle – melted onto him, then that too turned black. Robert stood there watching, knowing he couldn't do a thing. Not really wanting to. This was a replay of past events – slightly different, but still a replay. What he wanted to know about was the future, about his new enemies.

As if to answer him directly, the figure burnt brighter... and redder. It took a step towards him, and when it did some of the black crust fell away. What was beneath was red, and it merged with the fire: creating a figure that was crimson from the feet upwards. Robert's mouth dropped open as he witnessed this transformation. That's the only way he could describe it, a fiery Phoenix rising from the ashes. Dressed head to toe in red leather.

The build of the two men was similar, but Robert could see they were very different. This person was stockier, looked like he could really handle himself. Looked like he had seen some action in the past, not just ordered people to their deaths. And he looked... somehow regal. Like the campfire from the night before, the flames died down and when they did, the man pulled on his greatcoat. Then he placed the peaked cap on his head.

He smirked at Robert. There was no denying the intent was the same. He was here to destroy The Hooded Man, just as The Sheriff had set out to do. Was this the distant future, some kind of reincarnation perhaps? Robert had no idea, and no more time to ponder, because the fire surrounding them was also changing.

Robert looked to his left and right. There were faces there; faces painted white and black like skulls, with tattoos on their foreheads. *Yes, them! I came here to learn about them,* Robert told the dreamscape, told the forest. *I need to know how to defeat them. If I can defeat them!*

Except behind the figures were more people, faces without make-up. The faces of soldiers, who were carrying automatic weapons. The ground was shaking – Robert felt the vibrations up through his legs, into his guts. To his left, breaking through the ground and knocking charred trees aside, a huge tank shot upwards and then righted itself with a metallic clang. To Robert's left, an armoured vehicle did the same, followed by a couple of jeeps. In the centre of this burning scene there was suddenly an army made up of two factions. Impossible to fight alone.

Where were his people? Where were *his* troops?

There were shadows behind the man in red, stepping out. Two Asian women, Robert saw, and a man in a sharp suit. Each was holding a body by the scruff of its neck, which they threw to the ground in front of Robert. The first belonged to Tate, lifeless and limp. Then came Sophie, piled on top. Followed by Mary. Robert's entire body stiffened when he saw her tossed there, like a Guy on a funeral pyre. Her beautiful eyes looked up at him in death.

"Noooo!" he screamed. "You can't do this!"

A larger shadow emerged, carrying two bodies – one in each hand. But he could manage them well enough, the size that he was. Robert's jaw dropped again when he saw Tanek, the Frenchman's second, assumed dead but very much alive here (though hadn't De Falaise been standing there only moments before... living or deceased, it didn't mean a thing in this place).

The two last bodies were thrown over towards Robert, Tanek grunting – more with satisfaction than effort. Robert recognised who they were as they landed: Jack, defeated and deflated... and Mark. Finally Mark. Beaten to a pulp and with more than his finger missing.

Robert sank to his knees, tears flowing freely. He knew it wasn't a good idea to show weakness in front of his enemies, but couldn't help it. When he reached up to wipe the salt-water away, he found his face altered. There were antlers on the side of his head. He had a snout too. As he looked up again, Tanek was approaching with that crossbow of his raised, a bolt in the chamber pointing at him. The shot was fired and, though it entered Robert's temple, he could somehow still hear and see everything around him: the flames, the assembled war machine. Tanek crouching, letting go of the crossbow and taking out a knife with a serrated edge.

Robert's vision went black for a second then red, like a filter had been placed over a camera lens. Tanek finished his cutting, *sawing*, standing again with something in his free hand. Robert's... the stag's head.

He handed the gory thing to the man in leather, who took off his peaked cap and replaced it with the antlers. They looked for all the world like a pair of horns.

In spite of the fire's warmth, Robert felt cold. It spread quickly throughout his body. If this *was* a vision of the future, as he'd wanted, then he was sorry he'd asked for it. Better to be ignorant than live with the knowledge that they would all soon die.

"Vengeance," said a voice close to his ear, a figure he couldn't see whispering to him. It sounded... familiar. De Falaise, but not him; the voice softer.

Then he felt hands on him, moving him.

Moving his corpse.

It was a revelation when he found he *could* move – grabbing the hands that were shaking him. "N-Not dead," Robert mumbled. "Not dead!"

"Sshh. Keep it down," another voice, a different voice, whispered. "We're not alone."

Robert shook his head, clearing it. It had been a while since he'd slept so heavily, had a dream as intense. He'd forgotten how disorientating it could be. Mark was the person by his side – not the dead Mark with bits cut off, but the living Mark who he could still do something to save if he got his act together. Mark who had been trying to wake him for some time.

"People, circling the camp," he told Robert. "I caught a glimpse when I got up to pee. I managed to crawl across to your lean-to without them seeing, I think."

"How many?" asked Robert in hushed tones.

Mark shrugged. "A couple, maybe."

"That's the next lesson, then. Counting." Mark scowled, then Robert tapped him on his arm. "Come on, let's see what we're dealing with."

Grabbing his bow, arrows and sword, Robert emerged from the back of the lean-to with Mark beside him, using it to shield them both. Robert slipped the quiver and bow around his torso. It wasn't quite light, but the sun had started to come up over the horizon, giving everything a strange sepia look. There was also an early morning mist covering the ground, thin enough to see through close up, but out in the distance it could hide anything. Robert trusted the boy's instincts, because after years of living on his wits the lad had developed a sense about these things. He'd been the first to warn Bill about the attack on the market, and told Robert when Jack first entered Sherwood. Now he was telling him there was a potential threat in the woods and Robert took that very seriously.

This was *real* hunting.

Mark nudged him and gestured towards a nearby tree at 3 o'clock. He saw an elbow sticking out from behind the trunk. Robert nodded, then pointed across at another tree. He could tell Mark couldn't see it, but there was bark missing from one side, indicating that someone had scraped by it. Robert turned when he heard a noise behind him. Mark may well have dismissed it as a woodland animal, but he knew better. Even though it had been a while since he'd lived here, Robert still felt the rhythms of this place – could tell when there was something out of sync. So, he was surrounded, as in his dream. Robert just hoped the tanks and jeeps weren't about to shoot up from out of the ground.

He made a fanning out gesture to Mark, who nodded. He hated having to split them up – especially when he could still picture the boy's dead face – but he knew Mark needed to do this as much as he did. Robert pulled up his hood and began to stalk his prey, vanishing into the undergrowth.

Keeping low to the ground, he backtracked round to where he'd heard the noise. Robert closed his eyes and breathed deeply, attempting to *sense* where the intruder was. Where the disturbance in his forest was rooted. It didn't prove difficult, not when the attacker suddenly showed himself and charged at Robert. He opened his eyes in time to see a flash of machete blade, a painted face leering down at him. A Servitor!

Robert took hold of the rushing figure, at the same time dodging the man's weapon, then used his own momentum against him, flinging the Servitor into a nearby birch. "Damned Halloween freak," he snarled. The tree was slightly at an angle, so the robed man fell over it, landing on the other side. Robert was round it in seconds, bringing up a swift knee and clipping the cultist under the chin.

He was suddenly aware of two more attackers on either side of him. They appeared from behind trees and lunged at Robert, machete blades cutting through the morning air. He dodged one, then had to turn swiftly and duck another. But as he came up again, he brought his clenched fist with him, practically lifting the Servitor off his feet with the punch. The next swing, Robert met with his own sword: metal striking metal. Gritting his teeth, he pushed the robed man backwards until he hit a tree, winding him. Robert turned his back on the man, turned his sword around and thrust it backwards so that it slid into his attacker's side and out again very quickly, incapacitating him.

By this time the first attacker had recovered and was getting to his feet. Robert had time to quickly glance over and see how Mark was doing now their cover was well and truly blown. He saw the boy facing at least three of the freaks himself, and he'd already been relieved of his sword.

Holding the sword by the flat of the blade, Robert brought the hilt down heavily on the approaching cultist's head. It struck him dead centre and he fell to his knees. Then Robert swung the sword like a baseball bat and hit the man in the face, sending his head rocking back and a few of his teeth flying.

Unslinging his bow as he went, Robert pulled out an arrow and aimed across to where Mark was fighting, kicking the first Servitor who'd attacked to keep him down. Just as he was about to fire, though, a half dozen more of the men rose up from the mist or stepped out from behind trees.

"Crap," said Robert under his breath. Mark was on his own, at least for now. He turned the bow on the nearest of the approaching cult members.

The Afterblight Chronicles

What had been his first mistake?

Mark was asking himself this even as he realised it was probably the worst time to be doing so. It was only what Jack would ask him later, if there was a later, but the time for analysis definitely wasn't now. He'd blundered in, hadn't he? Gone for the guy with his elbow sticking out, thinking he was an easy target. But then he'd realised, when the figure stepped out and confronted him, that the Servitor had been expecting this strike all along. What the hell was the matter with him? Mark had been so quiet and nimble as a boy, slipping in and out of cities and towns for supplies, scavenging them and stuffing them into his knapsack. But creeping up on people? Not so great at that.

The noise had brought another one out of the trees, and now Mark understood what Robert had been pointing at. Another hiding behind an oak, the bark worn off. He should have taken one out at a distance with a rock then–

Swish!

Mark was suddenly stumbling backwards. This wasn't a training sword anymore, but the real thing, held by someone who really did want to do him some harm. He reached for his own blade, but had only got it part of the way free before he felt it being lifted out by a third cultist who had appeared seemingly from nowhere. The sword was snatched away and thrown into the snowy grassland beyond the trees.

Swish!

Again Mark only just had time to dodge the blow, as it whistled past his right ear. Stepping back did, however, have the added benefit of knocking the man behind him off balance, so that Mark could topple him fully over.

Now there were only two to deal with. And where was Robert? Mark saw that he was having fun with his own playmates; more and more rising up out of the ground itself, it seemed.

"You think you're always going to have a weapon to hand? Uh-uh. Nope. But your opponent might."

That's what Jack had said, and he'd been so right. Mark didn't have his sword but they each had one. Well, really big knives that you could probably call swords, but that was splitting hairs. *Think, Mark, think... how had Azhar done it again?*

Mark recalled the way that man had ducked and slid sideways to take the weapon from him. He had just seconds to react, to copy the move he'd witnessed. Now it wasn't a game, Mark found his body co-operating, his movements less clumsy. Mark grabbed his opponent's wrist and yanked, but the weapon wouldn't tug free. The cultist pulled back and readied himself for another thrust. Thinking fast, Mark let his backpack – only hanging over one shoulder – slide down his arm; then, as the blade came into range, he wrapped the thing in the material, yanking down until the machete fell out of the man's hands. As Mark bent forward to retrieve it, the first attacker fell over him and he instinctively followed through: standing and flipping him, letting the momentum of the move do all the work.

Snatching up the machete, Mark met the second attacker's swing; the clang made his teeth rattle. The third joined in and suddenly Mark had to block his attempt to kill him as well. That was one of the major differences between real combat and practising on your own: trees and fences didn't fight back. These people did, and by all accounts they didn't stop till one of you had stopped *for good.*

Mark batted away the attacks, using sheer desperation rather than finesse to carry him through. It was keeping him alive... so far. What he didn't know was how he was going to keep this going indefinitely, especially as the remaining cultist was rising from the floor. Rising, and searching around for Mark's sword.

What would Robert do in this situation? he wondered. What *was* he doing right now in fact?

That wasn't the right thing to ask, to get him out of this – so he asked himself quickly instead: *What would Dale do?*

What would Dale do if Sophie was watching?

And what would you do, Mark? What would you do to show her you can cut it?

Cut... cut... Mark grinned. He'd had an idea. Letting the pair he was dealing with get a little closer, though not too close, he pretended to trip.

"Mark!" He heard the anguished cry from across camp, Robert assuming he'd gone down because he was injured. Mark didn't have time to answer him. Instead, he lashed out at the men's legs, catching calf muscles and shins beneath the material of the robes. One spun around and Mark took the opportunity of hamstringing him, drawing the blade across where he judged the back of the heel to be.

It had the desired effect. Both men dropped, screaming.

Mark clambered to his feet, the smile spreading across his face.

"Mark!" came the cry again, and he couldn't understand why Robert was still calling. He'd taken down the two–

He remembered too late about the third, the one who'd been reaching for his sword. Mark pivoted, but at pretty much the same time the arrow flew past and into the fellow about to embed the sword in his head. The projectile's tip found the tattoo on the cultist's forehead, as if it were a bull's eye target, and he fell backwards.

When Mark looked across he saw the base camp littered with robed figures, arrows sticking out of various parts of their bodies. Robert was running over and waving something to Mark.

"...let them commit suicide..." The Hooded Man was saying. Mark didn't understand. Then he looked down at one of the men he'd crippled, saw him take his own machete with both hands, then ram it into his stomach. Mark felt his lip curling. The other one was doing a similar thing, except he was letting gravity do the work for him, lifting himself up as high as he could on his knees and just letting himself drop onto the blade.

Mark joined Robert, checking around to make sure no more were laying in wait. When he reached Mark saw he was crouching down next to one of the last cultists alive; the first proper rays of sunlight streaking through the trees onto the scene.

"And... and... He was cast... down," hissed the white-faced man with the arrow sticking out of his side, "on... onto the Earth... and His angels... were cast.... cast down also..." Then he took hold of his head and snapped it sideways, breaking his own neck.

Robert removed his hood and looked at Mark. "Are you alright, son?" Mark never tired of hearing Robert call him that. He nodded. "I didn't know there would be quite so many, otherwise I never would've suggested... But, you did well today. I'm proud of you. Jack would be, too."

"How did they find us here?" Mark asked when he'd finally got his breath back.

Robert stared down at the corpse. "I think we've made an enemy of these guys. They're keeping tabs on us now just like we've been doing with them. They're worried I'm going to stop their master from making His grand appearance."

"Master?"

"The Devil."

"Oh... What was he talking about just then, before..."

"Tate'll be able to tell us more about that. They seem to think they're fallen angels or something. Explains why they're not scared of dying. They probably believe they come right back again fighting fit."

"That's scary."

"Fanatics usually are. But that's not what scares me the most." Mark's puzzled expression drew the rest out of him. "I think there could be something else coming. Something much more frightening."

Mark didn't ask him how he knew that, because he'd heard some of the mutterings before he'd woken Robert from his sleep.

Besides, Robert hadn't been the only one who'd had dreams last night.

One more set of eyes had been watching the camp from close by that morning, had been watching most of the night.

They'd seen the Servitors make their way through the forest, taking their positions outside where Robert and the boy were spending the night. Had seen the boy get up to go to the toilet, spot something and then rush back to Robert's tent to warn him.

Had watched the fight with interest. More than interest:

Excitement. A tingling that had spread through the body until the last cultist had been defeated. It had almost been as good as being in the middle of it all, back in York.

From behind the oak, Adele let out the breath she'd been holding. And smiled. She'd enjoyed this little episode, but she knew there were tastier treats to come. And she'd be right there in the middle of those, definitely. There with the man she was after.

Right there with The Hooded Man.

CHAPTER TWELVE

He'd been hearing the rumblings of discontentment for some time.

Dale had debated about saying something to someone, but was faced with a dilemma. He was 'one of the guys', a member of the Sherwood Rangers who fought on the streets with his friends. Buddies that he'd made since coming to the castle last year. But he was also very close to Jack and Robert. If it wasn't for them, he might still be wandering around this country looking for a place to fit in. A former lead singer and guitarist in a band, whose life had fallen to bits after the virus struck, and who'd drifted from town to town, city to city, with a guitar in one hand and his other hand folded into a fist.

He often thought back to those days before everyone got sick: to the gigs he'd played with the other guys – Abbott on bass, Lockley on drums and Paige on keyboards. Only *she* hadn't just been one of the guys, had she?

Paige and he had formed 'One Simple Truth' together while

they were studying music in college. They'd been good mates throughout the course, and it just seemed like a sensible progression, especially as they'd just started going out. Paige had a real natural beauty, and she'd come along at a time when he'd just started to notice the opposite sex. She could be a bit serious sometimes, though, which is why, initially, he left a lot of the song-writing to her. It wasn't that he couldn't do it, Dale could make up stuff on the spot if he had to, it was just that she seemed to come up with the most soulful tunes.

When they advertised on the bulletin board for more band members they'd had all kinds of responses – some genuine, some just time-wasters. But they'd really gelled with the long-haired Lockley and bearded Abbott, especially in the improvised jamming session the first time they all got together. Jesus, how he missed them! The first few live shows at local pubs had been the pits, however, and Dale had almost called it a day at one point. Paige persuaded him to go on, and to his surprise they started to develop a fan base – particularly amongst the college and uni crowd.

Then came bigger and better gigs, and soon the money they were getting paid made attending classes seem moot. They were making it anyway, practising what their tutors only preached. It wasn't long before a talent scout with an eye for the next big thing spotted them. They were signed to a small indie label, but that automatically meant bigger gigs, and supporting turns for artists much higher up the ladder. Local stations played a couple of their releases and they even found themselves being aired on BBC Radio.

By this time One Simple Truth – and specifically Dale – had attracted another following entirely. Girls would hang out at the stage doors after gigs just to try and get an autograph. Or a kiss. Paige said nothing because she knew, at the end of the day, he was still hers. But during the course of their journey, Dale discovered his own simple truth: he found it impossible to be tied down to just the one girl. He loved the adoration his – granted – limited amount of fame brought him. And, girl by girl, tour by tour, he gave in to temptation.

Paige had confronted him, of course, and he hadn't even bothered to deny it. "What can I say? I have a weakness," he'd told her. When she'd threatened to walk from the band, he'd tried to talk her out of it, telling her she'd be slitting her own throat as well. "You're going to hold *this* against me, when we could be as big as Oasis or U2?"

The decision was taken out of her hands, because that's when the virus had struck. Dale watched his fellow band members die from that terrible disease, while he remained healthy.

Paige had been the first to fall ill, collapsing after a gig one night. She'd been rushed to hospital for tests – back before anyone fully realised what they were dealing with. "Tell me," Paige had said to him from her bed as they'd waited for her parents to get there from miles away. "Tell me you still love me."

He clasped her hand, but said nothing.

"Please," she whispered.

Dale had been about to lie to her when suddenly she'd had a seizure, coughing up blood onto the bed sheets. The doctors and nurses rushed in, flitting around. There was nothing they could do. They whisked Dale outside, but he'd already seen the worst – and when they came and told him half an hour later that she was dead, he couldn't believe what he was hearing.

He got drunk that night, asking himself what the hell was wrong with him. Why couldn't he have felt for Paige what she felt for him? Why couldn't he have committed to her when she was the one who'd been instrumental in getting them where they were?

His answer was to spend the night with some blonde girl he picked up in a hotel bar, someone who'd recognised him and he'd taken full advantage of the fact. He left early and hadn't seen her again. For all he knew she'd come down with the virus too, not long afterwards. Dale hadn't really paid it much mind.

He'd always been able to handle himself, a consequence of getting called a sissy for being interested in music growing up. The amount of fights he'd been in to show them, no, he wasn't actually a sissy at all and would happily rearrange their faces if that's what they really wanted... It had served him well after everything went to rack and ruin, and he'd had to defend himself from all kinds of dangers. He'd even stood up to gangs when he came across them, though sometimes came off the worst and crawled away to lick his wounds.

When he'd heard about what they were doing at Nottingham Castle, something seemed to click. It was a chance to be a part of a 'group' again, something that was being talked about and, yes, celebrated throughout the area. A major part of him knew he could do some good here, but how much of him wanted to join so he could be applauded again? So that he'd be sought after, not for his music this time, but because he could save the damsels in distress? If he could work his way up through the ranks, perhaps he would actually be a star once more?

Which brought him back to his dichotomy. Would keeping quiet about this hamper his relationship with Jack and Robert? Should he tell them about what he'd heard?

Not that Robert was here at the moment. He'd gone off with Mark, that little git who'd given him a bloody nose a couple of days ago. Dale realised that Mark would always be Robert's favourite – he'd heard the tales from the others about how the kid had been taken to the castle and tortured, then nearly hanged by the former sheriff. He was like a son to Robert, Dale got that. He also got that he himself was kind of a replacement for someone called Granger who'd been part of the final battle. Jack and Tate often remarked how much Dale reminded them of the guy, who'd given his life so that they could take the Castle. It was more than a bit annoying at times.

From his usual perch on the steps, Dale spotted Sophie walking through the grounds with Mary. Sophie. Now she was a prize worth possessing, a girl he thought he might be able to love. If Dale could actually figure out what love was. She'd shown more than an interest in him, that much was certain – but when push came to shove she'd always shoved him away. "Dale, don't," she'd said when he'd tried to kiss her the last time.

What was the reason? Was it Mark? The kid had feelings for Sophie, any fool could see that. But Dale had always assumed she wanted a real man, or at least someone old enough to vote and drink – not that laws about that stuff meant anything in this world.

The fact that Sophie was giving him the run around when all he wanted was... to show her how much she meant to him suggested that she must have feelings for someone else. What right did he have to interfere with that? If he hadn't been able to love Paige, then perhaps he couldn't love *anyone*, even Sophie.

Dale shook his head, this wasn't what he should be thinking about at the moment. The discontentment and the griping of the men; and whether he should talk to–

"Jack!" he was shouting to the large man before he realised he was doing it. "Hey Jack!" Now he was getting up and waving, grabbing his guitar and dashing down the steps to catch Jack as he came out of a side door of the castle.

"Hey Dale," replied his superior. As always, he had his staff resting over his shoulder. "You haven't seen Adele on your travels, have you?"

Dale told him he hadn't. And though he couldn't help it, a picture of that woman now flashed into his mind: her short, black hair, full lips. How he wished he'd been the one to save her that night in York rather than Robert.

Stop it, can't you see Jack fancies her? You just can't help yourself, can you?

"Not to worry," Jack said. Dale could tell he had more on his mind than where Adele was.

"Is everything okay?" he asked.

"Hmmm? Yeah. Well, no, not really. Did you want something?"

Dale thought about whether this was the right time, about whether he should even be speaking to Jack rather than Robert, but the words were escaping before he could contain them. "It's the men."

Jack turned to him. "What about them?"

"They're... I don't know how to say this."

"Just spit it out."

"They're overstretched, tired. They're beginning to moan about the workload, about patrols, about the last time they had any time off."

"Time off?" Jack said it like the concept was completely alien. "This isn't a damned holiday camp."

Dale held up his hands, his guitar flying out sideways. "I know that, and they do too. But, look, with this new thing – the cult – they've been run ragged trying to fight them. They're only human."

Jack gave a reluctant nod. "I understand. I just don't know what we can do about it. Maybe when we've got on top of this–"

"I don't know if you've got that long."

Jack sighed. "If you only knew." His face betrayed him. Dale could see he knew something else he wasn't passing on... or the troops.

"What? Tell me." He didn't really have the right to demand any kind of information, but was hoping Jack might tell him anyway.

"I'd rather wait until... Robert!"

Dale followed Jack's gaze down to the gate, where Robert and Mark had appeared on horseback, returning from their visit to Sherwood.

Jack made his way briskly down to the riders, Dale not far behind. He ignored the glare from Mark, using Robert's second as a justification to be there.

"Robbie, I'm so glad that you're back," shouted the big man.

"So am I. In some ways," Robert said, then looked over at Mark. Dale realised that more than training had occurred in Sherwood. More secrets he wasn't yet privy to.

"I've got something to tell you," Jack said, walking up to the horse and stroking it. "But maybe it should be someplace more private, y'know?"

"Could I just say something first?" Dale cut in.

"No," answered Mark without hesitation.

Robert gave the boy a severe look, then turned to Dale: "What is it?"

He studied them each in turn. "I know something's kicking off here. I just thought you ought to be aware that you could have some walkouts on your hands if you're not careful."

"Dale was just telling me that the men aren't too happy."

"Is that so?" Robert said, as he dismounted.

"I don't want to go behind anyone's back or anything, just thought you needed to know the score." Dale told him.

"To be fair, they are being stretched a bit thin, Robbie. Possibly even thinner soon."

That was another slip, and now Dale was desperate to know what Jack had discovered. If they were about to face something else on top of the Morningstars, then he and the others had a right to know. They were the ones putting their lives on the line.

"Okay, Dale," said Robert finally, "we'll sort this out later." Then before he could say anything else, the man in charge added: "I promise. Right now I need to speak with Jack, probably as much as he does with me." Robert turned to his right hand man. "Fetch Tate and Mary, too. If you're about to tell me what I think you are, they should hear this as well."

Dale watched as Mark got off his horse, and the three of them made their way back up the path. Things hadn't quite gone as he'd expected them to. In spite of jeopardising his standing in the ranks by telling Jack and Robert about the unrest, Dale still wasn't part of that inner circle. He'd been noticed by the talent-spotters, but not signed to a label yet. What made it worse was that Mark was turning as the group led the horses away, looking over his shoulder and glaring at Dale again. *He* was automatically included in the talks, as one of the core band that had come here. Could Dale's hard work all fall apart again because of a girl? Because of his messing about with Sophie, and Mark's feelings about that?

But Robert had promised to talk to him later, so he'd no doubt find out what was going on then. Better late than not at all.

Dale sat down on a bench and began to strum his guitar. One day when stories were written and songs sung about their exploits, Dale still intended to feature prominently.

They gathered in one of the rooms inside the castle: Robert, Mark, Tate, Mary and Jack. All the original members of Robert's team, barring one, but it wasn't long before he was mentioned.

"This afternoon we received a radio message from Bill," Jack told them. He'd kept up with his CB interests after moving to the castle, as a way of keeping in touch with places beyond Nottingham. "Actually, it wasn't from Bill himself, it was from one of his... I dunno what you'd call 'em, staff?"

Robert shrugged his shoulders. Bill was a bit of a sore point with him.

"Anyhow, turns out there's a force that's hit the coastline up near Whitby, Scarborough, Bridlington. They used hovercraft to get their vehicles ashore: tanks, jeeps, the whole deal. And they've been striking villages and towns as they make their way inland. Bill's been monitoring the situation through his network of markets, getting to places that have been struck and offering help. Otherwise I think he would have come here in person to warn us."

"I know," said Robert simply, and Jack, Tate and Mary all looked at him. "About the army, I mean."

"Me too," added Mark, and they switched their focus to him.

"How?" asked Jack. "I only got the call a couple of hours ago, and you've been off in the forest."

Robert looked at Tate, who blinked his understanding. "I think you've just answered your own question, Jack," the Reverend said, though the American looked none the wiser. "They were in Sherwood."

"The man in charge is Russian, I think," continued Robert.

"I'll be God-damned," Jack said, blowing out a breath. "The radio message mentioned Russian troops."

"There's another thing." Robert walked around the room; Mark was biting his lip in anticipation of what was about to be said. "Tanek's with them."

"What?" said Tate, having to rest on his stick.

"It's true, Reverend. Robbie's three for three. That was also part of the warning."

All the colour had drained from Tate's face. "Dear Lord. And they're making their way here... this force?"

"Seems like," said Jack.

"If Tanek's involved, he'll probably be out for revenge," Robert said.

"I need to warn Gwen," Tate suddenly announced. "He'll be coming for her without a doubt. She should be brought to the castle, don't you think? Her and Clive Jr?"

"If she'll come." Robert said.

"This is all we need on top of the cult," Jack said. "And if the men really are thinking about quitting–"

"What?" Tate virtually shrieked this. "They... they can't. We need them, now more than ever."

"Let's hope it doesn't come to that," Robert said. "We can't afford to lose a single fighter at the moment."

"Give 'em one of your patented speeches. Do the whole *Braveheart* bit," Jack suggested with a half smile, but there was little humour in his voice.

"The other thing is, we were attacked by members of the cult while we were in Sherwood. It was co-ordinated, intended to put me out of the picture." His eyes flitted across, searching for some kind of reaction from Mary, but there was none. She hadn't spoken, had barely been able to look at him since they'd all entered the room.

"You've rattled their cage," Tate said.

Robert ignored this and dwelt on Mary. "You've been very quiet, don't you have anything to say to all this?"

Mary looked him in the eye then, before speaking. "What's the point? You were in danger again in Sherwood. I know what you're going to do now about the army heading our way. It doesn't matter what I have to say, does it? You'll do what you have to do."

"Of course it matters, Mary," said Mark after a few moments, speaking for Robert because it didn't look like he was going to.

"I hate to say it, but the little lady's right – we are going to have to do what's necessary," Jack said.

"We're going to have to meet the army before it gets here," Robert stated. "We have to protect the people."

Mary nodded, then left the room.

Mark looked from the open door to Robert, his eyes begging the man to go after her, to fix this somehow. But both of them knew there was nothing Robert could say. Just as he'd been willing to sacrifice himself to save the villagers De Falaise was going to hang, now he was going to have to place himself between these new invaders and those who counted on him to protect them.

"Jack, call Dale. I need to sound him out about what's happening with the troops. I can't afford for them to turn tail."

"But Robert," Mark began. "Dale is–"

"Your personal feelings about him don't come into this," Robert interrupted, and Tate and Jack both stared. "I'm sorry," Robert said more softly. "He's one of our best, and he's very popular. If they won't listen to me, they might to him."

"He's popular all right," Mark said.

As the meeting broke up, each of them left except Robert. He walked over to the far wall and banged his fist against it in frustration.

What's the matter? You got what you wanted, didn't you? To be out there again, in action, in combat.

But even he wasn't sure whether he could win this time against such odds.

And he was frightened that even if he did, he might have already lost the one thing that meant more to him than any of that.

Robert left the room and searched the corridor for any sign of Mary. He caught a flash of a female figure and got his hopes up, decided that he would go and talk to her – try and explain himself.

Except as the woman moved into view, he saw it was Adele. She smiled at him, but he didn't smile back.

Robert continued on his way to the stairs. A man with a mission.

No, more than that. As he was constantly being reminded, he was a man with a *destiny*. One he could no more control than he could his love life.

CHAPTER THIRTEEN

It had been much quicker this time.

He'd cut a swathe through this country again – with a little help, admittedly – crushing resistance where they found it, making their presence known. It was all part of the plan. Tanek *wanted* Hood to know he was on his way, while Bohuslav and The Tsar didn't care about stealth because they were so confident in their victory. Nobody could defeat them, they were certain about that.

It was the kind of arrogance which often led to a fall, but Tanek didn't think that would happen this time.

They'd also become aware of another faction operating in their area. Tanek had extracted information from various people since returning to these shores, taking up his old hobbies with the burning hot pokers and pressure points. It wasn't quite the same, torturing people in houses rather than caves – or dungeons, as he liked to think of the cave system below Nottingham Castle. It lacked the proper atmosphere. But, he reminded himself, he'd been torturing people most of his life and enjoyed it wherever he happened to be. He'd just been spoilt, that's all.

He remembered one man in his forties, whose belly had hung down when stripped – and Tanek had taken great delight in snipping bits of excess flesh off with a pair of scissors to make him talk.

Bohuslav had walked in during one of the sessions and it had made even his face turn green. "I thought *I* was a sick bastard," he'd said, observing Tanek at work with a block of glasspaper: rubbing one woman's fingers until they were almost down to the bone. The thing was, they'd probably have told him anyway, what did they have to hide? But where was the fun in that?

As to the information: it seemed that a cult had sprung up in Britain. Or, depending on who you talked to, had resurfaced. They were sacrificing people in order to call forth their Lord from Hell, it seemed. What mattered was there were quite a number of them, and they were methodical.

"They might prove an obstacle," Tanek had said to Bohuslav. He still hated dealing with the toad, but in lieu of The Tsar he had little choice.

"Doubtful," Bohuslav countered. This was one of those times when his arrogance might stand in the way of preparing against a potential enemy. Tanek had found out what he could about their activities anyway: their preferred methods of hunting, their weapons, their skill at hiding when they didn't want to be seen (this last one could certainly trip up their forces – how do you fire at something that's made itself invisible?).

A good job then that Tanek had been with the first division to make contact. They were working their way through somewhere called Thirsk, as the light faded, when they were suddenly attacked. Tanek saw several scouts fall as they were walking up just ahead of the tanks and jeeps. The soldiers were dragged off the streets by men in crimson robes, and by the time the rest of the division reached them they were already dead – their throats slit.

Gunfire opened up behind Tanek; men shooting at shadows. They'd gone down as well, killed by men who looked like the walking dead. Tanks and jeeps were useless against them at this close proximity, and they knew it.

There was movement off to the side of Tanek, and he'd aimed and fired his crossbow in seconds. He nodded when he heard a muffled yelp, knowing his bolt had struck home. Then he was aware of a *swish* on his other side, something sharp cutting the air – about to cut into him. The clank of metal against metal followed and Tanek looked round to see that Bohuslav's hand scythe had met the machete blow intended for him. The serial killer would later explain that, should Tanek turn out to be the traitor Bohuslav thought, he wanted the pleasure of killing the giant himself.

For now, though, Tanek was grateful Bohuslav had blocked the attack; forcing the cult member back again with a thrust of his own blade. Before the robed figure could do anything else, Tanek had put a crossbow bolt in his head.

Confusion reigned, as their men fired into alleys, at houses, almost at each other. It was exactly what the cult wanted – exactly what guerrilla fighters would do. Tanek tried to get Bohuslav to order a ceasefire, but they were having difficulty making themselves heard. Soldiers were going down one by one. Tanek noted a guy not far away who was suddenly clutching at his neck as a powerful geyser of wet redness jetted out, a machete blow slicing neatly across his jugular, almost slicing his neck in two. Bullets riddled the robed figures whenever they appeared, but it didn't seem to deter them. It was as if they weren't bothered about dying at all. That, if nothing else, made them extremely dangerous adversaries. In spite of himself, Tanek found that he had quite an admiration for these people.

Then, as quickly as it had started, the fighting stopped.

Someone had appeared in the street, lit by floodlights from the armoured vehicles behind – like a magician materializing on stage. A man, flanked by two smaller figures. The man wore a coat that flapped about in the chill breeze, and the leather of his uniform beneath creaked. He adjusted the peaked cap he was wearing, before standing with his hands behind his back and gazing around. The women, for as they adopted a defensive position it was plainly obvious they were of the female persuasion, held their swords horizontally, protecting the man in the middle of them.

Tanek traded glances with Bohuslav, who appeared just as surprised as he was that The Tsar was present.

The time for asking questions would come later. Right now, what interested Tanek was the stillness this man inspired. He had some balls to walk out there in the first place – looking beyond the man, Tanek realised he must have pulled up in his own private jeep – but what was causing the cult to stay their hand? His own men, Tanek could understand. They would rather shoot themselves than risk hitting their glorious leader with a stray bullet. But why were these strangers holding off? It was quite a thing to witness.

Tanek's answer came when one robed figure emerged from a side street, and began to walk up the road. Bohuslav nervously shifted from foot to foot and Tanek was half expecting him to give an order to shoot. But The Tsar was gesturing with his hand that his forces should hold their fire for now.

When The Tsar began talking, it was in Russian. He soon realised his mistake and switched to his broken style of English. "You speak for your people, yes?" The twins were ready to spring on the figure should he put so much as a foot out of place. They needn't have worried.

"We are Servitor. When one speaks, we all speak." The robed figure dropped to his knees before he was anywhere near The Tsar. If the Russian was surprised, then he didn't show it. "My Lord." The man kept his head bowed, then added: "You are finally here."

Tanek saw The Tsar's eyebrows raise just a fraction. "Yes." Whether he thought the man was simply referring to his title – after all Tanek had heard the people under The Tsar call him Lord all the time – or he actually knew what the man was referring to was unclear. But the effect was the same. "Now call your men forth."

The robed figure did as he was told, rising and calling to the other members of his order. There were at least twenty of them, and they came tentatively out of hiding. It was only now that Tanek, and probably Bohuslav too, realised that they could have gone on fighting for hours and not got them all, they were too good at concealment.

What The Tsar was proposing was preferable to the conflict. A truce and a joining of forces. "We can... help each other," The Tsar explained to the spokesman.

"Whatever you say," he replied. He still wasn't able to look The Tsar in the face.

Later on, when Tanek had the chance to ask The Tsar about all this – and discover why he'd made the trip personally across the sea ("Like Richard the Lionheart in the Holy Land, I wished to see the 'conversion' of this country myself. And bring some additional firepower with me.") – he understood that the man hadn't quite anticipated that reaction from the cult leader.

"I was never in any danger. Apart from the twins, I had ample soldiers covering me. So I thought I might offer a proposition. I never knew they would mistake me for..."

For Satan? thought Tanek, finishing off what The Tsar couldn't bring himself to say. *In your red uniform, bringing fire and destruction with you?* It wasn't much of a stretch. But it did do them a favour.

It also meant that progress would be even quicker than they had anticipated. Soon they would be at Nottingham, at the castle's doors in fact. Tanek had persuaded The Tsar that the location was ideal for striking out at the rest of the country. It was what De Falaise once had in mind.

Soon, Hood and all those who followed him would be dead, and Tanek would be back where he belonged.

Perhaps then, his former leader's ghost would be able to rest in peace.

CHAPTER FOURTEEN

Robert had talked to Dale, who in turn had talked to the men, laying the groundwork.

Then, as Jack had suggested, Robert spoke to them all. He'd requested that as many Rangers who could be spared gather in the castle grounds first thing that morning. A transcript would be circulated for those who couldn't be there, and Jack was even recording it on the battery-powered tape player. Those present who could remember when he'd given the speech the night before the battle for this place, felt a certain amount of nostalgia. Tate knew their leader had been reluctant to say anything on that occasion too but, as now, he recognised that it was time to motivate.

Time to lay everything on the line.

He stood in front of the crowd of fighters, and it was obvious that looking over the swell of heads made him uncomfortable. They could see it was having another effect on him, too. The way his chest was puffing up, his eyes glassy; it could only be pride he was feeling when he looked at his loyal brigade. It made some of them, those who'd been complaining about how much work they were doing, feel more than a little ashamed.

Robert was casting his eyes down the rows, looking for someone. All those closest to him were there: Jack, Mark, Tate. All except one. Mary.

He began anyway, his voice cracking as he said his first few words: "T-Thank you all for listening to me today, I do appreciate it. In fact, even though I don't say this as often as I should, I appreciate everything you do, and have done, not only for this... well, I suppose some might call it a peacekeeping force... but also for the people of this area and beyond. Many of you probably know already that I didn't want this mantle of command, and don't even really see myself as your chief – or whatever you want to call it. Everyone's equal here, everyone's got something unique to offer. Some of us may be more inexperienced than others." Robert made a point of looking at Mark when he said this. "Some of us want to make an impression." Now he found Dale out in the audience. "But that's fine. As someone once said to me: we're a family. And I like to sort out any problems *within* that family.

"Now, I know that you're tired, that some of you are doing the jobs of three or even four people. A consequence of this new world we've found ourselves in, sadly, is that it takes time to build something. To find the people we need or for them to find us. And, believe it or not, we are building something truly special here. Something that's already being talked about throughout the country, and maybe even further afield. We're keeping ordinary folk safe from the likes of the Morningstars, from thugs and murderers and rapists. I don't know about you, but I'm quite proud of that."

There was a rumble of agreement from the crowd.

"The problem with gaining a reputation," Robert ventured on, catching Adele's eyes briefly where she stood not far away from Jack, "is that from time to time people are going to come and challenge us. People like the Frenchman we took this castle from; people who would destroy our homes, kill our loved ones. I'm standing up here today to tell those of you who don't already know – because I realise the rumour mill must be going into overdrive – that there's one such mobilisation heading our way. They landed about a week ago on the coast, and I'm not going to sugar coat this for you: we have it on good authority that they're well armed and in great numbers."

The rumbles turned into mumbles of shock and fear, as the troops in front of him turned to one another – some nodding at the confirmation of what they'd already suspected, some hearing it for the first time.

"They will reach us sooner or later, and countless innocents will die – are *already* dying as they make their way to Nottingham. The question is, do we meet them head on, attempt to stop them before they can slaughter anyone else, and before they reach the places and people we care about?" Robert paused to take in not only the faces of the crowd, but also the people who'd brought him out of Sherwood in the first place. As he did so, he saw Mary standing right at the very back. Their eyes met and from that moment on he was really only talking to her. "Do we do the right thing, or hope that someone, somewhere will do it for us? Personally, I believe we are the only ones who stand a chance of stopping them, of kicking them back to where they came from and making sure they never try anything like it again." He nodded. "Yes, I know how thinly stretched we are – mainly due to the threat the Morningstars have become. But if we wait, this could escalate further."

"The best defence is a good offence," Jack called out from the crowd. "That's what they always say back where I come from."

There were more murmurs from the crowd. Nobody wanted to face an enemy of this kind, but if they hid away behind the castle walls then they would have to at some point anyway. Was it better to pre-empt them?

"None of you are here because you *have* to be," Robert said once the crowd had quietened a little. "My way is not the way it was with the Frenchman, as some of you who served under him have discovered over the time you've been with me. I said this once before, but I've made my decision and I have to stick by it. I'm riding out to meet the convoy. How many of you choose to join me on this mission, I'm leaving in your hands. I've said this before, too. It'll be dangerous and there are no guarantees that anyone will be coming back." The pause this time was because Robert could see the tears welling in Mary's eyes, and his began to mist up in response. "So I wouldn't blame anyone for not coming. In fact some of you I *want* to stay behind to defend the castle, just in case we fail. But if you really wanted to leave us altogether, the door... well, actually the gate, is over there."

For a good few moments there was silence. No mutterings from the crowd at all, probably because many of them were trying to make up their minds about what to do. Divided between their loyalty to a man who'd given them refuge, given them a home, and their terror at facing what was to come.

It was Dale who broke this silence. "I'm with you Robert. Where you go, I'll be there." Azhar, at his side, put a hand across his chest and bowed. Then Dale turned and looked at the other fighters, in the hopes of shaming them into saying something. It seemed to work because they began to nod their heads and a buzz of positive noises filtered through. That buzz became a wave, which washed over the heads of those present. It wasn't long before some of the Rangers were holding up their swords and waving them in the air. Some might change their minds later, or opt to stay at the castle, but for now it seemed like the majority of Robert's men were on his side.

He thanked them and stood down, relief etched on his face – possibly because he knew he now had the support he needed, or even because he'd finished speaking in public.

Whatever the case, Robert knew that the hard work was only just beginning. If they were to halt the progress of this new army, they had to leave soon. And he had more than a few loose ends to tie up first.

He scanned the crowd for Mary as it broke up, but she'd vanished again. Before he could go and look for her, he was being pulled in several different directions at once. Being asked a million questions about the mission.

Though they weren't too happy about it, Robert insisted that Jack and Mark stay behind at the castle. "I need someone I can leave in charge here," Robert told Jack. "Someone I can trust." The fact that he'd seen them both dead in his dream also had something to do with it.

"I should be out there with you, Robbie," Jack complained, but when Robert asked him again, adding a firm 'please', the larger man relented.

Mark was more of a hard sell. "You're still not ready for that kind of combat," Robert pointed out, which wasn't the smartest thing to say.

"But you're taking Dale?"

"Yes."

"Because 'where you go, he goes,'" said Mark, mimicking the youth.

"Because I want you to stay and look after Mary and Sophie."

"Mary can look after herself. You know that."

That was true. "And Sophie?"

Mark thought about this for a moment. "I think she'd prefer to have Dale looking after her."

"You might be surprised." Robert looked him directly in the eye. "If anything happens to me, and the troops break in here, get Sophie and Mary out. Do you understand? You'll know where to go. That's the most important thing you can do, son." He gave Mark a tight hug, and when he pulled away again he could see the boy was fighting back tears.

Robert said the same thing to Reverend Tate when he spoke to him, that he should help to keep Mary, Sophie *and* Mark safe. "Plus Gwen and the little one," Tate added. He'd sent word to the woman at New Hope, letting her know about the army that was heading towards them, promising supplies if she would come to the castle to collect them. Word had it she was on her way with Clive Jr, and when she got to the castle Robert knew Tate was going to try and get her to remain there until the danger had passed.

"She won't stay, you know," Robert told him. "She'll want to be with her people. I have to say I can understand that."

Tate agreed. "All I can do is try."

"You do know I can't let her have any weapons?"

"I wasn't specific about what the supplies were."

"But that's what you've let her think."

The Reverend heaved a weary sigh. "Just as you do what you must, so will I. You know, I wouldn't normally be the one to say this, but are you sure you shouldn't take some of those things along yourself when you meet this army of yours?"

Robert tutted. "You're advocating the use of firearms now, Reverend? You sound like Bill."

"They were used in the battle for the castle," Tate reminded him.

"We'll do okay without them. Isn't that what you're always telling me, to have faith?"

"There's a difference between that and suicide."

"We'll be armed. Just not in the way they'll be expecting. The men have been trained well, and we'll have a few surprises for our friends."

Tate gave a tip of the head, then said finally: "Remember the story of David and Goliath, Robert. I think it's probably an appropriate one."

That just left Mary.

Robert tried to find her, but he knew that if he chose a quiet spot, she would eventually come to him... *if* she wanted to talk. That quiet spot was down in the stables as he was feeding his horse. They'd been through quite a bit together, and he'd be asking quite a bit more of the animal in the days to come.

When he heard the footsteps behind him, he hoped it might be Mary – so when he turned and saw Adele, he couldn't hide the disappointment on his face.

"You were expecting *her*, weren't you?" said the woman. "I'm sorry."

"That's okay."

Adele came a little closer. "It's just that, well, I figured I might never see you again. And I didn't want you to go before... That is, I really need to tell you something, Robert."

He pressed his face up against his horse, closing his eyes. "Adele, look–"

"No, let me finish. Please." He heard the woman come closer, now only a couple of feet away from him. When he opened his eyes he saw there was a figure just over her shoulder, her cheeks red from the cold, hair tied back. Mary. He was frightened that she would run off again, get the wrong impression about what was going on. But she didn't. Instead, she coughed politely, causing Adele to start.

"Jack's looking for you," Mary notified her when she turned around.

"But I was just... I needed to talk to Robert for a moment," she said, facing him again, in the hope he'd back her up.

"You should go and find Jack," Robert advised her.

Adele looked like she was going to say something. Instead she gave an almost imperceptible nod and left the stables. Mary watched her go, a mixture of concern and resentment in her expression. Then she focused on Robert.

"I..." he began, but realised he didn't know what to say. But he didn't really need to. Mary walked over, quickening her pace the nearer she came. Then their arms were open, and they held each other; grabbing on as if they felt the other person might just float away if they weren't anchored down. Robert thought about making a nervous joke, something along the lines of: 'You're not going to drug me this time, are you?' but thought better of it.

The time for jokes, the time for talking, the time for arguing and recriminations, was long over. They knew they may not be together again.

As they kissed, the world fell away. Both Robert and Mary wished that this moment would never end. She took his hand, and led him up to the entrance of the castle; then finally up the stairs to their room, where they would try and make the next couple of hours last an entire lifetime.

CHAPTER FIFTEEN

The army was using open ground to travel between urban locations, that much they'd been able to ascertain from radio messages. And they had a rough idea of where they were, too: somewhere between Doncaster and Gainsborough.

Robert had sent out advance scouts to get a proper sense of the route this war machine was taking now that they'd regrouped and were heading for Nottingham. It had allowed him and his men to lay in wait, to prepare for the confrontation to come. But, as dawn broke and they watched from behind a scattering of trees not unlike those he'd left behind in Sherwood, it would have been easy to mistake this for a normal winter's morning in the English countryside.

Holding up the binoculars, Robert scanned the horizon. There was nothing to see yet. He glanced over his shoulder at the division of men with him, some sitting on horseback, others standing leaning on their bows. He knew there were more ringing these fields, spread out to cause the maximum amount of confusion when the Russian troops arrived. Robert was just about to put the binoculars up to his eyes again when he heard Dale on the left of him say: "Listen... Do you hear that?"

Not only could Robert hear it, he could feel the vibrations coming up through the ground. Something was coming, something big. No, as he brought the binoculars up and focused on the spot he'd been watching, Robert realised that *many* big things were coming.

The jeeps were first, cresting the hill, bringing with them men swarming like ants – each one wearing a grey uniform and carrying a machine gun. Then came the back-up: tanks. More than De Falaise had dreamed of. More than Robert had ever seen, and there'd been a fair few at the Frenchman's command. But that wasn't all. Armoured personnel carriers and other armoured vehicles, some of which could be mistaken for tanks themselves were it not for the wheels instead of caterpillar tracks and shorter cannons. Then there were the motorbikes, their drone almost drowned out by their larger companions. They nipped in-between, churning up the grass beneath.

"Jesus," said one of the men behind Robert. "How are we supposed to fight... that?"

Robert had to admit, although he didn't show it, he'd expected something slightly smaller; more in keeping with what they'd dealt with before. A part of him was now wondering if he'd made the right decision, bringing these men – some of them only boys, like Dale – out here to face what appeared to be insurmountable odds. And Tate's words came back to him:

"I wouldn't be the first one to say this, but are you sure you shouldn't take some of those things along yourself when you meet this army of yours?"

Those things, those reminders of De Falaise and his rule... But when you were fighting men *like* De Falaise, shouldn't you meet them on a level playing field – even the odds as much as you could? Robert shook his head. That wasn't the way – he was sure of it. Old Eric Meadows had been sure of it... He just had to have faith that his plan would work, that they could catch bigger prey with the same methods he'd used back in the forest (keep well out of sight, always let them come out into the open – then deliver your surprise).

"We'll fight them," Robert said in answer to the man's question. "And as long as we stick together, we'll win. They won't be expecting an attack like this one."

"Too right!" said another Ranger. "Who'd be crazy enough to do it?"

Robert looked over his shoulder once more and grinned. "We would. Now ready yourself."

"Time to get up on stage and do our thing," Dale ran on, though all the usual cockiness was gone from his voice.

"Time to do our thing," agreed Robert.

If it was going to happen, it would happen here. Bohuslav was counting on it.

As he rode in the lead jeep, he surveyed the area in front of him, not with a pair of binoculars, but with his hawkish and unnaturally sharp vision. They were out there somewhere, he was certain. Did they not think that their little attack would be anticipated? Far from being herded into this stretch of countryside, he and his men were actually hoping to bring Hood's forces out into the open, let them do their worst, then wipe them from the face of the Earth. They'd *allowed* themselves to be seen, allowed the radio messages to get through without interference purely for this purpose. Hood's scouts had even been spotted trying to determine which direction their army was heading.

Oh, was he in for a shock.

Yet Bohuslav didn't really want to be here. As much as he loved the thrill of slaughter – though it would never replace the kick he got from capturing and killing people on a one-to-one basis – he was uncomfortable about this whole operation. He was proud The Tsar had left him in charge of such a legion, but couldn't help wishing he was with his superior right now. The thought of that bastard Tanek whispering in his master's ear was almost too much to bear. Bohuslav knew the swarthy giant was trying to worm his way in, but there was only room for one second, for one murdering psychopath on the team. Once this was all over, Tanek might well find his throat being slit in the night... If Bohuslav was quick enough to take him. He remembered back to the hovercraft, the knife Tanek was about to stab him with even as Bohuslav had his own blade poised to strike. Not much scared Bohuslav, but the thought of killing Tanek was terrifying and exhilarating at the same time.

But that was for the future. Right now, there was one small thing to do and he needed to keep himself sharp to accomplish it.

Before he could turn his attentions to Tanek, Bohuslav must rid the world of this new version of Robin Hood.

No sooner had Bohuslav thought this than he saw something down below, not much bigger than his thumb from this distance. It was a man on horseback – who had appeared, quite literally, out of nowhere. His head was bowed, but even if this wasn't the case, Bohuslav wouldn't have been able to see his features because he had a cowl pulled over them.

This man, Bohuslav saw, had a bow slung over his shoulder, and a quiver on his back. He also had a sword by his side, dangling near the horse's flank. He looked like he'd stepped out of a time warp. In no way, shape or form a match for any of Bohuslav's soldiers or their weapons.

Nevertheless, the sight of that lone figure gave Bohuslav pause for thought. He didn't fear him, at least not in the same way he did Tanek (though he would never admit it). But it made the serial killer at least think twice about giving the order to attack.

Is the man insane? he wondered – which was rich coming from someone who used to have imaginary conversations with his gagged and bound victims. *Or*, Bohuslav thought, *does he know something we don't? Does he have something up his sleeve?*

When all was said and done, this was the person who'd defeated De Falaise's army. A different fight, a different place, but Bohuslav couldn't help thinking: what if...

Then he smiled. If Hood wanted to play, he would oblige.

So Bohuslav ordered one of the T-90 battle tanks to target the man and blow him to kingdom come.

Robert held his position.

He knew they'd be firing any second, but this was more than a matter of drawing a line in the sand, showing both sides what they were up against. It wasn't about weapons, either, or about who was right and wrong. It was about courage, standing up for something you believed in.

Even if you were a solitary figure on the landscape.

Robert patted his horse's neck, holding her steady. Then, right at the very last moment, he pulled the steed around and rode her away, back out of range. He heard the shot from behind, the whizzing sound as the shell flew through the air.

It exploded in the spot where he'd been idling his horse only moments before. The animal protested, but was used to this type of noise. Robert urged her back round and they stood there again.

This time, though, Robert held up his hand – and dropped it again. Giving his order, just as the commander of these troops (the man he'd seen De Falaise morph into, or maybe Tanek?) had obviously done.

Like snowflakes they fell from the sky. But they were the wrong colour for snow. And they originated from the ground not from the air. Huge rocks rained down on the vehicles from strategic, hidden positions on either side. From catapults they'd brought with them, made over the last few months to defend the castle, but wheeled and easily transportable. The rocks landed heavily on the tanks, jeeps and other armoured vehicles, not doing a vast amount of damage, but proving that they weren't the only ones capable of firing projectiles.

It also had the effect of provoking the army into rushing them. Now the jeeps, bikes, tanks and Armoured Fighting Vehicles were moving forward into position. They began firing at the trees, at the point where the rocks had appeared – but Robert knew his men were camouflaged enough that they probably wouldn't be seen. The cannons might have fired ahead of them, but there was nobody apart from Robert on the battlefield to engage yet.

That's how it would stay for a little while, until they'd finished sending their message.

From the trees, now came hails of flaming arrows. These hit the vehicles, exploding on impact – their tips filled with a special sulphur brew. The flames spread across the metal, engulfing some vehicles almost entirely. Others were hit with mini-paint bombs, aimed specifically so that they would break against windscreens and viewing slats, obscuring vision. One driver rammed his jeep into the side of a tank, scraping along until it got in front and the bonnet of the smaller vehicle was crushed under the tracks of the other.

Meanwhile, the bikes, jeeps and other vehicles with tyres were discovering the presents Robert and his men had left. Clusters of barbed wire, which not only burst tyres, but tangled up around them, causing drivers to lose control of their vehicles. Bikes wobbled and keeled over, jeeps ground to a halt, armoured fighting vehicles could do nothing but sit there and offer covering fire.

Those that got away were introduced to holes the men had dug and covered over, much like the ones Robert had used to trap animals he survived on back in Sherwood. They didn't have to be really deep, just enough for the vehicles to dip forward into and be brought to a standstill.

Now came the second wave from the catapults: large gas canisters that hit the vehicles. No sooner had these landed than they were struck by more flaming arrows, igniting the gas. The landscape turned into a series of red and yellow mushrooms. Black smoke was laid down in front of Robert.

He took hold of his bow, grabbed an arrow out of his quiver and notched it, feeling the familiar tension of the string. Welcoming it like an old friend.

Armed men broke through the smoke. He shot the first one in the knee, the second in the shoulder. Given a choice and when not backed into a corner, he would always choose to incapacitate rather than kill – a throwback to his years in the police.

Robert nodded and his men broke free of their cover, some on horseback, some on foot. The firing started moments later, the

Russians letting rip with their machine guns.

Robert's men raised their shields; specially made by their blacksmith Faraday, steel plate more than 16 mm thick which their bullets would make a significant dent in, but not penetrate. Sparks flew as the bullets pinged off them. But several of the horses were hit and went down, taking their riders with them. Robert saw some of his men get hit and drop to the ground... only to wait until a Russian soldier was near enough and get up again, taking down the man with a series of martial arts moves.

He grinned again, knowing that each man had the extra protection of specially adapted vests – hard metal-plates fitted into ordinary bullet-proof vests like the ones armed response units wore, found during searches of police facilities. It would give added protection against machine guns and shrapnel. Robert himself was wearing one, and was glad of it too.

The smoke was clearing, making this a fight of bullets against bows. Arrows struck the Russian troops, hitting them in arms, legs, necks, taking them down swiftly. Flaming arrows set them alight and took them out of the battle altogether. Robert looked down and caught sight of Azhar engaging a couple of foot-soldiers, dodging bullets and slicing them with his sword.

Suddenly an AFV charged through, having driven around the trenches, its tyres ripped to shreds but ploughing forwards anyway.

"Dale," shouted Robert to the young man on horseback, "with me!"

Leaning forwards, they urged their steeds on through the combat. An explosion off to their right almost caused Dale's horse to rear up, but he kept control. The cannon on top of the AFV was spitting out shells one after the other. Robert nodded for Dale to give him covering fire, taking out the armed men on the ground now flanking the vehicle. The AFV turned and started ploughing diagonally through the fighting.

Robert pulled on the reins, then rode his horse up alongside the armoured vehicle. When he judged it was close enough, he jumped from the saddle onto the side of the thing, landing near the back. His horse rode off without him, away from danger. He almost slipped down and under the wheels, but his hands found purchase on the rails bolted to the metal. A stray bullet twanged off the plating near his head – whoever had fired it obviously reckoning that they couldn't do the AFV any harm but might be able to dislodge The Hooded Man. Robert risked a quick glance over his shoulder and saw Dale take out the shooter with an arrow to the back.

Shot! he thought, then concentrated on getting himself stable. Robert clambered around on the side of the vehicle, looking for a way in, but the hatches seemed to be sealed tight. The cannon on the top swung round in his direction, until he was staring down the black hole of the stubby barrel. Robert dropped down again just as it fired, almost slipping under the grinding remains of the tyres, but somehow swinging himself back along the side so that he was closer to the front. He kept himself low, avoiding the cannon, and climbed round so that he was now on the front of the vehicle – left hand gripping the rail there to keep himself steady.

Two metal flaps were open at the front, obviously so the driver could see. The AFV went over a bump, jolting Robert upwards. His shoulder took the brunt of the impact. He let out a grunt, but it just made him more determined to put an end to the vehicle's run.

With his free hand, he pulled out his sword – then, wincing as he did so, swung round and shoved the weapon into one of the viewing slats. He had no idea whether he'd hit anything, until he felt the end of the sword slide into something soft. When he pulled it out there was blood on the tip.

The AFV veered wildly to one side, away from the battlefield, heading towards some trees. Robert didn't have the luxury of waiting this time and launched himself off the vehicle, hoping he'd roll far enough out of its way that he wouldn't be crushed. He needn't have worried. The AFV was obviously stuck in forward gear, the driver probably slumped over the controls inside. The hatches opened as other men inside scrabbled to flee the vehicle. It hit a tree, but didn't stop. The second tree was too much for it, though, and the AFV shuddered to a halt.

Robert rose, barely having time to recover before he felt a presence at his side. Ducking and turning, the gunfire above him a dead giveaway that this wasn't one of his men, he brought his sword round and struck the man on the calf, digging the blade in and sending him toppling over.

Sheathing his weapon, Robert had his bow out again and was firing quickly: left, right and centre, putting as many of the armed men out of action as he could.

He noted, with some satisfaction, that his troops were all doing the same: picking targets either with the bow or, in close combat, their swords or knives. He also saw something that gave him pause – bodies of Rangers, laying there on the field. One's head had been blown almost totally apart, another had been practically cut in half by enemy fire. Robert dwelled on these for a second longer than he should have, but then ground his teeth, setting his jaw firm and raising his bow, felling another three Russian soldiers.

More jeeps and armoured vehicles – including tanks – were skirting the traps, wise to the barbed wire and trenches now. A group of Robert's men, about eight in total, charged the side of one tank carrying a tree-trunk like a battering ram. They rammed the wood into the tracks of the tank, jamming its progress. Another team did the same at the other side, given cover by arrows fired into the air above them. A further team was using Molotov cocktails against the vehicles.

Robert fired at a jeep heading in his direction, just as he had done the first time he'd engaged in combat like this, back when the market near Sherwood had been under attack. Then he hadn't been able to believe what he was doing, going up against a squad of the Sheriff's men on his own. Now, it seemed like second nature. And even though they were fending off an army, he wasn't alone any more. That made all the difference.

That might make the difference between winning and losing.

Were they winning or losing? Bohuslav couldn't even tell.

What should have been a cut and dried thing had suddenly

turned sour. Their enemies were using tactics the men had never come across before, but he certainly had. They were the methods of trappers, of hunters. What should have worked in his side's favour – the wealth of armament at their disposal, the sheer number of vehicles – was actually turning out to be their Achilles Heel. Hood's men were more manoeuvrable, running or riding – on fucking horses for sanity's sake! – between the behemoths, bullets bouncing off what looked like home-made shields. And body-armour! Tanek had conveniently left that detail out of the preparations... unless he hadn't known? It made them harder to kill, harder to kill *quickly* at any rate.

Hood's men were also able to handle close-combat fighting much better than his, probably because they'd never had to do it before. When The Tsar's troops entered an area, they usually obliterated everything in their path long before it got to that stage.

Bohuslav cursed under his breath in his native tongue, as another explosion went off outside the jeep.

He looked through the windscreen at what was going on ahead of him, and the certainty he'd had when he arrived began to wane. But there was something Hood and his men didn't know – apart from their plan, of course, apart from what was going on while they were all here. Bohuslav had hoped to settle this without having to fall back on them, but The Tsar had brought those special little toys over with him just in case.

Four Kamov Ka-50 single-seat attack helicopters, also known to those in the trade as 'Black Sharks'. Each one boasted laser guided anti-tank missiles located under the stub wings, plus 30mm cannons fixed semi-rigidly on the helicopter's side. One of the most lethal pieces of military hardware known to man. Granted, they weren't being piloted by the most highly trained individuals – at least not as highly trained as they would have been pre-virus – but they knew enough to get the job done.

The time had come to finish this, and if his ground forces weren't capable... Bohuslav reached for the radio, knowing now with complete certainty who would be the ultimate victors here today.

CHAPTER SIXTEEN

In the heat of the battle, even above the noise of gunfire and explosions, another sound could be heard. The distinctive sound of rotor blades in the distance.

Robert looked over the horizon to see four dark shapes advancing, like flying Horsemen of the Apocalypse. Helicopters unlike anything he was familiar with – certainly nothing like the Sioux he'd used to chase De Falaise through the streets of Nottingham. These had double rotors that afforded them a manoeuvrability most pilots could only dream of.

The two helicopters on the edges broke off, heading for the tree-line. Robert could see what was about to happen, but had no way of preventing it – apart from anything else, he was being attacked by two of The Tsar's men who he'd relieved of their machine guns with well-placed kicks.

Missiles were away seconds later, streaming into the trees. The height these monstrosities were flying at gave them a unique view of where the catapults lay. Not only that, they seemed to home in on the targets like a sniffer dog locating drugs. Robert dispatched the soldiers he was dealing with, then closed his eyes as the missiles hit home, killing the men he'd posted there.

Those Rangers closer by had – like him – paused very briefly to witness the lethal onslaught of these newcomers. However, as they did so they also saw more heavy rocks being launched at the chopper closest to the trees. It may not have been quite as accurate as whatever those pilots were using, but it was good enough to give the thing a bloody nose – a heavy projectile glancing across the bridge of the lowered craft knocking it momentarily sideways and off balance. Two more hit it in quick succession before another chopper came to its aid, firing off two missiles which put paid to that particular catapult. But it had already done enough damage to the first helicopter to make it beat a hasty retreat.

"That'll show 'em!" called out one of Robert's lads, a man called Harris who immediately drew back his bow and shot a Russian soldier in the thigh.

But there were still three helicopters left, more than enough to take out the rest of the catapults. Calling on anyone who was free to do so, Robert began to make his way forward, up the field, past the corpses of vehicles – firing arrows as he went.

One of the helicopters had bowed its front, sweeping forwards. Robert ordered his men to duck, shouting that anyone who still had their shield should crouch behind it. He himself dived behind the cover of an upended jeep, dragging a couple of his men with him – just as the chopper's machinegun began spraying the area. It seemed not to care whether its own troops were in the way, so long as it got Robert's men. Several were thrown back by the blast, losing their shields. Then, vulnerable, they were torn to shreds by the second sweep – vests no protection from this kind of intense firepower.

"Damn it all!" growled Robert. Then to his men: "Stay under cover!"

Before they could say anything, Robert had run out from behind the jeep, sprinting towards a tank that was still on fire. Bullets peppered the earth behind him, but he flung himself forward and, taking cover behind the metal hulk, he primed his bow, igniting one of the special payload arrows from his quiver.

Stepping out he took a second to aim, but it was all he needed.

The arrow was flying even as he took cover behind the tank again. The helicopter had no time to get out of its way, the pilot so overconfident that the arrow could do no damage to his craft that he stayed there and waited for the thing to hit. Then it struck its target, glancing off one of its remaining missiles, but in the process smearing the cocktail of heated chemicals across the casing. Seconds later the missile exploded, taking the entire helicopter with it.

Robert strode out from behind the tank in time to see the blazing ball go down, striking the earth nose first. He heard cheering from behind him, his actions prompting others to break cover, attacking the two helicopters as they had done the tanks, jeeps and motorcycles.

One of them was hit with a paint bomb across the windshield, obscuring the pilot's vision, forcing him to pull back. A tree trunk fired from what was probably the one remaining catapult then struck the side of that chopper. The pilot seemed to be trying to land, then attempted to rise up again. A couple of petrol bombs to the undercarriage were enough to persuade him to set down, and Robert saw him leap from the cockpit. Two arrows from Dale's bow – the lad still riding his horse into the action – were waiting for him, pinning him to the ground.

That left one last attack helicopter.

Robert broke cover again, hunting the thing before it got a chance to hunt him. He hadn't gone far through this nightmare of war – explosions going off everywhere; armoured vehicles still ahead; not to mention a good number of Russian troops – when the black beast spotted him. It hovered close into view before him. On the side of this one somebody had painted a shark. *Not a bad description for that thing in the right hands*, thought Robert. But where the shark was a thing of nature, this wasn't. It had no instinct, no cunning or guile: that was left to whoever was in control. There was nothing organic about its methods of killing at all, hiding behind all those guns and rockets and metal.

But The Hooded Man: he was another story entirely. He was living on instinct and adrenalin. A *true* force of nature.

He stood there, all Hell breaking loose around him. Then he raised his head, not revealing too much of his countenance. Bow slung over his shoulder, he coaxed the chopper to come closer with a crook of his finger.

The pilot was hesitating, probably because of what had just happened to the other chopper. Then suddenly the helicopter moved forward, nose down. Robert knew all its weapons must be trained on him.

Faith, he thought to himself. *If I just have enough faith.*

They seemed to stand frozen like that, an iconic scene from one of Jack's old action movies, everything happening in slow motion around them. Like two gunslingers from a western, each one waiting for the other to draw.

Robert reached around the back of his belt first, but as he did he could've sworn he heard the clicking of the machine gun, saw it moving and training on him. He waited for a blast that never came – whether the guns jammed or the pilot hesitated again, he had no way of knowing – but he took advantage of the seconds it gave him. Pulling out a bolas (the same design as the one he'd used for hunting in Sherwood, only now made from a length of metal chain) he tossed it at the base of the helicopter's lowest rotor. It got tangled up quickly, the small spiked balls – taken from two maces – sparking as they whipped up into the blades.

The helicopter pulled its nose up and veered to one side, firing its gun now but spraying the bullets into the air and hitting nothing. Robert watched from under the brow of his hood, as it drifted across the skyline sideways Then as it piled into a bunch of trees at the edge of the field, getting tangled up in the branches.

May not have been a slingshot, Reverend, thought Robert, *but it did the trick.*

He didn't have much more time to think about it, because something hit him. Something big and hard that came out of nowhere, sending him spinning.

Robert felt the pain in his side as he flipped around. Connecting with the ground, he continued to roll, his sword flattening against his side. He felt his vest catch on something and rip apart at the front, the metal plate slipping out; heard something round the back of him crack and hoped it was only his bow.

When he came to a halt, he was looking up at the blue sky, the clouds passing overhead. Then it was going dark... He was beginning to black out. *Not now, Robert. Fight it!*

He held on to the image of that blue sky, and for a few moments it felt like an ordinary day in the English countryside.

Then whatever had hit him drew up not far away.

And he heard someone climb out, approaching his battered and bruised body.

Bohuslav had watched the defeat of the helicopters and had to pinch himself in case he was dreaming. Not that he ever had dreams like this, his were much darker affairs. More personal.

It had all started off so well. The destruction of whatever was flinging those crude missiles was countered with the more modern-day variety, guided in on target and blowing them to bits. It was when the Black Sharks had got closer to the fighting that the problems started.

And him! *Govno!* That irritating little man with his Hood and his arrows and his sword. He'd actually taken down two – count them, two! – of the craft himself. Small wonder his reputation had spread. His men would blindly, and bravely it had to be said, follow him into the very depths of Hades itself if he asked them to. Perhaps Tanek had been right to broach his concerns that Hood might come for them one day. Definitely better to take him out of the equation now. Except they weren't doing such a great job, were they?

Bohuslav's fingers itched. He could see that the only way they were still going to pull this around would be for him to put The Hooded Man down personally. Cut off the head and the rest of the body withers – he had learned that at a very early age in his experimentations with animals.

Bohuslav ordered his driver to double back, come at the battlefield from the side. "Ram him," he commanded, pointing ahead to the lone figure who had just defeated one of the most sophisticated pieces of military hardware known to man, as if he was teaching a school bully a lesson. It would definitely be a challenge to fight this individual one-on-one, but there was no harm in stacking the odds in his favour. Bohuslav had no qualms about this, he preferred to pounce on his victims when they least expected it, so the fight would be brief.

This one would be too, he'd make sure. As the jeep slammed into Hood, sending him reeling, Bohuslav smirked. Then he got out of the vehicle, producing his handheld sickles as he strode over towards the leader of this rag-tag team that had held fast against their might.

Through watery eyes attempting to close, Robert saw him.

A blur at first, he blinked and, as the form took on more shape, Robert made out the man's attire. He looked so out of place here, in that sharp black suit, white shirt and black tie. But, looking beyond that, looking into the hawk-like eyes, Robert recognised what he really was: another hunter, a predator even. Not the main man himself, but one of the minions he'd seen in his dream.

The predator was holding in his hands two sharp weapons, like the Grim Reaper's scythe, only smaller and more curved. More deadly. It had been *his* vehicle that had run Robert over, intentionally wounding the prey. This monster liked his meat to be softened up before coming in for the kill. And Robert could tell he'd killed before, that he enjoyed it.

"Wake up, mudak!" shouted the man. He was using one of the sickle points to pull Robert's Hood back, exposing his face and head. "Yes, rouse yourself. It is time for you to die."

Robert tried to move, but every inch of him was protesting.

"Your performance was impressive, I will give you that," continued the suited man looming over him, "but ultimately you must have known you'd fail."

"F-Fail?" Robert half coughed, half laughed. "You... You must have been at a different battle to me."

"Ah, but this war is being fought on two fronts, my friend." There was a searing pain in his thigh as the man buried one of the sickle points into Robert's leg. "That's it, shout out. Let your men know all about it."

Robert clamped his teeth shut, hissing out the rest of his howl. The man twisted his blade and Robert had trouble keeping his agony to himself. But the man was leaning in, close.

Close enough to...

Even though he couldn't get up, Robert could still swing his fist – and he did just that. He couldn't get as much leverage behind the punch as he would have liked, but it had the desired effect of knocking the Russian back, and the sickle blade slid out of Robert's thigh as he reeled.

Robert struggled to get up onto an elbow, his torso and thigh in competition to see which could cause him more pain. With his free hand, he unsheathed his sword, just in time to hold it before him to meet a blow from the enraged Russian.

"That won't save you," promised the man, his piercing eyes flashing. "Nothing will." He struck again. Robert's blade clashed with two sickles this time, but he wasn't strong enough to hold them at bay. The man was leaning hard on the blades, the sickles getting lower and lower. "And nothing will save your friends at the castle, either."

Robert's elbow gave out, but he was quick enough to grab the other end of his sword. However, he was flat on his back, the man pressing down on top of him. The sickles were millimetres from his chest. Catching him off guard, the suited man suddenly put more weight on one side than the other, the left blade dropping – though not before Robert shifted slightly so that it entered his shoulder rather than his chest. Again, an excruciating white hot agony, and Robert let go of his grip on the sword.

Leaving the point of the sickle in Robert's shoulder, the man above him raised the other one high. He wasn't going for the chest any more. Now he was going to bring the sickle round in an arc, slit open Robert's throat, maybe even cut off his head.

There was a swish of air and Robert closed his eyes, steeling himself for the sickle to slice his flesh. Instead he felt something wet on his face and chest. Then came a cry.

When Robert opened his eyes he saw what had happened. Dale was standing off to one side, his sword covered in blood. The suited man was rising and backing off, clutching his hand... no, not his hand. Because that lay on the ground, still holding the sickle.

Blood was spurting from the suited man's stump and Dale was still on him. He lashed out with another stroke of the blade which the man had to duck to avoid. Robert heard him scream out something in his native tongue, cursing the person who'd cut off his extremity. Dale took no notice, waiting for the suited man to right himself before crouching and slashing crosswise. The man arched his body and it looked like Dale's attack had fallen short. Then more redness stained the white shirt, the bottom half of his tie falling to the ground as a slash in the fabric appeared. The man looked up at Dale, shocked, then down at this new wound.

Scrabbling back and holding his stomach, the man's face was growing paler by the second. Then he fell over, curling up in the foetal position.

Dale looked like he was about do some more damage when Robert let out a load groan, the first sickle still embedded in him.

"Hold on," said Dale. He put down his sword and took hold of the handle of the sickle. "Brace yourself, Robert, this is going to really hurt." He pulled out the blade, but it felt like the metal was still inside. Then Dale took Robert's hand and got him to apply pressure to the wound, while he saw to the leg. Robert heard, rather than saw – his vision was swimming – Dale rip a piece off his sleeve, tying a tourniquet around the wounded thigh.

"Son of a... I don't believe it," said Dale, getting up. Robert blinked and saw the blurry, suited man crawling back to the vehicle that had rammed into him. The Russian could just about move, reaching up in an effort to drag himself back into the passenger seat. Then helping hands pulled him inside, the driver setting off even before the suited man's legs were properly inside. Robert grabbed Dale with his free hand and shook his head.

"L... Leave him," he moaned.

Dale looked at Robert, as if about to disagree with him, then nodded. "He's half dead anyway," said the youth. "Let's see to you." He began ripping more material to tie around the shoulder wound.

"How... How are..." began Robert.

Dale frowned, then worked out what he was trying to ask. "It's pretty much over. The ones that are left seem to be scattering. We did it, we held them back."

Robert let out a breath, fighting to hang on to consciousness. His grip on the young man's arm tightened. "You... You have to gather the men..."

"I don't understand."

"Get... get them together... There's... there's another..." Robert forced the words out. "Another army heading for the castle... Tanek must be with them..."

"Fuck," Dale said quietly. "Okay, we can deal. Let's just get you sorted out first."

Another squeeze of Dale's arm, with all the strength Robert could muster. "Leave me."

"I... we can't do that, Robert."

"Leave me... Get to the castle... Mary... promise me... Mary..." Then his grip relaxed and Dale's features disappeared completely, fading from view. He'd been here before, when he'd been caught in an explosion, fighting De Falaise's men at Mary's farm.

Mary again.

He'd been saved by her that time. But now she was the one in trouble.

In the blackness, Robert heard Dale arguing with someone, with several voices, telling them they had to go.

Dale was following orders, just as he always did. Doing what Robert asked of him. "We'll send back help," were the last words Robert heard him say.

Then there was nothing but stillness – that and the smell of the English countryside – as he lost his grasp on consciousness completely.

CHAPTER SEVENTEEN

The first sign that something was wrong came when they lost contact with the sentries on the outskirts of the city.

"Could just be a fault in the radio equipment," Jack said to Mary when he visited her room, but the look on his face told her he didn't believe that for a second. When Robert's teams had originally infiltrated Nottingham, they'd kept up the pretence that the guards were still on duty, to retain the element of surprise. If the lookouts really were gone, then it showed that whoever was on their way didn't care whether they knew or not. "But I've already begun spreading the word among the men, just in case," Jack continued.

"We'd better gather people together," Mary told him, "Just give me a second." That second had been to grab a coat and fish out her father's precious old Peacekeeper revolvers, along with the bullets she had left. Robert hadn't even bothered asking her to give them up, as he knew what the answer would be. "Okay," she said, and they walked out together along the corridor.

Tate and Gwen hadn't been hard to find, they were still arguing down below.

"The fact remains, you got me here under false pretences! I thought better of you, Reverend." The auburn-haired woman was holding her baby in one arm, and jabbing a free finger in Tate's face.

"I never said anything about you taking more weapons back to Hope."

"*New* Hope," she reminded him. "We have all the food we need, what else was I expected to think?

"But you know, as well as I, Robert's feelings."

"Screw Robert. He's leaving my people out there defenceless!" snapped the woman, then caught sight of Mary and Jack from the corner of her eye. She stopped her rant, but didn't apologise.

Tate shook his head. "I only did this out of the best of intentions. Robert has gone to tackle this new threat, and I thought you'd be safest here."

"You may have underestimated exactly how safe we are," Mary told the holy man.

Jack explained about the lookouts to the baffled Tate.

"Then we need to break out those weapons right away!" Gwen said. "Start handing them out to your men and–"

"The men are capable of defending themselves regardless" said Mary.

Gwen rounded on her. "I thought you out of all of them had some sense, Mary."

"I do," she replied.

"And what's that tucked away there, a peashooter?" Gwen aimed her finger at Mary's belt, where one gun was stuffed in the front, the other out of sight round the back.

"That's different, it belonged to..." Mary didn't have time for this. "Look, have you seen Mark? We all need to stick together, keep inside the castle.

"And Adele," Jack said. "Have you seen her?"

Mary wasn't actually that bothered where *she* was.

"Last time I saw Mark, he was with Sophie outside," Tate informed them.

"Right," Mary said, making for the nearest exit and shrugging on her coat.

"Mary, let me-" Jack began, but she was gone before he had time to finish.

Outside, Mary looked for Mark and Sophie. She made her way around the castle, coming up with nothing. As she was about to make another pass, she stopped. Something was amiss. You didn't live somewhere for over a year - especially somewhere they'd originally taken over - without noticing subtle differences in your surroundings. This one, however small, was big in other ways.

The lock had been broken on one of the gates leading to the caves, the gate itself slightly ajar.

"Gwen..." Mary muttered to herself. She'd noticed a real difference in the woman since she'd returned to the castle, since she'd set herself up as a leader in her own right at New Hope. Mary had got to know her a little during the later stages of her pregnancy, during *and* after the birth, but the woman who'd driven in here late yesterday had been barely recognisable. She made some allowance for the fact that Gwen was being forced to return to the place where she had once been held captive. But it was more than that, Mary could see it in her eyes. They were colder, the determination she'd exhibited when she left had intensified a hundredfold.

Now she'd taken not a blind bit of notice of what Mary had said, gone down to retrieve the weapons anyway in spite of Robert's instructions. At first Mary hadn't really understood this herself, surely it did make sense - as Bill had repeatedly argued - to use the weapons they'd been handed on a plate? But the more she got to know Robert, the more she saw what kind of man he was and the more she loved him for his convictions. This wasn't an obsession with the past, as her own father had, but rather a revolt against the trappings of a world that spawned the virus in the first place. It had taken everything away from Robert, and left people like De Falaise free to use those kinds of weapons (weapons, she justified to herself, from a different era to her Peacekeepers). If they took up the same kind of arms,

Robert had maintained, how long before they were back in the position of country vs. country, with the threat of weapons of mass destruction hanging over their heads again?

That was why he'd gone off to face this Tsar character, completely mismatched some might think. But they'd be underestimating him, and Mary knew in her heart that Robert was anything but crazy. He believed it was something worth fighting for, a principle worth *dying* for. She just missed him and hoped he was okay.

It was also why she had to go down to the caves and have a word with Gwen, stop her from bringing up more of those weapons. They'd fight whatever was coming in the same spirit as Robert, not as the mad Frenchman would have done. Because he'd lost, hadn't he? And they'd won.

Mary began down the narrow, sheer steps that led into the cave system. The stone was slippery and it was dark. As she descended, though, she saw a flickering light. Someone had turned on the jury-rigged lamps which De Falaise had set up down here. For some reason she couldn't quite understand, Mary was as quiet as possible, loathe to give away her presence.

She turned a corner and saw it: the arsenal that had been carried down here not long after their victory, Robert's men disarming the Sheriff's troops and locking their toys away where they couldn't hurt anyone anymore. Until perhaps now...

Because Mary saw the female figure there in the shadows, hunched down, rooting through the weaponry like a dealer at a scrap metal yard. It was time to announce herself.

"And exactly what do you think you're doing, Gwe–" Mary cut short her sentence when she realised her mistake. As the figure righted herself, she saw that this woman had short hair, and it was much darker than Gwen's. Slowly, the woman faced her.

"Hello Mary."

"Adele." For a second or two, Mary's mind couldn't quite process this turn of events. "What are *you* doing down here?"

Adele just smiled that false smile of hers. "I... I heard about what was happening. And Jack told me about the weapons down here, so..."

"So you just thought you'd come and help yourself?"

"I was scared." But there was something in that voice which told Mary that Adele was anything *but* scared. This hadn't been a snap decision in the slightest, she knew exactly what she was doing. "Robert's not here and..." Robert again? "I'm glad you and him have patched things up," she tacked on, quickly. "Do you think he'll be all right?"

Mary frowned. What was she doing? Trying to change the subject, attempting to steer it away from why she was down in the caves after these weapons? Mary swept away all the confusion and let her instincts take over.

Don't trust her, Moo-Moo, said her brother's voice, so suddenly it almost made her start. *She doesn't care about Robert. Not really. She doesn't care about any of you.*

Nodding to herself, Mary then asked the most obvious question of all, the one she should have asked a long time ago. "Who exactly *are* you, Adele?"

"What are you talking about?" she said, a bit too hastily.

"Who are you? It's a simple enough question."

Now it was her who frowned. "I'm Adele," she confirmed, as if it answered everything. There was no response from Mary, so Adele began with: "I was born in Durham, moved away when I was old enough, travelled around... What more do you need to know?"

She's lying.

When Mary remained silent, Adele continued, like she was reading from a prepared speech. "Okay, I'm an only child, my mother brought me up on her own. It was... hard. My father... well, he left when I was very young. I never really knew him, but I would have liked to."

The woman was all caring and sharing now – why? So Mary would have sympathy for her? Another tactic? Were these more lies? Mary couldn't tell for sure, but Adele's eyes appeared to be welling up.

"I never really knew who he was until the end. Until my mother..."

Mary thought about what had happened to David, about caring

for him when he died.

Don't get suckered in Moo-Moo. Don't make this about me, concentrate on what she's saying. Listen, really listen.

"I found some stuff in an old trunk in the attic of the house," Adele went on, as if she needed to get this out, share it with someone after so long. "Papers, old photographs. I knew my father had been a soldier, but nothing more. I didn't even know his real name until then. Can you imagine?"

Was it Mary's imagination, or did Adele's voice sound different, as she was becoming more emotional?

"She told me he died in some accident while he was serving abroad. The bitch! Why? Why would anyone do that?" Adele was beseeching Mary, and now the tears did roll down her face. "Everyone has a right to know where they came from, don't you think?"

The more Adele talked, the more her accent was slipping.

Born and brought up in Durham my arse... said David.

"Everyone has a right to know their father, Mary! I'd lay odds that you knew yours," Adele almost snarled. "So I set off to look for him. I had nothing but a name. I did not even know if he was still alive. I mean, my blood was his blood, but then we live in such dangerous times. I must have toured the breadth of Europe in those couple of years. But on the streets you hear rumours, and it only took one person to tell me they'd heard that name. One person who'd come across my father. Apparently he had been travelling too. Making friends all over the place. Enemies as well."

Mary began to move her hand slowly, down and sideways.

"Then he headed across to England. I suppose he thought he could start again. I can understand him wanting to come, I spent some time here myself in my teens. Mastered the 'lingo' pretty well, too, don't you think?" For this last bit Adele's accent jolted back to British, but when she spoke again she didn't bother hiding her true voice, her native accent. "So I followed his trail. All I wanted to do was meet him, get to know him, *non*? But by the time I got over here it was already too late. He really was dead this time. He'd been murdered."

Mary's trembling fingers made their way slowly towards the Peacemaker sticking out of the front of her jeans.

"Strange thing was, he'd been killed by someone wearing a hood, carrying a bow and arrow. A legend. And why was he killed?"

"Because he was a sadistic scumbag," Mary said seriously. "Because he took delight in other people's pain."

Adele shook her head. "Spin, created by those who slaughtered him in cold blood. He had power; he was The Sheriff!"

"He was going to hang people, Adele – if that's really your name."

"It is."

"He kidnapped me and put a sabre to my throat."

"Having spent time with you, I can certainly understand that." Adele's false smile now looked even more wrong. "My mother kept me from getting to know my father–"

"Wise woman," Mary broke in.

Adele scowled. "Then you people kept him from me *forever*. Well, I decided it was time you paid."

"So you thought you'd worm your way in here, have us all at each other's throats? Was that the plan?" Mary's fingers inched a little nearer to the handle.

"Sort of," admitted Adele. "I believe my father used to use the same methods of infiltration, to get inside his enemies' lairs. But it was always going to come to this in the end."

"It was no coincidence that Robert picked you up in York, was it?"

Adele shook her head. "Hardly. I've been studying the cult's movements, and Robert's, for longer than any of you realise. It wasn't hard to put myself in harm's way, to orchestrate a little... rendezvous."

Her fingers were almost there, just a fraction more. *Careful, Mary,* said her brother, which made her even more on edge. He only called her by her real name when he was angry with her or feared for her safety. *She's crazier than her old man was.*

"I must say, I can see why you're attracted to him," Adele stared at her, the tears all but dried up. "Under different circumstances and if I didn't hate his guts, maybe... Wouldn't be exactly difficult to come between you two, not with all the problems you've both got."

"You didn't come between anyone," Mary said defiantly.

"Right," replied Adele in a tone that made Mary want to punch her in the face.

"Look, we don't have much time. We're all in danger from The Tsar and–"

"Ah yes, The Tsar. An interesting twist," Adele said, stepping forward. "Even I had not foreseen that. I thought I would have to do this alone, but now... Maybe he might want to join forces, do you think?"

Hearing her talk like this, and now seeing her face – her true face – for the first time, Mary couldn't believe she'd been so blind. But then, how could anyone have known about Adele's real origins? She'd been so clever at hiding them. And in a post-apocalyptic world what did anyone really know about anyone?

"Especially if I give him a little inside help. It was only what I was going to do anyway, now that a good portion of your compliment are absent... or dead." She said this last bit with such hope, Mary made a grab for her gun – pulling out the Peacekeeper, cocking it, and pointing it at Adele's head. Adele didn't seem surprised; in fact she smiled again. That same crooked smile. De Falaise's smile. Mary was hardly likely to forget it.

"I wouldn't do that if I were you," Adele told her, then brought up her hands, turning around and showing what she was holding. A live grenade. "The pin's already pulled, in case you were wondering. All I have to do is let go of the trigger. I go, you go with me."

Damn it, said David in her head. *What are you going to do now, sis?* Mary didn't have a clue. She couldn't even tell Adele to drop her weapon, or they'd both go up.

Adele offered a solution. "So, I suggest you let me walk out of here with these." She shifted to one side, nodding down at a bag on the floor. Open, because Mary had disturbed her in the act, it contained a rifle, handgun, some more grenades, and what looked to be a mini-bazooka.

"You're not coming past me," Mary said. God knows what kind of damage she'd do with those, and at a time when they might be under attack from the outside as well.

"I don't have to," Adele barked. "I know there are other ways in and out of here." She grabbed the bag then walked backwards, picking her way through the Aladdin's cave of weaponry.

Mary's gun arm wavered. "Don't."

"You are not in any position to give me orders."

Mary hated to admit it, but Adele was right. All she could do was watch her as she retreated. When she was a good way off, Adele smiled again.

"I would like to say it has been nice knowing you, but..." Adele let the sentence tail off, then tossed the grenade at Mary.

Instinctively, Mary took a shot, but the woman was already gone. Then her eyes dropped to the grenade bouncing into the middle of the arsenal.

"Nuts," said Mary under her breath.

Run, Mary, run! shouted her brother, but she didn't need to be told, her legs were already in motion. She pelted out the way she had come, making it to the steps and almost all the way up them when the explosion came.

The blast rocked the cave, blowing dust, sandstone, *and* Mary out with it, causing a section near the exit to fall in just behind her. She felt something heavy land on her leg, pinning her to the steps, pain following.

Mary could see the light above, the open gate, but couldn't move. She reached out her hand, yet in spite of the efforts of her brother to keep her awake, Mary found herself blacking out. It sounded like another explosion went off then, but that one was distant. She let it go, able only to focus on one thing.

Her final thoughts were of Robert, Adele's words echoing in her mind.

Absent... or dead

Absent...

Or dead.

CHAPTER EIGHTEEN

They were all dead.

Piled up, in front of The Tsar. And he was looking down on them with such a satisfied smile on his face. Mary, Tate, Sophie, Mark. And finally Jack, thrown down there by the giant Tanek, while the two Asian women looked on, swords drawn, ready to protect their Lord with their lives if necessary.

At The Tsar's feet was the suited man, crawling, half dead; one of his hands missing and blood staining his shirt from the belly wound that Dale had given him. All around them the forest was on fire. It was being attacked by the troops they'd found on the battlefield, trees mowed aside by armoured vehicles. The sound of chopper-blades could be heard overhead.

On his knees, Robert made an effort to get up and rush forward, to take revenge for the deaths of the people he loved. But he found he couldn't move. It was like he was stuck, his limbs unable to respond to his commands. His eyes were about the only things that could, and when he dipped them, he saw a light coating of fur on his chest, on his entire body (though he couldn't reach up this time – Robert didn't even think he had hands – he knew there would be antlers on his head). His shoulder was bleeding profusely, and so was his thigh.

But there was something else. A figure behind The Tsar. A woman. He recognised her short black hair, the pretty but tight features, instantly.

It was the woman he'd saved from the cultists. Adele. Indeed, the closer he looked at the soldiers flanking them, the more he saw their number amongst the troops: the robed men with machetes here and there, blending in with The Tsar's fighters.

Robert's attention was snapped back to Adele, though, as she draped herself over The Tsar, hands on his shoulders, lips to his ear. The Russian's grin widened, but his twin bodyguards looked like they wanted to run their swords right through her.

Then she came around the front, stroking Tanek's bicep as he joined them. There was something about the way she looked now, something that rang a warning bell. It was as if the layers were being peeled away, revealing the real face of this woman beneath her actor's façade. There it was in the eyes, in the crooked smile. He'd seen those features before, he'd looked into them as he'd been locked in a deathgrip. A relation? A cousin? A sister?

No. A daughter.

If only he had known earlier.

"Vengeance," whispered Adele in a French accent, now to the side of him. Now at *his* ear.

The *thrup-thrup* of an attack helicopter drowned her out, about to fire its payload as it had during the battle. The battle which he'd just fought and ended up–

Tanek, in front of him, was raising his crossbow – preparing to fire and then cut the antlers from Robert's crown. But those damned rotor blades, they were making such a row.

So close, so close.

Tanek raised his crossbow and fired...

...Robert's eyelids cracked open, then immediately closed again.

The noise of the rotor blades from his dream carried on. He must still be there, must still be in the dreamscape. Except, now he felt pain – real pain. The kind you could never feel in a dream. The kind that reminded him what he'd been through in the battle and the fight with the suited man.

Which meant that the sound of the chopper was real, too.

Robert forced open one eye. Yes, there was the outline of a helicopter. His lid snapped shut again. They'd taken out three of those things, but only incapacitated the first. It had to be that one returning to finish the job, the pilot intent on revenge, about to spray the field with bullets.

Robert kept as still as he could, *feeling* the shadow of the thing above him. But then his injured leg betrayed him, the pain there jabbing into him until the thigh moved of its own accord. That was just great; first he couldn't move at all, then his body was moving independently of his mind, giving him away.

He prised open both eyes, taking in the sight of the chopper directly above. If he was going out, finally, then he was going to meet death with his eyes wide open. Strangely, he realised he would miss seeing Mary's face much more than he was looking forward to seeing Joanna. It was a horrible, horrible thing, but true.

"I'm... I'm sorry," he muttered, but he wasn't sure which one of them he was apologising to.

Then Robert braced himself for those bullets.

He kept the helicopter level, coming in low and sweeping over the battleground.

What the hell had happened here?

He thought just how apt those words were, because Hell actually did look like it had happened to this place. This sleepy, wintry English meadow had been the site of some kind of rift, a portal connecting our world with–

He shook his head. That was cobblers. What had happened

here was man's work, not the Devil's. Two warring sides ripping each other to shreds.

The blackened and charred remains of tanks, jeeps, motorcycles and armoured vehicles littered the landscape. As did bodies, dozens of them. If he'd thought it was bad last time then...

"Judas bloody Priest."

When Bill had found out that something big was going down here, from a variety of his sources, he had climbed straight into his chopper and into the air.

He'd spent much of the time since the fracas at the Bay keeping tabs on the army that had landed, and what he was hearing made him sick to his stomach. These people made the Frenchman look like an amateur. They'd crash through cities, towns and villages like a juggernaut, treating those who could defend themselves and those who could not the same, killing both in equal measures.

Somebody needed to stop them, just like they'd stopped the Sheriff.

But with guns, tanks, jeeps and armoured vehicles of their own. Fighting fire with fire. It was the only way. Not like this, not with rocks, with arrows and swords. Not on horseback! It was the same old argument, one that had seen him leave these ranks in the first place and, looking around today, he was glad he'd got out in time.

Yet, as much as he believed that, Bill had to admit they'd fared damned well. Robert had again pulled something together out of nothing, led his men in an attack that any modern army would have been proud of. Seen off greater numbers and firepower with what looked like sheer force of will. There were more – many, many more – uniformed bodies down there than Rangers; which wasn't to say they hadn't taken heavy casualties as well. Bill spotted two or three corpses next to a small crater that looked as if they'd been melted down like plastic. Others had been raked with machine gun fire, their bows, arrows and swords laying uselessly by their sides. Robert couldn't have done all this with so few men, surely? Which begged the question, if there *were* survivors, where the blazes were they?

It was as he swept across this devastation that Bill saw something else. Someone he recognised down there, hood back and sprawled out on the ground. He was injured, that much Bill could tell – hasty field dressings made from strips of cloth covered his thigh and shoulder. But whether it was more serious than that, whether he was... Bill shook his head. He *couldn't* be, not Robert. Ever since Bill had first seen him in action he'd had a mental picture in his head of him being indestructible, and his reputation as a living legend did nothing to hamper this. But he wasn't some kind of superhero. He was just flesh and blood like the rest of them.

Which meant he could die. There, it was in Bill's head before he could shake it. But he wouldn't find out by staying up in the air like this. Quickly, Bill searched for a place to set the Gazelle down. It wasn't easy, everywhere he looked there were the carcasses of fighting machines or the ground was too churned up for a stable landing, but eventually he managed to find a small area of flat ground.

"Back in a sec, girl," he told the chopper, grabbing both his shotgun and one of his newly acquired AK-47s. He had no idea whether there were any Russian soldiers in hiding, waiting for someone to come along, so he wasn't taking any chances.

Cautiously, Bill picked his way across the field, hurrying when he got closer to Robert's position. Taking one last look around him, pointing the guns in every direction, he crouched on the floor beside Robert. Putting the machine gun on the ground, though still ready with his trusty double-barrelled shotgun if he needed it, Bill checked the side of Robert's neck for a pulse. For a second he couldn't find one, then he realised he was panicking, feeling in the wrong place. He calmed down and brought his fingers up higher, to the crevice between the chin and neck. There it was, a faint beat. Robert was still alive.

Bill let out the breath he'd been holding. They'd had their moments in the past, but this was still the man who'd saved his life. The man he'd gone into battle with at the castle. "Rob," he said, slapping the man's cheek. "Rob, can ye hear me?"

There was a flicker under Robert's eyelids.

"Rob?"

Robert opened his eyes, though they were still practically slits. "Not... not dead..." he whispered and Bill almost missed what he said. The man sounded surprised, like he'd been expecting to wake up at the Pearly Gates.

"Naw, but ye doin' a good impression of a dead man. Look at the state of ye, lad."

"B-Bill?" Robert managed, as if he'd only just realised who was talking to him. "Is that you?"

"Aye."

"W-What are you-?"

"Later," Bill promised him. "Along wi' the 'I told ye sos'." He felt bad right after he'd said it, but if Robert had only listened to him... "Right now I reckon ye need them wounds lookin' at. Get ye back to Mary."

"No," said Robert, louder than he'd said anything since Bill found him.

"No?" Bill couldn't understand that. Surely Mary would be the first person he'd want to see, they'd been as thick as thieves since they met. Plus she had all that medical knowledge.

"S-Sherwood," Robert said.

"Eh? What d'you want to go back there for? Ye really have lost it."

Robert wouldn't – or couldn't – explain. He just said: "Please."

"But–"

"*Please*," Robert repeated more emphatically, and placed a trembling hand on Bill's arm.

"All right, but let's get yer wounds dressed properly first. I've got a medical kit in the helicopter."

Robert nodded, then winced in pain.

"Ye know," said Bill, standing. "Yer one stubborn man, Robert Stokes."

"Look... Look who's talking," wheezed Robert, a slight smile playing on his lips.

Bill shook his head and went off back to the chopper.

CHAPTER NINETEEN

Mark had been having the most serious conversation of his life when it all hit the fan.

Stupidly, he'd figured now was the perfect time to talk to Sophie. Dale was out of the way – though it still smarted that Robert had chosen to take him along and not Mark – plus the place was more peaceful than it had been in weeks. Plucking up the courage had proved to be more difficult. He would rather have faced another dozen of the men in robes than come out and tell Sophie how he really felt. Fighting was much simpler than dealing with all these emotions.

But, eventually, he decided he couldn't put it off any longer. They were facing all kinds of threats; he might not get the chance to say anything later on. What was the worst that could happen? She could shoot him down in flames, that's what. Her emotional bullets doing more damage than real ones ever could.

Mark had thought about Sophie a lot, even before she came to the castle. He'd even wondered whether it was worth going out and finding her himself, to see how she was after he'd been dragged off by De Falaise's men. But then she'd followed him here. It had to be a sign, didn't it? Some kind of omen?

But Dale had come along before Mark had a chance to say anything. Dale with the good looks and stories about gigging; Dale with his guitar, making up songs to impress her. How could Mark hope to compete with that? For starters, Dale was older and much more experienced. He knew what to say to girls.

Whereas you'll probably make a balls up of this, he told himself as he went in search of Sophie. *Just like you do with everything.*

Then she'd found him again. Coming round a corner, he'd bumped right into her, almost knocking them both over. "Sophie!"

"Hey, it's all right. No harm done. Although if you do it again I might just have to retaliate, soldier boy."

Soldier boy, thought Mark. *There's that word again. That's all I am to her really, a boy. When we first met, all she'd talked about was The Hooded Man, though she didn't know then how old he was. Imagined him closer to Dale's age.*

"So," she continued. "Whatcha doing?"

"Oh, er..." Mark scratched the back of his head, losing his hand in his tangle of dark-blonde hair. "Nothing, I was just... Sophie?"

"Yeah."

"Can I talk to you?"

"I thought that's what you were doing," she said and gave another little chuckle. "No, I'm sorry, I'm in a daft mood today: go on."

"Somewhere a bit more, I don't know, private?"

Sophie looked around, there was nobody in sight. "Sure. Inside?"

Mark shook his head, then gestured for her to follow him. They walked down the steps to the overgrown grounds, the place that had once been a recreational park with a centrepiece of a Victorian Bandstand. That was still there, and it was where Mark chose to make his confession.

Sophie sat on a bench, then watched as Mark paced in front of her. "Sophie... I..."

"Mark, what is it? You can tell me." He looked at her; that freckled face the most beautiful thing he'd ever seen. How could he upset her?

"No. It doesn't matter."

"Obviously it *does* or you wouldn't have brought us down here."

He stopped pacing. "Sophie..."

"Come on, Mark, just tell me."

He swallowed hard. "Okay. We're friends right?"

She laughed again, only this time it was a kind of 'I don't believe you just said that' laugh. "Of course, silly. You're like my *best* friend, Mark."

His smile came out wonky. *Best friend is good. But is that all we'll ever be? And if I say this, will it ruin that friendship forever?*

"What's all this about, Mark?"

He decided to risk it.

"Sophie, I really love you." There, it was out.

"Well, I love you too."

Now *that* he hadn't been expecting. "What?"

"Course I do. We've been through a lot together, Mark." He couldn't believe what he was hearing. "We'll always be friends and I'll always love you to bits."

Now he could.

"Sophie, what I meant was... When I said I love you, I meant..."

She looked blank, then the penny dropped. "Ooh. I see."

Mark stared down at his boots. "God, this is awkward."

"Listen," she began, getting up to join him. "I don't want you to take this the wrong way. You're incredibly sweet but..."

Don't say it, please don't say it. You're loading up the gun, about to shoot. Soon there'll be flames everywhere. Crash and burn, Mark, crash and burn.

"...but I'm not looking for anything like that right now."

Mark looked up. "You mean with me?"

"I mean with *anyone*."

"Does that include Dale?"

Sophie laughed again, then she saw he was serious. "*Dale?*"

"He's older, you spend a lot of time together."

"Mark, there's nothing going on between me and Dale, I promise you. I'm just happy to be alive right now, happy to be here. I need to be around people who make me feel safe."

"But Dale-"

"Oh my God – Dale's a laugh, Mark. I like his company, that doesn't mean I'm going to jump into bed with him!"

"I didn't mean..."

"My sister went out with plenty of men like him, before..." She looked sad for a moment, remembering. "Trust me, I'm not looking for a guy like that."

"Then there's still a chance?"

Why can't you keep your big mouth shut, Mark? If you push it, she'll tell you – and this way you can live in hope.

"No... I don't know. Not right now anyway. Look, this is starting to make me feel uncomfortable."

"I just wanted to-"

"Mark, just drop it. Please." She made to leave. Mark stood in her way.

"Sophie, just let me explain."

"Mark, I said drop it!" Something in her eyes told him to do as she asked. This had gone from talking to arguing and Mark couldn't see the join. He got out of her way.

Almost immediately Mark changed his mind and went after her, but she had a lead on him and was heading for the steps. In fact she was racing up them; he'd really upset her.

His head was telling him to leave this alone, yet his legs were still carrying him forwards. Perhaps that was his immaturity. In the same situation Dale might let her calm down, talk to her later. But he wouldn't have created this situation in the first place! All Mark knew was that he wanted to make this right again.

He was part of the way up the steps when he heard the explosion, felt the earth tremble beneath his feet.

Sophie! was his one and only thought.

His legs worked harder, getting him to the top. His eyes scanned the area quickly, as he shouted Sophie's name. Then he saw her. She was on the ground, had been blown over by the blast. He raced across and checked her for wounds. She didn't seem hurt, just extremely shaken up. He couldn't help thinking about her words not ten minutes ago:

"I'm just happy to be alive right now, happy to be here... I need to be around people who make me feel safe."

"Sophie, are you okay?"

Eyes wide, she nodded. "Mary," she said, pointing. He followed her finger and saw the gate to the caves wide open, smoke coming from beneath. "I saw her. She was trying to get out."

Mark left Sophie and ran over. He had time to glimpse a figure on the stairs, with long dark hair, partly buried under the rubble. There was blood on the walls. His hands went to his mouth, but before he could do anything about it, there were more explosions – this time coming from near the castle entrance.

The first volley of shells hit the side of the castle wall, fired by tanks and armoured vehicles coming from two directions.

Mortars were also fired into the grounds, their purpose to send the enemy into turmoil, taking some out in the process. The guards positioned on the walls and at the castle's front gate did their best to fight back, but they were unprepared for an attack of this scale. Robert was supposed to have slowed the army's progress at least. The fact that they could have split into two, that they had enough weapons, vehicles and men to do that, hadn't been a serious possibility.

Until now.

It wasn't long before the side gates were breached, an AFV smashing through them, busting them wide, allowing smaller vehicles to follow; jeeps and motorbikes. The Rangers assembled in the grounds shot at the vehicles with flaming arrows, the concoctions attached exploding on impact. But seconds later machine gun fire from the mounted guns dropped many of these. Men entered the grounds, overrunning the place – not just soldiers, but men in robes. Members of the cult.

Robert's troops stood more of a chance against these, swords clashing with machetes, but again there were just too many. Slash after slash, those who were defending the castle fell, and a path up towards the castle keep itself was cleared.

A rocket blast hit the side of the castle, but oddly it didn't seem to come from the outside. It appeared to have been fired by someone in the grounds, its tail winding down towards the Middle Bailey. Masonry dropped on people below, taking out more fighters.

From an AFV near the back of the convoy, they watched all this with satisfaction: Tanek, The Tsar and the twins. Tanek was itching to get out there, to take his place with the men on the ground. To, as he put it, 'crack some skulls'. The Tsar insisted he wait a little while, at least until they'd put down the first wave of resistance.

Tanek huffed at that, and watched for his opportunity to leave the vehicle.

Tate, Jack and Gwen were still inside when the first set of explosions came.

Tate told Gwen to go to one of the rooms while they checked on the situation. Ordinarily, he knew she'd argue, but she had Clive Jr with her so she did as he suggested. She could protect him better inside.

When the Reverend and Jack stepped out of the castle, they could scarcely believe what they were seeing. Already the grounds were flooded with enemy foot-soldiers. "Where are they all coming from?"

Jack shook his head, and clutched his staff.

It wasn't long before they encountered the first couple of men, running towards them. Luckily they were cult members, not soldiers. Jack and Tate looked at each other. Each was thinking: since when was The Tsar in league with the Morningstars?

Then they were on them. Jack met a machete blow with his staff. Tate dodged his opponent, but seemed reluctant to fight.

In fact, he only just got out of the way of the second swing, his face a rictus of fear.

"Rev, look out!" shouted Jack, striking his man in the stomach, crumpling him up, and then slamming the staff down on the back of his head. Without drawing breath, Jack swung the staff around and smacked the cultist attacking Tate in the face. He went down backwards, dropping the machete. "Are you okay?" Jack asked Tate, who looked dazed. These guys really freaked the holy man out.

"I... I don't understand," the Reverend said finally.

"Me either. But let's figure it out later. Right now we've got to-" He dragged Tate down as a hail of gunfire tore into the wall behind them. The soldiers hadn't been that far behind, as it turned out.

Leaving Tate, Jack ducked and rolled, coming up and striking one of The Tsar's men across the legs, sending him toppling over. Another he whacked in the side, then brought the staff around again to catch a third across the chest. Not seeing another way to tackle those coming up the steps, Jack grabbed a Kalashnikov belonging to one of the incapacitated soldiers and shot over the heads of the approaching troops. They backed off instantly.

He returned to Tate, taking him by the arm. "Come on, we have to fall back!" It wasn't easy getting away with the Reverend's limp, and when they turned the next corner, Jack saw Mark and Sophie running to meet them.

"Jack, what's happening?" asked Mark.

"We're under attack, kiddo. And not just from those Russians – from the cult as well."

"What?"

"We don't have much time. Have you seen Mary? Adele?"

"Adele, no."

"But you've seen Mary?" said Tate. "She went looking for you."

"Oh no, did she?" Sophie was choking back tears.

"What is it?"

"There was an explosion," Mark told them. "In the caves. Maybe the soldiers got in down there, I don't know. But... I think she might be..."

Jack shook his head. "No way, not Mary!"

"I didn't get a chance to check, there were men coming up the steps," Mark told him.

"There are men *everywhere*," Sophie added, with a worried frown.

Jack gave Mark the rifle, then placed his hand on the lad's shoulder, squeezing firmly. "Anyone can see which way this is heading. It's *Assault on Precinct 13*, and you've gotta get out of here. Remember what Robert said if things went south."

"But–"

Jack looked at him sternly. "Do it, Mark – that's an order. Get Sophie out, get Tate out. I'll follow when I've checked on Mary and found Adele."

Tate's hand went to his mouth. "Gwen! She's still inside." As soon as he said it, the castle took a hit. The shell punched out the top corner of the building, opposite where they were standing. Mark shielded Sophie from the dust, as Jack and Tate turned their backs on it.

Coughing, Jack spluttered, "I'll find her too, now go!"

"I can't leave her alone, not again."

"*Go!*" repeated Jack, taking off himself.

Sophie and Mark took an arm each and tugged, but the Reverend was still reluctant to leave. Then more soldiers found them, bullets spraying the floor. Mark lifted the rifle, but he'd never fired a gun in his life – hadn't even trained for it. But he'd been taken by surprise and had no bow and arrow with him, no sword or staff. He had no option other than to use the weapon he'd been handed. When he tried to fire it, though, all he got was a click as he pressed the trigger.

Mark looked up and saw several soldiers all aiming their weapons in his and Sophie's direction. This was it. They were dead.

Then, suddenly, he was being relieved of the rifle, and bullets were fired from it. Tate aimed for the men's legs, wounding but not killing them. Mark's jaw dropped, but he didn't have time to ask where the Reverend had learned to use one of those things, nor how his aim was so good. There was another wave of attackers coming, a mixture of Russians and cult members.

Pushing Sophie behind him, Mark laid into the first one, a robed figure who ran at him a machete raised. Mark used his momentum against him, grabbing that arm and breaking it at the elbow. He relieved the screaming cultist of his weapon, just in time to meet a blow from another blade which was heading for Sophie.

Tate, for his part, was still firing at the soldiers – slowing their progress towards the castle. When the rifle ran out of ammo, he picked up his stick again and tackled the closest of the soldiers with self defence moves and well placed blows. When it came to fighting the cultists, though, Tate was still wavering; dangerously so, as Mark had to hack at one of their arms to stop a machete swipe from finding the Reverend's neck.

While he was doing this, his attention divided, Mark felt someone at the side of him. When he turned, a fist glanced across his chin. He stumbled, shocked, snapping out of it just in time to see a bayonet about to be rammed into his chest.

Then the attacking soldier was being struck, with almost as much force as the blow which had taken Mark by surprise. When the soldier looked to see who'd done this, he got a kick in the groin as well. Sophie nodded, as if telling the man to stay down. Mark smiled at her, and she smiled back.

"We've got to get out of here," he called over to Tate. "Before the castle's riddled with them. Jack said he would follow. Reverend? Reverend, we need you!"

Tate still looked like he was going to disagree, then at last relented, and the trio made their way towards the path that seemed to have the least amount of troops flooding it.

CHAPTER TWENTY

His place was with the men.

But his mind was also on the women in danger: Mary (who wasn't dead, no matter what Sophie and Mark had seen), Gwen and Adele.

Her especially.

Since she'd come to the castle, Jack had felt a certain connection with Adele. They'd talked and spent time together. She'd reminded him what it was like to be in the company of an attractive woman. Reminded him there were more things in this world than fighting the bad guys. Just as Mark was protecting Sophie, and Gwen was in Tate's thoughts, Adele was all he could think about. Where she was, if she was all right, how he could get her out of here. She'd said that she'd at last found a home after all that travelling, and now it was being torn down around her. Jesus, she must be terrified.

Jack paused to dispatch a couple of Russians, dropping and rolling along the floor so that he knocked the feet out from

under them; one of his favourite wrestling moves back when
he'd been on the circuit. This was usually the place where he'd
say, "You've just been Jack-Hammered, pal!" but it wasn't the
time for glib remarks. His newfound family was being attacked,
being threatened. Being destroyed. All that did was make Jack
angry. Really angry.

Suddenly, there she was. Adele. Down on the Middle Bailey,
soldiers crowding in on her. It looked like she was trying to
surrender, but they kept on coming. Jack made to get down
there as quickly as possible, but in the end he didn't need to.
Somehow, from somewhere, Adele had acquired a rifle of her
own. She swung this around, shooting the Russians dead.

As Jack watched, he saw two of his men come to her aid –
he recognised them as Wilkes and Ferguson – and she spun
fast, about to blow them away as well. "Adele, no!" he shouted.
"Friendlies!"

She turned to see who was calling, saw it was Jack, then saw
the men were there to help. As he hurried to join her, however,
his attention shifted to an armoured vehicle that had crested the
incline and was now on the Bailey itself.

As Jack stood there, he saw the hatch on top open, and a very
familiar figure clamber out. If his size hadn't given him away,
then his olive skin certainly did. They'd met once before, over a
year ago now. Back then the man had been shot by Bill after Jack
had taken a beating from him. He'd often wondered what would
have happened in a rematch, and it looked like he was about to
find out. Tanek was staring straight at him, and for a second or
two it seemed like he'd only ventured out *because* of Jack. Then
Tanek produced his crossbow and shot a couple of Rangers for
sheer sport.

Grinding his teeth, Jack made it the rest of the way to the
Bailey, hollering as he went: "Come on down, you big ape. We
got unfinished business!"

Tanek grinned, aiming the crossbow at Jack. Then he placed it
on top of the AFV before reaching inside the vehicle. He pulled
out what looked like a large metal spear, about the same size as
Jack's staff.

The olive-skinned man hopped down, and swatted away another one of the castle's fighters with the pike. Jack spun his own staff. There was no way this sadistic sonofabitch was going to get his hands on Adele or the others – he'd personally see to that.

"Come on then, let's see what you got."

"You. Talk. Too. Much," was Tanek's staggered reply, and he rushed Jack, hefting the metal lance high.

Jack blocked the move, his arms juddering with the vibrations of the blow. Christ, the man was strong; his 'death' had done little to change that. He was also as quick as ever, in spite of the limp – given to him, Jack knew, by Mark.

Nevertheless, Jack pushed him backwards, getting in a strike to the stomach with the end of his heavy staff. He might as well have been hitting concrete, because Tanek hardly even flinched.

Okay, thought Jack, *try this.*

He cut to the left and, at the same time, brought the staff up to strike the back of Tanek's neck: the same spot he'd punched Jack the last time they met – signalling the end of the fight. Tanek's pike was up in a flash, not only preventing Jack's blow from landing, but retaliating with one of his own – which caused Jack to roll forward. He came up poised to fight, narrowly avoiding the sharpen end of the spear.

Tanek tried again to impale Jack. As he shifted sideways, Jack noticed more people emerging from the armoured vehicle. First up were two oriental women in skin-tight black leather outfits, carrying lethal-looking swords. They climbed down like spiders navigating a wall. A couple of Jack's men had a go at them with their own swords and soon found out how outclassed they were, the women spinning and twisting as they slashed open necks, arms and thighs. One move from the girl on the right practically sliced some poor fighter's head – a young Ranger called Mundy – clean off.

The women stood ready to protect the next person getting out of the AFV. A figure who, straight away, put on his peaked cap before dropping down. In his long coat and maroon military outfit, it could only be The Tsar himself. Here to oversee the fall of the castle: and The Hooded Man's empire.

If Jack could take him out then –

But he had more pressing issues to deal will. Literally, as Tanek and he clashed weapons, each pushing against the other, neither willing to give ground. Jack's feet slipped a little on the slushy grass, but he dug his heels in, unwilling to let Tanek take an inch.

Although his identical bodyguards were there to protect him, The Tsar was not averse to getting his hands dirty, it seemed. Because Jack saw him take out his own sword: long and curved, Jack had seen its like in movies, but had never seen one being used for real.

The Tsar ran one of the wounded soldiers through, pulling out the blade and admiring the blood dripping from it.

He's just as sadistic as De Falaise... as Tanek, Jack thought, *possibly a fighter in the past, but now prefers the sure-fire kill. I might be able to use that, if I can get close enough.*

Then The Tsar's attention was drawn to Adele and the men flanking her: Jack's men. With the oriental sisters – twins? – in tow, The Tsar glided forward across the Bailey towards them.

Jack had to finish this right now. Had to get across to Adele before she ended up like Mundy.

That was easier said than done, because Tanek wasn't in the mood for quitting. The olive-skinned man flashed his teeth and gave one last shove, but Jack realised what he was doing and decided to give him that inch he wanted. In fact, he could take the whole Middle Bailey if he liked. Without warning, Jack took the pressure off his staff and stepped aside, causing Tanek to lunge forward, struggling to keep upright. As he passed by, Jack gave him a whack across the shoulder blades to help him on his way. Pitching him almost into the side of the steps.

He wasn't completely out of the game, but it would have to do for now.

Jack sprinted across the field, holding the staff horizontally to take out two more Russian soldiers, each end smacking into a face. He was going to be too late to reach Adele, because the twins were already closing in. And although she had a rifle, he knew that they'd still make mincemeat of her. Wilkes and Ferguson lunged forward, their intention to stop the women, but in reality all they could really do was try not to get *themselves* killed.

To begin with they did pretty well, holding their own against the two bodyguards, as fast as they were. And Jack was almost there when the first of them bought it: Wilkes receiving a savage slash to the side that bit into him to a depth of about four or five inches. He looked over at Jack, his eyes pleading as blood poured out of the wound.

"You bitches are gonna to pay for that," Jack promised, holding his staff by the end and swinging it so that it caught one of the bodyguards across the forearm. The shock of this bought him enough time to kick her over onto the ground.

Her sister looked across, and paid the price – as Ferguson got close enough to aim a punch at her head. The Tsar, instead of coming to their aid, pulled back slightly, raising his sword in a defensive stance.

The sister closest to Jack was recovering quickly, getting to her feet and taking a swing at him with her sword, then skirting past and making for Adele. "Where do you think you're goin', huh?" shouted Jack, grabbing her hair and yanking her back.

Ferguson had the drop on the second, raising his sword to bring it down on her. But she'd only been feigning weakness from his punch, and lifted her sword up to meet his, before kicking high and knocking him out of the way. Her path to Adele was now clear. Adele held the rifle up, then cast it to the side, attempting to surrender once more.

Jack dragged the first sister back and, jamming his staff under his arm, wrapped his other one around her neck – in a wrestler's chin lock – forcing her to her knees. "Back away from the little lady, sweetheart, or I'll crush your sister's windpipe." He hoped she could tell from the look on his face that he meant business.

The other bodyguard did as he asked, slowly backing away from the defenceless Adele. "T-Thank you, Jack," the woman called over to him. The look of sheer relief on her face was thanks enough. They weren't out of this yet, though. But as he glanced over, he saw Adele take a handgun out of her coat.

Attagirl, thought Jack.

She pointed it at the other oriental woman, covering her. Then a weird expression passed over Adele's face, a sort of calmness... as she pulled the trigger. Jack was stunned to see her do that, because he didn't think she had it in her. Then again, life on the streets post-virus could do a lot to a person. He expected to see the bodyguard fold up and hit the ground. Instead, she stood there – apparently as surprised as everyone else that she was still alive.

Then he saw it. Behind the woman, just off to the left of her, was Ferguson, who'd been coming up behind, to restrain her. Adele's bullet had put paid to that. Jack's head was spinning. She'd missed and shot Ferguson by accident, clearly not as used to a gun as she appeared. But the wound was slap-bang in the centre of Ferguson's forehead, a million to one shot for a mistake. She'd been *aiming* for him, and she'd hit her target.

Adele turned the gun on Jack. "Now let her go," she told him.

He couldn't take any of this in. "What are you doing, you can't–"

"I said let her go, Jack. Don't make this any more difficult."

Difficult? What was she talking about? Jack looked at the other twin, then at The Tsar. If they hadn't appeared as puzzled as him, he might – just might – have leapt to the conclusion that she was working for their side. An infiltrator. No, that was impossible. Not Adele. She'd just seen the way the wind was blowing, that was all. Had chosen to try and switch sides to save her life. All that time surviving out there alone, you put yourself first. But it didn't have to be that way, he'd show her.

"Let's talk about this. We can still get out of here, you and me. Don't–"

"Shut up," Adele snapped. "I'm not going anywhere with you."

"You're scared, I understand that, but–"

"You understand *nothing!*" she screamed, and this time it wasn't her voice. Not the one she'd spoken with before, anyway. Not the voice of the Adele who'd toured the castle with him, eaten with him as they'd gotten to know each other. This was the voice of a ghost. A voice he knew all too well. "I say again, Jack. Let her go."

For a second he almost did it, purely because he was so astonished. But Jack instinctively held on to his hostage. If he was walking out of here, it was with the Chinese woman as his captive. Not with Adele – or whoever she was – arm in arm, like in some stupid chick flick. Jack should have known better, he'd never had the greatest luck with women. But for her to turn out to be...

There was a sudden pain in his back. He was *forced* to let go of the woman then, because he needed to reach round, lessen the agony there somehow. Agony caused by being struck by something.

The Chinese bodyguard stumbled forward out of his grasp, towards her twin, rubbing her throat. Jack looked over his shoulder and saw Tanek standing there, pike held like a very long club, having just returned the favour of Jack knocking him on his ass.

Another blow and Jack was on his knees, his staff on the floor, kicked out of reach. Adele still had the gun trained on him and he couldn't decide which way would be better to go, a quick shot to the head – like Ferguson – or having Tanek ram that pointed piece of metal through him.

Through his broken heart.

The twins were edging their way towards Adele, and she was watching them out of the corner of her eye. Jack had no doubt that she'd turn the gun on them in a heartbeat if she thought she was in danger.

"Leave her be," Jack heard Tanek say to them. He'd recognised her as well, or at least a part of her. The part that must have come from *him*. The psycho who'd started all this in the first place. The reason they were all here today. As Adele came closer, still holding the gun out straight, Jack could see the same look in her eye now: an insane look. The look of a daughter out for revenge.

Jack gave a sad laugh. "I thought we had something there for a while."

"Oh, please," she said, then spat at him. "You were one of the men who murdered my father! How could I ever have feelings for you other than loathing?"

Jeez, do I have lousy taste in broads or what? Well, it's cost you this time, hasn't it, numbskull?

"Father?" asked The Tsar, now deeming it safe to come closer, though not before his bodyguards joined him again. "You don't mean that–"

Tanek nodded. "She is De Falaise's child." He exchanged a long look with Adele, who smiled. "The person I came here to find."

CHAPTER TWENTY-ONE

They'd been lies, pure and simple.

No two ways about it. Tate had lured her here under false pretences, as she'd told him repeatedly. When the message had reached her about the approaching army, one that apparently made De Falaise's look like a joke, she'd leaped at the opportunity to come to the castle for more weapons. If the soldiers passed through New Hope, then her people would need all the help they could get. It wasn't as if Robert was using them, was it? Gwen had to admit she'd been puzzled as to why they were suddenly going to give them to her, after denying them for so long, but she wasn't about to look a gift horse in the mouth. Telling Andy, Darryl, Graham and the others that she'd be back soon, she'd headed off for Nottingham with Clive Jr.

When she'd driven back through the gates and found the Reverend, he'd stalled her to begin with by offering her food and drink after her journey, then insisted that they should stay at the castle overnight as it was growing late. It was then that she discovered Robert and a good chunk of his men had gone off to meet The Tsar's forces, taking with them only rudimentary weapons.

"He's completely crackers, you do know that?" Gwen told Tate.

The Reverend said nothing, no doubt thinking God would be on the man's side. Oh well, it was his funeral – and it meant that there would be more *real* weapons for her to take back with her (and they'd damned well need them after Robert had finished agitating The Tsar). When she discovered that would not be the case, Gwen went ballistic.

She argued with Tate until she was blue in the face, but he refused to see reason.

"Is this about what happened before?" Gwen asked him. "About how you left me here?"

"I didn't..." Tate began, then bit his tongue. "I wanted to come sooner, but–"

"But you didn't because of Robert, right? Meanwhile that lunatic Frenchman was..." Gwen's eyes hardened, the memories too painful. "You want to help me, salve your conscience? You give me those weapons and let me return right now."

That hadn't happened, of course, and they'd been in the process of discussing it yet again when Mary and Jack had joined them. Apparently the army was coming to the castle. Robert's men had hardly slowed them at all. Tate had screwed up again, and he knew it. Now she and her baby had been placed right in the firing line, when she'd probably have been much safer back home.

There was a part of her that recognised Tate had only been doing what he thought best, that he genuinely did care about her. But he'd deliberately misled her and for that she would never forgive him. If only to protect Clive Jr, she'd done as he'd asked when he'd told her to go and wait in one of the bedrooms, while outside she could hear explosions and gunfire.

Gwen had sat there holding her child, telling him everything was going to be alright, but knowing that it really wasn't. *He's placed you in so much danger, little Clive*, Gwen said to herself, looking down at her son. *What in Heaven's name was he thinking?*

She peeked out of the window, and it was then that it happened. Something hit the side of the castle. The whole room shook and she grabbed Clive Jr, dashing out as quickly as she could. Gwen ran back up along the corridor, desperate to find somewhere safe. She'd brought a machine gun with her in case she'd been attacked on the journey, but that was in her jeep. Luckily, she'd kept her pistol about her person, in spite of the 'rules', which she didn't give a shit about. If Mary could break them just because of some sentimental rubbish, so could she.

Gwen reached around and pulled the gun out, tucked away in the back of her jeans, under her baggy jumper. No sooner had she done so than she heard voices below her, heading up the stairs. Russian voices.

She backed away, but Clive chose that particular moment to start crying. Gwen shushed him, but he cried all the more. She turned to run, only to crash into a figure that appeared in front of her.

The man was wearing dark red robes, a hood pulled up over his head. In his hand he held a lethal-looking blade.

He was not alone. There were two more dressed just like him. Gwen knew who they were. Members of the cult Robert had told Tate about. What they were doing here was another matter. She'd been expecting to see soldiers, not religious fanatics.

It wasn't important. All that mattered was they meant her and her son harm. Gwen raised the handgun. None of them even twitched.

"Don't move!" Gwen warned them.

The first, the closest, raised his hand.

"I said don't you fucking move! I'm not afraid to use this thing." She meant every word. It wasn't like the first time she'd held it, when she'd made her first kill: shooting the bastard who'd murdered her beloved Clive. She'd hesitated then, but she wouldn't now.

It didn't stop the cultist from continuing to raise his hand, peeling back the hood to show her his face, painted to look like a skull, a tattoo on his forehead, the one Robert had described. That fazed her momentarily.

But then the cultist on the right rushed forward, raising his machete. Gwen fired – twice – hitting him in the chest. He dropped to the floor, blood pooling around him.

The taller one, Skullface, looked down slowly at his fallen comrade. But if he was angry or upset by the man's demise he hid it well.

Gwen heard noises behind her. The soldiers! She'd forgotten all about them. And, as she pivoted, she saw uniformed men holding automatics, training them in her direction. Holding Clive Jr in the crook of her arm, she fired the gun with her other hand, causing the little one to cry out even louder. Gwen hit the first soldier in the neck and a red spray jetted powerfully out of the wound.

As Gwen spun round again, aware that she'd taken her eye off the cultists, she saw the man rushing forward, brandishing his machete. It connected with the end of her pistol and sent it flying out of her hand, over the rail of the stairs to fall somewhere below.

Now she was defenceless.

Gwen saw the machete blade rise again. "No, please," she implored. "Spare my son."

The robed figure didn't answer, but Skullface stepped forward, looking down at the crying child she was holding – and he cocked his head.

Yes, that's it. That's right. See Clive Jr as a person. See him as a person who could grow up and have so much potential, who could do so many things in this shitty world we've found ourselves in. So much good. Yes, that's it. See him. Really see him.

Gwen knew it might be the only thing that saved her child.

The lead cultist was staring at Clive Jr, dark eyes fixed on him. But other one was about to finish her off. If Gwen didn't do something now, it would be too late. "No, *please!*" she screamed.

"Wait!" ordered Skullface. "Look."

The machete hung in the air above her like the sword of Damocles. But then, slowly, it began to drop.

Gwen didn't have time to relax, though, because there were more Russian troops suddenly at the top of the stairs.

The cultist pulled Gwen and Clive Jr around, putting himself between them and the guns. Seconds later, she heard the *rat-ta-tat* of automatic weapons, and the man who'd protected them was toppling over, his body riddled with bullets.

Skullface rushed forward, waving his arms for them to stop – which they did, too late for the Morningstar who'd given his life to save them. Gwen looked down at the man, unable to figure out what had just happened. It was one thing for them not to be able to take a mother and child's life – though that still didn't tally with what Robert had said – but it was quite another to protect them from the Russians.

Why would they do that? she asked herself, and would keep asking herself, even as she was taken away.

Taken prisoner again in this castle.

The Tsar surveyed the devastation and laughed.

The battle, if you could even call it that, was over. They had crushed what was left of Hood's 'Merry Men' in less than twenty minutes. It was what they were best at, crashing in and stamping out all resistance. He stooped to pick up one of the arrows that had been used against them, turning it over in his hands. Now this place was his and, he had to admit, it felt good. He was glad he'd listened to Tanek, even to the point of coming over here himself to be involved in the final stages. Back in Russia, his empire was being run by underlings who knew that if they put even the merest hint of a foot wrong, they could kiss their private parts goodbye once he returned victorious from English soil, leaving similarly loyal subjects to rule here in his name.

Which he would, as soon as he had confirmation that Bohuslav had done the same thing to the rest of Hood's forces. Once he knew that The Hooded Man himself was dead. Maybe they'd put his head on a spike outside the castle walls, just as a reminder to others that The Tsar was now the great power in this region. And, in time, the greatest power in this country.

Then, perhaps, once he had more soldiers drafted in from England, and even Europe, they could think about turning their attentions to the US. Their real enemy.

The Tsar waited while his troops brought him progress reports on the mopping up operation, which included disabling Hood's people at the hotel prisons and assessing which of the prisoners might be of use. The twins were, as ever, by his side as he looked down on the grounds below. He'd feared he might lose them during the confrontation with the man with the staff – one of Hood's lackeys named Jack, he was reliably informed (who'd been taken away for Tanek to have his fun with a little later). But they'd been saved by an unexpected new ally.

De Falaise's daughter, who had gone off with Tanek to look for the other members of Hood's inner circle. The Tsar had to admit she was as deadly as she was desirable. When this was all over, he would seal their newfound alliance in the bedroom – in spite of how much that might pain Xue and Ying. Yes, she definitely looked like a woman who would respond well to his particular appetites.

It wasn't long before the pair returned, descending the steps to the Middle Bailey with a prisoner in tow. A woman being held up by a couple of his soldiers.

"There is no sign of the holy man, Tate. Nor of Hood's adopted son Mark and his little girlfriend," Adele said in that accent The Tsar found oh-so sexy. "But your men did manage to dig out this whore from the rubble." She looked at the woman being held up and spat on her. "I thought I'd killed the cow when I blew up the caves."

"Who is she?"

"Hood's woman," Tanek replied.

Hood's woman did not look very well. She was unconscious for a start, her face and arms battered and bruised, blood pouring from several wounds. One of her legs looked severely twisted. If she *was* still alive, then she wouldn't remain that way for long.

"She needs medical attention," Tanek confirmed, "if she is to survive."

"And why would we want her alive?" The Tsar said. "I thought the intention was to kill all those close to Hood, including the ones that you have clearly let escape."

"She might yet prove useful," Tanek retaliated.

"The big man will tell you where the others have fled, will he not?"

"Possibly."

"If your skills are lacking, my friend, then I'm sure Bohuslav will oblige upon his return."

Tanek shot him a contemptuous look. "I was thinking more in terms of leverage... against Hood."

The Tsar laughed. "Hood? I would not worry about him. He will soon be dead, if he isn't already."

"Don't underestimate the man."

"He's right," Adele said, siding with the brute who had once been her father's second. "Not that I want to save her, but I've seen the man fight, my lord."

The Tsar smiled. He liked the way that sounded coming from Adele's lips: *my lord.*

"Nonsense," he said. Then he gazed down and saw people being herded in through the castle's entrance, the first batch of prisoners from the nearby hotel, under armed guard in case they had any stupid ideas about fleeing. "We let her die. Look at her, she is well on her way already. She might even have died as we stood here talking about it."

Tanek looked her up and down and The Tsar was satisfied he'd made his point. Apart from anything else, there weren't many men with medical knowledge amongst his troops. If one of his men was injured, then he was of no use anymore and would either be left to die or shot right there and then. And The Tsar himself relied on Bohuslav to see to his personal health needs. With his detailed knowledge of anatomy, he was better than any doctor. But Bohuslav wasn't here, and even if he was The Tsar wouldn't waste his talents on this whore.

"Sire, sire!" This came from behind and The Tsar whirled around. It was the radio operator from the AFV they'd travelled in. "I have news of the other skirmish."

"Ah, excellent." The Tsar's smile intensified.

"Our... our forces have been..." The Tsar expected the next words out of the man's mouth to be 'successful', but instead the man said quietly: "Defeated."

"*What?*" The Tsar grabbed the messenger by his collar. "Repeat that, man."

"I... They have been defeated, sire."

"You lie!"

The man shook his head. "One of the remaining vehicles just checked in. Commander Bohuslav's."

Remaining vehicles? What the fuck was this cretin talking about? The Tsar had sent enough firepower to lay waste to an entire city. And what did Hood's men have? Sticks and stones! They didn't even fight using guns. How was this possible? Bohuslav. He was to blame. Oh, when he got his sorry hide back here The Tsar would personally punish him.

"He himself is reported to be extremely badly injured," the man blurted out, still petrified. "Near to death, in fact."

"Bohuslav?"

A nod from the mouse he was holding by the throat. The Tsar looked across at Tanek who was not only nodding in an 'I told you so' kind of way, he was also grinning, probably at the thought of Bohuslav's fatal wounds. "Impressive," commented the giant, "even for Hood."

The Tsar shook his man again, tightening his grip.

"They... they suffered heavy losses as well, majesty," he blurted, probably hoping this might spare him The Tsar's wrath, "including The Hooded Man himself."

At this news, The Tsar did let him go. The messenger dropped to the ground, landing on his backside. Without even bothering to get up, he crawled away in case The Tsar should change his mind.

"Not so impressive, after all," The Tsar countered, and forced a smile – though he couldn't help thinking it had taken all those tanks, armoured vehicles and men to bring down that one man.

"Can we be certain he's dead?" This came from Adele.

The Tsar glowered at her. "What is the matter? You seem disappointed."

She shook her head. "It's just that I hoped I might be the one to kill him."

The Tsar nodded, he could understand that. He'd never met the man and he wished he could have done the deed personally. Now they'd both have to settle for recovering the body and putting that head on a pike.

"Those left alive will return to the castle," Tanek said, showing no emotion concerning Hood one way or the other. Perhaps he didn't really believe it.

"But they will not be expecting us to be here. They will return, battered and exhausted, leaderless, demoralised, expecting a warm welcome... only to find guns jammed in their faces instead." It didn't worry The Tsar in the slightest. "We have more than enough men to stand against them, taking into account our new comrades from the cult and these prisoners."

As he waved a hand across to indicate the folk from the hotel, there was a sudden cry from one of them. A female cry. It was coming from a short woman dressed in scrubs, but with a Ranger's jacket on top. "Mary!" She'd broken ranks and was attempting to get to them, resulting in several automatic weapons being trained on her. But she was unarmed, and The Tsar was curious about who she was. He held up a hand to signal the men to hold their fire. She couldn't do much harm with the twins and Tanek standing so close by.

"Mary," cried the woman again, tears in her eyes. "Mary, what have they done to you?"

"And who might you be?" The Tsar asked.

She glared at him before answering. "Lucy Hill."

The Tsar looked across at Adele, who shrugged. She'd obviously not had much contact with this woman who'd been lumped in with the prisoners. Lucy took another step towards Mary, but it was one of the twins – Ying – who stood in her way this time, arms folded.

"Please," said Lucy, the tone of her voice changing from defiant to pathetic, "let me go to her. She's been training me as a nurse and-"

"Oh dear. If only you'd been here ten minutes ago," The Tsar cut in. "We have just learned that we have no further use for her. You see, Hood is dead."

"Robert?" Now the tears ran freely down Lucy's cheeks. "I don't believe you."

"Believe what you like. It is the truth."

Tanek placed a hand on Ying's shoulder, and was lucky the bodyguard didn't cut it clean off. "Let her go to the woman," he said, making it sound more like a command.

"But why?" asked The Tsar. "What purpose would it serve?"

He didn't answer, but that just backed up what The Tsar suspected. Tanek didn't believe Hood was dead either. He sighed and nodded for Ying to let the nurse through. What did it matter to him if Hood's woman was fixed up, only to be executed later? It was their time and energy they were wasting, not his.

Ying moved aside and Lucy went to Mary, immediately checking her over. Tanek moved to join her, but The Tsar was not quite finished with him yet. "I want to know where Hood's closest companions are," he told the giant, "that is your priority."

Tanek gave a brusque tip of his head, then continued on his path. Lucy said something to him The Tsar didn't quite catch, but the next thing he knew Hood's woman was being taken back up to the castle with the nurse accompanying her. Tanek and Adele followed on behind, but took a different route when they reached the steps, heading down instead of up.

"As useful as he has been, I think Bohuslav may have been correct about Tanek. The time is fast approaching when he will have outlived his usefulness. Do you not agree?" The Tsar said to Ying and Xue. The women concurred with silent nods. "And when that time comes, I will call on one of you to do the honours."

They both smiled at this, no doubt remembering the embarrassment of not being able to best Tanek back in Russia.

The Tsar would have smiled himself, were it not for the fact that he might have to give the same instruction about Adele, depending on where her loyalties lay. He hoped she would be sensible and see the benefits of life with him. Who knew, if she behaved herself and lived up to his expectations – in all departments – he might even give her this castle as a present. Call it her inheritance.

In the meantime they at least had something to celebrate.

The Hooded Man was dead. The Tsar was sure of it even if Tanek wasn't.

CHAPTER TWENTY-TWO

The man should be dead.

But instead of getting him back to Mary so she could treat his injuries, Bill had done as Robert requested. Once he'd cleaned up his wounds – stitching up the deep cuts in the shoulder and thigh before applying proper bandages and antiseptic – Bill had taken his former leader to Sherwood, bringing the Gazelle down in the car park of the old visitor's centre.

All the way here, Bill kept glancing over at him, as Robert drifted in and out of consciousness. *One o' these times I'm going to look and 'e won't wake up*, Bill thought. Robert was that bad. It wasn't like he hadn't seen Robert this way before, after an explosion at Mary's farm house. But even then he hadn't looked this ill, this close to the end.

Bill remembered them bringing Robert to camp – Jack carrying the man into his tent, Mary by his side, as she'd been ever since. Days later Bill was flying him into Nottingham for the final battle, where Robert took on the Sheriff alone. He shouldn't have been fit enough then, either. Shouldn't have recovered nearly as quickly as he did, even with Mary's attentions.

They'd been in Sherwood, though, hadn't they? *Robert* had been in Sherwood. So maybe he did have a point after –

Bill dismissed the notion. But he couldn't ignore the fact that the closer they flew to the forest the more Robert seemed to rouse from his stupor. He was muttering something, half dreaming, calling out Mary's name.

"Right, we're here," Bill informed him when the helicopter was down.

Robert lolled to one side. Then he opened his eyes wide and Bill saw him take a good look at the trees, before his eyelids began to flicker again and then close. Bill shook his shoulder gently.

"Let me take you back home, lad."

Robert coughed, then mumbled: "I *am* home." He was clawing at the door, fingers uselessly slipping off the handle.

Bill got out and went round. He opened the door and had to catch Robert as he fell out. "Judas Priest, yer in no fit state t'be goin' anywhere!"

Almost as soon as he'd said the words, he felt Robert stiffening, summoning strength from somewhere, forcing his legs to support him. Robert lifted his arm, pointing in the direction of the forest.

Bill had to half carry him down the path that led to The Major Oak. When they reached that ancient tree, Robert craned his head.

Then, nodding, he shooed away Bill's hands and leaned on the fence that surrounded it.

"Robert, come on. Enough's enough."

"Don't... don't try to... Bill, promise me you'll... stay here... The others... They'll... they'll be arriving soon..."

"What others?" Bill said, fearing he'd lost his mind completely.

"This... this is where it's going to happen... This is where they'll die unless..."

"Yer not makin' any sense, Robert."

"Promise me!" repeated Robert, his voice strengthening.

"Aye, all right. Bugger off, then!"

Robert was already pulling up his hood, and stumbling away, using the fence to keep him upright, then relying on nearby trees as he made his way into the forest. Bill nearly went after him, but something held him back. Something told him to go and wait with the Gazelle, even though he was almost certainly leaving The Hooded Man to die amongst the trees.

And his legend along with him.

They were pushing the horses too hard, even Dale could see that.

But he'd made a promise – and even as he was riding his mount across the next hillside, Dale wondered how Robert was. Robert, who he'd left in that field, bleeding to death but insisting that they go because the castle was – or very soon would be – under attack. Mary was in danger, that was the man's one and only thought, but how exactly was Dale going to explain to her that he'd left the man she loved?

"We'll send back help..."

He'd shouted that as they'd left and he'd meant it. As soon as they'd assessed the situation at the castle, tackled the threat – *and just how exactly are you planning on doing that? Take on another army with your own numbers depleted and no Robert to lead the charge?* – Dale would do it, he'd send medical aid and–

But Lord knows how long all that would take. Robert might be – definitely would be – dead by then. He'd lost a lot of blood from the sickle wounds, had been crippled by that jeep.

Dale squeezed his eyes shut, then opened them again, willing himself not to think about it. But when he closed his eyes all he could see was Robert's mangled body.

Quit it! He's relying on you to get to Mary, Dale. Now, I know you've never cared enough about a woman to sacrifice yourself like that, but it's what Robert's doing. His life for hers. So get on with it, get going, get to the castle!

Azhar was pulling up alongside him, having broken away from the pack behind, and was pointing to the horse he himself was riding; telling Dale what he already knew. Dale stabbed his own finger ahead. They were not stopping. The horses could rest when they arrived.

They had to reach the castle before it was too late.

Even during his days sneaking in and out of towns and cities to gather supplies, Mark had never pulled off a getaway like this one. He still wasn't quite sure how they'd made it out of the castle grounds, let alone Nottingham.

They'd surfaced from the caves out by the Brewhouse Yard, a reversal of what Reverend Tate had done to gain access when De Falaise had been in residence. Tate had a fun time negotiating the steps, but with Mark and Sophie's help he'd got down them okay. Of course there had been men stationed in the Yard, those who'd killed the Ranger guards, but Mark managed to creep up on them and took both out with blows to the head, hitting them with a fallen half-brick he'd picked up on the way.

The jeep had proved trickier, but while Tate and Sophie waited by the gate, he managed to creep up on the driver. Most of the vehicles had already entered the grounds, with some congregating up the top or waiting down side streets because they couldn't get in. They'd been lucky to find this one, very lucky.

Once he'd taken care of the driver, reaching in through the window and landing a well-aimed punch, Mark had climbed in and backed the jeep down to where his companions were hiding.

Sophie pulled the unconscious Russian out of the passenger side, and they'd climbed in, Tate having terrible difficultly getting in until Sophie helped out. That's why they'd had to steal something with wheels, because the Reverend wouldn't have made it half a mile on foot.

Mark had kept the engine idling a good few minutes, however, at the Brewhouse gate, expecting to see Jack come bounding down those steps, Gwen, Adele and Mary with him.

No, not Mary. Mark had seen her, seen what the cave in had done. If she wasn't dead already, she would be when The Tsar's men or the cultists got their hands on her. He gripped the wheel until his knuckles were white.

He'd wiped the tears away, but not before Sophie saw them. She reached across and put a hand on his forearm. "We have to go, Mark."

"Just a couple more minutes."

"Jack's resourceful. He'll find a way to get out, to meet up with us. He wouldn't want us to get captured. Would he, Reverend?"

Tate said nothing, but Mark knew she was right. They should get away, wait for Jack at the rendezvous point.

They had to head for Sherwood.

Mark's driving left something to be desired – having only been behind the wheel a few times before. He'd been too young to drive pre-virus, and Robert and his men went everywhere on horseback. Luckily, Bill had given him a few lessons before leaving. "Never know when it's goin' to come in handy," he'd said, tapping his nose.

Mark hadn't thought about Bill in months, and it was strange that he should do so now. Because, as they pulled in to the car park at Sherwood Forest, who should they see but the man himself, standing next to his helicopter, holding his shotgun as if he'd never been away. He was pointing it at their vehicle, squinting as he tried to make out who was inside.

For a second Mark thought he was actually going to shoot, so he stuck a hand out of the window. Bill kept his gun raised, but when Mark braked and shoved his head out, he smiled, lowering the weapon.

Mark hopped out and ran towards him. "Bill? Is it really you?"

"Aye."

They gave each other a hug as Sophie helped Tate out of the jeep. When the pair came over, Bill greeted them both. "How do?"

"What are you doing at Sherwood?" Mark asked him.

"Long story. Yerself?"

Like Bill, Mark didn't know where to start. He told him about the attack on the castle, and how they'd only managed to get out by the skin of their teeth. They were still hoping that Jack would make it, with Gwen and Adele.

"Well I'll be," said Bill when he'd finished. "It's a good job I didn't take him there then."

"Who?" asked Mark.

"Listen, I'm not goin' to lie to you. The bloke's in a pretty bad way, Mark."

"Who? Who's in a bad way?"

"Robert."

"You're here with Robert?" Tate rubbed his head. "I don't understand."

"Makes four of us, then, I reckon," Bill said. Then he went on to explain how he'd found Robert after the battle, badly injured and not making much sense. "Just kept on insisting we come 'ere."

"Where were the rest of the men?" asked Sophie, and Mark knew by that she probably meant Dale. "They weren't...?"

"Reckon you lost a fair few – bloody insanity goin' up against them things in the first place." He scratched his stubbled chin. "Tho' I will say this much, you lot gave them Russkies a good hidin'. Not sure what happened to the rest. Like I say, Rob wasn't makin' much sense by the time I showed up."

"How long's he been in there?" asked Tate.

"Good few hours. Wanted to fly 'im back to Mary, but... Do y'think she'll get out with Jack, then?"

Marked opened his mouth, then closed it again. He shook his head.

"What? Is the lass all right?"

Sophie suddenly burst into tears, and turned to Mark, pressing her face into his shoulder. Mark hesitated, then wrapped a comforting arm around her. He was having trouble holding back the tears himself. "Bill, we think Mary might be..."

"What?"

"I was the last one to see her. She was... crushed in a cave-in. Happened when The Tsar attacked. I think we've..." Mark sniffed. "I think we've lost her."

"Judas..."

"No," said a voice, so quietly it might have drifted in on the wind. The three of them turned, Bill automatically raising his gun.

There, in front of them, was Robert. Or rather, The Hooded Man: features still obscured by the cowl he wore. He was standing straight, in spite of the bandage on his leg, and when he took another step towards them he was hobbling. But this was nothing like the figure Bill had described.

"Robert?" gasped Mark. He'd come up on them so silently, he'd made all of them start. But then, he was good at that; self-trained in this very place.

"No," Robert continued in those hushed tones, ignoring everything but what had been said about Mary. "She *can't* be."

Bill was staring at Robert in disbelief. Slowly his gun dropped again, but he didn't say anything.

Mark nodded. "I think so. I'm really sorry. Everything happened too fast for me to..." He saw Robert's body stiffen, his back straighten. Then he saw the man's fists clench.

"We have to prepare ourselves," Robert said, his voice strong and sure.

"For what?" Tate asked, but didn't get a reply. Robert had already turned and was walking back towards the visitor's centre. *He* knew what was about to happen, of that Mark was certain – just as certain as he was that the forest had somehow healed Robert (though later Bill would argue that maybe he'd looked worse than he actually was). The forest had shown Robert what would happen, or at least what *might* happen without their intervention.

Mark looked at Sophie, then at Tate and Bill. Their confused faces said it all, but he knew exactly what had to be done.

They'd follow Robert, just like always.

So, as the sky began to grow dark and as a light mist started to roll in from the surrounding fields, they did just that.

Followed the lonely figure into Sherwood.

CHAPTER TWENTY-THREE

Sherwood Forest.

It was the most obvious choice, after all. Deep down Adele knew that's where they would go, because she'd followed them there once before. She knew that's where Robert belonged – if he was still alive (no-one seemed to be able to *confirm* it either way). So it was where Mark, Tate and Sophie would go, too.

They hadn't really needed the torture session with Jack at all: conducted in the smithy, in one of the archways adjoining the stables..

But it had been fun.

Adele – the... what was it Jack had called her just before his interrogation? Oh yes, the *femme fatale*. The pain Jack had experienced at the hands of this master craftsman, this artiste, had sent tingles through her entire body. He hadn't had time to do a complete number on the man, because The Tsar was demanding results, but it had been enough.

In lieu of his usual equipment, Tanek had made full use of the now dead blacksmith's furnace (after all, he wouldn't be needing it, now he was over in the corner riddled with bullets): the tongs, the poker, the red-hot coals spitting in that square metal tray with open sides, the kind they used in the old Hood's day. He hadn't even asked any questions to begin with, just inflicted his agonies on Jack – the screams of the big man so piercing they could be heard throughout the grounds.

Tied to a chair, and naked apart from a pair of boxers, Jack had looked up at Adele and the sense of betrayal on his slick face was incredible. It was like a physical thing, all adding to the torment the ex-wrestler was enduring. Adele knew that he had been starting to fall in love with her, in spite of everything she'd done to show her 'affections' lay elsewhere – or at least her obsession. With Robert. With his downfall. With his death.

Tanek had even let her have a turn with the irons, sweet man that he was. Her father's second, and now her protector. They'd hardly had a chance to talk since meeting earlier that day, but they hadn't really needed to. Tanek recognised her almost immediately, knew that she was from the great man's stock. And that allegiance continued even after Daddy was gone. Murdered by Robert and his followers; including Jack. It brought her great satisfaction to torture the latter, chasing any last doubts from his mind that she might be talked around or turned.

Or be his.

"Y-You... traitorous s-slut," Jack spat through clenched teeth, love turning to hatred.

She studied his face again, then she kissed him – because she knew that would cause more pain than she ever could with the irons. Adele bit his lip as she pulled away, laughing as the blood dribbled down Jack's chin. "Poor, deluded idiot," she said in her true accent, the one she'd been so careful to conceal during her time playing the helpless heroine.

"Where are the others going?" Tanek asked. Maybe he was uncomfortable with the way the session was going. Maybe he was just jealous. Was *he* hers for the taking as well? Adele had already observed the way The Tsar had been looking at her. But his time would come soon enough, she understood that. At some point she and Tanek would rule this army, or rather *she* would – with Tanek by her side. Whether that was as her willing slave, bodyguard or lover – or all three – remained to be seen.

"I saw how this went in *Reservoir Dogs*. Go screw yourself, pal," Jack breathed. That earned him a slap in the face. Adele could still taste the copper in her mouth as she continued to watch Tanek at work; now picking precise spots on Jack's body and hammering in horseshoe nails. It wouldn't kill him, but would deliver the maximum amount of lasting pain. Tanek hammered them home until Jack passed out. Then he threw a bucket of cold water over him.

But they were getting nowhere. "He'll never talk in the time we've got left," Adele said, and Tanek could see that she was right. Given a couple of days, he could get anyone to talk, even someone as loyal as Jack. But The Tsar was breathing down their necks and, like it or not, he called the shots.

"Let me try a different tack." She brushed a finger over one of the nails. "If you'll pardon the pun."

When Jack was awake, Adele ran a sharp fingernail down his cheek. "If you don't tell us where your little friends have gone, we will execute Mary."

Looking at her through a haze of anguish, Jack spluttered, "Don't have her... Mark said..."

"Oh, in spite of my best efforts she's still alive. Just. But how long she stays that way depends on you, my dearest Jack."

"How do I know you're telling the truth?"

She couldn't help but smile at that. "You don't, mon chéri. But you have my word as a De Falaise that she *will* die if you do not co-operate. Now, that really does mean something. That *is* important to me."

He thought about this for a second or two, weighing everything up and coming to the conclusion that if she'd done all this to avenge her father, then she would never take his name in vain.

"Tell us what we need to know," she'd pressed.

So, hanging his head in shame, he did.

She remembered the shame.

The nights lying awake as he snored beside her. Spent, after he'd done whatever he pleased with her. Of all the places the soldiers could have stuck her.

Focus on Clive Jr, not the room. Not the bedroom where De Falaise kept you locked up, where they are keeping you locked up right now.

Gwen screwed her eyes shut, then opened them. It was just a room, just a room in the castle. At least it was on the ground floor, with no chance of rockets hitting the wall. Not that there was any fighting going on anymore. The Tsar's forces had won, swiftly and confidently.

Perhaps he'll be like the Frenchman, her mind whispered. *Do you think* he'll *want to play games, as well? Dress you up and pretend, while you lay there, catatonic?*

Gwen felt sick to her stomach. If Tate was here right now, she might just put her hands around his neck and squeezed. Reverend or no Reverend.

But it could be worse. She was still alive, and so was her son – her one connection to home, to New Hope, to Clive.

Could be in the same state as Mary, she said to herself. Gwen had seen her being carried in, helped by Lucy, the woman who'd assisted when Clive Jr was born. She'd been training as a nurse. And Mary looked like she needed one, looked like she was barely hanging on to life. Gwen had exchanged a brief look with Lucy as they'd passed, and could see pure terror in the woman's eyes. Like she knew it, too. Like she wasn't sure she could pull Mary through.

Gwen had been bundled into the room then, the door locked behind her. As far as she could tell there weren't many other survivors, unless they were being held in different parts of the castle? Perhaps The Tsar had shot them all?

She wondered what might have happened to Jack, Mark, Sophie... and, yes, Tate. She did still care about him, in spite of herself. Were they all dead, or in the same state as Mary?

But the room. *Oh God this room.*

It looked different; had no bed in it for a start and had been turned back into some sort of office. Probably where Robert organised his little missions. Just who did he think he was, appointing himself the guardian of this land, withholding vital things like weapons from people who just wanted to protect themselves? Leading suicide squads of young men to their doom? He was lucky they'd go with him, though she had to admit he had a way of sucking people in. Didn't work on her, of course. Too bloody-minded.

Gwen rocked Clive Jr on her knee. "I won't let anything happen to you, sweetheart. Not while there's still breath in my body."

The door lock clicked and Gwen jumped. She watched as the handle slowly turned. When the door opened she felt a lump rise in her throat.

"Remember me?" said the man standing there.

Gwen said nothing.

"I had to see if it was true, that you were back." He grinned, but it came out more like a leer. A leer that stretched the scar across his jawline tight.

"Jace," she said.

"That's right," he chuckled. "You haven't forgotten me, then?"

How could she? He'd been her means of escape, the guard posted to keep an eye on her. She'd lured him inside, then stolen his clothes and knocked him unconscious with the butt of his own gun.

"But you were–"

"A prisoner? Just like you were back then? Fucking locked away when I hadn't even done nothin'."

Is that what you really believe? Yes, I think it is.

"Well, the new boss around here's letting all of the prisoners free who want to work for him. Good old Tanek vouched for me."

Shit, he's here as well? One big, happy family reunion.

"Hey, it'll be just like the old days, 'cept for the fact you've got a sprog now, eh?"

Gwen stood, holding Clive Jr close to her. "If you go near him, I'll–"

Jace pulled out a pistol and levelled it at her. "You'll what,

Duchess?"

Her eyes were fixed on the gun. Gwen was keenly aware that he'd pull the trigger in a heartbeat. He had a grudge not only against her, but this whole place.

"Now, take it easy and everything will be fine." Jace's eyes were crawling downwards, over the front of her jumper, just as they had that day when she'd deliberately enticed him into the room. He'd been distracted then, the horny little shit, and she'd been able to get the better of him. How was she supposed to do that now, holding Clive Jr and with a handgun pointed at her?

"I seem to recall that you got me to strip off the last time we met. So, how's about we start by you returning the favour."

"Please... My son."

"What about him?"

"You can't, not in front of him."

"Listen, I've been banged up in that fucking hotel jail the best part of a year, bitch. I haven't had any in all that time, so I'm going to make up for it. Just a happy coincidence that it's you, so I can kill two birds with one stone. Now, put him down so you can get on with things."

Gwen closed her eyes out of resignation. It was all happening again, wasn't it? It would happen in this room, just as it had before. But instead of the Sheriff it would be some wet behind the ears young thug. Only she'd changed so much, been *forced* to change. She'd do what he wanted, just until she could get that piece off him. Then she'd fucking well blow his brains out.

"I said *put him down!*" shouted Jace.

Gwen placed Clive Jr in the corner, telling him everything was going to be okay. Then she turned to Jace.

"Make it nice and slow. I don't want to miss nothing." He said.

Swallowing dryly, Gwen took hold of the bottom of her jumper and began to raise it. She took her time, like he said, but was apparently taking *too* long, because Jace jabbed the gun in her direction and told her to get the jumper off. "Now! I want to see."

Gwen pushed her elbow into the hem of the jumper and peeled

it off. It wasn't particularly cold but she shivered anyway, and thanked God she'd worn a bra today. It was the last thing standing between Jace's beady little pig-eyes and her nakedness.

"That too," Jace ordered, indicating the bra. He licked his lips, eyes glued to her chest. With his free hand he began to undo his belt, his trousers swelling where he was growing excited.

Gwen began to walk towards him. "Wouldn't you like to get a closer look, Jace? Maybe touch them?"

He straightened his gun arm and pushed her back. "I'm not falling for that twice. I'm not a moron."

Are you sure about that? thought Gwen. Quick as a flash she flung the jumper at him, knocking the gun sideways and allowing her a clear shot with her foot, to kick him between the legs. Jace managed to twist around, though, and the kick caught him on the thigh.

Angrily, he pushed her back, shrugging the jumper off his gun and pointing it at her again. "Gonna regret that."

Gwen tensed herself, but the shot didn't come. He didn't want to kill his plaything. Instead, he turned the weapon in the direction of Clive Jr.

"No, please. Not my son. I'll do anything."

"You will anyway," Jace reminded her. "Remember what you said to me last time, how was I going to do anything with my 'maggot'? Heh. When I've shut the kid up, I'm going to show you exactly what I can do."

Everything seemed to happen in slow motion. As she flung herself across the room – in an effort to put her body between the bullet and Clive Jr – Gwen noticed every tiny detail. Like the slight pressure on the trigger of the pistol; Jace's forehead crinkling as he concentrated on shooting her boy; the scar along his chin stretched tighter than ever. And the exact moment Jace's expression changed, his face creasing up in pain rather than concentration. At the exact same time a trickle of blood sprang from the corner of his mouth and began its downward journey.

Then there was the flash of metal and Jace was pitching forward, the gun falling from his grasp. He caught her eye as he followed it, dropping first to his knees, before coughing up blood. She knew he was thinking: *Why is this happening to me? I'm not such a bad guy.*

Gwen felt nothing as he collapsed onto the carpet, but she could now see the vicious blow that had caused his death. A long cut across his back, so deep it had probably severed his spinal column. And behind Jace, his attacker. The man she hadn't even seen or heard come in.

He stood there, blade dripping with Jace's blood, the hood he wore obscuring his features. But Gwen knew what he looked like. Knew it was *him*.

Knew that under that hood there was a painted face, a skull . Lifting the machete, he wiped the blood off on the edge of his dark robes.

Frozen in the process of running to Clive Jr, Gwen gaped at him, not comprehending. Skullface had just saved her, and her child.

Clive Jr! Gwen found she could move again and went to her son, gathering him up into her arms. She didn't once take her eyes off the cultist, though.

He had something in his other hand, the one not clutching his huge knife. He tossed it over, and when she held it up she saw it was one of their robes. "Put it on," he said. His voice was flat, robotic, but was she imaging things or was there a hint of humanity in there? (She thought this regardless of the fact this man had just killed someone in cold blood without showing a trace of emotion.) At first Gwen thought he might also be telling her this to cover up her dignity – as she was still standing in only her bra and jeans. Then she realised he had other plans.

"They will be coming for you soon," he stated. "You must leave the castle."

"Who will? The soldiers? Are they going to kill us?" Gwen placed Clive Jr down by her feet a moment while she slipped into the robes.

Skullface, who still hadn't removed his hood, answered: "They are taking you and the other women to the forest."

"What?" Gwen was more confused than ever. Why would they take them to the forest to kill them? And why just the women?

"You are to be bait."

Bait? She still didn't understand... unless Robert had returned to Sherwood? But then surely they'd take just Mary? Gwen cast her mind back to the hostages that had been on the gallows when De Falaise had been at the castle – Robert had been willing to come into the castle grounds alone to save them. Perhaps they were banking on him coming out because they had some of his closest friends? Closest female friends? The sexist shits.

It still didn't explain why this guy was helping her escape, why he'd stopped Jace from attacking them. From attacking Clive Jr...

"Why?" she asked as she scooped up Clive Jr again, joining the cultist at the door. "Why are you doing this for us? For him?"

"He must be kept safe," said the man in that monotone voice, tinged with the slightest hint of compassion. "Hide him under your robes."

Gwen did as she was told, covering Clive Jr as much as she could, before pulling up the hood to conceal her features. Their saviour led them out of the office and into the castle, where other robed figures were waiting.

She didn't have much option but to go with them, especially as they were able to move freely. Where they were taking her, she had no idea, but Gwen began to hope again.

For her there was *always* New Hope.

CHAPTER TWENTY-FOUR

It was already dark by the time they arrived, and they hit the mist about a mile outside Sherwood. The moon was on the horizon and Tanek recognised its red tinge instantly. He knew all too well what they called it.

Fog lamps kicked in and allowed the drivers of the armoured vehicles to see roughly a car's distance ahead of them. They'd brought three AFVs – a couple being Armoured Personnel Carriers, while theirs was a cannon-wielding BTR-90 – and a couple of jeeps. All they'd need to tackle a few fugitives.

Tanek rode with The Tsar and the twins. The Tsar had insisted on coming along personally, he'd said because he didn't want Hood and his men escaping this time. Tanek suspected it was more to do with keeping an eye on *him*. They were coming to a parting of the ways, anyone could see that, but it was fine. The Tsar and his men had played their part. Tanek was based back in Nottingham again. And, by a twist of fate, even that dolt Bohuslav was out of the picture. Which meant, if Tanek was to take control of this operation, he would only have to deal with the twins.

Only.

He remembered how adept they were. How skilled with those swords. One at a time, maybe. But when they worked as a pair, they were lethal.

Actually, everyone being in the same place, at the same time, might work to his advantage. If they were killed, he could blame the renegades – after killing them as well, plus any witnesses among The Tsar's men. Wouldn't be easy, but he'd pulled trickier things off.

Then he and Adele would have a little chat about how to move forwards. He could see her mind ticking over about what would happen once The Tsar was no longer in command. Ultimately Tanek thought she'd make a fine leader. *Eventually.* He'd already seen shades of his old master in her, especially the cruelty she'd displayed when torturing that scum, Jack. But she needed guidance. De Falaise had asked him to look after her, and he would. She'd take the reins only when he deemed she was ready.

She caught his eye as he was thinking this and smiled. Adele had come along as well because: "None of them know the truth about me. I can be another hostage." Along with a virtually unconscious Mary and the nurse, who'd managed to stabilise Hood's woman and splint her leg. The Tsar had at least told him he was right to keep her alive, because in spite of the fact Hood was dead – and Tanek still wasn't entirely convinced about that – the others would still surrender if their leader's woman was threatened.

Tanek had also been told that Gwen had been captured, and he'd ordered someone to go fetch her because she had a link to the holy man. Worryingly, they'd only found the body of ex-prisoner Jace in the room where she was being held. The grounds had quickly been searched, but there was no sign of her. Tanek wasn't surprised, not after the way she'd behaved on the day of the hangings. It really wasn't that much of an issue – just another loose end to tie up at a later point, like finishing off

Jack – but it irked Tanek all the same. She had been De Falaise's woman, so it was a matter of principle.

"How long until we are there?" Tanek heard The Tsar shout to the driver.

"We are almost at Sherwood, sire," came the reply.

The Tsar nodded, satisfied. "You see? Russian efficiency. We have made excellent time."

"We should have waited until the morning," Tanek replied. Night had fallen and now there was this mist. If the trees didn't provide cover enough, then both of those would. Except the plan was not to go *into* the forest – which would be suicide even at the best of times – but to force them to come out.

"And allow them to move on? We suspect they are here, right now. Why give them the opportunity to slip through our fingers again?" That last one was another dig at Tanek, even though he'd been busy dealing with Jack at the time of their escape.

"They won't leave Sherwood yet. It is where Hood will come when–"

"Hood? Hood again. Tanek, the man is dead. Will you not get that through your thick skull!"

One more crack like that and I will reach over and crush your windpipe, thought Tanek.

"Then we should have waited because of Hood's men. They will almost certainly try to regain the castle."

The Tsar waved a hand. "And do what? Shoot their little bows and arrows at my men?"

"It's what they did to Bohuslav's troops," Tanek retorted. It didn't do to underestimate Hood or his men, as they'd found out to their cost in the past. Tanek had a grudging admiration for the man, which he knew De Falaise would understand. It wouldn't stop him obliterating all of his followers, or indeed The Hooded Man himself if he still existed. Tanek had made a promise to avenge the man he had followed, not because of his lures of power, but because he had a vision. A vision which might yet be a reality.

Before The Tsar had a chance to say anything more, the driver informed them that they were pulling into the visitor centre's car park. It was empty, which Tanek knew didn't prove a thing. Any transportation the fugitives might have used would have been moved by now; that's if they'd even entered the forest from here in the first place. Sherwood was a big area, but Adele seemed to think this would be the best spot having followed Hood before.

"Turn the spotlights on," ordered The Tsar. The vehicles formed a rough semi-circle and trained their beams on the area just ahead of them, breaking through the mist. "This is where we will get their attention, yes?"

Armed men were already filling up the lit area, standing guard by the vehicles, and a rap on their AFV told them they were ready for Adele. Tanek opened up the hatch and climbed out, dragging Adele with him; the crossbow he was carrying pointing at her temple. They had to make this look realistic.

From another AFV came the small nurse and Mary. The latter was being carried by two soldiers, still pretty much out of it. The left leg of her jeans was ripped, the broken limb beneath kept straight between two pieces of wood. Her face was a mess, right eye swelled and black from bruising, but the nurse had managed to clean her up somewhat. There were plasters covering the wounds on her cheek and forehead, the edges of stitches poking out from beneath. She lolled between the two men as they dragged her along. Then they dumped her on the ground in the middle of the spotlights. When the nurse shouted something at them, she got a backhanded slap for her trouble.

"I am addressing the deserters who fled like cowards from Nottingham Castle," came The Tsar's address through the loud-speaker attached to his vehicle. "We are holding three of your friends in the entrance to Sherwood and *will* kill them one by one unless you surrender yourselves to us. You have one quarter hour to comply and then the first is dead."

Anyone on this side of the forest should have heard that, it had certainly been loud enough. Depending on where they were it should also give them enough time to reach the car park, unless they were deep into the trees. If they couldn't get there in time? Well, too bad. They'd execute the nurse.

Tanek scanned the edge of the mist for any movement. There

was nothing. So they waited.

When they'd been there almost ten minutes, The Tsar repeated his demands. Tanek looked at his watch. They were running out of time.

"We need to get Mary back inside!" said the nurse. "She's freezing out here."

"No one is going anywhere," Tanek told her, turning the crossbow on the woman.

His reward was a glower, but she stayed put.

Come on, Tanek said to himself. *Where are you? Make your move.*

Then someone stepped out of the mist. A figure wearing a hood, carrying a bow. On the ground, he saw Mary stir.

Tanek grinned to himself, not just because he could picture The Tsar's face in the AFV – and imagine him having to swallow his words – but also because he would now get the opportunity to kill Hood himself.

The Tsar's voice came over the speaker. "So, you *are* still alive after all? Then I will have your head for what you did this morning!"

Shots rang out, and before Tanek could tell them that The Hooded Man was *his* prize, bullets from one of the soldiers guarding Mary and the nurse peppered Hood's torso. He sank heavily to the ground. If he hadn't been dead before, then he certainly was now. Tanek swore under his breath and, turning, shot the offending guard with his crossbow. "He was *mine!*"

As he was turning back to the scene, though, Tanek's mouth fell open. Hood had climbed to his feet, bow and arrow poised. Adele stared in amazement too. What was he, indestructible? A ghost? He certainly looked the part with that mist swirling around him.

They'd hardly had time to recover from this when another figure stepped out of the fog on their right. This one also wearing a hood and carrying the same weapons.

Seconds later, there was another on their left. It was almost as if the man had cloned himself.

Tanek frowned. One of these *had* to be the real Hood – he'd just kill them all! With his bare hands if necessary.

Before he could do anything, arrows were fired into the circle from somewhere beyond the trio. They took out the spotlights on the lead vehicle, then the others.

"Shoot!" Tanek ordered. But, glancing around, he saw that a good number of the soldiers were already on the floor, unconscious. They'd been silently put out of commission by someone while their attention had been focused elsewhere.

Then he saw the culprit. Yet another hooded figure jumped from the top of an AFV, down into the small group guarding the hostages. He was dispatching soldiers with a sword, incapacitating them before they could get a shot off – slashing two across the face, then burying the end in another's shoulder before Tanek could blink. Once he had, Tanek raised his crossbow and fired.

The man stepped sideways, letting the bolt bounce off the metal of the AFV. He took out a knife and threw it at Tanek, where it embedded itself in his right arm. He immediately lost his grip on the crossbow.

More lights were put out, forcing the scarlet moon above to work harder. Everything was taking on a crimson shade.

The remainder of The Tsar's soldiers were climbing out of their vehicles, but were being picked off by the three Hoods who'd come out of the mist; moving forward and firing all the time. Weirdly, one was not using a bow and arrow, but instead had a shotgun.

Meanwhile, the Hood with the sword was helping the nurse get Mary to her feet – the gentle way he was holding the injured woman speaking volumes.

"Robert," said Adele.

Tanek indicated that the women should move off into the mist, where another figure had appeared; a fat, bald man. The mystery arrow firer, Tate.

Tanek pulled the knife out of his arm, wincing only slightly. He felt pain, just didn't show it, he never did. As the Hood who'd thrown it – the original, of that he was certain – came towards him, he grabbed Adele and put the knife against her throat.

"Tell them to put down their weapons. Or *I'll* put it to use."

Hood paused. "Go ahead."

Adele looked from Tanek to Hood. "How can you say that?"

"Because you're *his* daughter! The Sheriff's!" growled Robert. "Because you deserve the same as he got."

"Take cover," Tanek said to Adele and let her go. There was no point pretending any more. The only two hostages worth anything were getting away. But perhaps he could do something about that. Turning the knife around, he threw it at the escaping females. He had been aiming for Hood's pet, to put her out of her misery, but the nurse saw what was about to happen over her shoulder and positioned herself in the way. The blade slid easily into her back and she slumped forwards, falling on top of Mary.

Good enough, thought Tanek.

All around them The Tsar's men were falling – even those able to get off a round or two. The replica Hoods had revealed themselves now, hunting coats flapping open to show bullet-proof vests beneath. The first was the boy Mark, the other a girl Tanek had never seen before. Next, the farmer who'd shot him over a year ago.

Oh, there were many here who needed to be taught a lesson.

But first: Hood. He was coming towards him – was that a limp? – sword high, enraged at the attack on the nurse. Tanek braced himself to grab the man's forearm when he made his first swing. As it turned out, he didn't need to.

Hood's blow was blocked by another sword. One of the twins had eschewed the protection of the AFV, leaving her sister behind to guard The Tsar. Hood seemed taken aback, but not as much as when she lifted her leg and kicked him squarely in the chest. He flopped against the AFV, then slid down it.

Maybe I won't kill her so quickly after all, thought Tanek, in spite of the fact he knew she hadn't done it to save him, but rather in an effort to halt Hood's progress towards her precious Tsar. *She can keep him busy while I see to other matters.*

An arrow whizzed past him and he remembered there were still four of Hood's people out there. Picking up his crossbow and switching it to the other hand, he fired at the girl. It didn't matter if he killed *her* quickly, because it was the other two he really wanted to savour.

The boy dived across and pushed her out of the way, ending up taking the bolt in the thigh. At first Tanek was mad, but then he realised it was poetic justice. Payback for the bolt the boy had shot into his calf the last time they'd met.

"Oi!" came a call just off to his right. "Remember me?" It was the other one. The fucking farmer.

"Oh yes," said Tanek.

"Then you remember this, dontcha," the farmer raised his shotgun and let off a blast.

Not this time, my friend. Tanek ducked sideways to escape the shell's bite. "And you will remember this," he said, firing a bolt at his enemy. It hit the man's gun hand, nicking the back but not penetrating. Nevertheless, this was enough to cause him to drop his weapon.

Tanek was up and running towards him moments later, issuing a terrifying, bloodcurdling roar. He put his head down and rammed the farmer, lifting him up into the air and launching him backwards.

This, thought Tanek, *is going to be fun.*

Robert moved just in time to avoid the blade, which clanked off the side of the AFV. Dammit, she was fast.

Here was he thinking that the difficult part had been creeping up and fixing The Tsar's men while Mark, Sophie and Bill created their little diversion. Or getting Mary to safety... except she wasn't yet, was she?

Mary.

Words couldn't describe how he'd felt seeing her alive. He thought the dream was coming true (*it might still,* he reminded himself, *all of them dead; Jack probably dead already*). He wasn't going to let that happen, even if he wasn't quite back to full strength – and how he'd recovered so quickly was still something Robert didn't want to question.

He recognised the woman fighting him from the dream. One of The Tsar's bodyguards. But *only* one, which begged the question where was the other? Would she attack when he least expected it?

Robert silenced the thoughts – he needed to concentrate, to keep dodging this twin's swipes. Over her shoulder he saw Tanek shoot Mark and go after Bill. If he could get rid of the bodyguard, he might be able to help them.

This time he met her sword with his and it sent shockwaves up his arm, across his chest and into his bad shoulder – strapped up under his coat and bullet-proof vest. He groaned, and this seemed to spur the woman on. She beat at his sword, hacking it like a woodsman chopping at a tree. Each time the pain was tremendous.

Robert waited for her to do it again, then pushed forwards, hooking their hilts together and headbutting her. He tried to wrench the sword from her grasp while she was dazed, but it took her seconds to recover and she disentangled the swords with practised ease. He was woefully outclassed. Here was someone who'd spent years studying with this weapon, while Robert – in spite of this coming naturally to him – had only been using his a little over a year. Good enough to tackle machete-wielding cultists, but out of his depth with a true professional. He had to get that thing away from her before she–

Another swipe, this one slashing his combats, almost cutting into his good leg. He was just about managing on it, but if she wounded that one as well...

Spinning round, she came at him again. No respite, no pause for breath. Robert found himself being forced backwards, losing ground. He couldn't hold her off much longer.

Suddenly, she drooped. Something had struck her from behind and when she fell to the side Robert saw what it was. Tate had bashed her over the head with his walking stick, the hard wood still wet with her blood.

"Now Robert!" For a moment he thought the Reverend was advocating killing this woman, but Tate quickly clarified: "*Disarm* her, now!"

Robert brought down the hilt of his sword on her clenched fist, which opened like a sprung trap.

A thought struck him. If the Reverend was here, then who was watching Mary? Robert searched for her, zeroing in on the spot where Lucy had been murdered, brought down on top of Mary. Tate had at least managed to pull Mary out from under the dead woman, but now Robert saw Adele approaching her. And she had a gun. One of Mary's Peacekeepers in fact.

Shit! He began to go after De Falaise's daughter, but before he could move, he felt a presence behind him – vaguely heard Tate's warning cry of, "Look out." He instinctively knew the other twin was there, that she'd come to save her sister. That she was bringing down her blade on his blind spot.

About to cut into the side of his neck and deliver her master The Hooded Man's head.

Mary!

She heard the voice but it was dull, muffled.

Mary, you're in big trouble again. Even worse than before! Mary, you have to wake up. Have to get up! She's coming for you!

She would have asked her brother who, but Mary didn't care. Her whole body was numb, either from the cold or because of the last thing she really remembered: things, heavy things, falling on her.

Adele, David told her, *the harpy who did that to you. She's on her way over here with Dad's pistol – your pistol! – and she's going to finish the job. Mary! Mary, PLEASE!*

She told him to leave her alone. The blackness was calling again, regardless of the fact she thought she'd seen a glimpse of Robert.

David wouldn't leave her alone.

Mary, Mary, Mary, Mary. On and on like a stuck record, telling her that she was in danger, telling her that she was going to die. (Funny, she thought she had already.) Telling her that Adele was coming.

Adele.

That's right. The one who was all over Robert, who led Jack

*on. Who tricked you all, Moo-Moo. Lucy's already dead, she died
trying to save you.*

Lucy? No...

*Finally, an answer. Hallelujah! Now look, Adele's coming, so
you have to do something or Lucy will have died for nothing!*

But I can't move, David. I was blown up!

You can *move, it's just that you're telling yourself you can't.
You're giving up Moo-Moo, and if there's one thing I never
thought you were it's a quitter.*

It's so hard. *Too* hard.

*Bull. Get up Mary. Get up, or you'll just prove Dad right. He
always said that you could never do a man's job, that you were
weak.*

Mary felt her hand twitch.

*Do you think that's what Robert thinks, as well? Does he think
you're weak, not up to being by his side?*

Mary's fingers began to curl.

He thinks you're a: "Useless wretch. Look at you. This will
almost be a mercy killing, like putting down an animal." The
rhythm of the words, the accent, changed halfway through.
Suddenly Mary was listening to Adele. The woman was pretty
close – close enough to fire at any moment – but she obviously
wanted to vent first. "You were there, weren't you? When my
father's life was cut short. You were partly responsible. You and
that bastard who sleeps with dogs. Flea-ridden dogs like you!"

Mary's fingers balled into a fist.

"But both will die. First you, and how fitting it should be by
your own weapon. Then him. If there is anything left after The
Tsar's bodyguard has finished."

"Robert..." Mary gargled.

"What was that? Are you trying to speak? Are you begging me
for your life, Mary? Is that it?"

Mary said something else that was unintelligible.

"I did not catch that. You will have to beg louder." The voice
was close now. *Very* close.

Mary lashed out with her fist, connecting with the soft flesh
that could only be Adele's cheek. She heard a surprised shriek,

then a bang close to her ear as the Peacekeeper went off. There was a ringing in her head, but she said the words again, louder, not knowing or caring whether they were heard: "I said, shut your filthy mouth or... or I'll shut it for you!"

Then she opened her eyes.

It hurt like nothing he'd ever felt before. Not even having his little finger cut off compared.

Because that was quick, over in a flash and although the pain lingered, it dulled to a throb eventually. This? This was different. Every time he moved his leg it felt like someone sticking a knife into it. Not a knife. A giant splinter. Mark hissed through his teeth as he shifted position and the bolt in his thigh moved again.

"Oh my God, Mark. Shall I pull it out?" asked Sophie, squatting next to him.

Mark didn't know. Were you supposed to pull them out? Would he bleed to death if she did that? Mary would know, but... Mary was out of it at the moment. *Better than dead*, he reminded himself, as he'd told Robert she was. Imagine, thinking the woman you loved was–

That's why Mark acted when he saw Tanek pointing his crossbow at her. The same reason he'd protected Sophie back at the castle, and even when they'd first met. At least he'd had a chance to tell her. At least if they bought it, she knew. He looked into her eyes. Now she was *really* looking at him, and all the panic, the fear he saw in her eyes was gone. He saw only one thing. One thing that made him *want* to fight. That made him want to survive this and keep Sophie safe.

"Awwwwwgghhhh!" he cried out, the moment broken.

The bolt was being pulled, and he thought, to begin with, it was Sophie going ahead with the makeshift operation regardless. When Mark looked down, he realised his mistake.

There was Tanek, not only pulling, but twisting the bolt then shoving it back in. "How does it feel, boy? What you did to me?"

It felt bad, really bad. Not because of the pain, or because he'd shot Tanek back on that platform. Mark was actually regretting not being a better aim, not having another chance.

Tanek didn't look like he was going to give it to him. The big man had finishing playing with the bolt, and had slung his crossbow over his shoulder. He grabbed Mark by the scruff of the neck, dragging him round and hoisting him up.

Mark felt like he was on a very small, very intimate fairground ride – Tanek whirling him around like he weighed nothing. He lashed out, his fist catching the side of Tanek's head, but Mark suspected it probably hurt him more than it did the giant. Where was Jack when you needed him?

As if reading his mind, Tanek suddenly said: "First you, then the farmer... Nostalgic. Pity your tall friend is not here, but I think I broke him during our torture session."

Having been on the receiving end of one of those, Mark could well understand how. So, on top of everything else, he was worried about what this sadist had done to Jack.

"Now, boy, I break *you*."

Tanek lifted Mark up sideways, facing the sky. Although he couldn't see it, he knew Tanek had also lifted his knee, in preparation for dropping Mark across it. A thigh wound he might be able to get over, but a broken back? No chance.

"Yah!" Tanek let out, and Mark thought it was a cry of victory before letting him fall. Yep, he was being dropped, sharply, and Mark braced himself for the impact... which never came. Instead, his whole body fell and smacked flat against the concrete of the car park. It winded him, but at least he could still move.

For some reason Tanek had let him go. As Mark raised his eyes he saw the figure of Sophie on the giant's back, riding him like he was giving her a piggy-back.

She was clawed the sides of his head, raking his eyes with her nails. Tanek shouted again, "*Gah!*" Mark bet it was the closest they'd ever get to hearing him scream.

He was reaching up to grab Sophie's wrists, to prevent her from doing any more damage, but she was holding on like a rodeo rider. Desperate to keep Tanek away from Mark.

Saving *him*.

Though it was complete agony, Robert hefted his sword aloft, threatening to tear the rough stitches in his shoulder wound.

But he caught the other twin's blade just in time. Robert twirled, still locked with her blade, but she did the same and disconnected them. Then she took a swipe at his midriff, which Robert only just stepped away from. She was definitely pissed at their treatment of her sister. So much so that she'd left her master's side to come to her aid, probably fearing Robert would kill the sibling. It was no more than she deserved, but only as a last resort.

Probably should have, though, he thought when he saw the first twin getting up again. Not only that, but retrieving the sword and turning this on Tate. He blocked it with his stick, which was just about thick enough to take it – but splintered nevertheless.

They had to end this, and quickly, before either he or Tate wound up being skewered.

Meeting the blows of this twin's sword which, if anything, were harder than her sister's, Robert tried to manoeuvre her around. He hoped Tate could see what he was trying to do, but didn't have time to make sure. He was too busy trying to keep himself alive.

Clang, clang. Robert blocked another swing. *Clang!* And another. He couldn't keep it up for much longer.

He felt something press against his back. "Reverend, time for evil to face itself again."

"Agreed," panted Tate.

"On three... One..." Robert lashed out at the twin in front of him, expecting Tate to do the same on his side. "Two..."

"Three!" shouted Tate.

Robert dived to the left – he had no idea whether Tate was going that way or the other. It didn't really matter. The result was the same. Both twins had gone in for the kill, lunging in retaliation to Robert and Tate's swipes. Their blades entered each other at the same time – the one Robert was fighting taking hers slightly higher than her sister, just beneath the ribcage. They remained like that for a moment or two, eyes wide, staring at each other. Perhaps they couldn't believe they'd been caught out by such a simple trick. Or perhaps they were relieved they'd die together?

Simultaneously, both pulled their swords out. And, simultaneously, they fell.

Robert looked over to where Tate lay. The Reverend nodded that he was all right. Switching his attention to what was happening in front of him, Robert spotted that Mark and Sophie needed help. But his main priority was Mary.

He gestured for Tate to help with Tanek, while he made for Mary and Adele... even as he heard the Peacekeeper go off.

Robert feared he might already be too late.

CHAPTER TWENTY-FIVE

From his position inside the AFV, The Tsar had witnessed everything.

The death of his men, the execution of his precious Xue and Ying, killed by their own hands. He'd warned Xue not to follow her sister. Now they were both dead, and who would protect him?

You've spent too long letting people do that anyway, he told himself. Why, even now he was hiding inside this hulking metal beast while others fought. What had happened to the warrior who'd fought in Afghanistan? Who'd been one of the Mafia's most dangerous men? Who'd gone onto the streets armed only with a pistol and machine gun (all right, a fucking huge PK machine gun!) and built his own kingdom from the ground up? Was *he* hiding inside The Tsar?

If so, he wasn't coming out right at that moment. Ordering his driver to put the AFV into reverse, The Tsar set about giving the players in this little drama a leaving present. There was nobody left out there he cared about. Even the woman Adele was a delight he would have to do without savouring. She would probably have remained loyal to Tanek anyway.

The Tsar could still remember how to load up a shell.

He would blast them all to high heaven, then return to the castle where the rest of his army was waiting.

It was a grand plan, sure to succeed.

Bill shook himself.

It felt like a rhino had hit him at full speed, throwing him up and over into the trees. For a few seconds he'd flown without the aid of his helicopter. Might even have broken some ribs if it wasn't for one of those vests Robert had given him. That Tanek was as strong as he was fast, and he was mad as hell. Hardly surprising seeing as they were responsible for almost killing him.

Bill tottered to his feet. He felt like he was still in the air, unable to feel the ground beneath him. His hand was killing him, but he bit back the pain. Thank God the bolt had grazed it rather than going through. He started walking in the direction he'd come from. Bill picked up pace when he reached the edge of the mist and saw what was going on with Mark and Sophie. Tate looked like he was coming to help, but it'd probably take all of them to bring down Tanek. Even then it wouldn't be a walk over.

He spotted his discarded shotgun and snatched it up. Bill raised the weapon, hoping to get a clear shot at Tanek. But the big man kept dancing round, desperate to dislodge Sophie from his back. Bill couldn't chance hitting her by mistake.

By the time he reached them, Tate was already there – and had delivered a blow to Tanek's stomach with his stick that should have doubled him over.

Tate nodded a welcome to Bill as he joined him, and they both set about attacking Tanek. Tate with the stick, Bill with the butt of his rifle. He jabbed the man in the places he thought might hurt the most – including a wound on his upper arm that was still bleeding.

At last, Tanek managed to get a grip on Sophie, bending forwards and throwing her over his head to land in a heap on the floor. He was about to stamp on her, when Mark crawled between them and caught Tanek's foot.

Grimacing, he pushed and, with the help of Tate and Bill's battering, the giant was toppled. Bill swiftly struck him in the face with the butt of his shotgun. "Ram me, would ye!"

Tanek took the beating and more, holding up his huge forearms to protect himself. Then he reached up to swat away the annoyances. He grabbed Tate's stick and shoved, knocking the holy man over backwards. Then he rose and took hold of Bill by the throat, squeezing hard as he got first one knee beneath him, then both legs.

"Now, I finish this," he said, his face only inches from Bill's. So near he could smell the big man's fetid breath.

It was then they both heard a whistling sound from close by.

Robert was on his way to help Mary.

Not that she needed it. Somehow, she'd come to, and was grappling with Adele. Mary was trying to wrestle the Peacekeeper out of the short-haired woman's grasp. And, as Robert watched, Mary punched her in the face. Hard. He recognised that look, Mary was furious. Enough to spur her on, tackling the person who'd been a thorn in her side since day one.

Then came the noise. The sound of one of the armoured vehicles backing up, its eight wheels spinning, creating smoke that was soon lost in the mist.

So someone is still inside one of those things. Has to be The Tsar!

Robert saw that the cannon on top was swinging in their direction. The mad Russian was going to fire; obliterate him and his core group in one decisive stroke. Robert guessed Tanek and Adele didn't mean a thing compared to a win like that. Anxiously, he looked from Mary to the AFV.

He started after the vehicle, running as best he could with a leg that was far from healed. The AFV was reversing, backing into the mist. But it thudded into the hidden wooden dividing posts on the left-hand side of the entrance, where it juddered to a halt.

At the point of collision the cannon spat its load. Robert dropped to the ground. All he could do was watch as the shell flew overhead, whistling as it went. But the cannon's aim had been spoiled by the prang, and it flew over the top of the group. It cut through the mist, and exploded somewhere off in the trees beyond. But it was enough to blow those who weren't already on the ground off their feet, dust mixing with the mist coming in from the forest.

He had no time to check whether Mary, or indeed any of the others, were okay, because the hatch of the AFV was opening. A soldier, probably the driver, was climbing out. Or rather, was being *pushed* out. He was armed with a pistol, and began shooting in Robert's direction. Robert rolled over, bringing his sword close to his body. The bullets made a *ping* as they ricocheted off the concrete. Robert glanced up and saw another figure climbing after the first. The Tsar, using the driver to cover his own escape.

Robert swore loudly, then got up on one knee. Bullets came again and he rolled, sideways this time, so that he would end up underneath the AFV – out of the driver's range.

He waited under there, knowing the man would come down eventually, knowing that he would have been issued with precise orders to finish off The Hooded Man. Robert was only one guy, after all, and he had no gun. Sure enough, he saw two boots drop to the ground and the driver bent, shoving his pistol underneath.

Robert prodded his sword through the gap in the tyres, feeling the now familiar resistance of flesh against tip. There was a grunt. The gun went off, but it was already falling from the man's hands. He fell to the ground, clutching at his wound.

Robert scrambled back out, catching sight of a shadow disappearing into the mist off to his left.

He got up and, as quickly as he was able, gave chase.

The blast from the shell caught them all off guard.

Tanek let Bill go as they were both blown over – black smoke from the flames covering them along with the mist. From the far off hint of yellow and red, Tanek could see that the forest was on fire, or at least this part of it. Tanek coughed, then immediately surveyed the area to assess the situation. Hood's people were already stirring, as was Mary. Adele was laying motionless a little way from Hood's woman.

It was time to retreat.

The whole thing had gone to shit and he needed to get De Falaise's daughter to safety. He'd promised. Tanek got up, kicking the farmer across the face and grabbing his crossbow as he made his way to Adele.

"Time to leave," he told her, taking her by the arm and lifting her to her feet. She didn't complain, a ripe bruise flowering on her chin and eye. It seemed that Hood's woman still had some fight in her after all.

Tanek pulled Adele towards a jeep which had one working headlight. But, just as they were about to climb in, the sound of gunfire came from somewhere across the way – from the direction the shell had originated. Somebody was being shot at. Tanek hoped it was Hood.

Adele slumped forward, hanging heavily in his arms. She was staring up at him, as if shocked. When Tanek shifted his position to help her into the vehicle, he felt the wetness at her back.

More shots – only these were closer, in tandem with the others. Tanek traced them back to Mary, who was sitting upright, holding one arm with her other hand and shooting the Peacekeeper. Once the gun was empty she slumped – only having enough energy to perform that one, last act.

Adele was bleeding heavily from the wound in her back. Tanek lifted her into the vehicle and ran round to the driver's side. Gunning the engine, he pulled the jeep round and retreated, urging Adele to stay awake, telling her he'd get her back to the castle, get her fixed up.

"Hold on," he kept repeating as he drove past the stuck AFV and back onto the main road, cutting a swathe through the fog. He knew once he got far enough away from Sherwood, the mist would clear.

"Everything will be okay. Just hold on!"

As he stumbled through the undergrowth, the mist thickening, The Tsar couldn't help thinking that this was just like one of the old folktales, something parents would tell their children to stop them running off. Don't go into the forest, especially after sunset, because something might just come for you. Something might just be *hunting* you.

Well, something was definitely hunting him.

The Hooded Man, on his own turf. He knew every single one of these trees, whereas The Tsar was completely and utterly lost. They might only be within spitting distance of the road, but he couldn't see a thing. He ventured on, stumbling through the fog, his great coat flapping behind, waving his Cossack Officer's shashka blade ahead of him.

The Tsar tripped and crashed into a fence, breaking through the wood. He rose, tumbling forwards, the ground less grassy here. He banged into another fence and when he looked up, he gasped. The figure of The Hooded Man was towering above him. He was about to swing his sword when he realised it was just a statue, that the representation was holding a staff and was fighting with another, much larger figure. That the hood was down instead of drawn up.

Must be in the old tourist section of Sherwood, he thought, *the place where they honoured the first of* his *kind.*

The original, not this... this copycat who'd come along centuries later.

Even so, that mimic had managed to cripple his forces. Now had him on the run. The Tsar was searching for the warrior within himself, the man who'd fought so valiantly in the '80s, who'd beaten people up for protection money, taken assassination jobs.

You have grown soft, so used to luxury in your hotel back in Moscow, shielded from everything. Now you must fend for yourself because there is no-one else.

No-one else here to face him, Andrei, but you.

It was the first time in years he'd heard that name, his true name. Not Lord, or Sire, or The Tsar. The name he'd had as a child, an orphan. The name he'd used in the Russian army.

He remembered all those battles now, the bloodlust that had been in him, and the way he'd got rid of those enemies of the mafia during peacetime. Actually doing the damage himself instead of just watching others in a ring beating the hell out of each other.

The Tsar gnashed his teeth and trudged on, feeling his way along the sides of buildings, then up along an overgrown path. Suddenly, ahead of him, he saw the fire. His fire. The one he'd created with the explosion. He'd got turned around somehow and gone in a circle.

The fire was spreading through the trees, hopping from trunk to trunk, branch to branch.

"I'm coming for you, Tsar!" shouted a voice that echoed all around, full of fury. He'd invaded Hood's country, his city, killed his men and taken his women hostage. Now this: The Tsar had set fire to his beloved Sherwood.

But an angry man makes mistakes. *If I can just keep calm, keep my cool.* The Tsar let out a small laugh at the ridiculousness of that, while all around the fire raged.

Find the warrior inside, find that same fire in your own belly!

He stood up straighter, then called back: "Then come. I am read–"

The shape leaped out of nowhere, out of the flames. It dove headlong into The Tsar, shoving him sideways into the nearest tree. His shoulder stung as it connected with the wood and he let out a cry. Swearing, he shrugged off his greatcoat.

"What's the matter? Too warm for you? I used to be afraid of the fire," said a gruff voice from under the hood. "Afraid of the memories."

The Tsar stood again, swiping sideways with his curved sword and hitting thin air. "You should be afraid of *me!*"

"I don't think so." Hood lashed out now with his weapon, and The Tsar met the thrust. They exchanged blows against a background of mist, smoke and crackling flames. Then Hood rammed him up against a tree, this time crossing the blades so that they were either side of The Tsar's neck. Even as the man was doing this, The Tsar couldn't help noticing a wince of pain when Hood raised his arm. Some wound at his shoulder? A weakness?

The Tsar pressed the man back, then twisted the crossed swords so he could angle them sideways. He gave another push and the hilts smacked into Hood's shoulder. He let out a howl, fell back, and dropped his sword. Then he dropped to his hands and knees, gasping.

That is where you should *be!*

The Tsar kicked him in the side, rolling him over. As Hood clutched at the shoulder wound, The Tsar spotted blood staining the leg of his combats. He trod on this second wound and again. Hood let out a wail.

"So, you *can* be hurt. Not as invincible as you would have people believe, eh?" Hood lay there on the ground, with The Tsar above – sword at his throat. "All this will have been worth it just to kill you, comrade. Tanek was right, one day it would have come to this. Better that it should be settled here and now."

Hood didn't move, apparently helpless, The Tsar victorious over him. He finally felt like that warrior again. He, who had defeated Hood after the Frenchman failed; when his own tanks, guns and men had failed.

Then Hood grabbed the blade with his good hand. Though it must have been agony to do so, he levered it back – the sharp edges cutting into his skin, slipping slightly and causing even The Tsar to cringe.

"I agree," said the man, wrenching his head to the side and letting go of the sword. It dug into the soil behind, holding it there fast. But, as Hood slid from beneath The Tsar, he kicked the legs out from under him at the same time.

There was nothing he could do. He was falling, knowing what

was going to happen but powerless to prevent it. The metal hilt of the shashka, as smooth as it was, still went into him – helped by his own bodyweight and forward impetus. The Tsar grunted as he dropped down over the hilt, and onto the blade itself. Impaled.

He was still alive, just, when Hood picked up his own sword and walked round in front.

"You should have stayed where you were, *comrade*," he told The Tsar, spitting out the final word.

Then there was a final swish and The Tsar had to concede, in the end, that The Hooded Man had a point.

CHAPTER TWENTY-SIX

Heat. Fire. Pain.

It was all he could remember of the torture session. But, naturally, Tanek had left Jack a few reminders. Scalding burns, and several nails still digging into his body that hurt whenever he twitched. Though not even they hurt as much as the thought he'd let down Mark, Tate and the others. Not to mention Robbie. He'd given them up – granted, because they were threatening Mary's life, but she would have been the first to tell Tanek and Adele to take a hike. Mark probably lasted longer when faced with the olive-skinned psycho's attentions. Jack had also fallen for Adele, just how stupid was he? The daughter of their greatest enemy. Greatest till now, anyway. Not even De Falaise could have pulled off the stunts this Tsar character was responsible for.

Jack had passed out again a couple of times since the pair left, and night had fallen in the meantime. He'd also been left unguarded. They probably thought he didn't warrant watching any more. That he'd be going nowhere considering what Tanek had put him through.

They obviously didn't know Jack very well. He'd screwed up, big time, and he aimed to put things right. How, he didn't know, but he'd start with getting free of this fucking chair! Easier said than done when you were tied to the arms and legs.

He should have been freezing, stripped to his underwear. But they'd also been making use of Faraday's furnace. Jack recalled seeing the body of their blacksmith in the corner. How many more would be counted amongst his number by the time the day was out?

During the torture the furnace had been an instrument of terror; now, even though it had died down, it was probably keeping him alive. And might just be the answer to freeing him.

Mustering what little energy he could, Jack stretched his toes – the rope tying his ankles to the chair legs preventing him from placing his feet properly on the floor. As he strained, the cords in his neck tightened, and the nails that had been banged so methodically into his torso, arms and legs, sent more ripples of torment through him. Never, not even after all those rounds in the wrestling ring, had his body felt so battered and abused.

His toes brushed the cold floor, but he was going to have to do better than that. He stretched again, and this time they connected. He pushed down, enough to raise the chair slightly. Breathing heavily, Jack did it again, only this time he tried his best to lean to the side as well, angling towards the furnace. Just when he thought it wasn't going to go, the chair tipped, pitching him on his side. It knocked the square furnace over, sending a slew of coals and ash across the floor. The nail in his shoulder was driven even further in by the fall, and he bit back a cry of anguish.

Ignore the pain. You're not done yet, and someone might have heard all the racket you've just made!

Jack looked down and found that a handful of coals had rolled near to his bound wrists. They were no longer as hot as they had been when Tanek made use of them, but they might be hot enough for his purposes. Now, if he could just inch a little closer...

Jack wrenched his body sideways, lifting the chair off the floor, then threw his weight in the other direction. The chair moved a fraction across the floor. Dismissing the pain as best he could, Jack lifted the chair again, bringing it down closer to the coals. He was centimetres away, so he did it again. This time he landed virtually on the coals, and he yelped, but kept still because the rope was also on them. Slowly, they were burning *through* it. It took a few minutes, but he at last began to smell the smoke, as the heat left in the coals bit at the hemp. Jack held on a little longer, then couldn't take it anymore. The ropes were now loose enough for him to break free.

Making a fist, he tugged on the bonds, and was surprised when they gave first time. Quickly, he reached over, untying his other hand – then he did the same with the ropes holding his ankles. Jack collapsed on the floor, and crawled away from the sea of coals and ash.

Before he had a chance to pull out the nails still sticking in him, a Russian soldier appeared at the arched entranceway, barking something in his native tongue. He raised his machinegun. Part of Jack just wanted to lay there, let him shoot and get it over with. But people were relying on him. "T-Take it easy, buddy," he said, his voice hoarse. "We can work this out."

Just when Jack thought he was going to open fire, the soldier shouted something else, motioning with his rifle for Jack to come out. Jack held up a hand, rising slowly and wincing. "All right, all right. I'm coming." The man shouted again, and it was now that Jack revealed his other hand – flinging coals at the soldier, hitting him in the centre of his forehead. Before the soldier could fire, Jack had reached him and followed through with a punch in the face, knocking him spark out.

"Yeah, you sleep it off, pal," Jack muttered as the man slid to the floor. He dragged him inside, and began pulling off the soldier's uniform, tugging at the jacket and trousers. Jack braced himself as he pulled out the nails, so he could slip on the clothes: biting on his bottom lip to keep from screaming again. There were half a dozen or so, positioned like acupuncture needles all over his body. When he eased them out, they didn't bleed as much as he'd thought they would, but even after they were gone it still felt like the nails were there.

The jacket was a tight fit, but at least it was long, and though the trouser legs didn't go all the way down anything was better than freezing his butt off. Grabbing the rifle, Jack poked his head out of the stables. He couldn't see any more soldiers, so he ventured out. But just as he did, a squadron of men came up through the sloping tunnel, where the horses usually made their way to the nearby stables. He ducked back inside, opting to hide until they'd gone past.

Too late he realised he'd left the bare foot of the Russian soldier sticking out near the entranceway. All it would take would be for one of them to look sideways and they'd see it. Jack listened as boots stomped by, and breathed a huge sigh of relief when he couldn't hear them anymore.

He stepped out from behind the wall where he was hiding...

Only to see several more rifles trained in his direction, another smattering of Russian coming from the soldier in charge.

"Hi fellas," said Jack. "Don't suppose we could talk about this, could we?"

They'd entered the city under cover of darkness.

It was obvious when they found the dead men at the look-out points that The Tsar's army had arrived ahead of them. But he hadn't left any of his own men on watch. Which meant he either hadn't had time yet, or he'd already taken the castle and was supremely confident his forces could defend it.

Dale was hoping for the former, but if it did turn out to be the other option... Well, they'd already fought and won one battle that day against those very same forces. Okay, that also meant the men who'd come with him – who'd made that tiring journey, with no rest and not even a pit stop for something to eat – were not exactly at their best. Robert had already asked a lot of them, and now they were expected to fight another army, this time entrenched behind the castle's walls.

Dale was no good at making speeches. That was Robert's forte.

Could try singing to them, I suppose, he thought. In the end he managed to persuade the men to come with him and do a recce, scope out exactly what was happening. They left the horses behind and made their way up through the city, keeping to the shadows and conscious that The Tsar could well have posted armed men anywhere.

When they got close enough, they entered a building which offered a direct line-of-sight up Friar Lane, towards the castle. From one of the upstairs windows they observed through binoculars. Each one of them saw the devastation The Tsar's men had caused, illuminated by lights from the armoured vehicles parked both inside and outside the castle grounds. The castle itself had taken a hit, too, one top corner having been chipped away by a rocket or shell blast.

Once each member of the squad had taken a turn, Dale hadn't needed to give any speeches. This was their home – the only one a lot of them had known since virus times. They'd headed The Tsar's forces off because they'd been trying to prevent this. But the sneaky bastard had divided his troops and hit the castle anyway. Now, each and every one of the fighters with him wanted it back.

And they didn't care what it took.

"So Robert has somewhere to return to," Dale said to them, and they all agreed.

There had been no sign of any of those closest to The Hooded Man, though: Mark, Mary, Jack and Reverend Tate especially.

Or Sophie. Where was Sophie?

Dale had to assume they were being held somewhere inside the castle, because the alternative was just too horrifying.

All they needed now was a plan of action, and they were looking at him to provide one. He thought about what Robert would say if he were here.

"Okay, we'll divide into three teams," said Dale when they regrouped. "Hit them from the front and sides at the same time. We have our ropes, our arrows. We can scale the cliffside, the walls, and get inside. They haven't fixed up the mess they've made of the gate yet, so we don't even have to break in there.

We've trained for this, guys. We know that place inside out. *They* don't." He split the numbers, giving the cliff job to Azhar and his band, detailing how he wanted covering fire laid down for the frontal assault, and explaining how he would lead the third team in through those busted gates. "None of us are gettin' any younger – so let's do this."

Dale had played some gigs in his time, but this one had to take the cake. *One day*, he said to himself, *songs actually* will *be sung about what we've done... what we're* going to do *today.*

He just hoped he would be the one singing them.

"Before you start, you should know: I've had a really, really bad day."

Jack ducked back inside the stables a fraction of a second before he heard the first bang.

His reactions were definitely slower than usual, because a bullet nicked his arm. Compared with everything else he'd been through, it felt like a gnat bite. And it made him angrier than ever.

"Right," he said, taking hold of his machine gun. Reaching across himself, he poked the end out and treated the soldiers to a blast. After the first burst, the weapon clicked – either empty or jammed. "Goddamn!" shouted Jack, tossing the gun away.

He looked around desperately for something, *anything* to use in its place. Then he saw it: there was an old broom over in the corner. He edged sideways and grabbed it – pulling off the head and testing its weight. It was a far cry from his staff, but it would have to do.

Jack crouched and rounded the corner, this time holding his makeshift staff out in front of him – charging at any of the soldiers still standing and slamming the wood against their knees, bowling them over.

He stabbed the handle left and right, hitting one soldier in the temple and smashing another one's front teeth in. Jack let adrenalin take over, just like he used to in the ring.

One soldier attempted to get up, and Jack jumped on him.

Another was running off back down the slope towards the tunnel. Jack struggled to his feet, hefting the stick like a javelin, and threw it. The end of the wooden pole struck the fleeing man in the back of the head and he went down.

Jack moaned, only now feeling the mounting pain. He made his way down to the tunnel himself, willing his exhausted body onwards.

Picking up the staff, he checked the tunnel for the approach of any more soldiers – knowing that somebody must surely have heard the gunfire. But if they had, they'd be coming down the steps above him, not up the path, and so he was shielded for the moment.

Jack made his way down through the tunnel, pressing himself against the side when he got to the other end, seeing the armoured vehicles still on the castle grounds near the gatehouse. There were also clumps of troops – not as many as he'd been expecting (not as many as when they took the castle from De Falaise) but enough to cause him to groan in frustration. Not all were in uniform, some he recognised from the hotel prison – heck, some he'd even apprehended himself! They'd been given weapons as well, it seemed, drafted into The Tsar's employ. What he didn't see this time, strangely, were any of the cultists.

Suddenly there was shouting and Jack saw one of the troopers point up the slope in his direction. Then a squadron was heading his way, hefting their rifles.

They hadn't got halfway up the drive before they opened fire. Jack squashed himself flat against the wall, expecting bullets to spark off the stone. They didn't. And he could hear more gunfire, coming from another part of the castle, up and over to his right, over near the cliffside.

Jack looked again, and the group he thought were coming after him had veered off to the left, towards the gate. Then one of them was suddenly on fire. It was like he had spontaneously combusted, the flames spreading outwards from his chest to consume him. When he turned sideways, just before falling over in a blazing ball of orange, Jack saw the arrow sticking out of him.

Robbie! It had to be. The very thought that The Hooded Man had returned from fighting The Tsar's forces filled him with new energy.

More flaming arrows struck home, the soldiers they were hitting running this way and that, firing indiscriminately at shadows. That's because his men were following their training, sticking to the darkness where they wouldn't be seen; hitting their opponents hard and then retreating.

It was time Jack joined them.

He came out of the tunnel, just as a Russian soldier was running past him. Jack swung his staff, connecting with the man's face, knocking him flat on his back. Jack trod on him to get to the next soldier, hitting that one in the stomach as the man swung his rifle in Jack's direction. Jack struck the soldier's temple and he fell on top of his companion.

As he cleared the tunnel Jack looked up and saw other soldiers running from the castle, jumping down from the Middle Bailey, joining their comrades in the struggle. This time they were on the receiving end, but it was a stealth attack – not a show of force. And they'd been caught on the back foot.

Nevertheless, it was still machine guns against bows and arrows. And if they brought some of that other heavy weaponry into play... Jack had no idea how many allies he had out there – it was difficult to tell with a flash here, a flash there – but they had to cripple as many of The Tsar's men as they could, or this would be over as quickly as it had been the first time around.

More flaming arrows whizzed by ahead of him, but as he watched Jack saw these exploding in the grounds, flinging bunches of soldiers into the air as effectively as if someone had just tossed a grenade into their midst.

Soldiers ran around the grounds, confused. Nobody seemed to be in charge, and no-one apparently wanted the job. Jack guessed Tanek and Adele must have gone after Mark, Tate and Sophie at Sherwood. But where was The Tsar himself? Where were his bodyguards? Surely he wasn't so stupid – or overly confident – that he'd leave his castle with just his foot soldiers looking after it?

Somehow, over the top of all the gunfire, Jack heard the clack of a rifle being primed behind him. He turned, expecting to have his head blown off. What he saw when he made it round was one of the men he'd imprisoned in the hotel. Jack couldn't remember his name, but recognised him from his patchy beard. He'd caught him a few months ago picking on a group of teenagers who'd banded together, threatening them with a pickaxe if they didn't hand over their food. Now the man was out for revenge.

"Just wanted you to see who it was who offed you," said the man, venom in every word. He put the rifle to his shoulder.

"If you're going to do it, get on with it. Won't be the worst thing that's happened today, fella."

"Fair enough."

Jack waited for the bullets to hit home – with no archway to duck into, what choice did he have? But they didn't. Instead, the man's body jerked, his whole frame dancing like he was being electrocuted. His eyes went wide and he let go of his weapon, following it to the ground moments later.

Behind him stood a young man, his sword dripping with the bearded man's blood – which looked oddly black in this light. The youth beamed when he saw him. "Jack! You're alive."

Jack laughed, rushing up to Dale and clapping him on the arms. They didn't have time for a proper reunion though, as more soldiers happened across them.

Dale was on one of them in a flash, his blade slicing left and right. Jack handled another with the makeshift staff, forcing himself to ignore the tremendous pain he was still in.

More explosions nearby, and more gunfire. Jack's eyes flicked up to the castle again and saw troops being hit by arrows up there. "Your doing?" he asked quickly.

"Azhar," was all Dale needed to say.

As Jack's gaze was drawn towards the wall in front of him, he saw the black shapes of more Rangers clambering over. Some were immediately sprayed with bullets, tumbling over onto the top of the wall: dangling like lifeless marionettes. Others managed to get a foothold at the top, targeting the shooters with yet more arrows.

The grounds reflected how Jack's body both looked and felt; it had seen better days. But there wasn't an end in sight. Another wave of soldiers were coming from above, leaping down and firing into the dark recesses, covering any inch of ground their enemies might be hiding in. This lot seemed more together, and had obviously hung back to get a handle on the situation before rushing in.

"They're picking off my... Robert's men," Dale said, correcting himself.

Jack could easily see this kid leading his own division of the Rangers someday. He wanted glory, the adulation that came with bravery. But that was in the future. In Robert's apparent absence, Jack was in charge. "We need to round up as many of our lot as we can, bring them together and make a stand against The Tsar's remaining forces," Jack said, coughing and wondering how much longer he could hold out. This wasn't his first battle of the day – it wasn't his first of the week, or the month – and he'd been tortured by a maniac in the meantime.

Dale nodded, then whistled: a signal for the rest of the Rangers to converge, to make their way into the centre of the grounds. This they did, fending off the soldiers in their way with swords and arrows, fighting more valiantly than Jack had ever seen in his life – in reality or on the silver screen. It made him feel very proud.

They were still outnumbered and outgunned, but none gave up. It was quite a thing to see.

The remaining Rangers were gathering in the spot where Dale and Jack stood, forming a ring. They were being surrrounded by the numbers of soldiers and prisoners still swarming from every part of the castle and grounds.

Backs to each other, the Rangers fired arrow after arrow, stuck The Tsar's men with knives, struck them down with swords. But it was obvious who was winning. As Jack feared it would, the tide had turned, and not even the appearance of Azhar, swords in both hands, cutting and slicing his way through the mayhem, did any good.

"Always wondered what I'd choose for my final number," Dale

shouted to Jack.

"What?"

But the youth wasn't listening. He was singing. Lines from a song Jack hadn't heard before, probably one from Dale's old band, or maybe something he was improvising – he was good like that. The words were beautiful and poignant, though, and spoke of kinship, loyalty and of trust.

> "So we stand here on the brink,
> Hardly able to even think.
> Who'd have thought we could make it here,
> Together.
>
> What's waiting? Who can say...
> But we'll face it anyway.
> You can-"

He never got any further because the first of the explosions came. Their heads whipped sideways. These were coming from *outside* the grounds.

As Jack and Dale looked on, astonished, one of the armoured vehicles positioned at the wall blew up. The Tsar's troops had turned to watch as well.

"Is someone still outside?" Jack asked.

Dale shook his head. "We needed everyone for the assault."

Another explosion, another vehicle going up in flames. Now The Tsar's men were worried. They'd concentrated so much effort on the attack from Dale and his men that they'd taken their eye off the ball where the castle's defences were concerned. The result: somebody was having a merry old time blasting their toys to pieces.

The explosions died down and there was silence for a moment or two. Then:

"Invaders of Nottingham Castle. This is Robert... *Robin* Hood. Your beloved Tsar is dead."

"Robbie? Well, I'll be," said Jack. "Looks like you were only the warm-up guys, Dale."

The youth frowned and for a second Jack thought it was because of the crack. *Surely he can't be mad at Robbie for stealing his thunder, can he?* When Dale spoke again, it all became clear.

"I-I left him, on the battlefield. Jack, he was really hurt bad."

"Aren't we all," Jack pointed out.

"No, I mean... *bad.*"

Jack frowned. It did beg the question how in God's name he'd got from there to here, let alone what he was doing talking to The Tsar's men on a speaker system.

The Russians surrounding them were all exchanging blank looks, those who spoke English translating for the rest. It was clear none of them believed what this Hood character was saying.

"Unless you surrender, you will suffer the same fate." With that there was another noise. Not an explosion, but something overhead. The sound of a chopper's blades as it hopped over the buildings next to the castle to hover just above the grounds.

Jack peered up, hand covering his brow. "Is that... Holy smoke, it's Bill!"

The door of the Gazelle helicopter opened and something was dropped into the grounds. The Russians attempted to scatter, thinking it was some kind of grenade. But it was big, more like the size of those old bombs from cartoons. In any event it had landed before they could get very far.

It dropped with a dull thud and rolled into an open part of the grounds the soldiers had vacated.

Jack heard the first of the cries a moment later.

The Russians were backing away, as fast as if it actually *was* a bomb. However, when Jack, Dale and the others came closer, they saw it was white in colour; with features: eyes, a nose, a mouth.

Jack saw that it was the head of The Tsar.

"Now... get the *HELL OUT OF MY HOME!*" came a thunderous roar over the speaker. Some of the Russians dropped their weapons right there and then, holding their hands up in surrender. Others made a dash for whatever exits they could find. The prisoners who had been released, while not overly concerned about whether

The Tsar was alive or dead, recognised that the tide had turned. They fled, prepared to shoot their way out if necessary.

Dale and the Rangers began rounding up as many of the Russians as possible, but they were too few in number to go after both the soldiers and the escaping prisoners.

It wasn't long before an armoured vehicle came in through the already smashed gates, following closely by a jeep.

Surfing the AFV was Robert, bow in one hand and mike in the other, the cable stretching into the vehicle. He called for help and two Rangers came over. Soon they were carrying a half-conscious Mary from the vehicle. Sophie, who was driving the jeep, needed assistance as well, and a Ranger put an arm around Mark, helping the lad hobble out. Tate was also helped from the jeep, but waved the Rangers away once he was on his feet again. Up on the Middle Bailey, Bill's helicopter was setting down.

Jack and Dale went over, and the first thing Jack did was hold out his hand, which Robert shook gladly. "It's good to see you, boss," he told him. Jack watched Mary going past, saw Mark and Sophie's injuries, and he struggled to fight back the tears. "I'm sorry. This is my fault. I told them where you'd be... I mean, I didn't know *you'd* be there but they were threatening Mary and–"

"Don't, Jack. It's okay." Robert placed a comforting hand on Jack's shoulder; a hand wrapped in a bloodied bandage. "Really."

"How did you..." Dale began, then: "The last time I saw you, you were..."

Robert held up a finger. "Later, eh? I'll tell you guys everything then. Let's make sure the grounds and castle are clear first, then tend to our wounded."

"Like you?" Jack pointed at the bloodstains at Robert's leg and shoulder.

"We've all been in the wars," Robert said quietly, nodding at the state of Jack.

"Aye, that's one way o' putting it." This was Bill, joining them, and Jack hugged the member of their family he hadn't seen in so long.

Jack felt Dale moving away from his side, going off towards Sophie, asking how she was. Jack also saw the look Mark gave the lad. Even after everything that had happened, there were some things that still needed settling. Lots of things in fact.

But it would take a while, Jack knew that. They'd been here before. Yet that victory had felt so much cleaner, much more final. When they'd ousted the Sheriff it was after a lengthy campaign of terror on his part. The Tsar had managed to achieve more than he did in much less time. And they almost hadn't regained what was theirs. The price had been high. So many injured, including those closest to them. So many dead.

Everything felt broken.

Jack also knew what Robert would say to that. What was broken could be mended... usually. He just couldn't help thinking that the scars from today would remain long after the battles were just a memory. That the ramifications might prove tremendous.

Jack exhaled. He didn't have the energy to think about it. His body was crying out for rest, reminding him of every little thing he'd gone through. Like Mary, Mark, Robert and the others – even the castle itself – they needed to heal the physical before anything else.

Then, and only then, could they begin to find their way.

CHAPTER TWENTY-SEVEN

They'd all lost their way to some extent.

It wasn't until he took a step back from everything that he saw. It had taken so much to go wrong, before it could start to go right again. But then, Spring was here and it was the time for new beginnings.

Robert looked out over the flowers that were blooming near the war memorial. The place they'd buried the dead from the battle with De Falaise, and those who'd died when The Tsar's forces had – briefly – taken the castle. Those who had fallen in the skirmish with the suited man's legions (Robert had since learned his name was Bohuslav) were buried where they'd made their stand against them, once all the detritus had been cleared. Tate had performed a moving service at both sites.

They were still counting the cost, not just in terms of numbers but also morale. Those who were fit enough had been given the task of repairing parts of the castle that had been hit the worst. It had kept them focused on something other than training and fighting, given them a common goal of restoring their home.

Because that's what this place was to them. He'd said it himself over the speaker when they'd arrived back here, commandeering The Tsar's own vehicle to take the place back (he'd used it reluctantly, conceding that Bill was right and they had no choice on this occasion; they needed to get Mary back to the castle quickly *and* safely).

For the first time, he'd actually meant it. This was where he belonged, at least for now.

That didn't mean he was abandoning Sherwood – his *other* home. For one thing he was continuing Mark's training there. The young man had certainly faced his fears: faced Tanek, and taken his first steps towards becoming the person he was destined to be. And Robert would always need to return, in spite of what Mary had once told him about not belonging there. She understood a little more about that now, the more she saw of the place – after experiencing its strange effects herself when she was so close to death. Plus Robert would always carry a little bit of the wilderness inside him, he couldn't escape it. Now he knew that the dreams would come wherever he was. He just had to let them.

Relationships were being renewed, *re-forged*. From here Robert spotted Mark walking with Sophie, holding hands. Things had definitely changed between them since returning. It looked liked they'd finally worked things out with Dale, who seemed to have backed off to give them space. Mark had told Robert there'd been a conversation or two – between Dale and Sophie, Sophie and Mark – but he hadn't asked for details. He'd just been pleased that his adopted son was happy. Meanwhile, Sophie herself had turned out to be a pretty good nurse, with Mary's instruction and hours of dipping into text books on the subject. She'd definitely helped to patch them all back together when things had calmed down. Sophie said she'd always had an interest in medicine and now that Lucy was gone...

Poor Lucy. It hurt Robert to even think about her with the others near that memorial.

Bill, though he had things to attend to first with his market network, had agreed to come back and help with the general day-to-day running of the Rangers. He claimed Robert needed someone to "keep a bloody eye on him". This would allow The Hooded Man to go on more patrols, to be out there where he should be. "I still think ye should be armin' them lads properly," he'd said, Bill being Bill. But for now he seemed to have dropped the subject. For one thing he was busy fixing up one of the Black Shark attack helicopters they'd retrieved near Doncaster. "Look at that beauty," he'd practically drooled. "It'll be protection for the castle while you get your other defences up and running again..." Robert was too tired and too preoccupied to argue with him this time.

Bill would be helped by Tate, who'd moved back permanently. Robert felt the most sorry for him. They'd both gone out to New Hope, after hearing that Gwen and Clive Jr were alive and safe, that they'd somehow escaped on their own. But Robert and Tate had been prevented from entering the village by the armed guards at the entrance. After Tate told them they weren't moving until they saw Gwen, the woman had reluctantly appeared. At first she wouldn't even look at the Reverend, even after he apologised. Then, when she did, she told him:

"I never want to see you again. Don't come here any more."

Robert saw how much the words upset Tate – he'd only been doing what he thought best. The Reverend never spoke all the way home.

But even he hadn't moped as much as Jack. Robert's second had taken both Adele's betrayal and his own – he called it that no matter what Robert said – to heart. Or maybe it had been the torture; sometimes he woke the whole castle up at night with his bad dreams. Perhaps Robert's forthcoming wedding would take his mind off things. Who knows, maybe Jack would even meet someone from the neighbouring villages at that, because – like last year's summer fête – they'd invited all the people under The Hooded Man's protection.

Robert recalled now those agonising days waiting by Mary's bedside, with Sophie telling him he should still be recuperating himself.

"I *need* to be here," he insisted, and she'd left it at that.

Robert held Mary's hand and was there when her eyelids finally fluttered open, a smile breaking on her bruised, but lovely face. "Hey..." she'd croaked.

"Hey yourself."

"Did... did we make it? Back, I mean. What happened... with..."

"Sshh, shh." He stroked her hair, then kissed her forehead. "Everything's okay. We're at the castle. The Tsar's dead. Mark, Sophie, Jack, the Reverend, Bill, they're all..." He paused, but said it anyway. "They're all fine."

Mary nodded, then winced. "I feel dreadful."

"Well, you look beautiful."

"Liar," she said, laughing, then wincing again. "How about Tanek... and Adele?"

Robert shrugged. "Tanek I don't know. Adele you shot."

"Good old Dad, all those hours hitting tin cans were definitely not wasted. Yay me. Did you find the other Peacekeeper, by the way? In the caves?"

Robert nodded. "I know how much they mean to you, even though I don't technically approve. But yes, you have a pair again, now." He was skirting round what he really wanted to say, so he just got on with it. "Look, this probably isn't the right time or place, but, well, I've been thinking."

"That's dangerous," she said.

She must be feeling better. "I almost lost you, and I'm not sure if I could go through something like that..." Robert let the end of that sentence float away. "Mary, I guess what I'm trying to say is–"

"The answer's yes, you know. It always was." She smiled back at him. "You looked like you needed helping out."

And that had been that. They'd set a date over the summer, a special one that marked the anniversary of becoming a proper couple, and asked Tate if he'd perform the ceremony. His answer had been: "Nothing would give me greater pleasure." Now, if this quiet period would just hold out till then.

They'd had no more reports of invasions, nothing about the

Morningstars – it was as if they'd vanished, just as they did from the castle – no trouble yet from those prisoners that had got away, and that was how Robert hoped it would remain for the time being.

As Mary joined him on that sunny, but slightly chilly morning – still using a stick to get about – he thought about what he'd said, about almost losing her. Not even the castle had been safe; they *both* realised that now.

"When you're feeling up to it," he told her, slipping an arm around her waist, "how about we go out on a few patrols together. I know Dale would welcome the back-up. So would I."

"You old romantic," she said to him, slapping his shoulder. He gritted his teeth, feigning pain at the wound he'd received at the hands of Bohuslav. "Oh, I'm sorry, love."

"Maybe you should kiss it better."

Mary grinned. "I think that can be arranged. I wonder if the stables are free..." She took him by the hand and led him down the path.

As she did so, Robert realised that he didn't feel lost anymore. He been found, in more ways than one. He was both Robert Stokes – the man – and Robin Hood, the legend.

There were worse things in life he could be, and this woman had rescued him from that.

In a broken world, he said to himself, *what more could anyone ask for?*

The country had welcomed him back into her arms like a concerned mother.

One that also admonished him for ever wanting to leave. He comforted himself with the knowledge that none of this had been his idea. It had all been The Tsar's, the *old* Tsar's. Now that man was dead, along with Xue and Ying. Just as he had almost been.

As he stepped out into the cold, flanked by soldiers to the left and right, on his way to the combat arena from the Marriott, Bohuslav's wrist throbbed again, at the stump which he'd cauterised himself, almost passing out from the pain.

He felt the pull of the stitches at his stomach, the wound which would have seen his intestines spill out on the floor had it been a couple of millimetres deeper. As it was, he'd had to sew up the flesh with his one good hand – his driver useless at anything medical it seemed – dosing himself with antibiotics so there was no infection.

By the time he was fit enough to travel, news had reached them of the failure of their troops to retain the castle. Bohuslav had been numbed by the realisation that their entire operation had been a spectacular catastrophe.

There had been only one thing to do at that point. Waiting for them just off the coast were the fleet of empty hovercrafts, including The Tsar's, which he'd followed them in. He'd told his driver to radio that he would be returning, and that he would now be taking charge of the fleet – and indeed of The Tsar's entire army. They would return home to Russia to bide their time and replenish their forces.

It had been enough of a pasting to make him think twice about trying it again for a good while. Or at least without any major allies. One day, however, one day...

Because, as much as he loved his motherland, Bohuslav was also thirsty for vengeance. Not just on those who had done this to him, but also on the man who had lured The Tsar and his men across to that fated isle in the first place.

Tanek.

Even the name caused him to clench his fist as he climbed into the limo. He couldn't clench the other, as that position was now occupied by a handheld (Bohuslav would laugh at the inappropriateness of that, if it didn't remind him of the pain he'd endured) sickle, attached to the stump that was now aching so much.

Yes, one day he would meet both Hood and Tanek again. And when he did...

Bohuslav wondered where that cowardly giant had run off to after leaving his leader in the lurch. Reports were sketchy, but he'd apparently abandoned him at Sherwood after a confrontation with their enemies.

"Drive," he instructed the man in front, once his personal bodyguards were seated on either side. (They were no oriental beauties, but he knew they would give their lives for him.)

As the car pulled out into the snow-covered road, Bohuslav cursed Tanek, hoping that wherever he was, he was suffering.

For weeks now, he'd sat there, beside her, watching her suffer.

Quite how he'd managed to keep her alive was beyond him, not with the wound she'd suffered. He could put so much of it down to his skill with the blade, his knowledge of anatomy allowing him to perform the operation and remove the bullet – which had come so very close to penetrating her heart.

After leaving Sherwood, Tanek's plan to return to the castle had been waylaid by Adele, who had finally passed out from the loss of blood, in spite of the field dressing he'd applied. He needed to get her to an old hospital, anywhere he might be able to find replacement blood quickly. Tanek already knew her type: O-Neg. He consulted the map he found in the jeep they'd taken, and decided to head for King's Mill in Sutton-in-Ashfield because it seemed to be closest to their current position.

As he'd expected, the place was run down. People had picked over the stocks of drugs, but some of the medical equipment remained and the emergency operating theatre was still relatively intact – if woefully unhygienic after years of disrepair. They weren't in a position to be choosy, though.

Placing Adele on the table, Tanek went off and gathered what he could find – including tubes and needles for a transfusion, seeing as there were no stocks of blood that he could find. Running out of time, he'd hooked himself up and conducted the transfusion at the same time he began to operate. Not ideal, but necessary. There was alcohol in the medical kit from the jeep, so he'd been able to sterilise the bullet wound that way. He hadn't needed to knock Adele out with anything as she was totally unresponsive.

Tanek had cut into her with a scalpel that had survived the

scavenger hunts, searching for the bullet that was causing all the bleeding. Little wonder, because it had glanced off the ribs and come close to actually puncturing her heart. Tanek had managed to remove the foreign item, stemming the blood flow; stitching her up and treating her with antibiotics that were also from the jeep. But he knew they couldn't stay there for ever.

He was too woozy to drive that night, but once he'd recovered enough, Tanek carried her to the jeep and prepared to make the trip back to the castle in Nottingham.

He hadn't got to the city limits when he saw that Hood's men were back on point. Tanek knew what that meant – they'd taken back the castle. He was tempted to go there anyway, gun them all down, but realistically he wouldn't get very far. And he had to look after Adele.

The dreams, the promise... they were never far from his mind.

He needed somewhere quiet, out of the way, somewhere he could care for her. So he'd retraced his steps from over a year ago, returning to Cynthia's little house out in the middle of nowhere.

The door had been wide open this time when he arrived. Stepping cautiously inside with his crossbow raised, Tanek had searched the place for any signs of the woman or her fucking demon dog. There were none, just evidence of some kind of struggle. Obviously someone had stumbled upon this place and they'd either fled, or been taken away and killed. There were no corpses to indicate it had happened in the house. He neither knew nor cared.

Tanek had carried De Falaise's daughter up to the bedroom, placing her on the comfortable bed that was still untouched. Then he'd looked after her, continuing to give her the antibiotics until they ran out, mopping her brow as she sweated out the pain, and willing her to wake.

She opened her eyes only twice. The first time she asked for water, which he gave her. Tanek had been feeding her intravenously with a drip he'd found back at King's Mill, while he'd been surviving on what he could hunt in the nearby meadows: small animals mainly, some birds which he killed with crossbow bolts. He'd lived on less.

Adele told him she'd seen her father, that he'd talked to her.

Tanek nodded. She'd had the dream as well.

"He said I had to get better, had to... because..." She began to cough, and he gave her another sip of water.

"Take it slow."

"No, I must... must tell you... We have to... have to save..." That was all she could manage, then Adele lost her tenuous grip on consciousness. There was something wrong with her, any idiot could see that. Even in sleep, her face was a rictus of agony. Maybe he'd missed something internally, some fragment from the bullet that he hadn't spotted? Although he knew about the human body he was no doctor and hadn't had the best of facilities in which to work.

Whatever the case, it was too late to do anything but sit and wait.

The second time she woke, three days later, was the last. Tanek sat up when he saw her stir, especially when she'd grabbed his hand, gripping it tight. Adele looked at him, eyes wide, staring with an expression that only came when a person knew they were close to the end.

"He made me promise," she spluttered. "My father."

"Promise what?" Tanek leaned in. Maybe if he hadn't been able to keep his own pledge to De Falaise, he could fulfil Adele's. Would that make up for his mistakes?

"Save-"

"You said that before. Save who?"

The grip tightened again. "His child."

Tanek shook his head. He'd tried, he'd really tried.

Then Adele said her final words: "My brother. My little brother..."

She fell back on the pillow, letting Tanek's hand go. Tanek felt her neck; she was gone. It had taken this long but Mary had finally killed Adele with that bullet. He shed no tears, though. Not because it wasn't in his nature – he was just too preoccupied with what she'd imparted.

A brother, a younger sibling. But where? In France, over here?

A sudden thought struck Tanek. Perhaps the child De Falaise had been talking about in his dreams hadn't been Adele at all. What if it never had been?

Perhaps he was meant to save someone else? Meant to keep someone else safe?

It was a thought that would plague him even as he buried Adele in an unmarked grave. Even as he left Cynthia's house and drove on up the road again.

It was a thought that would continue to plague him for some time to come.

Gwen finished feeding Clive Jr, spooning the food into his mouth and wiping it.

She sat back and looked at her son, and not for the first time she wondered just how and why they'd been spared.

He must be kept safe...

That's what the cultist had said. A man she'd been led to believe was evil – who painted a skull on his face and had the mark of a sinner on him – and yet had actually saved her from Jace, smuggled her out of the castle when she was about to be used as bait, when Christ alone knew what was going to happen to her son.

What had he meant? She didn't have a clue, and hadn't had a chance to ask again. Because after they'd dropped her off near to New Hope, they'd all disappeared: Skullface and the rest.

Gwen had ditched the robes before walking into the village, Andy and Graham rushing over when they saw her. They'd bombarded her with a flurry of questions she either couldn't or didn't want to answer. But once she was safe again inside her own home, once she was sure she wouldn't be spotted or followed, she took Clive Jr and headed out to retrieve those robes.

They hung, even now, in her wardrobe upstairs. Gwen didn't know why she was keeping them. A souvenir of her escape? She doubted it, she wasn't the sentimental type anymore. Not since Clive...

Then why?

That wasn't all. Ever since she'd got back, every time she left the house to visit Clive's grave, or walk through New Hope, or attend meetings about the best way forward for the village – by which she and the others meant the best way to get hold of more weapons – she'd had the uneasy feeling she was being watched. Gwen would turn around quickly in the hopes of catching a glimpse of what was in the periphery of her vision. But it would always be gone.

Now, as she rose and walked to the window, hugging herself in spite of the fire that she'd made in the hearth, keeping out the dying breaths of winter, she thought she saw something out there in the dark. Just a quick flash, a figure perhaps, amongst the trees, wearing a hood. But not *him*: not the person she'd sent away when he'd brought Tate back to plead forgiveness.

No.

This was a different kind of Hooded Man altogether...

His presence heralding a different kind of future.

THE END

PAUL KANE has been writing professionally for twelve years. His genre journalism has appeared in such magazines as *The Dark Side, Death Ray, Fangoria, SFX, Dreamwatch* and *Rue Morgue*, and his first non-fiction book was the critically acclaimed *The Hellraiser Films and Their Legacy*, introduced by Doug 'Pinhead' Bradley. His short stories have appeared in many magazines and anthologies on both sides of the Atlantic, in all kinds of formats (as well as being broadcast on BBC Radio 2), and have been collected in *Alone (In the Dark), Touching the Flame* and *FunnyBones*. His novella *Signs of Life* reached the shortlist of the British Fantasy Awards 2006 and *The Lazarus Condition* was introduced by Mick Garris, creator of Masters of Horror. In his capacity as Special Publications Editor of the British Fantasy Society he worked with authors like Brian Aldiss, Ramsey Campbell, Muriel Gray, Graham Masterton, Robert Silverberg and many more. In 2008 his zombie story 'Dead Time' was turned into an episode of the Lionsgate/NBC TV series *Fear Itself*, adapted by Steve Niles (*30 Days of Night*) and directed by Darren Lynn Bousman (*SAW II-IV*). Paul's website, which has featured guest writers such as Stephen King, James Herbert, Neil Gaiman and Clive Barker, can be found at www.shadow-writer.co.uk He currently lives in Derbyshire, UK, with his wife – the author Marie O'Regan – his family, and a black cat called Mina.

ACKNOWLEDGEMENTS

Once again, a huge thank you to Trevor Preston for all his help with the weapons and military stuff – and for even knowing what thickness the metal should be for the Ranger shields! Cheers mate. A big thank you to Sue Pacey for the medical and drugs advice, who didn't bat an eyelid at my strange questions. My thanks once more to the staff at Nottingham Castle for that trip around the caves, and to Pete Barnsdale who gave us a private tour of the Castle itself. A thank you to Sherwood Forest Visitors Centre, and especially Mark for the archery lesson. To the staff at *The Britannia* – where Marie and I hosted our first FantasyCon as co-chairs, and the seeds were planted. Thank you to Simon Clark and Lee Harris for looking over the Robin Hood's Bay and York sections. A massive thank you to Richard Carpenter, one of my heroes, who let me use the quote from *Robin of Sherwood* at the front (for my money *the* best adaptation of Hood there's ever been). Thanks to Scott Andrews for the conflabs about where we're taking this future vision of Britain, and how we can cross over our characters. Thanks to my support mechanism of fantastic friends and loving family. To Jon Oliver for his great edits, Mark Harrison for the excellent cover artwork (I was a fan even before he started bringing Robert to life), and to my darling wife Marie, who was – as always – the first to read this and give me such insightful feedback. Love you more than words can say, sweetheart; you're the best.

THE AFTERBLIGHT CHRONICLES

Now read an exclusive short story set in the Afterblight
Chronicles universe...

THE AFTERBLIGHT CHRONICLES

THE MAN WHO WOULD NOT BE KING

SCOTT ANDREWS

Arthur St John Smith sat at a desk in a bland air-conditioned office, pressed the return key on his keyboard and wondered where it had gone wrong.

When the viral apocalypse wiped the world clean, he had been kind of excited. The terror, the wet beds and the months of self-imposed quarantine in his pokey flat living off cat food and, eventually, the cat, were a bummer, but he eventually came to see his survival as a grand opportunity to turn things around.

All his life he'd been in search of a calling. He was pretty sure that Data Entry Clerk (Croydon (South) Council) wasn't it, but he didn't know what was.

Maybe his new job as Survivor (End of the World) would lead him to his destiny.

His first foray into the devastated world beyond his front door was the most thrilling thing that had ever happened to him. He pulled on his gloves, stuffed his belt with kitchen knives, and bound his face and head with torn sheets, leaving just a slit for his eyes. Once he worked out that his glasses wouldn't balance on a cloth-swathed nose, he sellotaped them to his bindings and strode from the house, ready to do battle. In his head it was a grand narrative – meek suburban wage-slave reborn as survivalist hunter-gatherer, stalking the ravaged landscape, calm and ruthless, ready to fight looters and feral dogs.

Maybe there was a damsel in distress somewhere, in need of rescuing. He reasoned that such a maiden may have been even more reluctant to emerge than he, so he checked every house on his street, hoping to find a lissom beauty cowering in terror, just waiting for him to hold out his marigold-gloved hand and tell her everything would be all right.

He especially held out hope for number 34, where that mousey woman from the library lived. She had smiled at him once, a year ago, on the tram. It had been a Monday. But in her house, it was the cats that had done the eating. So he struck out into the wider world.

His big mistake, he now knew, had been stealing the car.

Before The Cull, he had walked past the showroom on his way to work and every day, without deviation, he would glance at the car as he walked past. He'd never stop and stare at it, that would be ridiculous, but he snatched glimpses of it out of the corner of his eye and nurtured a hard covetous knot in his stomach at the thought of it.

Once he was sure his road was empty of life, his first thought had been for the car. He strolled down the familiar streets, retracing his old route to work, marvelling at the changes in the landscape.

There was Mr Singh's corner shop where he used to buy his wine gums – two packs every Monday morning, enough to last him a week. The shop had been looted and set on fire; a charred corpse dangled out of the upstairs window.

There was the bus stop where the hoodies congregated. They'd jeered at him once as he walked past. Arthur pictured them dying horribly. He wasn't imaginative enough to conjure anything really gruesome, but the thought of them dying of the plague was satisfying. He chuckled. Served the vicious little bastards right.

There was the primary school. He ignored it; he'd never liked kids.

Finally, there was the showroom. His spirits sank when he saw that the windows were smashed and the cars were all gone.

His brogued feet crunched over the glass-strewn tarmac as he explored the wreckage. Nothing there. Out the back, however, he saw a garage locked up with a heavy chain. He paused. Should he?

His colleagues would have described him as bland. Not timid, but not dangerous. But with no-one to tell him off, no social disapprobation to keep him meek and mild, he felt a sudden rush of reckless freedom. Licking his lips in anticipation, he scoured the garages for a crowbar, then returned and jemmied the lock away, opening the garage doors to reveal his heart's desire.

A Lamborghini Murciélago, abandoned with the keys still in the ignition. The dealer must have thought to hide it when he realised things were going to hell.

Half full of petrol, untouched, jet black bonnet gleaming in the sunshine, the car invited him to take it for a spin. It was like some magic gift, so improbable it had to be intended. He looked left and right before he got inside, instinctively wary of discovery. But nobody yelled at him, or took a shot at him. The seat moulded itself to his saggy rear, allowing him to recline in the low slung vehicle. It felt right; it felt like a throne. This car was his now and why not? Didn't he deserve it?

He closed the door and gently, almost reverently, turned the key. The car purred into life. He placed his hands on the steering wheel, considered taking off his rubber gloves so he could feel the real leather, but decided to play it safe, pressed his foot on the clutch and then gently depressed the accelerator, revving the engine. The car growled, roared, came alive around him.

In that plush seat, enveloped in that purring, eager metal beast, he felt a rush of something new and strange.

Power.

He was free and alive and it felt good. He released the handbrake and let her rip, tearing down the Queensway towards Croydon town centre, weaving in between ruined and burnt out wrecks. This must be what it felt like to be a rock star, he thought. Like Chris de Burgh going smooth at ninety, feeling good to be alive; or Chris Rea, on the road to hell.

His drive lasted for thirty seconds, and now, two months later, as he scrolled down the spreadsheet preparing for another dreary morning of data entry, he looked back on that glorious half-minute and thought that probably it would be the most dramatic thing that had ever happened to him.

Because the men in the yellow hazmat suits had been searching the town for survivors, and he'd ploughed straight into a group of them outside Morrisons.

The ones he didn't kill were not happy with him.

He heard the office door behind him swing open, but he didn't turn to see who it was. No point; he knew already.

"You finished yet, Smith?"

"Ha ha, only just started, Mr Jolly." The fake laugh, perfected years before in the accounts payable department of Croydon (South) Council, came easily to him. It was his defence mechanism, a way of signalling that he wasn't a threat. If he were a pack dog, he'd be bowing his head, lowering his tail and whining.

Jolly was his supervisor, a whinging Wandsworth solicitor who'd landed himself a cushy little number running the bureaucracy in the main refugee camp for Kent. Supercilious, patronising and grey, he was identical in almost every respect to Arthur's boss at the Council.

"Be sure you're done by lunchtime," said Jolly. "The camp commander wants that list pronto."

"No problem, sir, be done in a jiffy."

Arthur's supervisor gave an oleaginous moan of assent and retreated. Arthur sniggered. Camp commander; that sounded gay.

He reminded himself to be grateful. The collectors could have killed him there and then, as he'd sprawled out of the Lamborghini, tearing at his bindings so he could empty the vomit from his mouth.

Instead, they'd thrown him into their van, with the corpses, and driven him here, to the camp. They'd been a bit rough with him at processing, but he was so terrified that he'd offered no resistance at all. Identified as a low level clerical worker, grade 5F, he'd been set to work in the offices, away from the barracks and the experimental wings, where all sorts of unpleasantness was visited on the survivors.

They were trying to find a cure, and they didn't care what it took, or who they hurt in the process. Who they thought they were going to cure, he didn't know and he didn't ask.

Barrett, the man who brought round the tea urn, reckoned that the government and royal family were all holed up in a bunker underneath Buck House, waiting for a cure so they could emerge and lord it over what was left. Arthur didn't really believe that.

Then he noticed the name of the next worksheet: Royal lineage.

He clicked it open and saw a list of all the people in line to the throne. It went through the obvious ones – the princes and princesses, the dukes and duchesses, but then it went further, into minor aristocracy and illegitimate offspring. The first column contained their names, the second their dates of birth, the third their last known addresses. And the fourth contained their blood type.

But when he scrolled all the way down to line 346 he gasped in shock. His hand shook and he felt momentarily dizzy.

Because it was his name. According to this, he was 346th in line to the throne of England. The fourth column contained a note: "Illegitimate offspring; unaware; unsuitable".

In a flash he remembered a snide comment his father had made to his mother over Sunday dinner, years before. Something about dallying with upper class twits. She had blushed.

Gosh.

He scrolled back up and started counting.

There were only eleven O Neg royals in the list above him.

He sat for a while, jaw hanging open, thinking through the implications of his extraordinary discovery. Then he came to a conclusion, sent the document to the printer, and stood to leave.

Finally, destiny was calling.

The King of England, John Parkinson-Keyes, knew damn well he was in line to the throne, and didn't care who knew it. It was why the boys at his private school had christened him Kinky - a bastardisation of King Keyes.

Not that he minded. He really was kinky and he didn't care who knew that either. Hell, it was practically a prerequisite for the job.

"Prince Andrew," he was fond of confiding to credulous hangers-on, tapping his nose as he did so, "has an entire wardrobe full of gimp suits. And Sophie's a furry!"

He'd nod in the face of their astonishment and then glance knowingly at his empty glass, which they would invariably scurry off and refill for him.

He didn't have hangers-on now, of course. Not after The Cull. Now he had the real thing: slaves. And he didn't need to invent tall tales to get them do what he wanted.

"Where's my bloody dinner?" he yelled at the top of his voice, which echoed around the vaulted wooden ceiling of the huge dining room. There was no response. He drummed his fingers on the table impatiently, then cursed and reached for his shotgun. He'd teach these bloody proles to keep him waiting. He cracked the gun open, checked that it was loaded, then snapped it shut and took casual aim at the door.

"OI!" he shouted. "Don't make me come and find you."

Again, no reply.

Christ, this was annoying. He was hungry. Resolving to teach that tempting young serving lad a hard, rough lesson in master and servant protocols, he rose from his chair and swaggered in the direction of the kitchens, gun slung over his shoulder.

"Parkin, you little wretch, where are you?" he bellowed as he pushed open the kitchen door.

He never even saw the sword that sliced his head off. Well, not until his head was on the floor, and he blinked up at his toppling, decapitated corpse.

The last thing he saw as his vision went red at the edges was a chubby little man in a grey sweater leaning down and wiggling his fingers in a cheery wave.

"Sorry," said his assassin. "Nothing personal."

King Keyes tried to call for his mummy, but he had no breath with which to cry.

The last thing he thought he heard was the portly swordsman saying: "Three down, eight to go."

The Queen of England, Barbara Wolfing-Gusset, hungrily scooped cold beans from a can with a silver spoon. The juice dribbled down her chin, but she didn't bother to wipe it off, so it dripped onto the dried blood and vomit that caked her best satin party dress.

She'd been wearing the garish pink frock for two months now, ever since the night of her 19th birthday party. Her parents had suggested that maybe a large gathering of people during a plague pandemic was not the best idea, but she'd silenced them with a particularly haughty glance, and invited practically everyone she'd ever met.

Turnout had been low, but that just meant more champagne for everyone else. Plus, that hatchet faced cow Tasmin hadn't been around, so Barbara had a clear run at Tommy Bond.

It wasn't fair; it had all been going so well.

Yes, Tommy was looking a little green about the gills, but Barbara had assumed that was the champers, and she'd dragged him away from the ballroom for a quick shagette in the scullery. And quick it was. What a disappointment. Tommy came in about ten seconds flat and, as he did so, his eyes rolled back in his head, he began to spasm, and then he vomited blood all over her, fell to the floor – withdrawing in the process – thrashed about until he cracked his head on the stone step and twitched his last.

Ungrateful bastard.

Barbara finished the beans and tossed the tin into the corner. She swung down from the table she'd been sitting on and headed for the door, aiming a kick at the dog, which was still gnawing on Tommy's straggly bones; she didn't want it to have all the meat, she was still planning on making a stew of her beau when she had a mo.

For now, though, her priority was the next chapter of *In the Fifth at Mallory Towers* and the resolution of the poison pen mystery!

Kicking her way through the remains of her fabulous party – mostly disarticulated bones and dresses stained with bodily fluids now, but still the occasional scrap of discarded wrapping paper and tinsel – Barbara went to the drawing room, humming to herself.

She stopped and stared, her mouth hanging open, when she saw the man silhouetted in the French doors.

"Barbara Wolfing-Gusset?" Said the man in a bland Croydon accent.

She nodded.

"Baroness?"

She nodded again.

The man raised his arms and Barbara saw he was holding a shotgun.

As the pellets thudded into her she realised two things. First, that no dry cleaners in the world was going to be able to salvage her best party frock; and second, that she'd never find out who'd written Moira those beastly letters.

The man walked across the room and stood over her as she gasped for air.

"Sorry," he said. Then he turned and walked away.

Barbara pulled herself out of the drawing room, leaving a thick, slick trail behind her. It was agony, but she fought her way back through the hall and into the scullery. After tremendous effort, she reached Tommy's rotting skeleton and rested her head on his ribcage. She closed her eyes and prepared for death.

Then she opened them again and shoved the dog away.

For now.

The smoke curled upwards from the embers of the Old Schools. No-one left alive in there, then.

Arthur panned the binoculars left and surveyed the wider ruins. The cultists – at least that's what he assumed they were – had done their job thoroughly, but had made his infinitely more difficult.

The message painted on the wall of the (latest, only recently ascended, blissfully unaware) King's house had directed anyone who was looking for him to his school. He'd obviously felt that it would provide a refuge. Arthur supposed it was a sensible idea; if the boy were safely ensconced in a stable community environment, it would make him far harder for Arthur to pick off. For that reason alone it showed common sense. And anyway, where else was there for the boy to go?

On his way to the school, Arthur had decided he would masquerade as a teacher from a similar institution. Computer Science; useless now, so unlikely to have to prove his credentials. If he could convince whatever passed for staff that he was legitimate – and damn, wouldn't you know it, he'd not got a copy of his Criminal Record Bureau check on him right now and it was going to be hard to get a replacement wasn't it, ha ha – then he could infiltrate the school, identify the boy and wait for an opportune moment to make his move.

Upon arrival, however, he'd discovered the school under siege by a ferocious band of naked, blood-daubed nutters led by some weirdo in a pinstripe suit and bowler hat. He'd stayed out of sight and let the siege play out to its inevitable conclusion – the complete destruction of the school and everyone in it. He was pretty sure there'd been cannibalism involved, but he'd avoided looking too closely once the gates were breached and the real savagery began.

Now, as he looked at the smouldering ruins of Harrow School, Arthur had difficulty deciding what to do.

If the boy king had made it to the school, he had almost certainly died in the massacre. But what if he'd been waylaid en route? What if he'd never made it here? There were too many variables, and Arthur had to be sure. He couldn't have a pretender turning up and causing trouble once he'd taken the throne.

Then a dreadful thought occurred to him: perhaps the boy had converted – he was pretty sure one or two of the boys had joined the cultists. Blimey, he hoped he wouldn't have to wade into that particular hornet's nest.

No, there was nothing else for it; he'd simply have to rummage around in the debris and entrails in search of identification. He might get lucky.

With a weary sigh, Arthur collapsed the binoculars, put them in the pocket of his coat, and stood up. He felt a slight nervous tingle as he broke cover and walked towards the wreckage. He might already be king, and he might find proof of that fact within the next hour. He could embrace his destiny by lunchtime. He felt lightheaded at the thought of it, and lengthened his stride.

Two hours later Arthur sat on a blood-soaked bench feeling deflated and nauseous.

Rifling through the pockets of half burnt – and in some cases half eaten - child corpses was not the best way to spend a morning. But, he told himself, if he was going to be king he had to earn the right, and facing up to difficult realities and making hard decisions was part of the job. Kings needed to be made of stern stuff. He was proud that he hadn't flinched in the face of such horror; he'd only thrown up twice.

But he'd found no proof of identity. A couple of bodies had been identifiable by library cards – held on to for what reason, he wondered? Habit? Some kind of totemic article of faith that one day there would once again be fines for overdue books? – but the majority of the bodies were anonymous.

This was not acceptable. He'd managed to find and eliminate ten obstacles with no doubt at all, but now, at the final hurdle, he was going to have to make a leap of faith. The boy was almost certainly dead but Arthur knew that scintilla of possibility, that maggot of doubt, would gnaw away at him for the duration of his reign. He'd never feel entirely secure upon his throne, he'd always be waiting for the day when the miraculously resurrected boy king, now grown up and riding at the head of an army, would rise up to challenge his rule and topple him from the throne.

Unconsciously, his hand rose to his throat as he contemplated Charles I's fate. Then he clenched as he recalled Edward II's.

No, he had to be sure. There was nothing else for it – he had to find the cultists. If he could talk to the boys who had converted they'd be able to tell him the boy king's fate. It was his final test, the last thing he must do to prove that he was worthy of his own destiny. He understood that.

But it really was going to be a pain in the neck.

The King of England, Jack Bedford, picked his way through the wreckage of his school.

Coming back to school had seemed like such a good idea when the world died. After all, if any school was going to survive The Cull, it would be Harrow, wouldn't it? As it turned out, only a few children thought of returning to school, so the community never had time to reach critical mass before their first big challenge.

When the Blood Hunters had turned up to kill and eat anyone who wouldn't convert to their mad creed, Jack and one of his classmates had escaped the slaughter by sheltering in a huge brick ice-house deep in the woods that made up a large part of the school grounds. They'd heard nothing in two days now, so Jack had emerged to scout the area.

He was shocked to see the school reduced to a pile of smouldering embers and a half collapsed stone shell. This was

Harrow, for God's sake. Was nothing sacred?

The Old Schools, chosen for a last stand in the event of attack, was still smoking, but he approached anyway. There had been twenty three other children and one teacher - the Head of English, who had proclaimed himself Headmaster - here when the cultists had arrived. Jack didn't hold out much hope of finding any of them alive, but he could at least bury any remains. There were no bodies here, though; everyone had been taken elsewhere during the bloodletting. Jack scrambled away from the still hot embers, ashamed at the relief he felt.

As he approached the dormitories he caught a whiff of cooking meat and a thick smoky stench of chemicals. He paused, thinking again. The sick feeling in his stomach hardened into a knot of fury and fear. He wanted to run as far as he could from this awful place, but at the same time he wanted to find a gun or a knife or a club, pursue the Blood Hunters and massacre the whole bloody lot of them.

He shook his head and sank to the grass, sitting down and wrapping his arms around his legs, resting his chin on his knees and staring blankly at the smouldering wreckage. Who was he kidding? He was fifteen, his arms were too long for his body and he kept bumping into things. Always the last to be chosen for rugby, Jack was not sporty or physically confident; he was gangly, awkward and beanpole thin. Give him a gun and he'd probably just blow his own foot off. He wasn't going to be massacring anybody, let alone a gang of heavily armed psychotic cannibals.

He sniffed and stuck his lower lip out.

Where could he go now? His family were dead, his school destroyed, the only friend he had left was that interloper Ben, who had remained in the ice house, asleep and unconcerned.

Jack sat there, disconsolate. He had no real friends, no family, no home, and nowhere to go. He was unwashed, hungry, tired and simultaneously terrified and furious.

He realise the simple truth of his life - he was prey, and that was all. A tasty morsel to be eaten up by whichever cult, gang or death squad ran him to ground. The best he could hope for was a squalid few months scratching a life in the wreckage and then a brutal and pointless death.

He felt tears welling up in his eyes.

Then he froze as he heard a noise. He held his breath and willed his heart to slow. There it was again. Sounded like someone behind him and to his left. He heard the faint sound of shifting bricks; someone was walking through the rubble of the Old Schools.

Instinctively realising that he had not been seen, Jack slowly raised his head and turned to look over his shoulder. A freestanding wall blocked the other person from view. He rose to his feet and moved away as quietly as he could, taking cover in the ruins of a classroom, peering out through the hole where a window used to be. He glanced down and noticed that his hands were shaking.

There was a sound of shifting stone and Jack saw the freestanding wall wobble dangerously. The unseen man must have destabilised it by accident. Jack heard him scrabbling to escape, but he misjudged it, because the wall toppled away from Jack with a slow, clumsy grace, and there was a loud cry of alarm and pain mixed in with the sound of crashing brickwork.

Unsure what to do, Jack stood there, stunned, watching the wreckage settled. After the sudden noise, silence fell again, for a moment.

"Oh... bother!" Came a voice from inside the rising dust cloud. "Damn and blast and buggeration!"

This did not sound, Jack thought, like the cries of a dangerous killer or a mad cultist. But still he did not move, waiting patiently for the dust to settle so he could see who he was dealing with. It took a minute or so, but eventually a silhouette hardened into the prone form of a chubby little man dressed in a v-neck sweater and a puffy green jacket. He was lying with his feet towards Jack's hiding place, but his legs were buried beneath piles of fallen bricks.

The man was trapped.

The man watching from the tree line cursed under his breath.

"Don't let me down now, Arthur," he whispered. "Not when we're so close..."

Then he reached into his backpack and pulled out a machine gun. Just in case.

Jack studied the prone man, trying to work out what to do.

The man didn't have a gun in either of his hands, and his bag had fallen beyond his reach. That left his coat as the only likely place for a weapon to be concealed. As he leaned forward and began trying to dig himself out, the coat fell open and Jack was pretty sure there was nothing heavy in any of the pockets.

Maybe this guy was friendly. He didn't look threatening. But what had he been doing here? Was he a looter, come to pick over the wreckage of his school, or something else?

He considered for a moment and then broke cover. He stood in plain sight but didn't move, waiting for the man to notice him. It took a few moments.

"Oh, hello, I didn't see you there," said the man, momentarily forgetting his predicament. He stopped trying to free himself and leaned backwards.

Jack licked his lips; he had a dreadful case of dry mouth.

"What are you doing here?" asked Jack, warily.

The man paused before replying, and Jack fancied that he could see cogs turning in the guy's head as he worked out his response. Subterfuge was definitely not this guy's strong suit. Jack did not think it would be wise to trust him.

"I'm on a sort of quest," he said.

"For what?"

"Not what, young man. Who."

"All right, for whom are you questing?"

"Oh very good. You must be an Harrovian, such good grammar." The man was eyeing Jack almost hungrily. Jack bit his lip nervously. What was this guy's game?

"I'm Arthur. Is there any chance..?" He waved at his trapped legs and smiled.

Still Jack didn't move.

"I asked you who you were looking for." He said.

"A boy. His name's Jack Bedford." The man's eyes were narrow, gauging Jack's reaction to this news.

And Jack was so astonished that he let a momentary flicker of that surprise show on his face before he said: "never heard of him."

Got him! Thought Arthur. He either knows the boy or – he looked him up and down; right age, at least – *is* the boy.

Arthur was good at subterfuge, though, and had played his cards close to his chest. There was no reason for this boy not to trust him. Plus, his legs hurt like hell, and may be broken, so he didn't think he presented an obvious threat. If this was the king, he could lure him forward by playing the helpless victim. His reached his right hand down, as subtly as he could manage, and wrapped his fingers around a brick.

"Oh, that's shame," he said. "I've got good news for him. Anyway, first things first, can you please help me free my legs? They really are rather sore."

"What news?"

Oh for god's sake, this boy was skittish.

"I'm sorry, I can only tell that to him. I promised." He was pleased with that last flourish.

The boy considered for a moment and then said "I can take you to Jack. I know where he is."

"You mean he's alive? Oh that's wonderful!" *Now help me move these bricks you snot-nosed whelp.*

He let go of the brick, and the boy moved forward at last, reaching forward to help release him. The poor idiot child had no idea he'd played right into Arthur's hands.

It didn't take long for Jack to uncover Arthur's legs. He worked in silence, unsure whether he should be doing this. He'd been shocked to hear his own name, and he couldn't pass up the chance that this man might be able to help him in some way. But he didn't trust him.

The best plan he'd been able to come up with was to take Arthur back to the ice house where Ben was waiting. He'd introduce Ben as himself and pull faces at Ben behind the guy's back to get him to play along.

Ben was more confident than he was, good at handling confrontations and problems. If anyone could turn this situation to his advantage, it was Ben. He just had to hope that he was feeling sharp today.

Jack heaved the last brick away and Arthur's legs lay exposed at last. There were spatters of blood on his trousers, but he cautiously flexed his legs and then shakily got to his feet.

"Well fancy that!" he cried. "No bones broken."

Jack also stood up, and kept his distance as Arthur hobbled over to his bag, picked it up, and slung it over his shoulder.

"Right then," he said. "Lead on... sorry, you didn't tell me your name."

"I'm Ben," said Jack.

Arthur reached out a hand, smiling insincerely. "Please to meet you Ben, and thank you for helping me."

Jack reluctantly shook Arthur's clammy, limp hand.

"S'this way," he murmured, and slouched off towards the woods. Arthur followed close behind.

"So, do you know Jack well?" asked the man, feigning small talk.

"He was in my house, but he was in the year below. So not really."

"Then how...?"

"We were just lucky. We'd been sent off to collect some firewood when the cannibals attacked. So we just hid in the ice house until they'd gone."

"Nice lad, is he?"

"Don't you know?"

"Oh no, never met him. I'm just running an errand."

"He's all right, I suppose. Bit annoying when you're cooped up in the dark with him for three days."

"I think maybe everyone is." Arthur gave a short, nasal laugh, which irritated Jack intensely. His fear had largely faded, now he was only curious.

The ice house was a small brick dome with a door that you had to crouch to get through; it looked like a brick igloo, sitting incongruously among the school's woodlands, swathed in ivy, better camouflaged than any pill box.

As soon as it came in sight, Jack stopped.

"Better stay here, let me warn him you're coming," he told Arthur. "He's kind of nervous and he's got a knife. We don't want you to get stabbed do we?"

Arthur gave another of his nervous, snorty laughs. "Heaven's, no!"

Jack walked towards the ice house, only just resisting the urge to run. As he stooped to enter, he glanced back over his shoulder and saw Arthur standing where he'd left him. The man smiled and waved.

The ice house smelled of damp leaves and dirt. It was dark inside, only a tiny chink of light penetrated the canopy of ivy that covered the small hole at the apogee of the dome. Designed to keep ice frozen throughout the year in the days before freezers, the majority of the ice house lay under ground; almost immediately you were inside, the ground opened up into a cavernous, brick lined hole. In the half-light, Jack could just about make out the sleeping figure of Ben. He was exactly where Jack had left him, curled up on the carpet of detritus that had accumulated at the bottom of the ice house in the hundred or so years since it had last been used.

Jack scrambled down into the hole and shook the sleeping boy awake.

Spotty, unkempt and decidedly common, Ben Wyman didn't deserve his place at Harrow. The Headmaster had insisted that the school should open its door to any refugee children they dredged up, and Ben had been the first. He claimed to be the middle class son of a school teacher from the local comp, but Jack had his suspicions about that. Ben had been wary of the Harrow boys and the haughty ease with which they carried themselves. He'd not been bullied, exactly, but he was ostracised by the other boys, including Jack. But he'd been appointed Ben's 'shepherd', which meant it was his job to show him the ropes and help him find his feet, so they'd ended up spending a lot of time in each other's company.

Even though Ben didn't much like Jack, and Jack didn't much like Ben, they were both too scared to be alone, so they'd stuck together.

Ben sat up quickly and rubbed his eyes. "What?" he whispered urgently, confused and still half asleep. "What's going on?"

Jack leaned in close and spoke quickly and quietly.

"Ben," he said, pressing his library card into his sleepy friend's hand. "I need you to do me a favour."

Arthur's incipient euphoria was enough to make him forget the pain in his legs. Even this close to his destiny, he chided himself. His ascent to the throne wasn't supposed to be easy, but he'd been so annoyed at the prospect of having to infiltrate the cultists that he'd felt himself to be unlucky. He realised that the wall had been a warning, a reminder not to be ungrateful. This was a test, he understood that, a baptism of sorts, and it was all to a purpose. Fate had plans for him, but it was not to be taken for granted.

So he stood, chastened, and waited patiently for the boy king to emerge from the ice house. He caressed the revolver in his jacket pocket lovingly. Soon, now.

He cocked his head to one side suddenly alert. The snap of a twig. Slowly, he spun through 360 degrees, scanning the surrounding woods, but saw no movement and heard no other sound. Must have been a deer.

His suspicions were instantly forgotten as he saw two boys emerge from the small brick dome. The King, Jack, was smaller than Ben, but carried himself with a confidence sorely lacking in his friend. It was obvious which of the two was of royal blood. It showed in his bearing as clear as day. Arthur was sure that was how he must look to others and wondered how it could be that no one had ever noticed his inherent regallness while he was working at the council. He decided that people lowly enough to be working in such mindless jobs were too stupid to notice such things.

The two boys stopped in front of him. The king stood slightly closer, his friend hanging back, timid.

"Hi, yeah, I'm Jack," said the boy, grinning as if he'd just said something incredibly clever or funny. "What can I do for you?"

And Arthur froze.

Here it was. The moment of his ascension. He stood there, transfixed by the enormity of what was about to happen.

"You had a message for me, you said?" continued the boy, his brow creasing in puzzlement.

Still Arthur couldn't move or speak. Unconsciously, his eyes widened and his mouth shaped itself into an idiot grin.

"Um, sir?" Now the king looked uncertain, and turned to his friend, pulling a funny face and shrugging.

Arthur withdrew the gun from his pocket, still grinning, and shot the King of England, Jack Bedford, in the head, believing him to be a useless commoner.

All the confidence of the boy standing before him evaporated into terror as he saw his friend fall to the ground, and found himself staring down the barrel of a gun.

Arthur was about to pull the trigger again when he hesitated.

"No," he said to the cowering, whimpering child. "Let's talk first."

The man Arthur believed to be the King of England, Ben Wyman, sat on his hands on the soft forest ground and tried to control his bladder. The madman sat opposite him, cross legged, gun in hand, regarding him curiously.

If he looked past the madman, Ben could see Jack's body. He was lying with his eyes open, staring at him in silent reproach.

"I never talked to any of the others, but there's one thing I kept meaning to ask them. Did you feel it?" asked the madman. "The moment you ascended to the throne, I mean. It was about a week ago, at two in the afternoon."

Ben didn't know what the correct answer might be, so he said nothing. Happily, the madman didn't seem to mind.

"I imagine you didn't," he continued. "It's not really your throne. You're not destined to remain King, you see. I am. I'll feel the moment of destiny because I'll make it happen. You were passive. Didn't have the guts to go out and seize your power, not like me. I've proved myself, you understand? Not like you, cowering here in this dungeon waiting for slaughter."

Still Ben said nothing. All those years in the care home had taught him the value of silence.

Suddenly the madman tutted, as if annoyed with himself. "Why am I wasting time?" he muttered, and raised his gun.

"Yeah, I felt it," said Ben.

The madman paused.

"Kind of like a hot flush, sort of thing," he elaborated.

The gun stayed where it was, neither lowered nor raised.

"Made me feel all kind of powerful and stuff," he added, unsure whether this was what the madman wanted to hear.

"And did you know?" asked the madman, his eyes narrowed, intensely focused on his answer.

"Of course," said Ben. "'Course I knew."

The madman nodded. "Interesting." He stayed sitting there, gun half raised, nodding pensively.

Beneath his right buttock, Ben made a fist, scooping up leaves and dirt, ready to throw them into the nutter's face if the chance presented itself.

"Did the other boys notice it, the change in you?"

"Oh yeah, natch."

"That's good. I'll need that, I think."

Ben cursed inwardly. Why had he agreed to go along with Jack's stupid plan to switch identities? It had seemed funny at the time. Jack was scared of his own shadow, and even though he resented Ben's confidence, he wasn't afraid to use it to his advantage. Just like a toff, thought Ben, not for the first time wondering why he'd thrown his lot in with these spoiled Harrow kids, refusing to admit to himself that he had been so scared of being alone that even a bunch of pampered prats had seemed like an attractive peer group. So he'd tried to adopt the accent and manners of the boys around him; he was good at blending in. He'd even begun to think maybe he'd found a home, until the cultists arrived.

He wondered if there was any point in protesting that he wasn't Jack. Probably not. The madman had killed Jack without a second's thought. Ben knew the only reason he was still alive was because the madman thought he was someone else. If Ben told him the truth, and if he was believed, he'd end up just as dead. Better to play along, to try and find some advantage. That was another thing he'd learned in the care home - if silence doesn't work, keep them talking, sometimes you can deflect them.

"Tell me about the others," asked Ben.

The madman shook his head briefly, forcing his attention back to the here and now.

"Oh, they were nothing, really," he replied. "Spoilt brats. Trustafarians. I should have realised that the lower down the list I got, the better they'd be. You're almost normal, like me. It'll be good to have a normal king, don't you think?"

Ben nodded. "So, let me see if I've got this right," he said cautiously. "I'm King of England, yeah? You're next in line to the throne after me. And you've gone around killing everyone in line before me. Now you've just got to off me and you become King. That about it?"

The madman's eyes narrowed, suspicious again.

"You know that," he said.

Ben nodded. "Oh yeah, just wanted to be absolutely sure we were on the same page." He was gobsmacked; he knew Jack had been posh, but he'd had no idea he was bloody royalty. "So, how many Kings have you killed?"

Could he persuade the nutter of the truth - that he'd got the wrong person, that he'd already killed the king and was in fact already the monarch? He cursed himself for speaking without thinking; no, he couldn't, because he'd gone and reinforced the madman's belief that you felt the moment your predecessor died, that becoming King was some sort of massive supernatural head rush.

There was nothing else to do. He was going to have to try and fight this guy. Ben knew he didn't have much of a chance, but if he didn't do something he was going to be shot dead at any moment. And he was damned if he was going down without a fight.

He clenched his handful of dirt and prepared to make his move.

"Kings and Queens," corrected the madman. "Ten in all. You'll be number eleven."

Ben ignored the nerves and the insistent pressure on his bladder, and rolled to his right, releasing his arms and flinging the forest mulch into the face of the madman.

"Like fuck I will!" he yelled, and then he was up and running.

Arthur wiped the muck from his eyes as he rose to his feet. The boy had already vanished into the undergrowth, but he was hardly stealthy and he could clearly hear him blundering away to his left. With a weary sigh, he gave chase. It was his own stupid fault. He should have just shot the boy when he had the chance. Then he would have fulfilled his destiny and ascended to invincibility. As it was, his legs hurt, his eyes stung, he had a stitch from running and he was starting to get really cheesed off. Time to kill the boy and be done with it.

He held tight to his gun as he ran.

Ben knew the madman wasn't far behind him, so he put his head down and concentrated on going as fast as he could. A bullet pinged off a tree right beside him, and he put on an extra burst of speed.

He was so focused on his pursuer that he didn't see the man who stepped out in front of him, only becoming aware of his presence when he ran smack into the heavy log the man was wielding.

He was unconscious before he hit the floor.

Arthur saw the boy lying on the ground and stopped dead. Had he tripped, or hit his head on a tree? He was pretty sure his hopeful shot hadn't found its mark.

He approached the boy carefully. Maybe he was playing possum, waiting for him to get closer so he could spring some trap. Arthur told himself not to be paranoid; there were no traps here.

Which was why he was so surprised when Mr Jolly stepped out from behind a tree and shot him in the gut.

Arthur stood there for a moment, his face a mask of stunned surprise. Then his gun dropped from his hand and he fell to his knees, clutching his stomach. He remained kneeling as his supervisor from the camp walked towards him shaking his head ruefully.

"And you were so close, Arthur" said Mr Jolly as he approached. "So close."

Arthur didn't understand. He was so shocked and confused that he couldn't even form a question. He just stared, baffled, at the man who had shot him.

Jolly knelt down as well, so he was facing Arthur.

"Of all the people I showed that spreadsheet too, you were the unlikeliest candidate," he said. "I'd almost given up."

Arthur registered that his accent had changed. The glottal stops of his Wandsworth accent had gone, replaced by round, plummy RP.

"I really didn't think you had it in you. The one before you, now he was a go getter. But when he saw his name on the list he just laughed. In all, you were the sixth person whose name I added to the spreadsheet, and by far the least promising. Or so I thought. Just goes to show, doesn't it? You never can tell about people."

"I..." gasped Arthur. "I don't..."

"Understand. Yes, I know. You've gone quite round the twist, haven't you? Poor love. I knew you'd finally lost the plot when you killed that reprehensible parasite Parker. Making him a paper crown, painting it gold, then setting him up in a tableau, in a big chair with a roll of silver foil as a sceptre... well, it was inventive, I'll give you that. But a bit bonkers, don't you think?"

"What are you... doing here?" Arthur was beginning to feel lightheaded, as if the world was spinning around him. Gravity suddenly seemed to be on the blink. He saw spots before his eyes and found it hard to draw breath.

"Oh do keep up, Arthur. I replaced my name on the line of succession with yours. Simple plan, really. Convince someone else that they're the rightful heir, they traipse off and kill everyone who stands in their way, and I sit back, watch the show, then pick off the hapless patsy at the end. That way I only have to kill one idiot, rather than eleven."

Arthur's head swam. Was this another test? Surely what Jolly was saying couldn't be true. No, it had to be a test. It was his destiny to be King. He knew that, more certainly than he'd ever known anything in his life.

"You used me?" he groaned.

"Well of course I did, dear boy. First rule of being King – delegate the nastiest jobs to the most expendable serfs you can lay your hands on. And you, Arthur St John Smith, are the most entirely expendable person I've ever had the good fortune to meet. Plus: murderous, delusional and now, very dead indeed."

Arthur laughed.

"Funny," he said, his voice little more than a whisper. "You see, I really am the king. I can feel it. You wouldn't know what I mean, of course. But it's in my blood. Don't you realise who I am?"

"Go on, surprise me."

"I'm the once and future king. Arthur, you see? My name isn't a coincidence. My parents must have known. Don't you realise? This is the moment of England's greatest need and I am come again!"

With that final pronouncement, Arthur's eyes rolled back in his head, he toppled sideways and lay motionless.

The King of England, Jolyon Wakefield-Pugh, tutted affectionately.

"Nutty as a fruitcake," he laughed.

He rose to his feet and turned to deal with the last bit of unfinished business.

But the boy was nowhere to be seen.

"Oh," groaned Jolyon. "Oh bugger."

Ben was woozy and concussed but he still had enough presence of mind to slip away quietly the moment he regained semi-consciousness. Once he was out of earshot he increased his pace, half falling forwards with every frantic step. He made for the school buildings, which seemed to offer the best chance of cover and safety.

The bump to his head had only made the events of the morning seem even more surreal and dreamlike. Had he really been attacked by two men who thought he was king? Had Jack really been shot down in cold blood right in front of his eyes? Could any of this be real?

He broke cover at the tree line and made for the ruins of the main building. There was a cellar there where he could hide.

But when he made it to the bricks he lost his footing and fell, sprawling on the ruined masonry. As he lay there he could feel consciousness slipping away again. The fear of death overwhelmed him, and he whimpered "Mum" before succumbing to the darkness.

Lieutenant Sanders, late of the SAS, now barracked at Salisbury with the remnants of the British Army, had all but given up hope. Six months spent chasing royalty, and all he'd found were corpses. Each time he found a new one he'd contact his superior officer and break the bad news. And each time he was ordered to go find the next person on the list.

Sanders wasn't much of a monarchist, but he had to concede that a figurehead would be a useful rallying point for the scattered survivors of post-Cull Britain. A heroic king or a stern but comely queen would provide a focal point for patriotism and a sense of allegiance that could help rebuild the nation.

It helped keep the army in line too, if they had someone they could swear an oath to.

So he'd scoured the length and breadth of the British Isles with a list of names and last known addresses, trying to find the rightful monarch. And each time he arrived, they were dead. He wasn't stupid, after the third body he'd realised that someone else was using the same list for a different agenda. A radical republican, maybe?

He skipped to number five on the list, but was too late. Then seven. Again, too late, and the body too long cold. Now he'd jumped to eleven. He had to get ahead of this bastard, whoever he was.

When he got to Harrow he went in cautiously, weapon at the ready. The school was still smoking, and he got a familiar sinking feeling. There was no-one alive here.

But just as he was about to give up and go on to the next name, he caught an impression of movement through the wisps of smoke. Moving cautiously, he stalked his prey.

Jolyon Wakefield-Pugh stood over the unconscious body of the boy he believed to be king and considered his next move.

More specifically: knife, gun or brick?

He eventually plumped for brick, reached down and grabbed one, enjoying its heft and solidity. He raised his right arm, ready to bring the brick crashing down on the boy's skull, ready to seize his destiny.

With his arm raised, the man presented a perfect target. Sanders knew nothing of his grievance or motive in wanting the boy dead, but he knew a murderer when he saw one. Martial law gave him the right to take action, and he was not afraid to do so.

He put three rounds into the chest of the King of England, killing him instantly, and he felt satisfied that he had done right.

Then he ran to offer aid to the fallen boy.

Sanders turned him over and felt for a pulse. Strong and steady. He was alive, but he had a nasty head wound that needed some attention. He had a medical kit in his jeep, so he leaned down and grabbed the boy's hands, lifting him into a sitting position, ready to throw him over his shoulder. As he did so, something fell out of the boy's pocket on to the ground.

He let go of the boy's right arm and reached down to pick up the library card.

He read the name on the card.

Then he looked down at the boy.

Then he looked back at the card.

"Well fuck me sideways, Your Majesty," said Sanders, grinning fit to burst. "Pleased to meet you."

He threw the child over his shoulder and walked back to his jeep, singing the Sex Pistols' God Save The Queen at the top of his voice.

Arthur St John Smith sat in the bottom of the ice house, pressed hard on his stomach wound and wondered where it had all gone wrong.

He had crawled away from the scene of the shooting, instinctively seeking a quiet sheltered place in which to die, like a mortally wounded cat. Now he sat on the soft carpet of moss and leaves, feeling his life seeping out through his fingers, waiting for the fair folk to come and carry him back to Avalon, to wait for the call to come again.

He knew they would find him. It was only a matter of time. He just had to be patient. His destiny was calling, he could hear it on the wind.

A fox peered in at the doorway, sniffing the air, drawn by something else the wind carried – the enticing tang of fresh blood.

Arthur heaved a stone at it, and it ran away.

For now.

Look out for Scott Andrew's Afterblight novel,
The Children's Crusade. Coming 2010...